JUL 2 9 2005   aug 17

P9-CDC-373

DEADLY SLIPPER

DOUBLEDAY CANADA

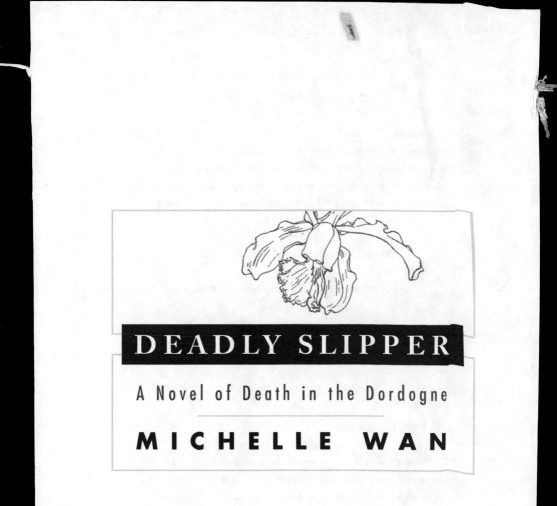

DEADLY SLIPPER

A Novel of Death in the Dordogne

MICHELLE WAN

Doubleday Canada and colophon are trademarks.

Library and Archives Canada Cataloguing in Publication
Wan, Michelle
Deadly slipper / Michelle Wan.

ISBN 0-385-66117-7

I. Title.

PS8645.A62D43 2005   C813'.6   C2005-901283-8

This book is a work of fiction. Names, characters, businesses, organizations,
places, events, and incidents either are the product of the author's imagination
or are used fictitiously. Any resemblance to actual persons, living or dead,
events, or locales is entirely coincidental.

Book design: Deborah Kerner
Printed and bound in the USA

Published in Canada by
Doubleday Canada, a division of
Random House of Canada Limited

Visit Random House of Canada Limited's website: www.randomhouse.ca

10   9   8   7   6   5   4   3   2   1

THIS BOOK IS LOVINGLY DEDICATED TO

TIM AND GRACE

ACKNOWLEDGMENTS

I am grateful to the many people who helped me along the way by providing local insights and factual information. I wish in particular to thank Alex Skelton for her friendship and valuable comments on the manuscript draft; Frances and Bill Hanna, Stacy Creamer, and Maya Mavjee for believing in this book; my sister, and Grace Anderson, whose generosity, encouragement, and wonderful house, La Charmeraie, were the beginning of everything. Above all, I wish to thank my partner, Tim Johnson, for his love, support, and botanical expertise. We have walked many paths together, and I look forward to walking many more with him. Among the many references used, Pierre Delforge's *Orchids of Britain & Europe* (HarperCollins, 1995) was my bible.

AUTHOR'S NOTE

The Dordogne (pronounced dor-DOIN-uh) is an administrative *département* of southwestern France. Its landscape is diverse and dramatic; its history and culture rich; its people warm; and its cuisine justly famous.

This is a work of fiction, based in the Dordogne. All characters are imaginary. Invented places have been intermixed with or based on real locations. For example, the place-name Ecoute-la-Pluie was fashioned from the wonderful *lieudit* Ecoute-s'il-Pleut (Listen-If-It-Rains) because this one was simply too good to pass up. The geological, culinary, and botanical details of the Dordogne are accurate. Above all, the orchids (with one exception) exist and grow in the kinds of environments described. Their beauty is there to be admired, photographed, and, above all, respected. Wild orchids everywhere are endangered. Please don't pick, trample, or dig up the flowers.

0　　1　　2 miles

0　1　2 kilometers

To Souillac
& Carennac →

Sarlat •

St.-Cyprien

ABRILLAC
FOREST

DORDOGNE

Beynac

RIVER

D703

D703

Siorac-en-
Périgord

Ecoute-la-Pluie

Belvès •

France

DORDOGNE

Sarlat

Périgueux

North

DEADLY SLIPPER

PROLOGUE

·

MAY 1984

 The Dordogne River springs out of the central highlands of France and flows westward through the region that bears its name, nearly five hundred
kilometers to the Atlantic. The river, in its middle
reaches, runs lazily through a narrow flood plain patterned with small farms. Here and there it swings between
deeply undercut limestone cliffs. Small villages and fortified
towns dot the landscape. Medieval castles rise from rocky
prominences. Everywhere the earth is densely clothed in
trees, for this is the heart of Périgord Noir—Black
Périgord—named for the darkness of its great forests.
Within their shadow, ancient footpaths wind over root and
stone.

A young woman was walking on just such a forest path
one day in the spring. Her stride was long, the stride of a seasoned hiker. On her back she carried a green canvas pack. She
wore jeans and a blue windbreaker, the hood of which was
pushed back, revealing dark, straight, shoulder-length hair
parted in the middle and fastened at the temples with metal
barrettes. Her ankle-high leather boots were caked with
chalky mud. A camera hung unsheathed from one shoulder.
Apart from the clatter of a nearby stream, the only other
sounds to accompany the woman's passage were her own soft
footfalls, the slight, rhythmical swish of her nylon jacket.

Her way now led uphill to an elevated meadow sprinkled
with yellow cowslips, violets, and pale bladder campion. The

woman paused, eyes searching until she spotted a scattering of odd-looking, greenish-red plants with hooded flowers, each formed around a deep throat. She approached to study them more closely, then took up her camera, slipping off her backpack at the same time for greater ease of movement. Carefully, she composed her shot, squatting low over one of the flowers, adjusting the lens meticulously for light and distance: first a close-up of the full plant, including basal leaves and inflorescence; then, shifting back with a crablike motion and refocusing to take in the immediate growing environment.

She capped her lens, gathered up her backpack, and walked on. Her path wound steeply upward over stony ground. Below her spread a rumpled panorama of wooded hills and valleys. Farther on, at the edge of a small clearing, she saw something that made her catch her breath: a plant bearing a single, fantastic blossom on a slender stalk. Her eyes widened and her lips curved in a smile as she crouched to marvel and admire. She prepared to photograph the flower at close range, adjusting her lens again, carefully pressing down the surrounding grasses for a better view. As she rose to back up for the longer shot, something—a streak of motion—cut across her line of sight. Startled, she looked up.

Talons outstretched, the buzzard struck so swiftly that the rabbit at the far side of the clearing had no sense of danger until it was pinioned with violent force. A shriek, a brief struggle, and the small animal was borne limply up beneath a beating canopy of wings. Raptor and prey disappeared beyond the trees. A moment later, a single feather, turning brightly in the air, drifted slowly to the ground. The woman watched transfixed.

Other eyes watched her.

1

"Maradonne," repeated the telephone voice. "I've been referred to you by someone who knows you, or knows of you—Monsieur La Pouge."

The accent was what he called straight-up American. Not a laid-back southern drawl. Not in-your-face New Yorkese, where "talk" rhymed with "squawk." But neutral, the tone slightly urgent.

"Ah," said Julian Wood, pushing his glasses up onto his forehead. He did not know any Maradonne. Or any La Pouge person, either.

"Because of your knowledge of wildflowers."

Julian thought hard. A fellow member of the Société Jeannette—Daffodil Society—the local wildflower amateurs' club? Or an enthusiast who had come across his book, *Wildflowers of the Dordogne/Fleurs sauvages de la Dordogne,* what he liked to think of as the bilingual bible on local flora?

He was standing in his slippers on the stone floor of his kitchen, which, since it was the best-lit and largest room of his ancient cottage, also served as his workshop. He fiddled with a sprig of dry-pressed pepperwort that he had been in the process of framing. He wanted to get back to it.

"I have a problem," continued the voice, "and I need your advice. That is, your expertise. I wonder if I could ask for an hour of your time? On a consulting basis, of course."

Consulting? Well, he could consult with the best of them, but what on earth was this woman on about?

"I'm afraid—what—um—exactly is it that you want?"

There was a pause. "I just need a little botanical information. Look," she insisted, "can I come out to see you now? You live in Grissac?"

"Just outside, actually," he admitted weakly. He belonged to that species of middle-aged Englishman made nervous by pushy females.

"I can be there by—shall we say four?"

Turning his head, he looked out the window at rain, a cold March rain slanting out of an ugly sky that had hung for weeks over this region of southwestern France. A sudden gust rattled his windowpanes (in need of recaulking). He wondered, not for the first time, where Edith had got to.

"All right," he heard himself say, and told this Maradonne person how to find him.

Julian took one look at her and had a premonition of trouble. She was small, coming below his shoulder, with straight, black brows, a pointed chin, and an air of determination. Her face brought on a rush of uneasy associations with other determined women, dimly remembered, whom he had known. She was also soaking wet. That was because she had run through the downpour from the road, where she had been obliged to leave her car. She stood, hair plastered to her head, water coursing off her onto the flagstones of his gloomy vestibule.

"Mara," she seized his hand damply but firmly. "Mara Dunn."

"Julian Wood."

Reluctantly, he helped her out of her raincoat and hung it on his wobbly tripod rack. She scrubbed vigorously at her short, dark hair, flicking water everywhere. The action left it upstanding and spiky, making her look oddly like a hedgehog and younger than she probably was. Forty? Forty-five? He wasn't good with women's ages.

"Well," he said with a stab at heartiness, "may as well come through. Awful day. Tea? Coffee?"

"Oh, tea, thanks, if it's not too much trouble." Her brisk voice grated already on his nerves.

She ignored his invitation to be seated in his front room. Just as well. Since he lived with no one but Edith, whose habits were bohemian at best, housekeeping was not a strong point with Julian. He had tried to make a fire, which was smoking unpleasantly on the hearth.

Instead, she followed him right into his kitchen where her attention was immediately seized by a contraption standing at one end of the room:

"What is that?" she laughed, waving at a series of bulky, rectangular frames fastened together with immense wooden screws. "Some kind of medieval instrument of torture?"

"Floral press, actually," he replied stiffly and slapped an aluminum kettle on the burner. "Nineteenth-century. I still use it. For preparing herbarium samples."

"Herb—what?" Her eyebrows arched.

"Dry-pressed flora. Once the only means of providing type specimens for horticultural classification and botanical study." The hedgehog had asked for his expertise—by god, she was going to get it.

She looked perplexed. He relented a little. "For drying plant material. In fact a microwave does just as well for most things, but I find the old-fashioned method gives a more antique finish. It's a simple process, really. Clamp the plants in the press. It's lined with blotting paper to take up the moisture. Tighten the screws from time to time. Whole thing takes about six weeks.

Thick bits like stalks and flower heads have to be pressed separately from petals and leaves and reassembled later. Then I mount and frame everything for sale."

He waved at an arrangement of flattened flowers and leaves laid out on a sheet of corkboard on his kitchen table. "It's my off-season trade. In summer"—he rinsed out a couple of mugs—"I'm a landscape gardener."

He eyed her warily as she approached his worktable to pick up a stiff cluster of pale-yellow blossoms.

"Cowslips," he told her. "What the locals call *coucous*. An early-spring bloomer found along hedgerows and shady footpaths."

"Oh!" Dark eyes swiveled to fix him intently. "Can you identify it like that? Where certain kinds of flowers grow, I mean?"

He cocked an eyebrow. "Well, yes and no. Most plants are habitat-specific. However, there are lots of hedgerows and footpaths around here. What do you have in mind?"

She took a deep breath, a diver about to plunge.

"Mr. Wood—"

"Julian."

"Julian. I'll get right to the point. If I showed you some photos of flowers, could you tell me—would you have any idea *where* they were taken?"

For a moment he entertained a suspicion that this was some crazy kind of test.

Quickly, she dug into her handbag and pulled out a thick brown envelope. "Please." She held it out to him.

With a sigh he slid his glasses down onto his nose and took it from her. It contained colored prints.

"But this is Beynac Castle," he objected, as the first shot revealed a fortified hulk perched on a cliff. It was a well-known local tourist site. "A few years ago, from the look of the cars."

"Yes. I left that in because it comes at the beginning of the roll. I thought it might give a general indication. There's also a *pigeonnier.*" She fingered through to a print of a tall stone dovecote standing like a gaunt tower in the middle of a field. "But the rest of the photos are all flowers."

He frowned and flipped through them.

"Well," he said finally, "they're field orchids."

She waited, watching him tensely.

He shrugged. "Temperate species. Cousins to the more dramatic tropical varieties most people think of when you mention orchids. These are more modest plants, but every bit as beautiful, in a smaller way. And damned easy to miss unless you know how to spot them. But look here, these photos are in terrible condition. Some are almost impossible to make out. You want me to tell you where these things grow?"

"If you can." She had moved close enough for him to feel the dampness rising out of her hair and clothing, to catch a faint scent of sandalwood. He found the proximity slightly disturbing. He cleared his throat.

"Well, I can't. That is, not specifically. I mean, most of these, from what I can make out, are pretty widespread throughout the region. Beyond the fact that some like shade, others sun, and most grow in calcareous soils, it would be hard for anyone to tell you exactly *where.*"

"But," she insisted, "you just said a certain kind of soil. Couldn't that be a clue?" She was not going to be put off.

"Calcareous?" He gave a harsh laugh. "Chalk. Pretty well describes the entire Dordogne Valley, certainly all of the middle reach, which is entirely underlain by chalky limestone."

The look of determination drained from her face, to be replaced by something like desperation. "You're absolutely sure there's no way?"

"Look," he said dryly, "I'm not a psychic." He returned the photographs. Her insistence was becoming irritating.

"No. Of course not." She slumped heavily into a chair.

Julian saw that, whatever her reasons, his visitor had placed a lot of hope in him. Now she was disappointed. More than disappointed. Crushed.

The kettle rattled on the burner. He turned away to make the tea, feeling mystified and thrown off by their exchange.

"Milk? Sugar?"

She did not answer. He put the teapot down and eyed her again. "Or something stronger?"

She stirred, looked up dully. "No. Thanks. Look, if you don't mind, I think I'll pass on tea. Anyway, I'm interrupting your work." She rose jerkily, dropped her bag, picked it up, and fumbled in it. "Can I—can I pay you something for your time?"

"Good god, no." He felt insulted.

"Well, if you're sure . . . ?" She regarded him uncertainly. "Then I'll be on my way."

She did not wait for him to help her with her coat. He stood by as she struggled into it, feeling somehow that he had failed this odd, impulsive woman with her unreasonable expectations. She shook his hand stiffly.

"Thank you. You've been very kind."

Through the bull's-eye window in the vestibule Julian could see rain sheeting off the overhanging roof.

"Er—do you want an umbrella?"

She forced a brittle smile. "I'll sprint."

He opened the door for her. She pulled up her collar and stepped out. In the next instant something struck her full in the chest. With a scream, she skidded backward, threw up her arms. Her handbag flew, hitting the ground for the second time. Before

Julian could catch her, she landed hard on the wet flagstones. A large, writhing form straddled her while a vigorous lash repeatedly struck the rickety coatrack, knocking it from side to side until it, too, went over with a splintering crash.

Julian waded in, lunging and grabbing.

"Dammit, Edith," roared Julian Wood, finally getting a hand on the collar of a large, very wet, exuberant dog. "Get off, you bloody beast! Get off!"

She had twisted her right ankle and had to be helped, carried by him really, back into his front room. It was an awkward, bumpy trip, and Mara was intimately aware of Julian's long, angular body, his thick pullover smelling slightly of damp wool, his rough, badly trimmed facial hair. She recalled his look of dismay—or was it shock?—when she had first entered his house, dripping water, mascara undoubtedly running down her face, and acknowledged with embarrassment that her attempted exit was even less graceful.

He deposited her on the sofa. Edith, a black-and-white short-haired pointer, was dragged away and shut up. Mara could hear her barks, whines, and frantic scrabbling from the back of the cottage.

"Better get that up." Julian swept away several days' accumulation of newspapers from the sofa so that she could raise her leg. Then he was gone again, retrieving her bag, placing it beside her, darting away into the kitchen, calling as he went, "Sorry about the dog. She just wanted to get inside. She hates the rain. I was wondering when she'd turn up."

He reappeared moments later with ice cubes wrapped lumpily in a tea towel. "Here. Get the swelling down. Nothing broken? Do you want a doctor?"

"No, no, I'm fine," Mara lied. Her ankle throbbed. Edith's howls were making the pain worse. "You ought to do something about her, you know."

"What? Let her out?"

"I meant, get her under control," Mara told him severely. "She's a liability."

He grinned, a sudden, attractive, boyish grin that illuminated his saturnine features. "Not guilty. Not my dog. Belongs to a farmer down the road, old Hilaire. Lets her run loose. She lives with me when she feels like it, and when she doesn't she buggers off somewhere else."

He shot away again. Mara closed her eyes. His comings and goings were making her dizzy.

However, the improvised cold pack was dulling the sharpness of the pain. She adjusted it around her ankle and looked about her: a low, small room full of mismatched furniture, threadbare carpets, and lots of litter. Pots of flowering plants crammed the window ledges. The walls were entirely taken up with books. Their worn spines suggested that all were well read.

He was back with a mug of tea and a couple of aspirins. "Here. Take these. When you feel better, if you can't drive, I'll run you back wherever you want to go."

Mara managed a smile. "Thanks. I'll be okay."

"No problem, really. Where are you staying?"

"Ecoute-la-Pluie." She opened her bag and gave him her card: *Mara Dunn—Interior Designer/Décoratrice ensemblière.*

Julian looked surprised. "You're not a tourist?"

She shook her head. "I'm sorry. I should have made that clear. I'm Canadian, but I live here."

"Ah," he said, as if that explained something. "Of course." He lowered himself into a leather easy chair—obviously his favorite since the arms and seat were badly worn. "And the photographs?

Look," he said, against his better judgment, "don't you think you'd better tell me what this is all about?"

Wearily Mara let her head fall against the sofa back so that she gazed past him at an indeterminate spot on the ceiling. "Yes," she said at last. "The photos." Briefly she closed her eyes. "You see, nineteen years ago, my sister Bedie—Beatrice Dunn—I think my sister may have taken those pictures."

He stared at her blankly, waiting for her to go on.

"In 1984, my sister, Bedie, disappeared in the Dordogne." Mara had told this story many times. With each telling, the recital became bleaker, more mechanical, reducing the people in it to mere essential facts. "She'd come over with her boyfriend, Scott Barrow, for a hiking holiday. They were camping not too far from here at a place called Les Gabarres. It was early May, and they'd had a lot of rain. Scott wanted to push on. Bedie wanted to stay. They had a fight about it, and Scott packed up and took off." Mara was silent for a moment. "When he came back to the campsite a couple of days later, Bedie was gone. Scott waited around for a few more days. He was sure she'd be back because, although she'd taken her backpack and camera, a Michelin guide, and a book on flowers, the rest of her things were still in the tent. We—none of us—ever saw her again."

Her eyes wandered to the windows. Darkness, the early darkness of remnant winter days, was closing in, but the rain was letting up. "The police launched a massive search. It was in all the papers. They questioned everyone in the area and followed up with campers who'd left during the critical period, anyone who might have seen her or given her a ride. A German family said they saw her go out of the campsite the morning after Scott left. Alone and on foot. No one else knew anything."

Throughout this narrative, Julian had been regarding his visitor with an increasingly troubled gaze. Now he stirred, rising to poke mechanically at the dying fire. He spoke with his back to her. "What about the boyfriend? Surely he must have had some idea where she might have gone?"

"No. In fact, for a time Scott was a prime suspect. The police were sure it was a *crime passionel*. They put him through hell, poor guy. Why did he leave? Why had he waited so long before reporting her missing? Scott told them that he had simply hitched a ride to Bordeaux and back, and that he hadn't been particularly worried about Bedie, at least not right away, because, as anyone who knew her could tell you, Bedie was perfectly able to look after herself. The police didn't believe him. On the other hand, they had no proof of foul play. There was no body, you see.

"My parents and I came over as soon as we were notified. We stayed on for three months, looking for her. Scott stayed, too. We showed her picture to everyone—hikers, campers, waiters, shop-keepers, farmers. My father offered a reward for any information about her. We had dozens of leads that went nowhere. Finally, the police told us we were complicating things by trying to run our own investigation. They told us to go home."

"And then?" Julian turned back to sit down again.

"And then, a couple of months later, in the fall, the French police contacted us again. Someone had found a woman's body in a wood near Carennac, over in Quercy. Her skull had been bashed in. They wanted dental records. But it turned out not to be—to be someone else. The woman was later identified as a Dutch tourist. Bedie just went on . . . missing."

Julian scratched his beard. "It could have been an accident. The entire region is full of underground fissures and pits. She could have fallen down one of them. Or—or drowned in the river."

"We went through all that. We thought of mental break-down. Amnesia. I pictured my sister wandering mad and nameless through the streets of Marseille. For years we all hung on to the hope that somehow she would just turn up. Eventually, my parents just found it easier to accept that she was dead."

"And you?" His tone was tentatively probing.

She shook her head. "It hasn't been that simple for me. You see, we were very close. Closer than ordinary siblings. We're twins."

She fumbled in her bag for a photograph, cracked and ragged at the edges, encased in a plastic sleeve. It was Mara's face, the same oval shape, straight brows, and pointed, determined chin. But taken long ago, frozen in time. The hair was different, longer and worn pinned severely back at the temples by metal clips. The eyes gazed out at the world with a challenging, quizzical stare. *Find me,* they seemed to say.

"I see," Julian spoke quietly. Unlike most people to whom she had shown this photograph, he did not display intense interest, merely glanced at it, then back at her, before placing it with a hint of distaste on the low table between them. He cleared his throat. "And so you came back to look for her?"

Mara shook her head. "Not right away. I got on with my life. I married, I divorced, I moved around. Finally, I realized I couldn't go on like that. I had to find out what happened to her. That's when I decided to make the move. My parents loaned me the money to set myself up in business here. I pushed to have the case reopened. The police haven't been very helpful. I tried myself to follow up old leads, but most were cold by then. The campground at Les Gabarres doesn't even exist anymore. People we had talked to at the time were dead, or moved away. It was hopeless, after so many years. But at least I was doing something. It made me feel somehow closer to Bedie, that I wasn't letting her down." She paused. "And then, a few weeks ago, I found the camera."

He raised his head sharply. "The camera?"

She nodded. "Last month I stopped off in Villeréal to check out a *brocanteur* I sometimes use—I'm always on the lookout for antiques for my clients, to go with their renovated barns and farmhouses. They like the genuine thing, or at least the appearance of it. Anyway, there was a big basket of junk. Dishes, figurines, books, and a camera, an old Canon. It was in pretty bad shape, the leather case all mildewed, like it had been stored for a long time in a damp place. It caught my eye because it was exactly like the cameras our parents had given my sister and me for our high school graduation. I looked at it more closely, and I realized, incredibly, that it was in fact the twin to mine!"

Julian regarded her doubtfully, eyebrows jacked up to the top of his head. "How could you be so sure? There must have been thousands of tourists with cameras like that coming through the Dordogne in the past—what did you say?—nineteen years."

Mara hesitated, then gave him her proof: "There were initials written on the inside of the case. *B.D.* Beatrice Dunn."

"Ah."

She set the ice pack aside, swung her feet to the ground, and sat facing him squarely. "But that wasn't all. Needless to say, I bought the camera. After I got it home, I found *there was still film in it!* I didn't try to have the film developed myself. I didn't want to risk a commercial lab. After all, it might be evidence, and the film was bound to be in a fragile state. I took everything to the police in Périgueux. They weren't very interested in reopening a missing person case nearly two decades old. However, I finally persuaded them to examine the film and have it processed in their lab."

"And these," he surmised grimly, "were the photos you showed me?"

She nodded. "It was a roll of thirty-six, intact, although in pretty bad condition, as you saw."

"Well, did the police at least try to trace the camera? What about fingerprints?"

"There were residual prints on the film, but they were too deteriorated to be analyzed. The police did try to trace the camera but got no further than I had. The *brocanteur* in Villeréal could only say that it had come from a clear-out of someone else's stock, an old junk dealer named la Camelote who died last year. The police kept the negatives but gave me back the camera and a copy of the prints. They aren't willing to take it further."

Julian grunted. "I suppose to them it's an old incident. Cold file."

"That's right. Most of them weren't even around when it happened. However, there's one man I've had contact with on and off. Lieutenant La Pouge. He's retired now, but he actually worked on Bedie's case. I looked him up again. He wasn't very encouraging, though. He dismissed the initials as coincidence and said the photos could have been taken by anyone who'd done the usual tourist circuit and who liked wildflowers."

"He may have had a point."

"But that's just it," Mara cried, her frustration breaking through. "That was the most important part. Once I found out what the flowers were, I realized that was the link. *Bedie, you see, loved orchids!* She was what you'd call an orchid freak."

"I see," said Julian. He thought a moment and then nodded his comprehension. "Sure. Orchid fever. Gets in your blood. With some people it's an obsession, especially the tropicals. Fanciers spend big money on them. The field varieties you get around here are free but, for my taste, just as addictive. I know a Dutchman who hikes around France every spring with a donkey, just orchid hunting. His wife remains in Amsterdam. I'm not even sure they're still on speaking terms."

"Well, I'd say Bedie was obsessed. I tried to explain the importance of this to the police. I got nowhere. And that was when he thought of you."

"Who?"

"Lieutenant La Pouge. He'd heard you were something of a local authority."

"Oh well!" Julian lounged back in his chair.

"So, you see, I thought if you could help me . . ." She locked her gaze on his. "Julian, I'm not only convinced these photos were taken by my sister, I believe that somehow they're a clue to where she was before . . . before whatever happened to her."

He looked startled, almost aghast. "But they're just photographs of flowers. There's nothing in them that could indicate—"

"Maybe not directly. But I was hoping they could serve as a— a kind of signpost . . ."

She trailed off, not saying to where, but she could see him thinking it: a shallow grave?

"Please," she said after a long silence, "these photos are the only lead I have. Won't you have another look at them?"

2
.

There were thirty-four of them, each numbered on the back in order of exposure. Julian sat down next to Mara on the sofa and laid them out in a line on the coffee table. He put his glasses on and scanned the array. As he had noted before, all showed some degree of damage, streaks and staining, as if by light or moisture. Not surprising if they really had been taken by Mara's sister, with the camera lying about god knows where for nineteen years. It was a bloody miracle that the film had survived at all.

He was able to identify most of the flowers easily: dainty Helleborines; pink, conical Pyramidals; frilly Lady Orchids; white Butterflies. The final frames were the hardest to make out. They had suffered the greatest deterioration because they had formed the overlying tail of the film.

"What do you think?" Mara asked.

He sighed. "Well, I'll say this much. Whoever took these—your sister—knew something about orchids and had some experience documenting floral material. Look, each one's been photographed at least twice, once up close as a full-plant shot, showing the flower and the leaf base. That's important for identification. And then again from a few meters back to show the growing environment. For example"—he picked out a portrait of a compact spire of creamy florets lightly tinged with maroon—"this is *Aceras anthropophorum*, Man Orchid, so called because the labellum is shaped like a little man."

He saw that he had lost her, so he explained: "Orchids have

three petals, surrounded by three sepals. The sepals are like—like a kind of cup holding the petals in place, you might say. One of the distinctive features of orchids is that the middle petal, the labellum or lip, is specialized, sometimes in fantastic ways."

He jumped up to fetch his botanist's loupe and held it out to her. "Here, see for yourself. The photo's got some bad patches on it, but you can just see that the labellum of the Man Orchid has four prongs, like arms and legs, with the sepals closing over the top to form a little head."

Obediently she peered through the lens.

He went on. "Now, the close-up is fine, but it's not that informative. All you get is the flower. So it's the habitat shot that's going to be the most useful for what you want." He pointed to the next photograph in line. "This is a middle-distance shot of the same plant. Here you can see that it's part of a scattered stand of Man Orchids, growing on a patch of rocky, sloping ground. So this tells us we're looking at, say, an eroded hillside, which would account for the lay of the land and the stones at the surface."

He skipped to a view of a grassy field awash in purple blooms. "Or this one. These are some kind of Marsh Orchids, which only grow in wetlands. So this has got to be a water meadow. The dark line there is probably a stream, and you can make out a wood in the background. This is an identifiable place. Of course, exactly *where* is the problem."

He continued scanning slowly, pausing with a grunt of approval over a portrait of a single brownish-yellow sprig. *"Neottia nidus-avis.* Bird's-nest Orchid." The grunt changed to a low whistle when he saw the companion photo. What he had initially dismissed as a badly stained exposure now proved to be a view of an extensive carpet of the plants. How big he couldn't exactly tell, because the plants filled the entire frame.

"Nice," he muttered admiringly. "A bloody great stand of them. Certainly bigger than anything I've seen."

Mara peered through the lens at a swarm of pale, fleshy specimens. "Those are orchids? They look like some kind of fungus."

"In fact," he nodded, "they live on fungi, and they're that browny-yellow color because they have no chlorophyll, no green in them at all. It's their matted roots that give them their name. Bird's-nests aren't that uncommon around here, but a big colony like this is extremely rare. Again, the problem is finding the location. If it even still exists," he added doubtfully.

He pored lengthily over the remaining photos. Suddenly, through the staining and speckling, he saw something that made him stiffen.

"My god!" he uttered.

"What?"

He grabbed the loupe from her to squint intently at a flower. It was taken in close-up, a startling plant bearing what looked like a deep-pink, swollen median lip flanked by two long, thin, spiraling, dark-purple petals. A blackish-purple dorsal sepal, arching forward like a hood, gave the flower an almost sinister appearance. Unfortunately, the picture was so badly damaged that he couldn't tell if he was truly seeing a slipper-shaped labellum.

"If I didn't know better"—he sprang up and carried the photo to where he could study it under better light—"I'd say it was some kind of *Cypripedium*."

Mara frowned. "What's that?"

He was at his shelves, pulling down reference books.

"*Cypripedium?* The French have various names for it—*Sabot de Vénus,* Venus's Shoe. *Sabot de la Vierge,* Virgin's Shoe." He thumbed rapidly through Delforge's *Orchids of Britain & Europe.*

"In English we call it Lady's Slipper. The only known Western European species is *Cypripedium calceolus*." He flipped through a few pages and came over to show her a picture of a handsome flower bearing a bright-yellow slipper flanked by two twisted maroon side petals and backed by sepals of the same hue. "Here. The color and shape of the one in your photo are different, but it's definitely in the same genus. I'll be damned if I've ever seen the like of it, and certainly not around here.

"The problem is," he went on, more to himself than to Mara, "it's impossible. *Cypripedium* doesn't grow in the Dordogne. In fact, it's been wiped out in most places in Europe because of picking and habitat destruction.

"It's got to be the photo that's misleading me." He scowled irritably at the blackened print, slammed Delforge shut and plunged into Landwehr's double volumes on wild orchids of France and Europe. A serious orchidologist, he was sorely tempted to put the matter of Mara's missing sister entirely aside, itching as he was to pin down an identification. But there was only the single portrait of this tantalizing flower, and it was the last shot. Filming had stopped before the end of the roll. From what he could tell, the final couple of frames had not been exposed. He stood for a long moment, lost in thought.

Mara's voice brought him back. "If it's not a Lady's Slipper, what is it?"

He shook his head. "Damned if I know."

It was a question he would have gladly given everything he owned to answer.

·

They were sharing an omelet, the only food Julian had to offer. The bread was day-old, but the eggs were fresh, bought that morning from Madame Léon next door, the shells in fact still crotted with dung and feathers. He also had a decent bottle of

Pécharmant on tap and a bit of chèvre, from another neighbor (Edith's putative owner), who made, in Julian's opinion, the finest goat cheese in the region, smooth and mild, not rank and gritty like some.

Julian had finally coaxed the fire to life. They ate companionably before it. Edith, released from captivity, lay dreaming on the hearthrug. Mara, with her ankle propped up again, was in less pain now and looking better. Julian was aware of the way she sipped her wine, the rim of the glass pressed against her lower lip, the flickering flames glowing in her dark eyes, lending color to her cheeks.

"Julian, I need to know," Mara said. "Am I asking the impossible?"

He hesitated and then answered, "Yes. Apart from this"—he tapped the photo of the mystery *Cypripedium*—"most of these orchids are pretty widespread throughout the Dordogne. Even the Bird's-nest could potentially grow in any forested glade. This makes pinning down an exact location pretty hard. Also, although you have the sequence of exposures, there's no way of telling if your sister took all of these pictures within the space of a few hours—say, on a walk—or over several days. If she took them all in one go, that would simplify things because it would limit their range to a given area, whatever she could do on foot, assuming she was on foot. You could then try to find places where all of these flowers grow together and use the photos to create a sort of continuity—"

Mara cut in eagerly, "That was exactly my idea. I thought, if somehow I could find a starting point, I could use the photos as a kind of—of map to retrace her steps."

"But what"—he had to point out the other possibility—"if they were taken at different times? That means they were also probably taken in different places. Look, the lighting in this photo of Beynac Castle is dull, the road and stonework look wet. But the flowers were shot in dry, sunny conditions. That suggests that these were taken at different times, on different days and possibly in different locations."

"Or that it rained in the morning and cleared up in the afternoon. The weather in these parts can be very changeable, everyone knows that." She was not prepared to accept his complications. She fixed him with an obstinate regard accentuated by the set of her pointed chin.

He shook his head. "You also have the problem of this." He returned to the Lady's Slipper. "If this really is a *Cypripedium,* it's very doubtful it was taken anywhere around here at all."

"But Beynac Castle shows that the photos were taken locally."

"However, not necessarily the orchids, or at least not all the orchids. Your sister could have begun the roll in the Dordogne and finished off in—in the Gorges of the Tarn, for all I know."

"But I found the camera in Villeréal," she objected. "That's no more than thirty kilometers away."

Julian shrugged. "Junk travels."

Then he gave her the coup de grâce. "The real difficulty is that you're hoping to follow your sister's footsteps using floral landmarks of nineteen years ago. A lot could have happened in that time, Mara. Orchids are extremely vulnerable to changes in their environments. Their propagation patterns could have shifted. Their habitat could have been destroyed. You could be looking for something that no longer exists."

She was silent for a long moment, taking this in.

"All right," she said doggedly. "What about this?" She held up the photo they had so far ignored. The pigeon house. It was a distance shot, taken from an elevated point: a round stone tower, some fourteen meters high, with a rough, gray conical roof. It stood by itself, surrounded by poplars, at the bottom of a soggy-looking field. The specific features of the structure were hard to make out because of a large patch of speckling covering much of the print, but it appeared to have at least one window, a low door, and numerous holes for the entry and egress of birds.

"True," he had to admit. "In any case, a *pigeonnier* is a more permanent marker and a lot easier to spot than orchids. But, again, the Dordogne is full of these things. Every farm has some kind of a dovecote. Where do you start?"

She stared at him unhappily. "You think I'm crazy, don't you? Or maybe obsessed." She gave him a small, tight smile. "You don't have to be polite. I've heard it before. I have a friend—she used to live out here. She's gone back to New York now, but we still stay in touch by e-mail. She says it has to do with our twin psyches. She says I have a misplaced sense of guilt. Why Bedie and not me, that kind of thing."

"Sounds like the stuff of psychoanalysis," Julian grunted.

Mara gave a dry laugh. "Pretty good. Patsy is a psychoanalyst. And she may be right. But I think it's more than guilt. It's—it's something almost tangible, as if Bedie and I each had hold of a piece of string. Her end has gone slack, but I can't drop mine because I'm afraid if I do I'll lose her forever. So I have to keep hanging on. Sometimes I feel that if I could only follow the string out to its end I'd find my way to her . . ." She trailed off. "What I'm trying to say is, if I could only find out what happened, then we could all get on with our lives—Mum, Dad. And Scott. Because it's been worse for him in many ways, living all this time in the shadow of guilt."

"And you?" Julian prompted.

"I?" She paused and then said simply, "I could put an end to my nightmare."

"Ah," he said, as if he understood, but he wasn't sure if she were speaking literally or figuratively. This woman had an uncomfortable knack of knocking him slightly off balance.

Mara sighed. "You see, Julian, I have a recurring dream. A nightmare. In it I see my sister walking along a forest path. I'm behind her. I can make out the details of her jacket and the green canvas backpack she carried, the barrettes she always wore. She's walking very fast, and I'm hurrying after her because I have to warn her she's in danger. I shout her name, but she doesn't hear me. I start to run. Then, just as I'm about to catch up with her, she vanishes around a bend. I reach the bend, but she's gone. Now I'm alone in the forest, and I'm very frightened because I suddenly realize that the person behind my sister all along wasn't *me* but *someone else*. It's like I've been seeing her through *his* eyes, and now *he's* behind *me*. He walks very quietly, but I know he's there, and I can sense him closing in. I grab a stick, or sometimes it's a rock, to defend myself, and Bedie, too, because if I can stop him I can save both of us. I scream and swing around to face him. And then I wake up. I've had this dream dozens of times since Bedie disappeared. It's always the same dream, and it always ends like that."

He studied her silently for some moments. "Nineteen years of it is a long time."

Mara nodded somberly. The fire crackled. Edith whimpered in her sleep.

·

The rain had stopped. A strong wind had driven the clouds before it, leaving a half-moon and a sprinkling of stars in command of a clear night sky that promised fine weather on the following day.

Although her ankle was very stiff, Mara insisted on driving herself home. It was not far, half an hour at most. Julian walked her down the long path leading from his house to the road, shining his torch ahead of them on the wet cobblestones. When they reached her car, parked beneath the dripping branches of a chestnut tree, she touched his arm in a gesture of parting.

"Thanks again, Julian. For everything. You've been really kind."

He shrugged. "Least I could do. But"—it seemed only natural for him to place his hand on her shoulder—"if you want my opinion, I'd say forget the photos. Leave your sister where she belongs. In the past. Move on." Even through the impersonal fabric of her raincoat he felt the shape of her, alive and warm. The sensation was both exciting and deeply disturbing. Easy, boy, he warned himself. Take your time with this one.

With unaccustomed gallantry, he reached out to open the driver's-side door. A terrifying, feral snarl erupted from the darkness within. Julian gave a panicked yell and dropped the flashlight, which went out with a sound of breaking glass, as something big lunged out to clamp his forearm with bone-crushing force.

Mara shouted, "Omigod! Jazz! No! No!"

There was a confused struggle, ending with a deep grunt, before Julian was freed from an excruciating grip of teeth that stopped just short of breaking flesh.

"Oh, Julian," Mara cried. "I'm so sorry. I totally forgot he was in the car. Are you all right?"

"Just a severed limb." Julian was still recovering from his fright. "What in the name of hell was that?"

"My dog," she said sheepishly as a large, muscular body bounded from the car, fortunately with no further display of hostility. With a brief flash of tail it raised a leg against the rear tire of the car and let loose an urgent, copious stream of urine. "He wouldn't have bitten you."

"Thank you, the effect was just as good. You ought to do something about him," Julian told her severely.

"It's just that he's very territorial. A lot of dogs are protective about their space when they're confined, and he gets very cranky if he's left too long. . . ."

"Get him under control," Julian declared angrily. "A dog like that's a bloody liability."

"*Touché!*" she acknowledged, laughing softly.

3

April came on fitfully, with windy skies, bright patches, and sudden showers. Julian stood in the open doorway of his kitchen. The sun for the moment shone warmly. Wisteria bloomed on the crumbling stone wall between his land and the walnut plantation of Madame Léon, from whom he got his eggs. The cherry tree at the bottom of his garden was in full and glorious flower. A cuckoo rang out in the valley.

He should have been feeling satisfied with life. The sale of two dozen herbarium frames to a hotel in Le Bugue had replenished his bank account. The prospect of a new landscaping client (referred by Mara Dunn, and rich from the sound of it) made his immediate financial situation look even better. But he was restless.

First there was the *Cypripedium*. Its weird, beguiling beauty haunted him. Orchid fever, he had called it. Where tropical species were concerned, it drove a multibillion-dollar industry. Nice, ordinary people were compelled by a dark-side lust to possess these plants, to engage in the costly, competitive, and secret business of searching for and breeding them. For two centuries, European and American orchid hunters had trekked, at no little risk to their necks, into the jungles of the Amazon, Borneo, Sumatra in search of new, undiscovered species. Temperate-clime orchids commanded a less extravagant piece of this botanical market. All the same, the fanaticism of fanciers and collectors was no less acute. The possibility that a totally unknown species of Lady's Slipper grew in some hidden corner right there in the Dordogne made Julian almost frantic with desire. If it still existed, he knew he had to find it. But where to begin?

And then there was Mara Dunn. He recalled the flicker of firelight on her face, her dark eyes, the set of her chin. Not the kind of person, he sensed, to leave things as they were. He had been surprised and then relieved when several days had passed without a phone call from her. Nevertheless, he felt her looming ominously on his horizon. The thought brought on an unpleasant pressure behind his eyes, which always foreshadowed a headache.

He had been toying with a plan, more out of self-defense than a desire to help her. Now seemed the time to put it into action. Except that he wasn't sure if he should venture seeing Paul so soon. He hesitated, then made up his mind. Not bothering to lock his door—he rarely did—he set off down the road.

It was a brisk, fifteen-minute walk from Julian's cottage to the village of Grissac. Along the way, Edith loped up to join him. Pleased to have company, he gave a token scratch to her silky ears—much her best feature in his opinion. The vagabond bitch was exactly the kind of female that suited him: handsome, wayward (she came and went as she pleased), but constant (she always turned up at mealtimes); full of her own plans, yet often willing to give him the pleasure of her company for long rambles or drowsy winter evenings by the fire. Best of all, she was not his. Not his responsibility, not his blame.

Grissac consisted of a few dozen houses built in the style typical of Périgord Noir: tall, two-storied structures of warm, honey-colored limestone, narrow windows flanked by heavy wooden shutters, and roofs steeply pitched to bear the immense weight of overlapping layers of *lauzes,* rough-hewn limestone slabs, the traditional roofing material. Its main features were an incomplete thirteenth-century central arcade surrounding a grassy square, which doubled as municipal parking lot and marketplace (Thursday mornings), an elementary school, and the Chez Nous bistro. It was Friday, past noon, and, apart from the voices of children behind the high playground wall, there was little sign of life.

Chez Nous, a large, square building on a deep plot of land, was situated just off the *place.* Julian found his friend Paul Brieux at the front, washing winter's grit from the windows.

"Missed a bit there," Julian observed, playing the jolly kibitzer. His French was good, although it bore remnant traces of his English background. At the moment he was unsure of his welcome. In last Saturday's friendly rugby match (there had been nothing friendly about it), he had failed to stop a try in the final minute of play, which had put the dreaded team from Les Eyzies on top. It wasn't good rugby—mostly middle-aged men, short of wind and gone to fat, who met in occasional inter-village matches organized by Paul—but the play was serious. *Le rugby* being one thing sure to rouse passion in the breast of the otherwise phlegmatic Périgourdin, Julian was not an especially popular man with his teammates at the moment.

"I'm not talking to you," snarled Paul, wringing a rag into a bucket of soapy water. A bull of a man, son of a farmer near Issigeac, he played right-hand prop to Julian's fullback.

"Come on, Paul," Julian pleaded. "Christ, it wasn't my fault. Those guys from Les Eyzies are out of the Stone Age. How would you like having le Trog pushing *your* face in?" The one they called le Troglodyte was Les Eyzies's horrendous center, a brute with a forehead like a cliff and small, piggy eyes. "He nearly bit my ear off last year."

"You chickened out," Paul accused in a seriously aggrieved voice.

"I wanted to live!" Julian recalled his feeling of extreme vulnerability as le Trog advanced on him, head lowered, arm outstretched like a battering ram, fully intent on flattening Grissac's last remaining line of defense: Julian. Why did they call it a "line" when it always boiled down to one lone man?

"Anyway, why do I always get stuck with fullback?" He knew the answer: the position was his because no one else wanted it. Since their forward defense was not particularly good, he frequently found himself alone, deep in home territory, scrambling for the ball while a rush of attackers—loggers, farmers, abattoir workers—converged darkly on his field of vision. Admit it. He was getting too old for the game.

"All right," conceded Paul. "What do you want?"

"Well, I just stopped by to say hello," said Julian, feeling as wounded by Paul's unfriendliness as by the pounding he had suffered. He still showed the bruises.

"Go bother Mado."

"I intend to," said Julian, relieved to see that he had been forgiven.

"And leave that bloody thief outside," Paul roared, meaning Julian's canine companion, but Julian and Edith were already through the door.

Chez Nous could just as well have been called Chez Paul, or Chez Madeleine, but when the couple had first set up the establishment, they could not agree on whose name should go on the sign. "Chez Nous" was the compromise. In fact, Chez Nous had evolved, through economic necessity, into more than a bistro. It served Grissac also as *tabac*, newsstand, post office, general store, and community hall. The Brieux lived above all of this and worked below in the various capacities implied. If Chez Nous had failed so far to rise to the height of culinary fame originally intended by the pair, in fact the cooking was very, very good.

Julian ate there at least once a week, as much for the company, which he genuinely enjoyed, as for Mado's confit of duck or Paul's *feuilleté au citron*. Despite his bulk, Paul had the lightest hand with pastry in the region.

There was no one in the front area, which served as the store. The bistro was through a bead curtain off to the side and consisted of a bar with stools, a dozen or so tables, and a mixed collection of chairs. Julian had a look in. The only person there was a morose type named Lucien Peyrat, who delivered bread to communities too small to have their own baker. The man was eating an early lunch. Julian gave him a perfunctory nod and wandered back to the kitchen. The appetizing odor of frying garlic filled the air.

"What's cooking?" he asked in both senses of the word, sticking his head through the door. Edith stuck her head in, too.

"Ah," cried Mado, a statuesque redhead with tawny, leonine eyes, *"c'est toi."* She was at the stove, pan-frying river sprats to a golden crispness, moving the fingerling fish about with swift, sure motions. She wore a loose knit jersey, which draped a magnificent bosom and left bare a pair of voluptuous arms.

"So—we haven't seen you for days," she accused. "Gone off my cooking?"

"I lust after your cooking and I was here last week," Julian defended himself. He had purposely let six days elapse before venturing back to give Paul time to cool down.

"For a miserable *apéro*," snorted Mado. She cared little for *le rugby* but could be as cranky as Paul when the mood took her. Julian fancied her in an off-limits kind of way, largely because she gave him a taste of what it would be like to live dangerously with a woman driven by temperament and steaming sexuality.

She jerked her chin in the direction of the bar. "Serve yourself. I'm busy. *Tiens, bibiche,*" she baby-talked the gourmand pointer, tossing out a tidbit which Edith snapped up midair. Mado adored all animals: dogs, cats, ferrets, donkeys, rabbits, although she had no qualms about gutting, skinning, and stewing the latter. She and Paul had no children.

"Thanks, love," Julian said, and wandered off to make himself a pastis at the bar.

By one o'clock, the bistro was busy. Julian had the prix fixe of the day: a terrine of aubergine for starters, followed by the sprats, hot, crisp, and dressed in garlic and coarse salt. They were accompanied by potatoes and spring asparagus poached in butter. He ordered a *pichet* of local white.

Paul, who had donned an apron, was now serving tables. A group of cyclists, dressed in colorful spandex, sun goggles, and aerodynamic helmets, pushed through the bead curtain. All walked with the mincing step of men treading on cleats who have been straddling bicycle seats too long.

"Messieurs, dames," they gave the standard greeting to the room at large.

"Damned spacemen," Paul muttered to Julian in passing. "Think they're training for the Tour de France. Drink nothing but Badoit."

Julian finished up with a dessert of crème brûlée. He drank a well-sweetened coffee and read the paper. Eventually, when the bistro cleared, Paul joined him at his table, followed by Mado.

"Listen, you two." Julian drained his cup. "I need to ask you something."

"What's up?" rumbled Paul. Mado lit a cigarette, dragging at it deeply.

"Do you remember a case involving a missing hiker, a Canadian woman, nineteen years ago? She was last seen at Les Gabarres. It's possible she disappeared in this area."

"Vaguely." Paul pulled a face. "Long time ago. Why?"

Julian told them about Mara Dunn and her sister.

"She should lean on the police, lazy *salopards*," Mado said. "She could be on to something with these photos. Why won't they take it seriously?"

"There's no real way of proving her sister really took them, except for some initials on the inside of the camera case, but those could be anyone's."

"The flowers tell you nothing?" Mado took another deep drag, tilting her head back to blow smoke upward to the ceiling, eyes half closed. Mado's smoking, Julian thought with pleasure, was an object lesson in sensuality.

"Probably not. However, there's a shot of a *pigeonnier* in the middle of a field. Something like that is a lot easier to place than a bunch of flowers. It's long odds, I know, Paul, but you're from around here. I thought if you could look at the photo . . ."

Paul stared aghast. "*Bigre!* Do you know how many *pigeonniers* there are around here? In all the Southwest? For five hundred years, farmers have been building pigeon houses. Pigeon shit used to be worth its weight in gold, you know, as fertilizer. France was built on pigeon shit."

"Well, even if you don't know the *pigeonnier*, you might be able to recognize the general locality," Julian persisted doggedly.

"Oh, what can it hurt?" cried Mado, stubbing out her smoke with a quick, imperative gesture.

"Just look at the photograph," pleaded Julian.

"You know what you are, my friend?" uttered Paul. "You're a raving lunatic."

But he promised to have a go.

•

The drive to Toulouse took Mara much longer than if she had gone by the A20. But today she preferred the minor roads. She needed the soothing progression of villages and farms and rough, newly planted fields, of towns with names that rolled off the tongue: Villefranche-du-Périgord, Fumel, Tournon-d'Agenais, Montaigu-de-Quercy. Her dog, Jazz, also a lover of country drives, occupied the passenger seat, his broad head hanging joyfully out the opened window. The wind was heavy with the smell of wet manure.

A few days before, Mara had sat on a hard, upright chair in police headquarters in Périgueux, pleading again with Commissaire Boutot for the reactivation of Bedie's case. The Commissaire, a sad-eyed man with a drooping mustache, told her mournfully that the camera was very little to go on, the police had already made what inquiries they could with no result, therefore, *désolé*, there was nothing more they could do. "After all, madame, nineteen years!" His entire demeanor gave a weary conveyance of the Gallic shrug.

Depressed, Mara had e-mailed Patsy Reicher, her psychoanalyst friend in New York:

> *So once more things are at a stop. I told you I drew a blank with Julian Wood. Knows his flowers, but a bit of an oddball and in the end no help. Oh, Patsy, why did I have to find that damned camera? Just when I was beginning to let go, I'm plunged right back into it. I haven't told Mum and Dad yet, or Scott. Afraid to raise their hopes. Sometimes I feel as if Bedie were still alive, playing a game of hide-and-seek, daring me to find her. <*

For five years, tall, wacky, gum-chewing Patsy had been Mara's only real confidante in the Dordogne. The problem was that Mara's other friends were also her clients, and experience had taught her that business and intimacy—particularly something as heavy as Bedie—didn't mix well. With Patsy, however, it had been different. Mara pictured her—gangling, fifty-something, with frizzy, badly hennaed hair showing gray at the roots, a broad, freckle-splashed face, ironic green eyes—and missed her badly. But Patsy's time in the region had been a temporary midlife fling at sculpture. Her work, humorous, free-form, and too large to command a market, now stood moss-covered and forlorn in Mara's back garden, where it had resided since Patsy's return to New York and psychoanalysis. *Know when to cut your losses*, was Patsy's motto, a guiding principle she also applied to men—her marital career, like her art, being somewhat free-form.

From her uptown Manhattan office, Patsy had fired back:

> *Easy, kid. The only player here is you, and the game is solitaire. Yes, you can let it go. Finding out what happened won't bring Bedie back. Besides, you might not like what you dig up. <*

It was true. So focused was she on the hunt that perhaps she had not sufficiently considered its possible consequences. Suddenly the countryside she drove through took on a more forbidding aspect: wild woods and fields, a scatter map of isolated farms and small communities. The rough, clustered dwellings of the villages seemed to draw in on themselves, stubbornly closing down on secrets that the outsider would be hard put to dislodge. Terrible things could happen within their precincts and no one would be the wiser. Which one, she wondered, and where?

•

Mara's business in Toulouse included an importer of ceramic ware, a fat, voluble Spaniard named Pablo who had his shop in the old Fish Market. She had not dealt with him before. He gazed at her with warm, coffee-colored eyes while Mara gave him a purposely exaggerated notion of the size of her clientele, all with bathrooms and kitchens that they, as today's purchasers of picturesque Perigordian cottages, were disinclined to leave in the sixteenth century.

"Bueno." He drew back thick lips, disclosing square, yellow teeth, and offered her a negligible discount and a bag of sample tiles.

Lunch was a quick *croque-monsieur,* half of which she shared with Jazz, followed by a pass through the antique dealers on the Left Bank. The only thing she found of interest was a dusty bolt of vintage yardage that in the end wouldn't do for draperies because on unrolling it she discovered that it was water-damaged. All in all, a disappointing day.

She drove home in the gold-blue twilight, tired, still depressed, mechanically making the turnoff to the hamlet of Ecoute-la-Pluie. Translated literally, Ecoute-la-Pluie meant Listen to the Rain. Nomenclatures in those parts tended to be rendered in a kind of rural shorthand, reduced simply to the names of residents, or, in this case, to their prominent characteristics. Ecoute-la-Pluie referred to a small water mill that had once operated there—or, more whimsically, to the miller himself (as Mara imagined him), ear ever cocked for the sound of rain that would swell the little stream that powered his grindstone.

The hamlet consisted of a handful of dwellings, strung out along a bumpy gravel lane. At the head of the lane, someone had left a battered white Peugeot van, badly parked on the grassy verge. She veered around it. Her house was the third down, a rambling eighteenth-century structure. She loved her house, its honey-gold stone, its roughly tiled roof, its many windows. It was her one solid point of reference in a life that to date had been busy with making her business go, haunted by the imperative of Bedie, and too little given to comprehending where she herself fit in all of this.

She parked along the side and got out, breathing in the sweetness of lilacs that filled the evening air. Jazz dropped heavily to the ground behind her, did a dog's version of a full-body stretch, and sauntered off to water a bush. As she rounded the corner of the house, a tall figure broke from the shadows. She froze. Jazz was suddenly beside her, tail stiff, ears erect. He gave a low growl.

"Ah," said the figure, stopping mid-stride. "Julian Wood. You came to see me about some photographs. Is your—I've forgotten his name—is he okay?"

"Jazz," said Mara, slightly annoyed with herself for being frightened. In fact, now that she had recovered, she was glad of a visitor. She hadn't been looking forward to an evening of her own company. "Don't worry." She waved a reassuring hand. "He's very friendly, actually."

"I'm sure," said Julian with palpable skepticism.

•

"I just happened to be passing," Julian said, stepping bemusedly into her front room. Right away he didn't like it: a showcase of period furniture and objets d'art, all positioned for effect. A large floral carpet (genuine Aubusson? if so, worth a small fortune) lay on the highly polished walnut floor. The whole place had an uncomfortable, upmarket air, redolent of the sweetish smell of beeswax polish. He looked at her, and his discomfort deepened. This was not the hedgehog woman who had come to him for help the month before. Instead, a person to match the room, bone dry to start with, coolly professional, tailored silk dress belted at the waist, wedge sandals, hair artfully clipped. Stood to reason, he thought sourly. As her business card had announced, she was a designer, an arranger of the natural scatter of things.

And then there was her dog, a large, tawny beast, probably of pit bull extraction. In any case immensely strong, with a broad chest flashed with white and a very big head. It took up a protective position beside her on the Aubusson. Its eyes, Julian noted, were remarkably intelligent, golden-brown, and outlined in black.

Julian hadn't really been passing by. He had driven out on purpose. It was necessary to his plan that he see her in person. Not knowing which house was hers, he had parked at the top of the lane and ambled down, peering in the dusky light at names on mailboxes until he saw her sign. Now, taking in her furnishings, her dog, he decided to cut his visit short.

"Um, thanks, but I can't stay," he said in response to her offer of a drink and a chair (a hard-looking Louis Something fauteuil). "I really came by because I was wondering if I could have another look at those photos."

She tensed immediately. "Have you found out something?"

"No," he admitted. "I just thought—"

She didn't wait for him to tell her what he thought. "Come out to my studio," she said, and led him quickly across the room and out the back of the house through a set of double doors.

He had anticipated manicured turf and topiary to match her interior decor. He was surprised to find instead an unkempt ground studded with oversized statuary that made his patch look like the formal gardens of Versailles. Her studio was even worse. Housed in a converted stable, it resembled a bomb crater. The floor was littered with what looked like salvaged material from wrecking sites. A chipped marble mantelpiece and bolts of cloth leaned against the walls. There was a broken-down armchair loaded with manila files, a large workbench buried in paint samples, plans, and sketches. The only relatively clear space was an L-shaped desk with a phone/fax, computer, and printer.

"Sorry," she apologized. "This is how it really is. What you saw out there is my storefront, where I impress my clients."

"I was impressed," he admitted grudgingly.

She laughed, a clear, friendly laugh. "You were meant to be. Everything in it is for sale. My cleaning woman treats it like a holy shrine. Honestly, she polishes the floor on her hands and knees with a brand of encaustic that smells like churches."

She went straight to the desk, pulled open the bottom drawer, and removed the now familiar brown envelope. Beneath it lay a dark rectangular object covered in plastic.

"Is that the camera?" he was moved by curiosity to ask.

She nodded, lifting it out, unwrapping it, handling it like a holy relic. He took it from her. The black leather case was brittle, crumbling slightly at his touch. Gently he unsnapped the top. A dusty smell of mold rose to his nostrils. The metal mounting and other hardware were corroded, but the box and lens looked intact. On the interior of the cover flap, he saw the letters, clearly printed: *B.D.* At that point, she took the camera back from him, as if his scrutiny had somehow become too personal.

Julian removed the photos from the envelope and fanned through them, purposely ignoring the Lady's Slipper, singling out the shot of the pigeon house.

"Look," he said, "would you be willing to make copies of this print?" And he told her about Paul and Mado Brieux.

"Paul's from around here, you see. I thought, even if he doesn't recognize it, he has a lot of contacts, agricultural salesmen, farmers, market vendors, people who travel around the region every day. I've talked to him. He's willing to pass copies of this print around."

"Julian, that's brilliant!" Mara cried. Her pale face glowed with sudden hope.

"Oh well," he said, speculating on where the admiring light in her eyes might lead. "Nothing may come of it, of course. Still, no harm in making, say, a couple dozen copies, letting Paul hand them out, and seeing what happens." He was standing close enough to her to catch a remembered scent of sandalwood, to see the faint flutter of a pulse in her throat. It made him slightly uneasy.

"I can't begin to thank you—"

"Yes, you can," he said, taking a deep breath and stepping back. "Because I want something in return."

"Oh?" She was suddenly wary. "What?"

"A full set of these prints."

She looked surprised. "But the photos are awful. You said so yourself. Oh . . . I suppose you're interested in the Lady's Slipper?"

"Be crazy not to be," he admitted. "Something like this is a botanist's dream."

She frowned. "But why do you want . . . Wait a minute, I thought you said it was impossible to use these photos to trace my sister."

"Well, yes, there's really no way—" he began, but she cut him off.

"But you're going to try to find this *Cypri*—this flower. Using Bedie's photos. That means—"

"Now, hold on, Mara," he broke in. "No one said anything about trying to *find* the *Cypripedium*. After all, what are the odds? It's probably a mutant that bloomed once a long time ago and died. I just want a photo of it for, well, call it scientific curiosity."

"Fine," she said coolly. "If that's all you want, then you can have it. I'll make you a copy. But only this one. You don't need the rest. Not if, as you say, you're really not trying to track this orchid down."

He felt a sudden spike of anger. "For heaven's sake, this is ridiculous. It's not a lot to ask, and I would have thought—"

"You help me," she said, her awful chin snapping up, "and I'll help you. After all, in a way, we're looking for the same thing, aren't we?"

The admiring light in her eyes had hardened to a bargaining glare. The pulse in her throat pumped aggressively.

She had him.

"All right," he gave over. Bloody woman. At that moment, he felt like strangling her.

•

Julian got out of bed the next morning feeling terrible. He had slept badly, and the shadow headache of the day before, taking on substance, seemed to be trying to hammer its way out of his skull. A real thumper. Strictly speaking, his headaches were not typical migraines. He did not have, thank god, the nausea, the incapacitating pain, but they were bad enough. He stumbled blindly into the bathroom, groped for his pills, and swallowed them down with tap water. Seeking Mara out had been a big mistake, like dropping a rock into the placid puddle of his existence. Grudgingly, he had to hand it to her. She had seen through him pretty damned quickly. With a sigh he shambled unsteadily into the kitchen to make himself a mug of tea. Stirring in four sugars, he squinted dizzily at his list of appointments—there was only one, but he wondered if he really would feel well enough to make it. It also occurred to him that Edith hadn't been around for her morning snack. In fact, he hadn't seen her for a while. She was in heat. Probably off coupling with every dog in the valley, the slut.

By eleven o'clock, the pills had kicked in and Julian was feeling better. He slicked down his hair, put on a clean shirt, and drove out to meet the new client whom Mara had referred. She proved to be a glamorous, retired Chinese American advertising executive named Prudence Chang. Looking over her property, Julian cheered up considerably. He fervently hoped the woman had money to burn. If he was given his way, her renovated farmhouse, fronted by a wonderful walled-in cobblestone courtyard, was about to become *la plus belle site de la région.*

The client, standing with him in the sunny courtyard, listened while he enthused over the microenvironment of walls, the characteristics of *Rosa gallica* versus heady floribunda. He was developing a theme of wisteria over the archway of the double gate when she tipped down designer sunglasses and looked at him with tired, slim-line eyes.

"Look. Julian. I've got two questions. How much is this gonna cost, and do I get to see any of it before I die?"

Sadly, he realized that what she really wanted was instant garden—hostas, bedding plants, and *pret-à-porter* hanging baskets. It was like that with most Americans. She read the disappointment on his face and offered a compromise.

"Okay, listen. I'm giving a bash here next month. You get things looking nice—I don't care what—just whip it into shape—in time for my party, and you can plant roses up the ying-yang for all I care."

"Fair enough," he said. But he wondered what "whipping into shape" meant to a woman like Prudence Chang.

.

There was a message on his *répondeur* when he returned to his cottage: *Julian, Mara. I've made two dozen color photocopies of the* pigeonnier. *Can I bring them over?*

She turned up at the end of the day, accompanied inevitably by Jazz. They went straight round to Chez Nous, where they found Paul working in his *potager,* turning the soil carefully around herbs that had wintered over, and setting out tomato and lettuce seedlings with a delicacy that belied his size. He gave Mara a muddy fist to shake, scratched Jazz's ear, and jerked his head toward the house.

"Apéro," he stated rather than asked, and led the way inside.

Mado was within, talking at the bar with Gaston, the fat, big-nosed postman, who was finishing up his rounds with his usual *coup de blanc.* Lucien Peyrat, as thin as the baguettes he sold, was also there, eating a solitary ice cream at the back of the room.

"Her husband's in the hospital," Gaston was saying. "Liver. It's serious."

"Ah, Paul, did you hear? Yvette's old man is dying." Mado pecked Julian and sized up Mara before saying briefly, *"Bonjour, madame."*

They sat down near the window. Julian had a pastis, Mara accepted coffee, Paul drew himself off a *pression,* Mado smoked a cigarette, and Gaston, who himself looked like a candidate for a serious liver complaint, joined them for another *coup.*

Mara gave them a shortened version of her sister's disappearance and her discovery of the photos, more for Gaston's benefit, since Paul and Mado had already had it from Julian. It was the first time Julian had heard her speak French. She was fully fluent, although he found that she had an oddly flattened accent and a way of swallowing her vowels that he could not immediately place.

"Wait a minute." Gaston scooted forward in his chair, his beetroot nose quivering with emotion. "I remember! Years ago. *La canadienne disparue—c'est ca?"*

"Yes, that's right," cried Mara eagerly. "The Vanished Canadian. That's how the papers described her."

"And she was your sister? A terrible business, madame. To come all the way from Canada to disappear like that. Montreal, wasn't it?"

"Yes," replied Mara. "We're from Montreal."

"Ah," said Mado knowingly. "Montreal."

Gaston went on, "I remember because all of us *facteurs* were told to be on the lookout for her. Or anything suspicious. For me, that was the bad part. I have daughters, you see. It could have been someone from around here. It made me think, I tell you."

"The countryside is full of cretins and perverts," snapped Mado, drawing hard on her cigarette.

They all looked at the photocopies of the pigeon house that Mara handed round.

"It's a very bad photograph," said Gaston. "Eh, Lucien," he called to the thin man as he slid past on his way out. "You seen this?"

Lucien, who had pale eyes set very wide apart, giving him the look of a startled horse, stared at Mara rather than at the photo-copy that Gaston held out. He shook his head, left money on the bar, and slipped like a shadow through the bead curtain.

"Scared of his own farts, that one," Gaston grinned, as Lucien's battered vehicle shot off in a spurt of gravel.

Paul, who had been studying the photocopy intently, blew out his cheeks. "Needle in a haystack," he concluded. Absentmindedly he fondled Jazz's massive head. The dog gazed up at him ador-ingly, great jaw agape in an idiotic grin. A moment later, however, something on the wind caused the animal to tense and shoot out the door.

Mara said, "Isn't there anything—those poplar trees, for ex-ample—that could give you a clue?"

Paul said, "There have been half a dozen big windstorms in the past ten years alone. Poplars grow fast. Then they rot. They could have all blown down. Or been cut for firewood."

"Nothing at all distinctive about the *pigeonnier*?"

Gaston pushed his lower lip out. "Plenty like it. This one might not even be still standing."

"Or recognizable," added Paul. "Big ones like this are being converted into holiday homes nowadays."

Mado had been studying one of the copies with slit eyes

through a cloud of smoke. She tapped it with a red-enameled nail. "That's a sheep."

They all craned forward. The object she indicated was faintly outlined and could have been anything because it was largely obscured by a stain.

Julian had to admit that he hadn't spotted it before. "Looks more like a goat to me."

"Sheep, goat. So what?" said Paul.

"Not everyone raises sheep," said Mado.

Paul said, "It's *one* sheep."

Mara asked, "Is there any record of—of sheep farmers in the region?"

"Are you kidding?" This was from Gaston, who had slumped back in his chair.

"You have to find someplace with a *pigeonnier*, poplar trees, and sheep—nineteen years ago. It won't be easy," Mado concluded, not unsympathetically, nodding in Mara's direction.

"I'm prepared to offer a reward." Mara sounded desperate. "One thousand euros."

"Seriously?" asked Gaston, sitting forward again.

"Seriously."

Gaston's bulbous snout twitched. "Not bad, that."

Paul shrugged. "Still a needle in a haystack."

Gaston drained his glass and stood up. "Well, I'm off." He held up a copy of the print. "Can I take one of these? I'll ask around. You never know."

He saluted the company and went out, also leaving money on the bar. They watched as, a moment later, his canary-yellow minivan, with *La Poste* scripted on the side, trundled down the road.

"Poor Gaston," said Mado. "He has seven kids. All girls. On a postman's salary."

Julian and Mara rose to leave. Paul walked out the front with them and around to the side of the house, where Mara had parked her Renault.

"Look, I'll show my father this picture. He may come up with something, or one of his cronies may remember this *maudit pigeonnier*—" He broke off abruptly. For a moment he stared unbelieving at what was happening in his beloved *potager*, then stuffed the photocopy into his back pocket and gave an outraged bellow.

Jazz was humping Edith lustily among the newly planted lettuce and tomatoes. For her part, the bitch, tail flagged coquettishly to one side, appeared to be trying to walk away, requiring Jazz to hop athletically behind her and causing a widespread trampling of young seedlings. Human attempts to move or separate the coupling dogs—the scene by then had attracted a small but interested crowd—only resulted in worse damage. There was little to be done except stand back and let nature take its course. It lasted nearly half an hour, during which time the dogs wound up end to end before Jazz finally came free. He was panting hard but looking smug.

"Oh, Paul, I'm so sorry," Mara moaned, surveying the wrecked garden in dismay.

Paul seemed to come out of a trance. Slowly he shook his head. *"Quel dogue!"* he breathed in admiration.

"Swine," muttered Julian.

•

"I'm going to have to persuade Prudence to hire Mado and Paul to cater her party," Mara said as she drove Julian back to his cottage. "It's the only way I can make it up to them for their garden."

Jazz, tongue lolling, lay splayed out across the backseat. Edith, who had never in her life accepted a ride home, had trotted off on business of her own.

"Oh, don't worry about Paul," said Julian tartly. "He'll get over it. Besides, he liked you. Did you notice the way he wouldn't look at you? Whenever he refuses to look at a woman, it means he fancies her."

"I've never heard anything so ridiculous in all my life!" Mara laughed. "However," she said after a moment, "Mado has her eye on you."

"Eh? What makes you say that?"

"The way she checked me out. She regards you as her property. You two haven't got something going, have you?" Her tone was bantering.

"I hunger for her cooking, not her body." Julian replied with mock dignity. Nevertheless, his conscience twanged as he spoke the words. There had been one or two occasions, usually when he had drunk too much on a Saturday night after rugby, when he had found himself swirling like a drowning vole in the vortex of Mado's powerful attractions. "Besides, Paul's one of my best friends, practically family."

"That's why they call it a *ménage à trois*," Mara said.

"She's French Canadian," Mado said to Paul when they were alone. "Did you hear her accent?"

"What accent?" Paul sat on one side of the bar, studying rugby scores in the local daily, while Mado dried glasses on the other. In a region where people spoke a lazy patois and where all words were drawled out to end in "ng," an accent was hardly a thing to be remarked on.

"*Joual.*"

"What're you talking about?"

"*Joual.* She speaks *joual.*"

"What *joual?*"

"It's the Montreal argot. That's how they say 'horse.' They eat their words, so *cheval* winds up sounding like *joual*. I think she's got her eye on Julian."

"About time somebody did." Paul buried himself more deeply in his paper.

Mado watched him. "Are you going to show that photo around?" she asked a moment later.

"Sure. Why not?"

"Well, like Gaston said, it could have been anyone around here. You'll want to go carefully. Don't forget, the man was never caught."

"How do you know for sure it was a man?"

"Use sense. It had to be."

"Well, who?"

"Anyone. Lucien Peyrat, for example. It's usually the re-pressed type."

Paul looked up. "For Christ's sake, he's a bread man, not a murderer."

"Or old Benoît. Being a butcher, killing would have been easy for him. Even you."

"Are you joking?" Paul gaped, incredulous.

"All I'm saying is, you could stir up something. Especially if she's really offering a reward. A thousand euros is a lot of money."

"Hou!" Paul went back to his sports page. "I'll wave the photo under people's noses. No one's going to identify this *bougre* of a *pigeonnier*. Besides, the boyfriend probably did it, even though they couldn't hang anything on him. Or else the sister drowned in the river or fell down a hole."

Mado shrugged. After a pause, she resumed, "She's not his type, you know."

"Who?"

"This Mara. She's all wrong for Julian."

Paul threw his paper down at last to squint ferociously at his wife.

"What's right? The problem with Julian is, he's got no staying power. He takes up with a woman for a while, and just when things start to look serious, *fsst*. It fizzles out. Sometimes I think he doesn't really like women. He wants them, but he doesn't like them."

"He likes me," pouted Mado.

"You're different," her husband pointed out. "You're safe."

"Safe?" The redhead bristled.

"Unavailable. Married. He can fantasize without running any risks. In any case, he has no idea what makes a woman tick."

"You do?" Mado challenged, rubbing the glassware hard.

"At least I'm not scared of them." Paul retreated from possibly thin ice. "Anyway, if this Mara's putting moves on him, she's as good as any. Julian needs a woman, any woman. He's going to seed. You should have seen him watching that dog of hers hump Edith. Pure envy."

Mado gave a throaty laugh, put away her towel, leaned across the bar, and nuzzled her husband's ear.

"Poor Julian," she whispered throatily. "Poor, poor Julian."

4

He had been christened Armand some fifty years ago, but round about they simply called him Vrac. The name meant "in bulk" or "loose goods." He grew up large and brutish, with an oversized head, slack mouth, and pale hair that stood up in tufts. He lived with his mother in a grim farmhouse, eking out an existence from a few hectares of soggy land in a valley below the village of Malpech.

The mother, Marie-Claire Rocher, otherwise known as la Binette, was herself no beauty: a hulk of a woman, with a massive jaw rising out of a creased dewlap, and a livid birthmark covering one eye. Her nickname suited her, for the word *binette* meant "hoe," an implement she had once nearly decapitated a man with for trespassing on her land. Its more archaic meanings, "visage" and "wig," could equally be taken to refer to her unsettling face or to the coarse yellow clump of horsehair that sat on her head like a turkey's roost.

Of Vrac's father, nothing was known. Everyone suspected it had been old Rocher himself. "*Mon dieu,* his own daughter and barely thirteen!" they had exclaimed those many years ago as the smock front of the young Marie-Claire grew daily shorter for all to see. Over time, Vrac the child and Vrac the man came simply to be accepted by the scattered farming community as an unpleasant feature of existence, like bad weather or mud. If he was shunned—children ran when they saw him, and women crossed themselves at his approach—he was at the same time tolerated and even protected by the fierce local loyalties that defined a region where in times past a person's entire universe was measured by how far he or she could walk out and back in a day.

In fact, it might even be said that Vrac enjoyed a kind of ill-favored celebrity. Local farmers sometimes employed him to fell trees and heave tractors out of ditches, for he was enormously strong. He also had a certain understanding of the darker side of machinery and was often able to bludgeon exhausted and antiquated farm equipment, which normally would have been left on a hillside to rust, into some level of fitful functioning. These odd jobs gave Vrac cash in his pocket, a tenuous claim on society, and a kind of preposterous self-conceit.

All the same, Vrac understood murkily that he was not wanted. Even his own mother called him names. These rejections filled him with an inarticulate rage that erupted from time to time in crude acts of violence perpetrated randomly against inanimate objects and living things that chanced to cross his path.

Like a bear, Vrac covered a vast territory, killing and taking at will, poaching on reserves and fishing on private land where the streams and rivers of the region formed pools attractive to pike and perch. There was only one place that he avoided—a deep pond in the forest where tall reeds whispered and frogs and small fry abounded. For reasons known best to him, he would not eat things taken from its muddy depths.

La Binette was a more complex being. She assessed the world about her with a cynicism that usually worked to her benefit. Her son she treated like an animal, with a bitterness that arose from her belief that he was a punishment for past sins. He was of her making, and he never should have been made. Nevertheless, need arising, she probably would have defended him to the death. And if she attended but minimally to his bodily needs, it must be said that she did no more for herself.

For the rest, la Binette tended her sheep and made a surprisingly good cheese from ewe's milk. In fact, her *brebis* was something of a local specialty, which she sold at nearby periodic markets, arriving with much backfiring in an ancient wood-paneled truck. Occasionally, she augmented the household income by picking up unwary hitchhikers or motorists in distress, driving them not to where they wanted to go but to some isolated spot where she demanded a *forfait*, usually what cash their wallets contained, for "transportation services rendered." Most paid and were then dumped, shaken but relieved, to make their way back to civilization as best they could.

Curiously, mother and son slept together. Whether they joined in an incestuous relationship was beside the point. The point was that, apart from routinely cooperating out of necessity to till the soil or harvest or slaughter, these two creatures went their own way from dawn to dusk. At night, however, like beasts made uneasy by the dark, they drew together, sharing a sagging double bed. Vrac had slept with his mother since his first day of life, when she had given him the breast, the only bounty he had ever received from her, and continued to do so unthinkingly into adulthood and middle age.

In a region where places took the names of the inhabitants, the Rocher farm was simply referred to as La Binette. Its narrow fields lay between the forest and the road. The house, built over a byre, a style more typical of Quercy than Périgord, stood in a wooded combe.

The byre, once used for stabling animals, served la Binette (the woman) as a cheese cellar and Vrac as a storehouse. There Vrac kept his fishing tackle, gutting knife, shotgun, and other items—a book (he could no more read than fly, but he liked the pictures of the flowers); a dog collar; a canvas backpack; old boots; a green bicycle bearing the stamp *Phoenix Made in China,* which he occasionally rode.

For the most part, the mother was incurious about the son's treasure hoard, her only interest being the possible value of a given object. However, one day many years ago, la Binette happened to notice that a camera had been added to the collection. She picked it up and examined it because it looked to be expensive. Then she heard a noise behind her. Turning, she saw her son's form, framed in the low doorway of the byre, blotting out the light.

"No," Vrac croaked hoarsely, hands dangling heavily at his sides. "Put."

Dropping the camera back onto the pile, la Binette pushed roughly past her son to the outside. Sometime after that, she saw that the camera had gone.

•

High on a prominence above La Binette (the farm) and at the top of a tortuous road, stood the grand but decrepit château of Les Colombes. It, too, was heavily screened by trees—from most angles, nothing more than its numerous chimneystacks could be seen. To the northwest, it looked across a broad valley to the village of Malpech. In all other directions, it was surrounded by forests and fields.

At one time all of the land for leagues around, La Binette included, had been part of the Seigneurie of Les Colombes, owned by the powerful de Sauvignac family. However, over the course of ten generations, the Seigneurie had been so parceled, hacked, sold, and ceded that only the château, with its adjoining woodland, remained. Nevertheless, the fact that the estate was still in the hands of an unbroken line of de Sauvignacs was a matter of local pride.

How la Binette's father, a drunken day laborer with never two sous to rub together, had come to acquire a corner of Les Colombes was a mystery. "Silence is golden," the more cynical locals said knowingly, tapping the sides of their noses, suggesting that the scoundrel Rocher had rooted out something about the family worth the price of a parcel of land. When Rocher died— "Fetched by the devil," they said, for he had been found in a ditch one winter morning, frozen stiff, mouth wide open as if mid-shout—the farm had passed to his stony, antipathetic daughter and her son. And so things had continued over the years, with la Binette and Vrac tending their sheep and wresting their harvest of root crops from the wet, exhausted soil.

La Binette was on the big-nosed postman Gaston's route. For years, his canary-yellow minivan had bucketed past the place, making only infrequent stops. There was rarely any mail for the residents, mostly circulars and bills that the *facteur* deposited in a rusty iron box set on a cairn of stones at the roadside. Never had he needed to negotiate the narrow track leading from the road to the farmhouse itself. Just as well, for Gaston, like others, preferred to stay well clear of mother and son.

However, on this afternoon there was a delivery requiring a signature. From the Electricité de France, so it had to have something to do with the electricity. As he turned off onto the muddy, rutted lane, Gaston reflected that, in all the time he had come down the valley, he could not recall actually having spoken to either of the La Binette pair. Today, he wondered nervously if Vrac would be around. Of the two, he thought he would rather deal with the woman. Once or twice he had seen Vrac standing on a hillside roaring unintelligibly at the sky, or glimpsed him in the rain, moving like an animal among the trees. Besides, he didn't think Vrac could read or write, let alone sign his name.

Gaston pulled up in front of the farmhouse. The day was turning overcast and windy, with the suggestion of an impending storm. Reluctantly he heaved his bulk out of the minivan. A crow rose flapping from the roof.

"Allo?" he shouted from the bottom of the six deep steps leading up to the front door. In addition to its unusual style, he noted that the house was built of darker stone than normal, giving it a damp and secretive air.

Laboriously, he climbed up to the elevated stoop. He knocked. Silence. The front of the house had one window. Peering through grimy glass, he could make out nothing of the darkened interior.

Not here, he concluded, considerably relieved. He wondered if he could get away with putting the EDF envelope and the signature form in the mailbox at the roadside with a note instructing la Binette to sign the form and leave it for him to pick up the following day. He wasn't really suppose to do that, and he had no reason to believe she would comply. Ah well, he supposed he'd just have to try again.

As he turned to descend the steps, he saw, with a sense of shock, that la Binette was waiting for him at the bottom. She wore overalls tucked into knee-high rubber boots, and a black jersey with the sleeves pushed up. With her massive forearms and her birthmark obliterating one eye, she reminded Gaston uncomfortably of a beached pirate.

"Ah, madame," Gaston stammered. Perhaps she had been in the byre at her cheesemaking, for her hands were wet, and her wig, the color of dirty straw, was tipped askew over her forehead. Fleetingly he wondered what had become of her own hair, not that he would have dared to ask.

"What?" she said. Her voice was hollow and harsh, like wind blowing down a chimney.

"Er," he said, "it's this. For you." Tentatively he held out the electricity board envelope.

She ignored it, glaring balefully into his face.

"What do I want with that?"

"*Eh bien,* how am I to know?" he gabbled apprehensively, realizing that it was probably a final notice of arrears. "However, as you can see, it requires your signature."

She spat, aiming for a spot just off his right toe.

"Madame!" Gaston pulled his foot back. "I am only doing my duty."

At that point Vrac appeared, rounding the corner of the house and stopping up short behind his mother. Together the pair of them blocked the *facteur*'s way like standing stones. Gaston thought how much bigger Vrac seemed up close. He wore dungarees over a greasy sweater and a pair of steel-rimmed sunglasses with one lens missing, giving him a patch-eyed look and the bizarre appearance of parodying his mother's birthmark. The expression on his large, misshapen face was not friendly, and he smelled strongly of sheep.

Gaston tried affability. "Come. I'll leave it here, shall I?" He placed the envelope on the third step. "And if you'll just sign this. A mere formality." He extended the required paperwork.

Vrac gave a sudden, braying laugh. He moved close enough to poke Gaston hard in the chest and plucked the form from the postman's hand. Scowling, he goggled at it upside down and right side up, turned it over, and gave another burst of mirthless laughter. Momentarily, Gaston was taken in by this dumb show. Then he caught a gleam of malicious cognition in Vrac's eye.

"Monsieur," he cried, somewhat shrilly but with all the dignity he could muster, "I really must—"

But Vrac merely stuffed the paper inside the bib of his dungarees and stalked away.

"Madame," Gaston appealed to the mother, who still barred his path, "I regret to trouble you, but I must have that back. With your signature."

"*Toi.*" Her eyes had never left his face. "*Va t'en foutre,*" she directed, telling him crudely what he could do with his form and his signature together.

It was not a hot day, but Gaston found as he edged past—she left him barely enough room to get by without actually having to brush up against her—that he was perspiring heavily. Defeated, he scrambled into his minivan and drove rapidly away.

⋅

Les Colombes was also on Gaston's route. He had no mail for the de Sauvignacs, but after his experience at La Binette, Gaston felt that he owed himself a stop at the château. He needed something to calm his nerves. He was so shaken that he ground his gears twice as he downshifted to take the steep ascent.

The château was, of course, altogether a different matter, for the de Sauvignacs had once been, and for many remained, the first name in the land. Henri de Sauvignac père, now long dead, was still remembered with affection as a dotty old gentleman with a passion for botany. The son, the present Henri de Sauvignac, was a more worldly character, known in his heyday for his elegance, high living, and appetite for women. He had taken his wife, Jeanne Villiers that was, a willowy, compliant creature, from a well-to-do bourgeois family. In the sixties, the couple had made a handsome grouping with their two little boys, driving about grandly in a shiny new Citroën with hydropneumatic suspension, the first of its kind in the area.

Of the two de Sauvignac sons, Alain, the elder, had grown up, studied civil engineering, and gone abroad to work in places like Gabon and Cameroon. Patrice, the younger, had not grown up because he had drowned in a pond in the woods below Les

Colombes when he was seven. It was a terrible tragedy, and some said that Jeanne de Sauvignac had never fully recovered from the loss.

Now in their seventies, the de Sauvignacs lived almost like recluses but still commanded respect. Aristocratic folk, Gaston called them, with an old-fashioned sense of *ce qu'il faut*. Even on days when he had no mail for them, he frequently made the steep drive up just to look in on the old people. In winter Monsieur was often good for a small tot of rum, in summer a refreshing *coup de blanc,* either of which Gaston took standing on the stone floor of the cavernous kitchen.

In return, the *facteur* gave them the latest local gossip and ran the odd commission, rub for Madame's rheumatism from the pharmacy in Belvès, cigarettes and newspapers for Monsieur from the Chez Nous emporium in Grissac.

The de Sauvignacs still had their Citroën. Like them, it had grown old but retained a certain dusty cachet. From time to time, Monsieur might still be seen puttering sedately along the roads, raising a hand in greeting to the locals, and stopping occasionally to offer, with seigniorial courtesy, directions to lost motorists and rides to bewildered hitchhikers passing through his *territoire.*

•

As he neared the top and turned onto the path running up to the rear of the great house, Gaston remembered that he had been meaning in any case to ask the de Sauvignacs about the *pigeon-nier.* If nothing else, it would give them something to chat about and be good for his *coup de blanc.*

He had shown the photocopy earlier in the week to his fellow *facteurs* (keeping quiet about Mara's cash incentive), with no luck. Now, standing in the vast, damp stone kitchen of the château, he watched anxiously as Henri de Sauvignac studied the, by now, much-wrinkled photocopy. Before looking at it, the old gentleman had first taken his glasses from his jacket pocket and polished the lenses with care before setting them on his beaklike nose. A once imposing man, he was now stooping and cadaverous, but still meticulous in his habits.

"Hundreds like it in the region, m'boy." He shook his head and passed the photocopy to his wife. Jeanne de Sauvignac, trailing several layers of shawls, looked about for her glasses, could not find them, and ended by squinting ineffectually at the paper at arm's length.

"Dear me," she murmured with an absent, lopsided smile that always made Gaston think of village idiots, even though he was ashamed to harbor such a disrespectful thought in association with someone belonging, if only by marriage, to the first family of the region.

"You'll have a time finding one among so many," Monsieur observed. "Things have a way of blending in. One gets so used to seeing them, buildings, people, one no longer in fact sees them, not for what they really are." He seemed to imply that Gaston would be destined to pass by that particular *pigeonnier* every day of his life and never recognize it.

Gaston thought disconsolately that this might be true. He tried to envision all the pigeon houses that he routinely encountered. Many were attached to houses. Others, like the one Mara was looking for, were solitary, freestanding towers. It could have been one of them or none of them. Pity the detail was so hard to make out. *Merde* of a print. Why couldn't the *pigeonnier* have been one of the really distinctive ones, like that self-important cross-timbered block set on six stone pillars he'd once seen in Quercy?

"She's offering a reward." Gaston felt it appropriate to impart the information to the de Sauvignacs. A thousand euros wasn't to be sneezed at and would establish that his inquiry was serious.

"Hmmm," said Henri judiciously. "As much as that. But you have only her word that she'll pay up."

"She seemed sincere," Gaston ventured cautiously. "Of course, I know with foreigners it's say one thing, do another. Still, it's worth keeping one's eyes open."

"Of course. You do that, m'boy," agreed Henri and offered Gaston the longed-for *coup*.

"But what does this person want with a *pigeonnier*?" Madame's watery blue eyes goggled at the postman. Her dry, yellowy-gray hair was as faded as her face. "Will she buy it?"

"Ah. There's a story," exclaimed Gaston, enjoying the cool trickle of wine down his parched throat. And he then spun the de Sauvignacs his version of Beatrice Dunn, enjoying their scandalized attention.

"Funny how life brings things back around," he wound up his narrative with a deep, philosophical sigh. "First *la canadienne disparue*. Now, all these years later, the sister."

"Indeed," Henri said dryly.

Jeanne, bony beneath her shawls, stirred restlessly.

"Well," said Gaston, feeling it was time to change the subject, "what do you hear from—where is he now?"

"Douala," Jeanne said at once.

"Ah, yes," Gaston nodded knowingly. Their son, Alain, was off in Africa, constructing roads. It seemed to the postman that he could have built a superhighway all the way around the continent, he'd been at it so long. For twenty years at least, Gaston had carried up letters bearing colorful stamps from places like Abidjan and Libreville. "Still building things?"

"Bridges." The mother gathered her draperies primly about her. "He's their, what do you call it, washout expert. Very important work."

"Head operations engineer, actually," corrected her husband.

"It rains a lot out there, you know," Jeanne confided. "Bridges are always washing out. He works terribly hard. Of course, it has its compensations. He's much in favor with influential people in the Cameroon. He's been to the *presidential palace*, you know." Her rusty voice pealed with pride. "And he speaks the local patois quite well."

Gaston had heard much of but never clapped eyes on this prodigy, who seemed to like living in places where things collapsed in the wake of tropical storms. For his part, the *facteur* couldn't understand this preference for the jungle, with mosquitoes and snakes, over the healthy *dordognais* countryside.

"His contract has just ended, so he's coming back to be with us." Madame's puckered cheeks went pink with pleasure. "For a visit, before he lines up something else. He'll be home any day now."

That was another side of the Dordogne, Gaston reflected. Young people fleeing for lack of work, only the old remaining. A countryside abandoned to foreign holiday cottagers, or people from Paris who spent two weeks a year in run-down family houses that stood empty and shuttered the rest of the time. How many were like the de Sauvignacs, left stranded, waiting eagerly and pathetically for the next visit from children who had moved on to other lives, other worlds?

Although, in the de Sauvignacs' case, Gaston had heard that it was some problem between father and son that had caused Alain to leave home and stay abroad. Something to do, perhaps, with Alain's objection to his father's profligate ways, his chronic fondness for a bit of skirt. No doubt about it, the old fellow had been a spender and chaser in his day. Women from Limoges to Bordeaux, until his wife's money had given out. It was rumored that this was the bone of contention: Henri de Sauvignac had run the estate into the ground, and the son sweated in Africa to keep Les Colombes in de Sauvignac hands.

Outside, it had grown very dark, even though it was the middle of the afternoon. A wind was building up. Tendrils of ivy tapped fretfully on the small panes of the kitchen window, and Gaston could see trees swaying in the distance. He drained his glass, saluted—for some reason with the de Sauvignacs he always raised a respectful forefinger to the side of his cap by way of greeting and leavetaking—and hurried out to his van.

The first drops of rain were already smacking down, forming big craters in the dust on his windshield. He looked back. Husband and wife seemed to be clinging together in the obscure opening of the kitchen doorway, Madame's draperies whipped by a moist wind. He had the impression of a pair of ragged crows balancing precariously on their perch.

Rapidly he backed out of the overgrown courtyard, where in better times tradesmen had called with crates of champagne, oysters in season, truffles, and foie gras; and where nowadays few but Gaston, with his belly and beetroot nose, ever came.

In the cover of the shrubberies at the corner of the house, a large shape stood motionless as the postal vehicle bumped off down the narrow lane. Vrac stepped out onto the weed-choked, rain-spattered flagstones.

Jeanne saw him first and uttered a startled cry. She stamped her foot. "Go away. Shoo!"

Henri looked up and frowned. Then he said, "Ah, it's you. Come here."

5

•

"You've got a *fouine*," said Mara.

She was balanced precariously on the courtyard wall, peering at the rough tile ends of Prudence Chang's roof. Down below, Jazz was whining and trying to scramble up after her.

Prudence, dressed in a smock like the figures in the Quimper ware she collected, frowned. Sunlight gleamed on her faultless casque of black hair. "I'm from L.A.," she complained. "The only wildlife you get there is Homo sapiens. So what's a foo-een in *anglais*?"

"A marten. Like a weasel." Mara shooed Jazz off and jumped down. "They like old stone houses. Look, you can see where it's been getting in. That hole right there. It's made its den in your roof."

"Oh, swell," said Prudence.

Like many of the expatriates coming back to the region for the summer, Prudence had called Mara first. If the toilets didn't work, if mice had chewed the wiring over the winter, if renovations were needed, Mara knew exactly what to do and whom to contact—fixers like Edouard, who would block up Prudence's roof; Kranz, the plumbing whiz; masons and painters who attended to damage done over the winter by wind and water. She also subcontracted work to a quaint trio of unmarried sisters in Limeuil who specialized in custom sewing.

"You'll have to leave it," Mara advised, brushing her hands off on her jeans. She had stopped by to check on a delivery of tiles from Pablo for the renovation of Prudence's kitchen. The stainless-steel double sink had been installed, but the new tiles for the counters had not arrived, despite the dealer's fervent promise to expedite them.

"Leave it?" Prudence objected. "Mara, it crashes around up there at night like a drunk husband. I'm losing my beauty sleep. And it smells."

"It'll smell worse if you close the hole up now. It's rearing a litter up there, and the lot of them will die. Wait until the babies are grown and leave the den. I'll get someone to seal it up for you then."

"Oh goody," said Prudence unenthusiastically. "I can hardly wait."

"By the way," said Prudence, walking Mara to her car. "That landscaper you set me up with."

"Julian Wood?"

"He's been asking questions about you."

"Oh?" Mara felt her cheeks go warm. "Like what?"

"Like what do I know about you. If you're attached. I think he's interested. Sweetie, you're turning pink."

Mara gave a snort of laughter. "He's fixated on orchids. I doubt if he thinks about anything but flowers. Besides, he's not my type. And I haven't turned pink."

Prudence cocked an Oriental eye at her. "What's your type, then?"

Mara was sure that the pink was now a dark red. "Oh," she said evasively, "someone a little more urbane. Less—less botanical. For heaven's sake, Prudence, I don't know."

"That's your problem," Prudence said, stepping back to regard her severely. "You really don't. I've known you now for—what?— two years? And in all that time I don't think I've ever seen you with a man. I mean, not seriously. What's wrong, gone off them?"

"Not at all." Mara was now on the defensive. "But I've been there before, don't forget. Marriage, divorce, the whole bit." And she had. Hal, her ex, had been a brilliant architect specializing in old stone structures. Everything she knew about restoring houses she had learned from him. Hal also had an ego bigger than the buildings he worked on and a love affair with the bottle that she simply couldn't compete with. Other relationships had followed for her, none of them satisfying. For some reason, she seemed to gravitate toward men who, though outwardly unlike Hal, inevitably revealed the same underlying trait: 150-proof self-worship. Although Julian didn't seem eaten up by conceit. Or was he? She knew nothing about him, really.

"Time to move on, don't you think?" suggested Prudence.

"When I'm ready," said Mara, ending the conversation.

•

Spring was Julian's favorite time of year. The lilacs were just finishing, but the locust trees, coming into bloom, gave a heady sweetness to the air. The hillsides were burnished with golden *genêt,* the local variety of broom, and poppies brightened the fields of newly planted wheat. Edith, Julian noted, was beginning to take on a sleek, self-satisfied look.

Spring was also Julian's peak time for gardening. He had a dozen or so properties that he maintained regularly. Throwing in Prudence Chang's courtyard, which was requiring a lot of work, he found himself hard at it from dawn to dusk. Not that he didn't welcome the business. He knew that things would die down for him later, when it got too hot to do more than nurse seedlings along. Business would pick up slightly in September and October, with fall plantings and beddings down, before dropping off entirely for the winter.

When he had time to think about anything else, his mind was taken up almost entirely with the *Cypripedium.* Almost, because it was hard not to think about Mara, too, given that she was so tightly bound up with this botanical puzzle. He felt a little sorry for her. But also resentful because her position amounted to nothing short of blackmail. Much good it would do her. He knew his chances of tracking down the Lady's Slipper were close to nil, which was exactly the odds he gave Mara's hopeless search for her missing twin. The thought filled him with a certain spiteful satisfaction.

More than a week had passed since Mara had distributed the photocopies. She knew that Julian would have phoned if the *pigeonnier* had been located, so she assumed he had no news. On the other hand, if he had been asking questions about her, as Prudence had said, she wondered that he hadn't found another reason for calling. She thought things over and decided to take matters in hand.

He was just pouring himself a late-morning mug of tea when the phone rang.

"Julian? It's Mara. Are you busy?"

It was Sunday morning, Julian's day of rest.

"Er—no," he said and wondered what he was letting himself in for.

"Well, I was hoping to invite you to lunch."

He was pleasantly surprised. "In that case, entirely at your disposal."

"Great. I'll pick you up at noon. And by the way, I hope you don't mind, there's someone I'd like you to meet."

"Oh?" He was wary once more. Whom did she mean? A boyfriend?

"Look, I've got to run now. Tell you about it when I see you. *A bientôt.*" She rang off.

Julian put the receiver down. What the hell was she up to? It was something he really disliked about her, always tipping him off balance, speaking fluent French, albeit with peculiar vowel sounds, having a dog that lunged out of the dark to take off your arm, turning nasty over the photos. And now inviting him to lunch so she could introduce him to somebody else. Still, she was paying. He showered and put on a clean pair of slacks—well, they had a couple of not-too-visible splotches on the knee (Mado's crab mousse?)—and a freshly laundered shirt.

He waited for her at the roadside to save her the walk to his front door. She pulled up, and he got in. She looked glamorous in dark glasses and an orange short-sleeved dress. Her arms were slim, her neck graceful. Had she done something to her hair? It was shorter than he recalled, sleeker.

Jazz was in the back seat of her Renault, but no one else. So where was this person she wanted him to meet? He risked the French cheek-to-cheek greeting, keeping an eye out for any sign of jealousy from Jazz, but the dog only favored him with a careful exploration of the back of his neck with a cold, wet nose.

"So—where are we going? Or am I allowed to know?"

"Bergerac. There's a restaurant there I'm dying to try. And then Duras. Didn't I say?"

"No, you didn't." Bergerac first and then Duras? That would take the rest of the day. Really, Julian thought, feeling a little put out by her easy assumptions regarding himself. To make matters worse, her dog was now resting his heavy head on Julian's left shoulder.

"Sorry." She executed a three-point turn. "It's just that the person I want you to meet lives in Duras. Louis—although he prefers to be called Loulou—"

The boyfriend, Julian confirmed with irritation and shoved the head away. It returned with a gust of malodorous breath.

Why on earth invite him to lunch and drag him to Duras just to introduce him to a clown named Loulou?

"—La Pouge," she finished. "The retired policeman I told you about. The one who put me on to you."

"Ah." The one who had referred to him as—what was it?—a local authority. That was all right. Mollified, he reached back absentmindedly to scratch Jazz's neck.

"I phoned him yesterday. He wants to meet you." She braked before turning onto the main road. "I figured we could swing by Duras on our way back from Bergerac. It's not much out of the way. He's the one who was involved in investigating Bedie's disappearance. I told him about your idea of handing out copies of the *pigeonnier* photo, by the way. He said it was a very clever strategy."

"I'm afraid I haven't heard anything from Paul or Gaston," Julian had to admit.

"It's early days yet, Julian." She turned to him with a smile. The dark glasses flashed. Her voice had a huskiness that got him in the base of his spine. "Anything could happen."

Anything could, he thought, and warmed to the possibility. Suddenly he felt quite happy to be rocketing—she drove too fast—across the countryside with her. Glad about lunch in Bergerac, glad about Duras and Loulou.

•

Cyrano de Bergerac had nothing to do with Bergerac. Still, this did not prevent the Bergeracois from embracing Rostand's romantic hero as their own, even raising a statue to this fictional character, nose and all.

Roadwork was going on around the statue when Mara and Julian arrived. Workmen were once again tearing things up. Consequently, traffic was snarled and parking impossible. They had to leave the car below the Ancien Port and walk back up along the quai where in times past *gabarres,* the workhorses of the Dordogne, had discharged lumber from upcountry for making barrels and taken on casks of Bergerac wine. Nowadays it seemed the boats were mostly used to shunt tourists about.

Their destination was in the old town, a small restaurant called, with a grammarian play on words, Le Plus-que-Parfait, the Pluperfect. An elderly waiter waved them in and seated them at a shady table on the terrace at the rear. With a dignified tread, he brought Jazz a bowl of water on a tray before even considering Julian and Mara's needs. The French were like that. Nutty about dogs.

The lunch, living up to the restaurant's name, was more than perfect. Julian started with grilled foie gras of duck topped with thin parings of summer truffles and went on to a fish dish of *merluchon* baked in cream. Mara had oysters, followed by quail in a delicate pastry basket. She chose the wine, a crackling dry white Bordeaux. Cheese was roundels of *cabécou,* lightly grilled, dessert fresh Garriguette strawberries dipped in dark chocolate and topped with crème anglaise. Julian took the opportunity to point out that the strawberry, unlike most fruit, wore its seeds on the outside.

"The red pulpy bit that we think of as the strawberry is actually what's called the pseudocarp."

"No kidding," Mara commented with her mouth full.

Jazz sampled everything except the oysters, which Mara said made him sick. Mara liked the way Julian let her handle the wine, deferring to her choice. So many men she knew seemed to need to take charge of the wine, as if it were some kind of male preserve.

Their conversation throughout the meal was relaxed, verging at times on intimate as they disclosed to each other selected details of their lives.

"My people? Oh, your garden-variety Brits." Julian leaned back with a pleasant feeling of repletion. "I grew up in Essex, oldest of five. Did a degree in horticulture at Wye. In those lighter, swifter days of my youth," he sighed with exaggerated but perhaps not mock regret, "I played wing forward for my college rugby team."

Had he ever been married? Well, yes, he had. At the age of twenty-three, he had fallen hard for a stunning French au pair and moved with her to the Dordogne. It was the seventies, life was easy, and theirs the romance of the century. Unfortunately, like so many relationships, it hadn't worked out. Véronique had developed other interests. By then, however, he had taken root in French soil. He had been gardening in the Dordogne ever since. If Julian neatly glossed over how deeply the au pair's defection had hurt him, the chaos it had made of his life, and the anger he had experienced, still felt sometimes, he did so because that had been twenty-five years ago, and, where Véronique was concerned, the less said the better.

Mara described her background. Grew up in Montreal. Crazy hybrid family, Scottish father, French-Canadian mother who came from a tiny place in Quebec with the unlikely name of Saint-Louis-du-Ha! Ha! She explained that the "Ha! Ha!" (complete with exclamation marks) had nothing to do with laughter but was an old French word for "dead end." Many archaic terms no longer used in France still survived in Quebec.

"Mum's *pure laine,* one-hundred-percent *québécoise,*" she informed Julian, "and a staunch separatist. Wants Quebec out of Canada. Dad says, Dream on, it'll never happen. They argue endlessly about it. It's their way—" She paused and drew breath "—of not talking about Bedie." She turned her wineglass about slowly, concentrating on the shifting level of the liquid.

"You know," she said, "when we were kids, Bedie and I hated

being twins. We fought a lot, and we were horribly competitive. If I beat her at tennis, she had to beat me in skiing. We were always trying to put distance between us."

"Isn't that typical?" offered Julian. "I mean, with twins?"

She shrugged. "I suppose. Anyway, I left home in the seventies, did a couple of years at the Ontario College of Art, got a job with a design firm in Toronto. Bedie stayed on and did a degree in wildlife biology at McGill. After a few years apart, I think we realized, like it or not, we were joined. It was only then that we began to be friends."

After Bedie's disappearance, Mara had drifted, freelancing in Ottawa, Vancouver, and Montreal. She touched briefly on her failed marriage to Hal. Like Julian, she felt the less said the better. Bedie continued to haunt her dreams. Cutting ties in Canada to come to the Dordogne had not been easy, especially since it meant she had to start up anew in a place where she was unknown and where she knew no one. However, timing had been in her favor. With the boom in holiday cottages and the influx of expats, her line of work was now very much in demand.

"I have something for you," Mara said over coffee. Ceremoniously, she presented Julian with a duplicate set of the photographs.

"Ah," he said. "Thanks."

Tucking them in his shirt pocket, he had to acknowledge that she had come through with her end of the bargain. Now he would have to make some sort of effort, even if halfhearted, to do his part. A deal was a deal.

6

They reached Duras around four in the afternoon. The buildings of the town ambled pleasantly along a breezy escarpment above the broad, green valley of the Dropt. Vineyards stretched away below them. Mara parked in front of a narrow stone-faced house just off the main road. They left Jazz in the car, head thrust disapprovingly through the open window. Julian sincerely hoped no one would pass within lunging distance of the vehicle.

"So, madame, we meet again!" Loulou La Pouge swept Mara an exaggerated bow. He pumped Julian's hand, greeting him in rapid, voluble French. He was a tubby, energetic man, pushing seventy, with remnant strands of hair plastered across a speckled scalp and a round face creased from smiling. Julian thought that he looked less like a retired cop than a superannuated cherub.

"Entrez. Entrez." He led them into a narrow parlor crowded with furniture. An upright piano stood at one end of the room. Family photographs took up every available horizontal surface. There were more photographs on the walls. "Sit down. Sit down."

Julian and Mara perched stiffly on small overstuffed chairs while their host brought out a chilled Monbazillac.

"You know this wine?" Loulou held the bottle aloft. "Pure nectar. A specialty of the region. Gets its sweetness from a fungus, what we call *la pourriture noble,* the noble rot. It makes the grapes split open and shrivel up, a horrible sight, but it creates a very high sugar content. Did you know the harvest is done grape by grape, with special clippers?" He trotted away and came back with little glass dishes of shelled pistachios.

"*Santé!*" Loulou plumped his sizable haunches onto a plush-covered sofa and raised his glass. "Now we have our little chat, eh?" He poked a forefinger at Julian. "You must, of course, wonder how I got on to you in the first place. Well, I saw your slide show, eight, maybe nine years ago. In Bergerac. The wife talked me into going. She was keen on flowers. When she was alive. You gave a talk at the public library. Something about orchids. Unforgettable."

"Ah." Julian was gratified but unremembering.

"You tripped on the cord—ha-ha! The carousel went on the floor. Slides flew everywhere." The cherub gestured expansively.

"Ah," repeated Julian, placing the event.

"Everything was out of order. You kept saying, Sorry, sorry. All the same, when Mara looked me up, I remembered you. Thought maybe you'd be able to spot something in those photos. Couldn't recall your name, of course, but a fellow at the library was helpful. Still, I expect you'll have a time trying to trace those flowers."

Mara cut in, "Julian's very knowledgeable about orchids."

Loulou chuckled, as if she had just told a mildly funny joke. "Of course. However, as I already told you, your first problem is establishing that the camera really was your sister's in the first place."

Mara's chin shot up. "I'm positive it's the twin to mine. I'd know it anywhere. Besides, her initials were on the case."

"*Alors,* the famous initials." The cherub twinkled mirthfully. Another joke. "But we must look at the facts, eh? You found this camera where? A junk shop in Villeréal. How did it get there? Part of a lot purchase from another dealer. Where did this other dealer get the camera? Only *le bon dieu* knows because the person in question is now dead, and when she was alive, la Camelote showed up at every estate sale from Bordeaux to Toulouse. First the undertaker, then la Camelote. Where did she get it? She left no records of acquisition, that one! It could have been part of another lot purchase from another *brocanteur,* for all we know. I sympathize, but you must understand that the lads in Périgueux need more to go on than hearsay."

"Hearsay!" Mara was indignant. "Loulou, I'm convinced Bedie took those photos. This is the first positive lead I've had, and if the police aren't willing to do anything about it, I"—she glanced quickly at Julian—"*we're* going to follow it up."

Julian caught her shift of pronouns and fidgeted uncomfortably in his chair.

"*Très bien.*" Loulou threw up his hands. "Let's say, for the sake of argument, that's how it was. Then let's review the course of events. Before her disappearance, your sister and the boyfriend, Monsieur Scott Barrow, were camping at Les Gabarres. According to him, they had already visited—let me see—the Caves of Lascaux, Sarlat, Domme, La Roque–Gageac, Castelnaud. To get around, they walked or hitchhiked. Then they have the falling out. He wants to move on, she wants to stay. He goes off on the eighth of May, she remains at Les Gabarres. He comes back two days later, on the tenth. Their tent and equipment are still there, but your sister is not. On the thirteenth, Monsieur Scott becomes worried and calls the police.

"Now, if Mademoiselle Beatrice took those photos"—Loulou held up a finger—"mind, I don't say she did. But if she did, then she could only have done so *after* she and Monsieur Scott separated because in his *déclaration* he made no mention of having been to Beynac, which is on the first couple of frames of the film."

Mara shrugged. "Why not? It's a major tourist attraction. It was fairly near the campground. And, don't you see, the fact that she and Scott *hadn't* already visited Beynac is a kind of negative proof that Bedie took those pictures. Because if Bedie had already been there she would have had no reason to return."

Julian found her reasoning unncessarily complicated.

Loulou merely looked unconvinced. "But how much better if the photographs actually tied in with places your sister was definitely known to have visited? Or, better still, if there were a shot of her in front of the castle keep?"

Julian spoke up, realizing as he did so that he was nailing down Mara's earlier use of "we," but something, he knew, was expected of him. "Look, in my opinion, what you've really got to deal with is the *discontinuity*."

"Comment?" asked the ex-*flic*.

"I mean, after Beynac the quality of the light changes from overcast and wet to sunny and dry. Okay, admittedly, the weather can shift pretty rapidly in May. But also, and what's more important, the film goes from a castle in a built-up area to flowers that mainly grow in forests and undisturbed areas. Now, I know orchids pop up in the damnedest places—roadsides, airfields. Nevertheless, it really seems to me the critical piece is how Bedie got from Beynac to wherever she photographed this lot."

"Bravo," cried Loulou, clapping Julian on the shoulder. "You, *mon ami*, will make a detective yet." He tipped a handful of pistachios into the red hole of his mouth and scooted forward in his seat. "So," he said, munching loudly, "this suggests an interesting scenario. Mademoiselle Beatrice meets someone. They get to talking. She tells this person she's interested in orchids. He says, I know a place where the ground is covered with them. She goes with him. They drive to some isolated spot. Then—*tac!*"—both Julian and Mara jumped—"he does away with her."

"But not right away," objected Julian. "Don't forget, she had the chance to take thirty more photographs. If this person intended to harm her, why wait?"

Loulou shoveled more nuts in his mouth and considered. "Maybe he didn't mean to. Maybe something happened along the way. Our man makes a pass. Mademoiselle Beatrice resists. Or perhaps he simply needed to lure her to a sufficiently isolated spot . . ."

Mara shuddered. "All the same," she persisted, "if this person knew where to find the orchids, then it means he must have been local, from the area. And if we can find where those orchids grew, it's possible they could lead us to him."

Loulou pulled a face. "What's local? Do you remember the Dutch tourist we dug up in Quercy? Hanneke Tenhagen, student from Eindhoven, twenty-one years old." He addressed himself to Julian. "Let me tell you something about Mademoiselle Tenhagen. Multiple fractures to the skull, as if the killer had been in a frenzy. Possibly raped. Her corpse was pretty badly decomposed when we got to it. A truffle hunter and his dog found her. Shallowly buried and then covered over with branches. Maybe the killer was disturbed in the middle of concealing the body. How did she get there? We interviewed an elderly couple who remembered picking up someone fitting Hanneke Tenhagen's description at the beginning of August outside of Millau. Drove her as far as Rodez. Three months later, her body turns up in the woods near Carennac, one hundred and twenty kilometers away, *mon dieu!* And between Carennac and Beynac, it's another eighty kilometers. So you see"—Loulou pivoted back to Mara—"your idea of local doesn't work. If he had a car, our killer could have come from anywhere, gone anywhere."

"He has a point," Julian conceded. Mara glared at him.

Loulou continued: "Even if you find out where those photos

were taken, where do you start? Do you question everyone in the vicinity? Do you dig up the forests? You must comprehend, Mara, your sister's case was difficult because there was no evidence of a crime. I was working in Missing Persons at the time. We had very little to go on. I'm afraid she simply remained for us *la canadienne disparue.*"

Mara felt suddenly tired. The visit was taking a discouraging turn that she had not expected. Had Loulou invited them merely to justify the lack of interest on the part of the police? She glanced at Julian, who seemed disappointingly willing to capitulate. She was thinking of terminating their stay as politely as she could, when Loulou raised a hand.

"Of course, you haven't yet asked me the most important question."

Mara blinked. "What's that?"

"So far we have Mademoiselle Beatrice and the Dutch woman. But *were they the only ones?*"

Mara and Julian stared at him.

Mara found her voice. "There were others?"

Loulou savored his moment, rising to pour another round of wine and taking care to give the bottle a half-turn each time, to avoid drips. "Have more nuts," he said maddeningly.

"You see, my friends"—he addressed his guests but spoke as if a much bigger audience filled the room—"after I talked with you yesterday, Mara, I got to thinking. I used to keep a journal, rough case notes, to help me on the job, so to speak. I thought, who knows, maybe one day I'll write my memoirs. Well, anyway, I looked through them last night, just to refresh my mind." He paused, bottle in hand.

"And?" they asked in unison.

"*Eh bien,* there were *subsequent events* that might interest you."

They both sat forward. "Subsequent events?"

He nodded, pleased with his effect. "Just that. At intervals, spaced out over the next fourteen years."

"Bodies?" Julian asked.

"No," Loulou admitted regretfully, "but vanished, like Mademoiselle Beatrice. One was a woman from Souillac, Julie Ménard, thirty-five, married. Summer of '89 it was. Another was a middle-aged spinster, Mariette Charlebois, from Le Buisson, July 1993. Then there was a teenager, Valérie Rules, from the hamlet of La Bique, set out after school one day, never arrived home. That was in June 1998."

"They've never been heard from since?"

"Missing to this day. Every one of them." Loulou had the self-satisfied air of a magician making rabbits disappear. What he actually did, however, was to put the bottle down and go over to the piano bench. As he lifted the top, Julian and Mara could see that it was filled not with sheet music but with square copybooks with shiny red covers, such as schoolchildren used. "It's all," he said, proudly displaying his archive, "in here." Despite the cheap melodrama of it, they were impressed.

"Naturally," Loulou went on, "we did the usual routine questioning—family, friends, employers, teachers, parish priests. Even talked seriously with a couple of *types*."

"Well?" Mara pressed.

"Phut!" He dropped the piano bench lid with a resounding thud.

"Wait a minute." Mara turned suddenly to Julian. "La Bique. Isn't that just down the road from you?"

Julian, about to help himself to pistachios, paused. "Well, yes. Yes, it is. Oh, I see. Valérie Rules. Now that you mention it, I do remember hearing about her. I believe she went to school in Grissac. Everyone said she ran away from home."

"Who knows?" Their host pulled up a chair opposite them and sat down on it. "Let me tell you something. I'm speaking as a cop now, with many years' experience. With missing persons, psychology is very important. Julie Ménard, the woman from Souillac, husband claimed she went off with another man. Personally, I always thought the husband did her in. But her clothes were gone, and she did have a certain reputation. Or la Charlebois. Nursed her invalid *maman,* vicious old trout, rich to the gills, but never let her daughter have a life of her own. So one day poor Mariette just walks out and doesn't come back. Who can blame her? As for *la petite* Valérie, alcoholic father, neurotic mother, she could have run away. Kids do that. Is she dead? Or working the streets in Marseille?"

Loulou leaned forward. "Even Mademoiselle Beatrice. She and her boyfriend had a quarrel serious enough to cause Monsieur Scott to leave. Maybe your sister, out of spite or disgust, simply went off, too."

"But we would have heard from her," Mara cried out. "She would never have left us without word all these years—" She bit her lip, deeply troubled.

"But of course." Loulou waved a hand. "Undoubtedly, something unpleasant occurred." Mara found it a perverse kind of comfort. "The question is, what? You see, Hanneke Tenhagen aside, where the other women are concerned we have to consider the possibility that *no crimes were committed at all.* Valérie, Mariette, and Julie could have simply left for reasons of their own. Beatrice could have met with an accident—"

"No," Mara objected. "The camera changes all that. Whoever found the camera would have also found her body and reported it."

"Not necessarily, if she dropped the camera first. Picture it.

She slips, drops the camera, tumbles off a cliff into the river, her body is never recovered. My point is simply that some or all of these missing women may still be alive."

"You don't believe that!" Mara cried.

Loulou tugged meditatively at the fatty wattle beneath his chin. "No," he said finally. "I don't. And this leads me to the second possibility and my little theory. Because, you see, if we say that these women, including your sister, are all dead, then we must also consider the possibility that their deaths were not unrelated."

Mara tensed. "Are you saying that we're dealing with a serial killer?"

Loulou cocked his head to one side. "It's something to think about, *n'est-ce pas*? And it leads us to an interesting speculation. Taken all together, the disappearances tell us a little about the person, if it is one person, whom we seek. *Primo,*"—he stuck up a big, flat thumb—"it was certainly a man, and one who chose his victims at random. Why? Because only Beatrice and Hanneke Tenhagen had anything in common. Both were tourists, similar age and build, both hitchhiking. Little Valérie Rules, on the other hand, was a schoolkid, fifteen, no breasts, skinny like a stick. La Charlebois, forty-two, fat, face like a cow pat. Julie Ménard, thirty-five, glamorous in a cheap way, liked the bright lights. So he took them as he found them.

"*Secundo,*"—a forefinger shot out to join the thumb—"he probably was, how should we say, comme il faut, presentable. Maybe even"—he grinned at Julian—"an orchid amateur like yourself. Oho! You are discomfited. But it's logical. Who better to attract someone like Mademoiselle Beatrice, who loved orchids and who would be easily approachable by anyone who shared her interest? Tell me, were you in the Dordogne nineteen years ago, monsieur?"

Julian looked aghast. "Was I—? Well, yes, I was."

"And you undoubtedly heard about *la canadienne disparue*?"

"Of course I did," cried Julian irritably. "It was everywhere on the news. But there was absolutely no mention of orchids at the time."

"True," admitted Loulou. "That's something that has only come to light just now. Always assuming, of course, that the photographs were taken by Mara's sister."

"They were," said Mara doggedly.

"Regardless," Julian persisted, "you can't honestly believe—"

"*Assez.* Enough," Loulou chuckled. "Just my little joke. All I say is, whoever it was, his victims must have trusted him. Hanneke Tenhagen was hitching rides, very possibly Mademoiselle Beatrice and Valérie Rules as well. Would any of them have gone willingly with Quasimodo?"

Julian parried, "He could have forced them or taken them by surprise."

"You mean followed them to a lonely spot and then—*couic!*" Loulou drew his forefinger sharply across his throat.

Mara winced.

The ex-cop shook his head. "It doesn't fit. Take Mariette Charlebois, fat, asthmatic. Or the Ménard woman. Unlikely that either of them would have been wandering alone in the forest. More probably our predator met them in a more conventional way. Say la Charlebois is sitting disconsolately in a *salon de thé,* dipping a macaroon and thinking about her horrible mama. A stranger befriends her. He is *sympathique,* offers her a ride somewhere. Or Julie Ménard. Picks her up in a bar.

"*Tercio,* it's probable that our man lived or worked somewhere in the region, or traveled, for whatever reason, within Périgord-Quercy. And, finally, he must have had some form of transportation because the disappearances were widely distributed."

Julian developed this train of thought. "So you have a body in Carennac and four others missing, last seen in Souillac, La Bique, Le Buisson—and Beynac, if we accept that Bedie was there. All of these places lie in an east-west line *exactly following the Dordogne.* Have you considered that the person you're looking for might work on the river? A barge hand, for example. Or someone who works on those tourist *gabarres.*"

"Hmm," said Loulou. "Yes, we thought of that. Except my theory is, it's not the river but the road. Every one of those places is also on the D703, the major east-west artery, or the D25 where it joins the D703. Who knows, maybe he was a trucker with a delivery route along that stretch."

Mara came in. "The dates of these incidents. Except for Bedie and the Dutch woman, which occurred in the same year, the others were—what?—roughly four or five years apart? You said the last one was Valérie Rules, in 1998. So nothing's happened since then?"

"Not within the region. Not so far." A hard glint came into Loulou's eyes. "Makes you wonder, doesn't it?"

"Yes, it does."

"But surely women have gone missing in other places," Julian objected.

"*Certainement.* Over the years there have been disappearances elsewhere—Limoges, Bordeaux, Biarritz."

"Then maybe your man's not from around here after all. And maybe the four-to-five-year gap doesn't hold, either. In fact, as you pointed out, every one of these women could have gone off for their own reasons. You could be looking for a killer and a pattern that don't exist."

"Hanneke Tenhagen was most definitely and brutally murdered," Loulou reminded him sharply.

"Of course," Julian conceded, looking vaguely troubled. "I wasn't referring to her."

"And my sister," said Mara. "She didn't disappear of her own volition. I'm sure of that. I think Loulou's right. I don't know about the women in other places, but for my money, Bedie, Hanneke Tenhagen, Julie Ménard, Mariette Charlebois, and Valérie Rules are connected somehow. I think there's a killer loose in the Dordogne, Julian, and he's probably looking for his next victim right now."

They were all silent for a long moment.

Julian was the first to speak. "All of this is very interesting. But what are we supposed to do with it?"

"Do?" Loulou looked startled. "In my opinion, nothing. But of course, that's up to you." He peered closely at Mara and shook his head. "I fear, however, that Madame is very much the one for action."

"I'm convinced the orchids are trying to tell us something, at least where my sister is concerned," she said.

"*Eh bien,* what about you, Monsieur the Orchid Expert? Do these flowers also speak to you?"

Julian blinked. "Well," he said after a moment, "it so happens the section of the Dordogne Valley between Souillac and Le Buisson is a part of the region I know well because of the mapping and field research I did for my book." Not in his wildest dreams had he ever expected *Wildflowers of the Dordogne/Fleurs sauvages de la Dordogne* to be put to such a bizarre application. "Offhand, I'd say that most of the orchids in the photographs could be found there. Trouble is, they can also be found in other places, scattered pretty much throughout the region." He shook his head. "When all's said and done, it's precious little to go on."

By the time Loulou saw them out, the day was coming to a

spectacular end. A fierce sunset bathed the western face of the town, lingered redly in the windows of the houses. The vineyards in the valley below stood in shadow.

"*Bonne chance!*" Loulou shook hands energetically with them. "I think you have much work ahead of you. Keep me informed. I'll be very interested to know how you progress." He added gravely, "But be careful. You realize, do you not, Mara, that you place yourself in great jeopardy?"

"Me?" Mara was startled.

"But of course. If our killer is still operating in the area, you could come as a nasty shock." And since she still looked puzzled, he explained: "Your face, Mara. Your face. You will remind him unpleasantly of a woman he murdered nineteen years ago. Our man will not be happy finding you on his trail. Having killed before, how easy it will be for him to kill again." Loulou regarded her searchingly. In a moment of genuine solicitousness, he took her hand once more.

"If you really want my advice, I say give it up. Take it from me. Some things are better left alone."

"I'm not sure how useful that was," Julian grumbled as they left Loulou's house. "All we know now is that four other women, apart from Bedie, have gone missing, and the police haven't been able to find them. And I'm not including Hanneke Tenhagen."

"But there's the possibility that one person might be behind the disappearances," said Mara. "It puts everything in a different light."

"Humph," said Julian.

As Mara drove out of the town, she reflected that Julian had played it rather cagey about Bedie and Valérie Rules. He clearly remembered the cases well enough but for some reason had been reluctant to admit his knowledge. Was he just one of those people who didn't like talking about unpleasant things? Or was there something more behind his reticence?

"Are you going to take his advice about giving it up?" Julian asked, noting that she had gone quiet.

"Of course not," said Mara, downshifting into a turn.

Far away, against a fiery sky, a buzzard circled lazily, on the hunt.

7

Mara e-mailed Patsy:

> *Look, Patsy, I know you don't do criminal psychiatry, but do you have any thoughts on what the profile of a serial killer might look like?* <

In her Manhattan office, housed on the third floor of a dignified if dingy brownstone, Patsy frowned as she read Mara's message. She rubbed her nose, made a noise that sounded like "Sheew!," and tapped out a response.

> *Not until you tell me what's behind this, kiddo.* <

> *Loulou La Pouge, the ex-flic I told you about, thinks we may be dealing with a serial killer. He's collected information on other women who have gone missing from the area. Bedie and Hanneke Tenhagen, whom you know about, both date from 1984, but after that there was someone named Julie Ménard from Souillac who disappeared in 1989, then a Mariette Charlebois from Le Buisson in 1993, and a schoolgirl from La Bique in 1998. The problem is, except for Hanneke Tenhagen, there was no evidence of a crime in any of the cases, they're all simply missing persons. Nevertheless, Loulou thinks they were all the victims of foul play by a single perpetrator.* <

> Okay, I get you. Look, like you said, I'm no forensic shrink. There's a range of psychiatric disorders that can turn nasty, given the right push. But what you're talking about is a whole different twist. However, at a guess, I'd say your subject would probably present as someone with a lot of unresolved anger, obsessive, a loner, socially inept. Although not necessarily a geek. In fact, this person might have to be capable of projecting a lot of charm in order to get near his victims. Don't forget, some of the most horrific mass murderers have behaved like thoroughly nice people. At least at first. <

> Right. My next question is, what would drive this person to seek a victim at regular intervals? The dates of all these incidents are roughly four to five years apart. <

> Hoo boy. You don't want much, do you? At a guess, and this is no more than a guess, I'd say any situation that causes the demons to rise, say an adverse life change or some sort of personal crisis. On the other hand, it might be as simple as noncompliance with medications. Say we're dealing with a severely paranoid individual on antipsychotic drugs who quits taking his Thorazine every so often and starts hearing voices. It could also be something that moves this person periodically out of circulation. Say a series of prison sentences or a history of repeat psychiatric hospital stays. Then again, maybe he simply goes by an inner clock. However, the real question for me, Mara, is not the timing, but what makes a serial killer in the first place. Is it simply hard-wiring? Some kind of significant precipitating conditions? A combination of both? Answer that question, kid, and you could make psychiatric history. <

It was something to go on, Mara reflected as she read Patsy's reply. Except how did she set about commandeering the incarceration and release records of every person who'd served time in a French jail since 1984, or the admission-discharge information of psychiatric patients? She doubted Loulou would be willing or even able to twist arms to help her. And what about Patsy's question. Was the killer she sought triggered by cyclical events? Or was he driven by an inner impulse, like a spring wound tighter and tighter until it caused the mechanism it governed to burst apart?

Paul gave out the photocopies of the *pigeonnier*. Like Gaston, he did not mention Mara's money incentive. He did not see his father until the following week, when he and Mado went to the family farm outside Issigeac for Sunday lunch. His uncle Emile and Sylvie, Emile's wife, were also there.

Paul's mother had prepared a haunch of Quercy lamb, lightly rubbed with garlic and so tender it made one sigh. They had, in addition, fennel in cream sauce with pan-roasted potatoes, a compote of prunes, a plate of local cheeses, and a Savoy cake, light and moist as only Tante Sylvie, a Savoyarde from Bonneville, could make it. The wine was a robust red from the family's own vineyard. Fresh figs finished off the meal. Paul's mother believed, for reasons of her own, that figs would help Mado to conceive.

"By the way," Paul said as the women cleared the table for coffee and Armagnac. He pulled out a crumpled copy of the dovecote photo and handed it across to his father and uncle. "Does this look familiar?"

His father adjusted his glasses, smoothed out the paper, and peered at it. "It's a pigeon house," he said finally, handing it on to Emile.

"Right," said his brother, who suffered from a left-veering amblyopia.

"I mean," said Paul, "do you know it?"

Uncle Emile, bad eye wandering up the chimney, reached for a toothpick. "Sure."

"You do?" Paul sat forward. "This very one?"

"Well, maybe not this very one. *Zut!* You can stand on a hilltop and see half a dozen like it any day."

"Not so much around here, though," said Paul's father.

"What's wrong with around here?" asked Paul.

"Well, they didn't go in for pigeons as much. Pigeons eat too much grain."

"And the roof of this one is different," offered Uncle Emile.

"How so?"

"It's made with *lauzes*. Around here it's mostly tile."

"What's so special about this one, anyway?" Paul's father tapped the photocopy.

"Nothing," said his son, "but if you can locate it, there's money in it."

Father and uncle looked interested for the first time. "How much?" they asked together.

"One thousand euros. Split two ways, five hundred for me, five hundred for whoever can tell me where to find it."

"One thousand euros." Uncle Emile screwed up his face in the effort of converting currencies. He still thought in francs, would never get used to euros. "*Bigre!* That's almost seven thousand francs."

Both older men looked more carefully at the photocopy.

"Where do you come in?" asked the father after a while.

"Brokerage fee," grinned the son, leaning back in his chair, content for the moment to digest his excellent meal.

Slowly breasting the hill, the ancient wood-paneled truck came to a groaning, fumy halt at the summit. The young German hitchhiker ran forward gladly, swinging his rucksack onto his back.

"Sarlat?" he inquired with a broad smile, naming his destination to the driver.

The driver, a farmer in a shapeless, broad-brimmed hat, barely glanced at the hitchhiker, gave a grunt and a nod, and signaled with a thumb for the young man to climb onto the bed of the truck.

"Danke! Merci!" the youth shouted. He trotted back and hoisted himself lightly up over the tailgate.

The vehicle revved up with a shuddering jerk, moved forward, and gathered speed on the downhill run. The German, whose name was Hans, slipped off his pack and lowered himself beside it, squeezing down onto the floor of the truck bed between a stack of empty crates and an assortment of muddy tires and dented milk cans. On the other side of the crates was a heap of dirty sacking. A thin, good-looking youth traveling *auto-stop* through France for the first time, Hans had been lucky. From Carcassonne, two rides in swift succession had brought him this far. He calculated that this lift would bring him to Sarlat within the hour. He leaned back against the wooden slats of the side frame, stretching his long legs out before him, and congratulated himself on his good fortune. With the heel of his boot he shoved one of the crates aside to make more space. The sacking next to it moved. Hans was startled to see that he was not alone. A hand flapped in the air, as if driving away flies. Then the sacking sat up. Hans saw a flat, misshapen face perched neckless on a massive pair of shoulders. One eye was obscured by a dark lens. The other glared at him balefully.

"Bitte," said Hans faintly, forgetting momentarily what little French he knew. The uncovered eye continued to fix him unpleasantly.

"I go to Sarlat." Hans struggled. "You go also to Sarlat?"

The face gave no indication of intelligent reception.

Hans smiled weakly. Nervously, he dug into his rucksack for his guidebook and made a great display of poring through it. Sarlat-le-Canéda, the German text informed him, boasted some of the finest examples of medieval secular architecture in the Dordogne. The town had grown up around a ninth-century Benedictine abbey. The thirteenth and early fourteenth centuries were the golden age for Sarlat, which waxed in importance as a market town. But the Hundred Years' War left it weakened and depopulated.

Hans stole a nervous glance at his companion, who had not left off staring at him in a way that made the young German increasingly uncomfortable. It was at this point that Hans realized that they had left the main highway and were bouncing crazily over a dirt road, headed in a westerly direction, trailing a plume of dust behind them.

"Hey, wait a minute," he shouted in German. "Stop! Where are you going?"

If anything, the truck picked up speed. With difficulty, he stood up, steadying himself against the side rail, and worked his way forward. In order to reach the cab, he had to step over the legs of his fellow passenger.

"Bitte," he said again and banged with his fist on the metal roof. *"Halt!"* The wind cut at his blond hair as he stood swaying with the side-to-side motion of the vehicle. *"Stopp! Stopp!"* The landscape of Black Périgord, which he had so recently been prepared to admire, flew past him, wild and unfriendly. Then the truck took a sudden turn that sent him sprawling over the other

man, upsetting the crates, which, being loosely stacked, went spinning against the tailgate. The patch-eyed man, with intentional malevolence, seized the hapless German by the collar and shoved him backward with a force sufficient to land him winded against the opposite side of the bed.

"Hey!" shouted Hans, terrified but prepared to defend himself. "What did you do that for?"

For answer, Vrac gave only a hoarse, unpleasant laugh.

Hans took in the size of the man's hands and the fact that they were now jolting through alien forest over a deeply rutted road. Tall trees rose up gloomily all around. Mutely, he sank to the floor of the truck bed.

After what seemed like an interminable time to the young German, the truck came to a rocking halt. The cab door slammed, and the driver got out and came to the back.

"Listen." Hans rose to his feet and stopped. He now perceived that the driver was not a man but a woman, but that did not improve his situation. Seen full-on, hat pushed back, her aspect, with its gargoyle features and a purple mark over one eye, was enough to make his mouth go dry.

"Wh-what do you want?"

"Cash." La Binette held out a blackened hand as hard and horny as a hoof. She never took traveler's checks or credit cards.

"Haven't got any," Hans squeaked, which was near enough to the truth.

"Your wallet," la Binette demanded.

"I give you money, and then what?" he demanded spiritedly in his rudimentary French.

Again, Vrac gave a loud, braying laugh. "Give!" he roared, rising to his feet.

Frightened though he was, Hans was a quick thinker. Also a fast sprinter.

"All right," he said and picked up his pack as if to comply. In one fluid motion, he leaped over the opposite side rail and was off through the trees, running like a hare.

Vrac gave a tardy bellow and lumbered forward.

"Leave it," snarled the mother. The German was already lost to view. With a stoical grunt, la Binette climbed back into the cab, turned the truck around, and set off in the direction they had come. Vrac lay down again and resumed his nap. His mother drove until they rejoined the D703. She turned onto it and proceeded slowly west. At this time of year there wasn't much traffic, and fewer hitchhikers. From June on, she knew things would improve.

8

She stood still, her heart pounding. Once again she heard the sounds, a soft rustling in the undergrowth, the snap of a twig.

"Who's there?" she called. And turned, staring wildly about her.

From the dark shadow of the forest there came only breathless silence.

Panicked, she groped for a stick, a rock, anything with which to defend herself. Then she glimpsed it moving behind the screen of trees. Slowly it broke into view, coming on her with an implacable tread. In horror, Mara saw for the first time the large, shapeless thing that had been behind her, the creature through whose hungry eyes she had watched her sister on the forest path. Desperate to buy escape for Bedie, Mara did the only thing she could do. Shouting an inarticulate challenge, she ran straight at it.

She awoke with a thundering in her head. *A dream*, she told herself. *It was only a dream.* Abruptly, she sat up in the darkness, breathing hard.

And then she froze in terror. *It had been no dream.* There was something in the room with her, a black, featureless form standing motionless at the foot of her bed. She opened her mouth to scream. Nothing but a strangled whimper came out. As she cowered there helplessly, the thing raised its arms, and she saw in that awful moment that it had no head. In a rush it was on her, enveloping her in a sudden, suffocating wave of red.

Mara lay facedown, drenched in sweat, heart hammering in her chest. The blankets were twisted around her legs. Gradually, familiar sounds reached her. Jazz's light snoring beside her on the bed. The early-morning sound of birds. She raised her head. Gray, misty dawn filled her window.

With a sob, she stumbled out into the cold, damp air, ran barefoot across the wet grass, fumbled with the latch of her studio door. Once inside, she switched on her computer with trembling fingers, dialed up and pounded out her electronic cry for help.

> . . . *My god, Patsy, what does it mean? Why headless, why red, and why now, after all these years?* <

•

Patsy Reicher opened Mara's e-mail hours later, at the start of her day by New York time. She ran her fingers through her crazy gray-red mop of hair. Thoughtfully, she moved a wad of gum from one side of her mouth to the other. The air in her office was stale. She got up from her desk, shoved open a window. The smell of the day, the grind of traffic, a sudden blare of car horns reached her from the street below. She returned to her desk and tapped out a response:

> *Calm down, Mara. Headless because so far he's faceless. Red? Well, he ain't Santa. Try red for danger, red for predator. Hunters always wear red, don't they? And why now? Because you've got new information, you're processing it, and you're beginning to believe that things are finally breaking open on Bedie. Maybe they are. Go carefully, kiddo. You may not like what you find.* <

•

She was at his door again, sweeping past in a rush of air, taking possession of his front room. "Julian, we need to make a start."

"Eh? What are you talking about?"

It was nine o'clock on a Friday evening. Mara's knock had jerked him out of an armchair doze, dog-tired as he was from a day of heavy labor. He had been assisted in this enterprise by his neighbor's grandson, Bernard, whom he employed casually, partly because Madame Léon was a lovely old girl, partly because he valued fresh eggs, and partly because Bernard was the closest thing Julian had to a bulldozer. He really didn't want to deal with Mara.

"Our search for the orchids. And the *pigeonnier*." She was depositing an assortment of maps on his dining table.

Christ! There it was again, this coming at him blind-side. Julian shook himself awake. He needed to take control of the situation.

"Look here, Mara, you simply have no idea what you're asking. Do you know how much area we'd have to cover? On foot and bending from the waist?"

She paused, clearly lacking the faintest notion of the enormity of her demand. "Why bending from the waist?"

"Because, dammit, terrestrial orchids aren't that bloody easy to see! They grow in tall grass and among other plants. They're widely scattered. Anyway, I already told you, you're looking for a specific place that might never have existed, where a certain sequence of flora grew. Nearly twenty years ago. It could have been plowed up, grazed over, or wiped out by herbicides. Or simply buried under a meter of cement!"

She was taken aback by his vehemence. "But you agreed to help me. I can't do it alone. You know the terrain. You've got the field notes."

"Okay. Sure. But I'm telling you, it's not that bleeding easy."

"Right." She raised her hands, palms forward. "That's where I thought the *pigeonnier* would come in. I've worked out a system. We'll look for it first, as our main point of reference, you see? Once we find it, we can use the orchids to work from there."

"*If* we find it, don't you mean? Don't forget, Paul, Gaston and god knows who else have been looking. So have you, so have I—"

"Well, I've just figured out a way of making the job easier," she announced, waving at the maps. "The Série bleue. I got one for every section of the Dordogne and including the western part of Quercy. They show everything. I don't know why I didn't think of it sooner."

Julian was fully familiar with the Série bleue maps. They were a necessity to someone like him, whose customers resided on isolated hilltops, in the hidden folds of valleys, and down unmarked lanes. The maps, on a scale of one centimeter to 250 meters, and based on National Geographical Institute surveys, depicted not only contour lines, geological features, land use, and types of vegetative cover, but every road, every footpath, every man-made structure on the landscape. He could, for example, pick out his own cottage—fifth dot on the right on the road going west out of Grissac. But it was difficult to say, unless you knew beforehand, what was what.

"Look," he pointed out, "they show everything, sure, but these maps aren't foolproof. Or what if the *pigeonnier* we're looking for no longer exists? Besides, on paper, buildings show up only as black dots. Things aren't labeled 'house' or 'barn,' you know. How will you be able to tell a dovecote from a—a pigsty or a *cabane*?"

"Simple. The *pigeonnier* we're looking for is in the middle of a field, away from other buildings. All we have to do is look for isolated dots in the middle of open spaces."

"All we have to do—? Mara, there must be thousands of isolated dots in the middle of open spaces all over the Dordogne. Are we going to check out every one of them?"

"Listen," she said, a flinty edge coming into her voice, "we had a deal. You got your photographs. Now help me find my sister. Or at least the path she walked before she disappeared."

He gave in. In a perverse sort of way, he was even relieved that she had kick-started the process. He had been sitting on the fence for days, wondering how to deal with her, what to do about the Lady's Slipper, wanting it but knowing it to be impossible. Now she had given him a possible means to resolve both issues. But he'd have to work fast. Orchids had a limited flowering season. It was already coming on to early May. It had been a hot, wet spring, with early flowering, meaning that many of the specimens captured in the film would not be much longer in evidence. Using the maps to identify possible *pigeonniers* made sense. At least it shortened the odds.

"All right," he said. "Give me a couple of days. I'll see what I can do."

•

Thus, Julian found himself spending his Saturday afternoon after rugby (Grissac won for a change, twenty-three to fifteen, in their "friendly" game against La Grotte) at home, instead of celebrating at Chez Nous in the company of teammates. Forgoing Mado's mouth-watering veal pie, he settled down at his kitchen table with the photographs and a solitary, sorry lunch of tinned cassoulet, washed down by quite a bit of wine.

The only way through an impossible task, he decided, was to be systematic. He got a pad of paper and lined off the top sheet into three columns. In the first column, he listed the orchids in the photographs by common rather than taxonomical name and in order of their appearance. There were fourteen different species in all. The first seven—Helleborines, *Limodorum*, Common Spotteds, Military Orchids, Bird's-nest, Butterfly, and Pyramidal Orchids—were followed by the *pigeonnier*. Then another seven: Marsh, Bee, Lizard, Man, Lady, Tongue, and Fly Orchids.

Finally, the Lady's Slipper. Next to each, in the second column, he jotted down what he knew of the growing environment. Orchids were habitat-specific. Each required well-defined growing conditions: sun, dappled light, deep shade, varying degrees of dampness and soil conditions. Some proliferated on hilltops and open meadows; others grew shyly in woodlands and forests. Some occurred in conjunction with certain trees; some were transitional plants, occupying the edges of clearings; still others could only be found in wetlands.

When he had completed this task, he saw that the information, organized in this way, told more of a story than he had realized. In fact, he had created a specific progression of landscapes, like beads threaded on a string. However, the problem was locating where this particular combination of habitats was to be found. For the region in its entirety provided endless possibilities: pine and deciduous forests, grasslands, fields, swamps, seepage zones, scree, scrubland, all characterized by the calcareous, alkaline soils on which most of the species he had listed thrived. Again, he was ominously aware of the immensity of the undertaking ahead of him.

His only recourse was to fall back on actual sightings. These were documented in field notes that he had made over the years, as well as hundreds of prints and slides, everything stored topsy-turvy in an old metal cabinet.

He began by pulling out anything related to the orchids captured on the film and entering known locations in the third column. For most, he had numerous sightings, and in some cases this proved more problematic than helpful. For example, the purple Pyramidal Orchid, an aggressive colonizer, grew everywhere. Next to it he simply wrote: *widespread, abundant.*

Then it occurred to him that he really needed to focus on sightings dating from around the time of Bedie's disappearance in 1984. Here he met a more serious roadblock. In those days he had not been particularly systematic in charting floral distributions, except for the notations he had done for his book, and even these were casual scribbles on the backs of envelopes and so forth.

"Merde!" he uttered, shoving his glasses up to the top of his head.

Inevitably, his thoughts drifted to the *Cypripedium*. He rose to stare in fascination at a blowup of the print that he had pinned to his kitchen wall. There was now no doubt in his mind about the slipper-shaped labellum, although a more objective observer might have pointed out that the stain running across the print made identification iffy. A remarkable flower under any circumstances, magnified five times it seemed almost nightmarish. The deep-pink labellum looked swollen, veined, and slightly obscene, although some of these effects could have been owing to the graininess of the enlargement. Two wildly twisted lateral petals, springing stiffly away from the slipper, resembled fantastical, blackish-purple mustachios.

"Merde!" he said again, turning away from the blowup in frustration. Why did this have to be the worst of the lot, and the only one to lack a habitat shot? Not that this in itself would have pinpointed a location, but at least the surrounding growth and leaf litter might have furnished him with something to go on. It occurred to him (he was in a maudlin mood) that it was all too emblematic of his life—doomed to clutch hopelessly at the things he wanted most, desired objects dangling just out of reach. More wine reconciled him to his fate.

He was slumped in an attitude of defeat when Edith appeared in the open doorway. She looked at him speculatively. Julian considered the fag end of his dinner, congealing palely on his plate.

"All right, you opportunistic bitch," he muttered and scraped the remains into her dish. Watching the pointer gulp it down, Julian gave in and decided to call for help.

•

"Allo?" Géraud Laval's voice thundered at him through the telephone.

"Géraud? Julian. Julian Wood. What? No. Géraud—yes, yes, I know. Géraud, look, I've—er—got a problem. No, not personal, floral. I said floral. Are you and Iris busy? Well, I don't want— Oh, all right, if you're sure. Great. Be there in half an hour."

Julian did not like Géraud. Put plainly, the man was insufferable. He was also Julian's main rival in the Société Jeannette's Bring and Brag, as Julian called it. The club, which attracted wildflower enthusiasts from Mussidan to Rocamadour, met monthly in different locations. The end of each meeting was always set aside for members to show off important botanical finds. Julian vied bitterly with Géraud for primacy in this area.

On the other hand, Géraud Laval was the only person who could help him. A vastly knowledgeable orchidologist, he bred tropicals in a hot room attached to his house and grew plantations of temperate species on his property near the village of Malpech. Géraud lived with Iris Potter, a cheerful woman from Lancashire whom Julian did like, in a long-standing but on-and-off relationship. That is, every now and then Iris declared Géraud to be impossible to live with and moved out. Her goings were always noisy, with everyone taking sides; her returns surprisingly uneventful, word simply going round that Iris was back. She had been back, as near as Julian could reckon, for nearly half a dozen years.

Resignedly, Julian grabbed his notes and Mara's photographs (imagining Géraud's sneers at the poor quality) and headed for the door. Then a better idea struck him. A malicious grin spread over his face. He turned back and reached for the phone. There was no reason, he thought, why Mara shouldn't help to bear the brunt of Géraud's obnoxious personality.

•

Mara had spent a frustrating day. Wealthy American friends of Prudence had purchased a charming nineteenth-century manor house and were now complaining about the rudimentary state of just about everything, especially the water closet. Their problem was now Mara's headache, since she had agreed to put things right. It came with the territory, she had to admit. Without people who bought things they ultimately couldn't live with, she would be out of business. Her difficulty at the moment lay with Kranz, the plumbing whiz, who had stubbornly voiced several objections, mainly structural, to her redesign. Stare as she might at the sketch before her, she could see no other way of repositioning the narrow little recess that currently housed the toilet. She was glad, when Julian called, for a reason to quit her studio.

Now she was crammed into the front seat of his van, feet on a coiled hose, knees jammed against a plastic sack of fertilizer, as they sped off in the direction of Malpech.

"Géraud Laval's a retired pharmacist," Julian informed her. He swerved around a pothole. "And, to hear him talk, the world's leading mushroom authority."

The edge in his voice made Mara look at him sideways. She had been in the region long enough to know that pharmacies routinely dispensed, along with pills and enemas, advice on the edibility of wild mushrooms. From late summer onward, the woods swarmed with people in search of apricot-hued chanterelles, black-capped *têtes de nègre,* and other edible cèpes. Every year, people got sick or even died from failing to distinguish an innocuous fungus from a deadly cousin. The easiest way of knowing was to consult your local pharmacist. So maybe this Géraud's claim wasn't as far-fetched as Julian made it sound.

"He's also as vain as a prima donna," Julian went on. "And twice as temperamental."

"Then why are we going to see him?"

"Because," Julian admitted grudgingly, "he's as good as they get where orchids are concerned. Breeds fancy tropicals and has a fine collection of European orchids right in his own backyard. Which he got from rootstock, not seed, I might add."

"Meaning?" His tone was ominous, but the significance escaped her.

"Meaning the bugger digs up wild plant material rather than gathering the seed and growing his orchids in vitro, as any"— Julian downshifted angrily—"decent conservationist would do. And by the way, Mara, while we're there, it might be better if you let me do the talking."

"Let you—? Oh, be my guest!" Mara rolled her eyes. Really, if he wanted her to keep her mouth shut, why bother having her along?

•

Iris met them at the door, a short, dumpy person with a round, weathered face, very blue eyes, and wispy gray hair. She wore a paint-smeared smock over baggy trousers, and her broad, flat feet were strapped into leather sandals.

"So glad you came," she welcomed them in English after Julian made the introductions. She gave Mara a friendly but frankly curious once-over before adding, "Visitors. Always relieves the tension." Not bothering to lower her voice, she informed them as she led them in, "He's been absolutely awful these last few weeks, you know. Honestly, I really think it's time I left him. What do you think, Julian?"

"By all means." Julian seemed to take the question in his stride.

Mara did not know what to think. She focused instead on the walls of the front room, which were covered with bad impressionistic floral paintings that seemed to match the condition of Iris's smock.

"You're the artist?" she inquired.

The other woman giggled. "Awful, aren't they? But they sell surprisingly well. Come on. Don't want to keep his nibs waiting."

"Ha! Julian Wood!" roared a short, powerfully built man, emerging from the depths of a glassed-in area attached to the back of the house. *"Entrez, entrez!"* The space was crowded with moss-filled hanging baskets and clamorous with blooms.

Iris left them, and Julian made more introductions, this time *en français.* Everything from that point on switched to French. Conversations in the Dordogne, which was rapidly filling up with English-speaking expatriates, were apt to be like that, a mix of languages according to the speakers.

"Enchanté, madame," Géraud boomed. He stared avidly at Mara, then bowed and kissed her hand. His prominent head, bald on top, was made fantastic by wild sprouts of white hair springing like horns from the sides. Tufts of darker hair grew out of his ears. Mara wondered if they impeded his hearing, causing him to shout the way he did. "Are you as well an orchid amateur?"

"Débutante," Mara admitted. "What lovely flowers. But why is everything hanging from the ceiling?"

"Because," said Géraud smugly, "these are tropical epiphytes. *C'est-à-dire,* in their natural jungle habitat, they grow on trees to get light, and their root systems are designed to capture airborne nutrients. I mimic here the same conditions. Whereas orchids that grow in the ground, such as our local species, put out tubers or rhizomes. Do you know," he leered, "why I consider the orchid to be the most sexual of flowers?"

"I have no idea," said Mara, not liking the leer but enjoying the look of disgust on Julian's face.

"Why, because the tubers are—ahem—testicular in shape, hence the name 'orchid.' From the Greek, *orchis,* you see, which means testicle—"

"Yes, yes." Julian moved in to stem Géraud's verbal foreplay. "While you're at it, why not tell her that 'orchidotomy' means castration, and 'orchialgia' means pain in the balls?"

Géraud glared at him. "Come." Skillfully he steered Mara away. "Let me show you my new *Paphiopedilum.*"

Proudly, he walked her over to a large, glossy flower rising imperiously from a slender stalk. A tropical species of Slipper Orchid, it had a greenish, tubular labellum, ripple-edged side petals, and a yellow dorsal sepal that flared up showily, like a sultan's fan.

"*Que c'est belle!*" Mara exclaimed, sincerely impressed. Julian's expression as he trailed along behind was decidedly sour. Serve him right, she thought, for that crack about doing all the talking. She laid it on thicker. "*Absolument magnifique.* Did you—er—breed this yourself?"

"But of course," the other preened. "Bulldog hybrid. Just in bloom."

Their host took advantage of her show of interest to point out other of his botanical achievements. At one point, Julian simply left them. When, at last, Géraud led Mara out to a terrace at the rear of the house, Julian was already there, seated at a wooden table with Iris, a half-empty, sweating bottle of sparkling Vouvray between them. An unopened second was on standby in a bucket of ice.

"So—what's this all about, eh?" boomed Géraud, seating Mara with an excess of gallantry.

"We need," said Julian, "to draw on your knowledge of local flora to place a certain sequence of orchids." He made a show of informing Mara, "Géraud's terrifically knowledgeable about terrestrial as well as tropical orchids. If anyone can tell you what you want to know, it's Géraud." It was a shameless priming of the pump, and they all, including Géraud, knew it. Julian laid out the photographs in order on the wooden garden table.

Their host squinted at the array. "What's this? Terrible quality. Who took this rubbish?" He glanced at Mara, then turned on Julian. "And you expect me to tell you where this muck grows? What's this all about?"

"Treat it like a botanical puzzle," Julian evaded. Mara caught the warning glance he shot her. Bringing Bedie into the conversation, the look said, would simply sidetrack the purpose of their visit. She raised a hand: *Your show.*

"Oh, goody," cried Iris. "A mystery. I love mysteries."

Géraud gave his visitors a suspicious glare.

"Come on, Géraud," Julian wheedled. "I just need some information from you. My notes don't go back far enough."

Grudgingly, Géraud picked up the first photo, a composition of dainty white Helleborine florets springing from a single stem. The habitat shot included a cluster of similar plants against a shaded backdrop of beech saplings.

"*Cephalantheria longifolia,*" their host declared, holding fussily to taxonomical names. "Bah. Impossible to place. Grows along every footpath in the region. You ought to know that."

Julian said with forced patience, "I was hoping to identify a possible location through *all* of the orchids, taken together."

"Hmmph. So you said. What's next?" The older man frowned at a portrait of a dark, leafless stalk bearing deep-violet flowers tightly braided up the length of the plant. This was followed by a middle-distance view showing a trio of the same, blossoms beginning to unfurl. They stood in a light-dappled litter of conifer needles. *"Limodorum abortivum,"* he identified.

"It's growing here among what looks like Scots pine—"

"I can see that for myself, thank you."

"—but my notes show it mainly in conjunction with oaks and chestnuts, especially along tree-root systems—"

"Quel merde," scoffed Géraud. "You're about to tell me *Limodorum* is parasitical."

"Who said anything about parasites? They're saprophytes."

Iris leaned forward to peer at the photo. "Well, for that matter, *I've* only ever seen it growing near rotting stumps."

"You wouldn't recognize *Limodorum* if it bit you," Géraud snapped. "Look, take it from me, *Limodorum's* mostly found, when it's found, in mixed deciduous-coniferous woodland. That describes most of the Dordogne. So where does that get you?"

Not very far, Mara acknowledged silently. Julian looked grumpy.

Géraud grunted dismissively at the shots of *Dactylorhiza fuchsii* and *Orchis militaris,* but his attitude changed abruptly when he saw the Bird's-nest Orchids. Startled, he reared a pair of tufted eyebrows. *"Mon dieu!"* he shouted. *"Épatant!"*

"Thought you'd be interested." It was Julian's turn to look smug.

The eyebrows waggled. "And why not? *Neottia nidus-avis* is not that common. A stand like this is entirely remarkable. Whoever took this photograph was damned lucky—not you, was it? No, couldn't be. You wouldn't be here picking my brains. Well, as you undoubtedly know, *Neottia* likes damp shade, so this would have had to be found under forest cover, most probably deciduous."

"I don't suppose you've ever seen anything approaching this size?"

Géraud stuck a lip out. "Well, not quite this big." A quick look at Mara, as if assessing how much she knew. Then at Julian. "You?"

"Oh, couple of sightings." Julian's tone was casual.

"Wait." Géraud appeared to think hard. "Maybe."

Julian grinned. "I'll tell if you will."

The other glowered. *Julian one, old fart nil,* Mara marked the score with amused interest.

"Go on," rumbled Géraud.

Julian referred to his notes. "One fair-sized scattering, Forêt de la Bessède, south of Urval, just below the junction of the main logging roads. And a small growth along the footpath north of Doissat. Your turn."

"Hmm." Géraud rubbed his chin. "Abrillac Forest."

"You couldn't be a little more precise, could you? Abrillac covers a big area, as you well know."

"Near Le Double," Géraud revealed cautiously.

Mara felt a quickening of the pulse. She had once done a small job for someone near the hamlet of Le Double. "That's just north of Beynac," she broke in.

"Date?" Julian persisted as if she had not spoken. "I'm interested in anything around 1984."

Géraud frowned. "Why?"

"Oh, just curious."

"Very well. Nineteen eighty-two."

"How can you be so sure?" Julian objected. "Just a moment ago you said you didn't have anything—"

"Of course he has," crowed Iris. "He has stacks of notes, all in Latin and Greek and teensy-tiny coded numbers so no one else can read them. He's terrified someone will steal his precious information. Go on." She gave her lover a hearty shove. "Show the lad."

Scowling murderously, Géraud strode off into the house. He returned with a long wooden file drawer. It was labeled *E–N*, suggesting a wealth of other material spanning the rest of the alphabet. The older man riffled through tightly packed, minutely inscribed index cards while Julian looked on with obvious envy.

"As I said"—Géraud surfaced after a moment—"nineteen eighty-two." And since Julian was eyeing him meaningfully, he reluctantly imparted minimal directions.

This interchange put their host in a bad mood. He sneered at the shots of *Anacamptis pyramidalis*—"Common as straw!"—and quarreled angrily with each of Julian's subsequent identifications.

"*Platanthera bifolia*, Lesser Butterfly Orchid," Julian said.

"*Bifolia* my elbow!" This aimed at a graceful stalk of spiky white blooms. "It's *Platanthera chlorantha*, or Greater Butterfly, if you must. Use your eyes, *mon vieux*. Regard the positioning of the pollinia!"

"You can't *see* the pollinia. At least, not very well. I make it out to be *bifolia*."

"Rubbish. When was this taken?"

"Early May."

"That proves it. *Clorantha* blooms before *bifolia*." Géraud flashed a look of triumph in Mara's direction. Julian looked huffy.

One–one, Mara tallied over the rim of her glass.

Iris created a temporary diversion by snatching up the next photo in line and interjecting, "Ooh, look, a *pigeonnier*! I once lived in a converted pigeon house."

"You would have," intoned her temperamental consort through gritted teeth.

"I also painted a lovely series of them. For greetings cards. Sold very well."

"Did you?" Mara was immediately interested. "You don't recognize this one, by any chance, do you?"

"Oh dear." Iris studied it lengthily. "I don't think so. I mean, it was years ago, and there are so many, and one is very like another, don't you think?"

But the two men were off again, sparring over the distinguishing features of subspecies of *Dactylorhiza* and arguing heatedly about a plant that Julian said was one variant of Marsh Orchid and Géraud another. Géraud's temper grew shorter as the condition of the photographs deteriorated. "What did you do with this film? Flush it down the toilet?"

Iris, on the other hand, was unperturbed by the awful quality. She crooned over a discolored clutch of fat, velvety blossoms. "Bee Orchids. The darlings, so sweet, with their little furry bodies. And Snakes!" She pounced on a blackened portrait of a tall spike just coming into bloom, the lower blossoms of the spike releasing what looked like pale, wildly flying ribbons. "My absolute favorites."

Géraud closed his eyes and pushed air noisily out his nostrils. "Do me a kindness. *Himantoglossum hircinum.* What you English refer to as Lizard Orchid, although the locals call it *orchidée bouc* because it smells damnably like a billy goat in rut."

"Don't be pedantic, dear. Snakes, Lizards, whatever. But so dramatic, don't you think, with their twisty things?"

Géraud glared. "Those 'twisty things,' as you call them, happen to be much-elongated median lobes." He said for Mara's benefit, "Thinly but widely distributed. They typically populate open fields and sometimes roadside verges, but where, my dear, is anyone's guess."

He waved in disgust at the rest of the shots. "What the devil do you expect me to do with these?"

Julian said acidly, "Well, I was hoping you had some sightings."

"Sightings?" Géraud threw up a pair of short, hairy arms, demonstrating that he had reached the end of his limited patience. "*Parbleu*, what do you think? I have been hunting orchids in the Dordogne for forty years. Of course I have sightings!" Fulminating, he picked up and slapped down each of the remaining photographs in turn. "*Aceras anthropophorum?* At least three dozen stands between here and Bergerac. *Orchis purpurea?* Ditto. Aha, *Serapias lingua*, what my beloved here would call *Tongue Orchid*"—he roared out the word "Tongue"—"well, I can give you a damned fine spread of them on a hillside above Le Grand Mas dating back to 1972, but the land was bought last year by some Belgians, so you can't get in there anymore!"

Iris shook her head at Mara. "You see? Absolutely impossible. I really shall have to go. I was saying, dear"—she raised her voice over her lover's bellows—"that I shall have to leave you. Oh, no point looking like thunder, Joujou. It's for your own good." She turned back to Mara: "Always pulls him up short, and gives me a break. He's as good as gold after."

Julian struggled to get the conversation back on track. "I was talking about sightings that could tie in with the others."

"*Bof!*" Géraud slammed his hand down on the table so hard that the glasses jumped. Then he said what Mara was most afraid of hearing: "What you're asking is impossible. You can't seriously expect me to take this garbage and give you a location."

At that point Iris leaned forward confidentially. "If I tell you something, you two, will you promise to keep it a secret? There's a lovely little cluster of Fly Orchids right behind the Chapel of Our Lady of Capelou that I can show you if you're interested. I visit them every year around this time, when I go to get spring water."

"*Ah, ça, enfin!*" exploded Géraud.

There was one photo left: the Lady's Slipper. Géraud seized it irascibly. Mara held her breath.

"What in the name of *le bon dieu* is this?"

"It's probably," said Julian carefully, "a very bad photo. I was just curious to know what you make of it."

"Julian thinks it's a Lady's Slipper," Mara cut in, tired of the verbal fencing.

"What?" Géraud roared.

Julian said stiffly, shooting her a furious glance. "Well, yes, I did rather think it might be—er—some form of *Cypripedium.*"

"Impossible!"

"I know. But you have to admit the structure is awfully similar."

"You're mad. First, *Cypripedium* is exceedingly rare. Second, it doesn't grow here. It likes cooler, subalpine conditions."

"Only the labellum isn't yellow but deep pink," Julian persisted. "And these appear to be unusually long lateral petals. I thought maybe a mutant, and if so, did it propagate, and where?"

"*Balivernes!*" shouted Géraud. "Absolute rot! I tell you it doesn't grow here. If it doesn't grow here, how can you have a mutant?" He paused, frowning intensely. Despite himself, he was intrigued. "*C'est ça?* No other photo?"

"Unfortunately, no."

"And you think you've made a rare find. What do you plan to call it? *Cypripedium woodianum?*"

The tone to Mara's ears was viciously mocking, revealing a seriously nasty side to Géraud's intense competitiveness about floral matters. As he held the photo up to catch the light, the reddening sky behind him outlined his head with its hairy horns, giving him an infernal, demonic look.

"Oh, Julian." Iris clasped her hands in suppressed excitement. "A find. How wonderful for you!"

"Cease the raptures, woman," Géraud muttered wearily. "And this, I suppose, is what the charade has been about? If you wanted me to help you locate this dubious specimen, why didn't you say so straight off, man?"

"Come on, Géraud. Admit you're fascinated."

The other glared at the photograph again. "Let me put you out of your misery. If this is some kind of *Cypripedium,* I can tell you it wasn't taken here. *C'est final.* Don't get visions of grandeur yet, *mon vieux.* Come." He reached into the ice bucket for the second bottle of Vouvray and turned to Mara with a ghastly grin. "We've had enough of orchids and execrable photography, wouldn't you say, my dear? More wine."

•

"You didn't make things any easier," Julian said coldly as they drove away, "telling him I thought it was a Lady's Slipper."

"Oh dear," snapped Mara, "and here was me thinking that was what it was all about."

•

By the time they had picked up a selection of deli items from a charcuterie and returned to Mara's house to assemble their findings, an unspoken truce had been established between them. They ate their food hurriedly, sitting cross-legged on the Aubusson, which in Julian's opinion was a damned sight more comfortable than her chairs. The Série bleue maps were spread out edge to edge before them, showing the entire region in cartographic detail. They were able to follow the lazy looping of the Dordogne, flowing west through a patchwork flood plain of fields and farms. Its ancient bed wound between limestone cliffs crowned with stark medieval fortresses (black dots) and pleasure châteaux (more black dots) built by the gentry over the centuries. *Gentilshommières,* they were called. Julian traced the path of the D703 with his finger. It followed the contours of the river from Souillac as far as the town of Siorac-en-Périgord, where it swung north. Westward traffic was carried along the D25 on the next map of the series, until it turned south at Le Buisson. Jazz, banished to the hardwood floor, looked on, deeply offended.

Julian got right down to business. "We have to make a critical assumption: that Bedie took the photos in one go. After visiting the castle in Beynac"—he circled the town on one of the maps with a red marker—"your sister somehow found herself on a shady footpath. *Where* is the question, and how she got there, of course, the missing piece. But once there, she was likely walking through light woodland, say, something like a second-growth copse, which is where she found the Helleborines, *Limodorum,* Common Spotteds, and Military Orchids. From there she went into dense tree cover for the Bird's-nests." He gestured widely, indicating numerous green areas on the maps affording a plentiful choice of forests.

He went on. "But then she came out into open country again. That's indicated by field dwellers like the Pyramidal and Butterfly Orchids."

"And after that," Mara put in, "she found the *pigeonnier.*"

"Right. Then the water meadow, where she saw the Marsh Orchids. The maps show contour lines and elevations, so they'll be some help in locating low-lying bogs. The rest of the flowers suggest a transition onto higher, drier ground, and again we can use the contour lines: Bee, Lizard, Man, Lady, and Tongue Orchids are all pretty adaptable, but they prefer sunny, well-drained areas—hillsides, high meadows, embankments, that kind of thing."

"And the Lady's Slipper?" Mara asked.

Julian frowned. "The Lady's Slipper would have probably grown on even higher ground, say a cool, shady, north-facing ridge. And that," he finished abruptly, "is where the trail ends."

Mara stared at him. "But—but that could be anywhere!"

"It's what I've been trying to tell you." Julian found her dismay intensely satisfying. "Worse than that. If Bedie took the photos at different times and in different places, then, like I said before, we have no continuity at all, and even less to go on. Which brings us back to the Lady's Slipper. You heard Géraud. He thinks I'm mad to even think it was locally occurring mutant of *Cypripedium calceolus*. So we have to consider the possibility of another discontinuity—your sister found it in an entirely different location. Or we're looking at something quite different."

"Are you saying it's *not* a Lady's Slipper?"

He shook his head. "More like an unknown variant of Lady's Slipper. You see, the genus *Cypripedium* consists of around a hundred and ten species. Only one, *Cypripedium calceolus*, is native to Western Europe. But who's to say your sister didn't stumble on an unknown, highly localized type that grows in one spot in the Dordogne and nowhere else?" For a moment Julian let his mind drift as he considered the possibility. "Blimey, wouldn't that shake up the botanical world!"

Mara regarded him somberly for a moment and then called him back to more practical considerations. "So how should we go about this?"

He sighed. "Right. Well, we have three distinctive photos to go on. First the *pigeonnier*. Then the *Neottia* or Bird's-nest Orchids. And, finally, the Lady's Slipper. Let's try your idea of identifying possible pigeon houses using the maps. But, rather than looking for any isolated dot, we can narrow things down a lot, at least at first, by focusing on dots in the vicinity of known sightings of Bird's-nests. We've got three sightings, two of my own and one from Géraud. Let's start with Géraud's. It's just about here, above Le Double"—Julian drew a red "X" on the map—"which, interestingly enough, is only about five or six kilometers north of Beynac."

"I tried to tell you that."

"What? Oh. Well, I hope you realize it's the only useful piece of information that bloody man gave us, and you saw how I practically had to pull worms out of his nose to get an exact location. Now, if we concentrate on a walkable area within a radius of, say, ten or twelve kilometers around this point—"

"That's walkable?" Mara asked faintly.

"Nothing for an experienced hiker," he replied breezily and penciled in a rough circle around the "X." "What does that give us in the way of single black dots?"

Together they scanned the map.

"Here's a couple outside Le Glandier." Mara pointed at two specks that Julian duly marked. "And one there, north of La Fage, and another south of Lavergne."

In all, they found a dozen candidates. Several Julian rejected straightaway. "Too big for a pigeon house. Things may not be labeled, but they're more or less to scale. And these are probably cottages. You can tell by their orientation to the road. Luckily, we'll be able to check most of these out by car, or with the aid of binoculars. Except this one." He tapped a spot on the map. "It's in the middle of woodland. Have to walk in for that." He eyed her severely. "You'd better come prepared to trek, you know. Even if we're lucky enough to find your pigeon house among this lot, we'll still have to hike in for the *Neottia*."

"I don't see why, if we have the *pigeonnier*," she objected. "Why not just go from there? Look for the orchids that come after it?"

"Because finding both will help us establish that Bedie took these photos in a single walk, which, don't forget, is the critical assumption. The other orchids, except the Lady's Slipper, are simply not rare enough to go on. Also, the pigeon house and the *Neottia* together will give us the direction of Bedie's approach, since we know the Bird's-nest is before the *pigeonnier*. Any evidence of orchids that come after the *pigeonnier*, say, like the Marsh Orchids in the water meadow, will help us fix her forward path."

Mara was silent for a moment. Finally, she said, "It all boils down to the Lady's Slipper, doesn't it?"

Julian frowned. "Unfortunately, yes. Without that, we can't really know where she ended up. We're always faced with the possibility that your sister began the roll of film in this area, and finished up somewhere else, like in the Lozére."

She said somberly, "I don't think you understand what I mean, Julian. You told me Bedie was systematic about photographing her orchids. She took them close up and at a distance, right?"

"Sure. It's standard practice."

"Except the Lady's Slipper. She only took one shot of it. I've been asking myself why. There were at least a couple of frames left on the film. It occurs to me that the only explanation is that something must have interrupted her. Julian, I think the reason Bedie didn't take any more photos was that she couldn't." Mara paused. "By then she may have been dead."

9

They agreed to meet at eight the following morning behind the Parc Archéologique in Beynac. Mara arrived first. She parked her car and let Jazz out to mark trees while she leaned against the front fender of the Renault. A thin mist, rising from the river, hung delicately in the air. Below her, the town, stacked against the face of a jutting cliff, still slept. The tour buses would not appear for another two hours. A fat woman in slippers came out of one of the houses, threw open the ground-floor shutters, and waddled inside again.

Above Mara soared the massive ramparts of Beynac Castle. French stronghold during the Hundred Years' War, the fortress glared upriver in the direction of equally hulking English Castelnaud. Both fortifications had played key roles in the bitter fighting. At Castelnaud, Mara had once seen a full-scale working model of a *trébuchet*, a giant medieval catapult, with which the English had once hurled boulders at the French. She had found the brutish engine of war daunting, even at a remove of five centuries.

Mara wondered how the day would go. She felt energized, finally having something concrete to focus on: Géraud's *Neottia* and a scattering of black dots. At the same time, she was wary of entering Julian's turf, his world of leaves and flowering plants. Julian had a deadly seriousness and quick irascibility where botanical things were concerned. Would he tell her to keep her mouth shut while he stared at the ground? Make her walk until she dropped? Would he even notice? She was sure that the only thing that mattered to him was his damned Lady's Slipper. Fixated, that's what he was. And, curiously, alone. Like her, she had to acknowledge. Her world was bound by work, the reconstruction of dank water closets and primitive kitchens. And Bedie, nineteen years gone. It occurred to her that, viewed from this perspective, she and Julian had a lot in common after all.

He came roaring up twenty minutes late with a bump and a screech of brakes. He jumped out, looking harried.

"Sorry I'm late." He traded quick pecks with Mara and sidestepped Jazz's snout, directed at his crotch. "Had to get Bernard started on some digging for Prudence. The lad works hard, but he's got a very short attention span."

He wore jeans, sturdy boots, and a wide-brimmed hat. He bristled with equipment: binoculars, camera, compass, canteen, rucksack. She wore cotton slacks and light canvas running shoes. Her only provisions were a tube of sunscreen and a couple of ham sandwiches that she stowed in Julian's pack.

They left her car and went in Julian's van, Mara navigating them along the edges of the Abrillac Forest, down bumpy lanes, past wood lots and pale-green fields of newly planted maize. It took them over an hour to locate six dots, all of which they could see from the car. Two were in fact *pigeonniers,* but square structures unlike the one they sought. The others were a barn, a couple of sheds, and a conical shepherd's hut built of darkly weathered stone.

"It's down to this one," Mara said, studying the map.

Julian leaned over to peer at the final dot, situated in forest.

"Hmm. I make it about five or six kilometers north of Géraud's *Neottia.* I suggest we go back to Le Double and hike in for the orchids first and continue from there on foot."

He let out the clutch, and they started off down the road. As they approached the hamlet, Mara read out Julian's scribbled notes of Géraud's directions. " 'Bark'—no, 'park bend in road.' Slow down. I think this may be the spot we're looking for."

Julian pulled off onto the narrow shoulder and set the hand brake with a jerk.

" 'Path N,' " Mara continued, squinting at his cryptic scrawl, " '2 k. Function'—? Oh, 'junction—W 2 k.' Then something 'oak.' 'BN 100 m S.' "

"We have to look for a footpath on the north side of the road," Julian interpreted. "We follow it for two kilometers until we hit a junction of trails. Then we branch off west for another two kilometers until we find a very large oak tree. The Bird's-nests are off-trail, about a hundred meters in a straight line south."

A beige Deux Chevaux was parked farther down from them. At the roadside, a big man in a blue jacket was stringing a length of orange plastic tape around a framework of wooden stakes. The man looked up, recognized Julian, and waved.

"*Salud!*"

"Bother," muttered Julian. "I'll have to say hello."

As they approached, Mara could see that the framework surrounded a clutch of what she was pleased to be able to identify as Lizard Orchids. They were tall plants, most still tightly in bud, but two had already begun to unfurl gaily twisted labella, like pale-pink party streamers, to the breeze. It was the first time Mara had seen them in the leaf, as it were, and she was impressed by their dramatic oddity.

Julian introduced the man as Maurice Bourdon, secretary of Les Vigilants, dedicated to the protection of endangered flora.

"The mowers will be coming through next week," Maurice explained for Mara's benefit. "The barrier alerts them to leave the orchids. Trouble is, they don't always cooperate. You see," he went on, his broad red face earnest, "one has to act. Orchids are vanishing from our woods and meadows. Most people don't care, so it's up to the few of us who do to do something. With force, if need be." And he cited instances of violence, of greed and corruption driving the development of lands where protected species grew. "I tell you, these canailles will stop at nothing. You don't believe me?" He rolled up a trouser leg. Mara beheld a massive, hairy shin cut across by a jagged weal.

"See this? Last year, three of us were guarding a pair of Summer Lady's-Tresses. They're dying out everywhere, you know. We were taking it in turns, just until they had time to bloom, because roadwork was going on, and we were planning to move them to a safer spot. Construction crew came through, trucks and earthmovers. I told them to bugger off. Cracked me on the leg, the bastards did, with a shovel."

Julian cut off the flow of further tales by asking Maurice about the Bird's-nest and the *pigeonnier.*

The other shrugged at the photocopy of the dovecote. One was much like another. As to the *Neottia nidus-avis,* he thought they might find a few plants round about, but nothing like what they were looking for.

"Your trail head is over there." He directed them about twenty meters farther down. "It's marked by another one of those damned *bornes.*" The entire region was criss-crossed by ancient cart tracks and paths. Some, like the one Julian and Mara sought, had been designated with markers as hiking trails by the Dordogne Tourism Service, a phenomenon that Maurice vigorously cursed. "It's just inviting more destruction of orchid habitat by hikers and those *fichu* all-terrain bikes." He waved his arms to take in the surrounding countryside in a gesture of despair.

They left him to his taping.

Their trail ran between pastures and newly planted fields that shaped themselves to the contours of the surrounding hills. The air was rich with the smell of overturned earth and dung. Cattle stared placidly at them from the other side of electrified ribbon fencing. Jazz rushed them, and they lumbered off, hooves squelching on the muddy ground. Along the way, Julian was surprisingly chatty, pointing out common wildflowers for Mara's benefit. The tall flower there, looking like a tiny purple candelabra, was tassel hyacinth. That was wild sage; if she crushed the leaves between her fingers, she could smell its pungent aroma. Buttercups she knew, but she didn't know that the locals called them *boutons d'or,* or gold buttons. Mara warmed to his brisk authority, his long, swinging stride, and hurried to keep pace with him.

They entered a meadow awash with Pyramidal Orchids, hundreds of purple cones made up of small, tightly packed blossoms balancing atop single stems. Mara knew the flowers—they grew plentifully in fields near her house—and wondered that she had never before stopped to admire their beauty. She bent to pick one. Julian's hand closed over hers swiftly.

"Lesson number one, Mara." His face was very near hers. A vein in his temple flickered. "Never pick an orchid. Look, photograph, but don't touch. *Ever.*"

"Sorry." She backed away. "But there are so many of them. And you pick flowers. What about your herbarium samples?"

"I only take common plants," he said coolly. "Never vulnerable species."

Farther ahead, as they clambered over a fallen tree, he waved despairingly at a cluster of withered Lady Orchids.

"This is what we're up against," he complained. "Things are going fast. In a few more weeks we may not see much in bloom."

"Think positively," she grinned, to lighten things up. "I need you at your very best."

He glanced at her slyly. "Botanically speaking?"

"Of course."

They walked on. Then something caught his interest. "Look." He grabbed her arm and pointed to the top of an embankment.

She saw a scattering of slender plants topped with plump, dark blossoms. "What is it?"

"*Ophrys apifera.*" He climbed up, placing his feet with care, beckoning her to follow. "Bee Orchids. You have some on your film. Here, if you look closely you can see why they're called that." He selected a flower, cradling the labellum gently, almost intimately. Standing close beside him, Mara made out a furry, blackish-brown lobe with yellow markings.

"But," she marveled, "it looks exactly like a bumblebee."

"Exactly." He uncapped his camera. "And there's a reason for that. It's— Wait!" he broke off tensely. "Don't move!"

For a panicky moment Mara thought she was about to tread on a snake—she had heard there was some kind of poisonous viper in the Dordogne. But it was only a bee, the real thing. Hastily, she waved it away.

"For Christ's sake, Mara," Julian hissed furiously. "Don't do that! Look, just stand back, will you?" He scowled and crouched, camera at the ready, waiting for the circling insect to return. After some moments, it alighted on an orchid. Waggling its body, it mounted the fleshy labellum, probing its head down the flower's throat, tiny feet treading busily. She heard the snick of the shutter. "Got it!" Julian exclaimed.

"Got what?" she asked resentfully. It was an aspect she didn't like about him, this overbearing, downright tetchy underside to his congenial surface.

"Pseudocopulation. False mating. Well, you said you wanted me at my best botanically."

"Oh, absolutely," she replied. "Do go on."

He gave her a searching look. "All right. You see, the sexual reproduction of orchids is very complex. Some orchids try to appear like other kinds of nectar-bearing flowers in order to attract pollinators. In fact, you often find them growing among the flowers they model. Now, with the Bee and Fly Orchids, which belong to the *Ophrys* genus, it's different. They've evolved flower parts that not only mimic the bodies of female insects but also put out pseudopheromones to lure males into false copulation. The live insect lands on the fake one, gets covered in pollen, which it carries to other orchids, which of course is the whole point of the exercise. Am I boring you?"

"Not at all," she told him coldly. "It's fascinating, all this pseudocopulation and fake pheromones. Makes one quite dizzy. Tell me, are the orchids that do the attracting male or female?"

"What? Oh, both. That is, orchids are hermaphroditic. In fact, they're quite capable of pollinating themselves."

"Now, that," said Mara softly but with meaning, "is boring."

•

They set off again. This time Julian did not bother to help her over logs but strode ahead, leaving her scrambling to keep up. Jazz ran, nose to ground, back and forth between them. The sun, riding high overhead, was hot. She found herself lagging behind. She wished she'd thought to wear a hat.

"Julian. I need a rest."

He allowed her a brief pause and a swallow from his canteen.

Then he was off again. "Come on," he called over his shoulder. "Chop-chop. We've got a lot of ground to cover."

"Look, I'm going as fast as I can."

"Well, don't complain. This was what you wanted."

She was grateful when they plunged into shady woodland. Helleborines, each plant bearing clusters of delicately nodding white bells, embroidered the shoulders of their path. Eventually, beech and pine gave way to a dense forest of oaks and chestnuts whose branches met overhead, creating a greenish net of light that shivered down through the leafy canopy. Here great vines hung like curtains, and ferns carpeted the forest floor. The air was fresh and cool, redolent of leaf mulch and growing things. Mara leaned against a tree, breathing hard. Julian drew up beside her.

"Forests," he murmured softly near her left ear. "Mystery, creation, and evolution." It was poetically, almost seductively said, and she turned to him in surprise. His eyes, brown flecked with gold, held hers for a moment. He placed his hands on her shoulders. Her heart gave a leap.

"Look," he whispered, turning her about, and pointed out purple spears of *Limodorum abortivum,* rising from the litter of the forest floor. "You see how they follow the root system of this old beech tree? One up on old Géraud."

•

Their chief difficulty lay in finding Géraud's landmark oak. There were so many, all clotted with balls of parasitic mistletoe, but not a *Neottia* in sight. An hour of off-trail searches into likely growing areas produced nothing more interesting than a giant bracket fungus adorning a tree like a huge, fleshy lip.

"We're not going to find it, are we?" Mara said, seating herself wearily on a rock. Jazz flopped down panting beside her.

"Wouldn't put it past the old fox to have purposely misled me," Julian fumed.

They abandoned the search and ate their sandwiches. It was a bizarre kind of investigation they were conducting, Mara thought, taking in her leafy surroundings. One in which the sole witnesses to Bedie's disappearance were silent and ephemeral, their only evidence the existence of a *pigeonnier* and a certain pattern of plants. How, she wondered in bemusement, do you question a flower?

"Do you suppose," Mara mused aloud after a long silence, "that what Maurice said is really true?"

"What?" Julian, deep in his own reflections, surfaced.

"That people commit violence over orchids?"

He replied cautiously, "It's been known to happen. I've heard worse stories than Maurice's—double-dealing, even murder—but mainly to do with tropicals, the showy ones that collectors go mad over. Avid fanciers can get pretty unbalanced. Why?"

"Well, supposing it wasn't a serial predator that Bedie met but an orchid fanatic. Supposing this person never really meant her any harm. Only she did something, accidentally, to an orchid that he was trying to protect . . ."

"What, stepped on it?" Julian was incredulous.

"Or say Bedie found a rare species, like the *Cypripedium*, that this person wanted to keep secret. Bedie might not have been exactly cooperative if she thought the world should know about it. This person could have seen red, struck out blindly—"

"You mean Géraud?" Julian looked interested. "Admittedly, he's bloody obsessive about his favorite stands . . ." He trailed off, frowning, then shook his head. "I don't see it," he concluded regretfully. "Géraud's a right prick, but not even he would go to that extent. Anyway, what you're saying puts every amateur orchidologist in the region under suspicion. In fact, every bloody member of Société Jeannette—I can give you the subscription list—to say nothing of Maurice's Vigilants lot."

"Well, there *is* something else. Iris says she leaves him periodically."

"What's that got to do with it?"

"The four-to-five-year cycle. Adverse life changes. Her departures could set him off."

"What are you saying, every time she walks out he goes on a rampage?" Julian gave a sharp bark of laughter. "Oh, he's impossible to live with, I'll give you that. In fact, I don't know how Iris puts up with him. But that doesn't make him a serial killer. And anyway, you keep saying 'he.' It could just as easily have been a woman. Females can be pretty violent, too."

Mara sighed and took off her shoe to examine a developing blister.

"It was just a thought," she said.

Julian opened the map and took a bearing with his compass, orienting them toward their final dot.

"Rather than go all the way back to the main trail, what say we save time by angling through the woods and picking it up farther ahead? It'll mean some crashing through the bush, if you think you're up to it."

"Sure," Mara agreed, although she was quite certain she wouldn't enjoy the crashing part.

Farther on, as they plunged deeper and deeper into forest, Julian remarked, "You know, peasants used to give this area wide berth. It's full of swamps and once had a bad reputation as the hideout of brigands and wolves. Even werewolves."

"Brrr."

"Of course, that was a hundred years ago. Still"—he paused to glance back at her—"even today you wouldn't want to get lost here."

"No. I would not."

But she did get lost. It was after Julian had led them over a ridge and down into an extensive bog. Dragonflies hovered thickly in the air. The earth was spongy and full of standing wa-

ter. As usual, he strode ahead of her. Soon he had vanished behind a gray-green wall of willow bushes. Jazz, off on business of
his own, was nowhere to be seen. Mara found herself struggling
through high swamp brush that obscured her view, cursing the
ankle-deep, sucking mud, and falling farther and farther behind.

It was an eerie, claustrophobic place full of rustling vegetation. A frog erupted suddenly in front of her, landing on her foot.
She choked back a yell of alarm as she shook it off. Not, of
course, that Julian would have heard her. Where was he? She
fought her way forward. Quite unexpectedly and with a feeling
of immense relief, she broke through into an open water
meadow.

"Julian?" she called, shading her eyes to look around her.
"Jazz!"

The meadow grasses rippled in the wind. She was utterly
alone.

"Julian," she shouted, louder this time. She stood still to listen. Silence. A slight feeling of unease gripped her. On the far
side of the meadow, a dense wood rose up. A gap in the trees revealed a path. *Dammit,* she thought, *he could have waited.* Furious,
she made for the trailhead.

"Julian?" she called doubtfully, peering into a tunnel of greenery that led uninvitingly into a twilight world.

"Bastard," she muttered and started unwillingly down it.
Suddenly a brownish blur exploded in front of her. She screamed
and ducked. The thing passed so close to her head that she felt a
great rush of air lift her hair. She had an impression of rapidly
beating wings, an open beak, cruel, bright eyes. Seconds later, she
realized that she had startled a buzzard from its perch. She saw
it now, through a gap in the trees, lofting powerfully, angling
sharply against the sky. Shaken, she stumbled back out into the
sunshine.

"Shit!" It was as much an exclamation of fear as of real anger with herself for being afraid. Anyway, it was ridiculous to think she was lost. Somewhere along the way, Julian would find her. In fact, he was probably looking for her at that moment. And if he didn't, well, screw him, all she had to do was to return the way she had come until she found the path they'd taken when they branched off in their search for the Bird's-nest Orchids. Working back through the swamp, as much as she disliked the hissing world of towering reeds, would be easy. She could simply follow the swath broken by her original passage. But finding her way through the uncharted forest to rejoin the signposted main trail might not be so simple. She had not paid particular attention to the way they had come, merely followed Julian as he pushed through the understory of the trees.

"Shit," she cried again and recrossed the water meadow.

She almost stumbled on him, crouching behind a thicket of willows.

"Julian," she cried out, half in relief, half in exasperation. "Where were you?"

He peered up at her. "What do you mean, where was I? I was here."

"Well, *I* was lost. Didn't you hear me shouting for you? You— you left me behind!"

"I did no such thing." He sounded indignant, but she thought he looked a little guilty. "And no, I didn't hear you. Or, if I did, how was I to know you were lost? I mean, how could you get lost? All you had to do was follow me. Anyway, look what I've found." He pointed triumphantly to a pair of tiny, green spires rising bravely out of a saturated patch of moss.

"*Hammarbya paludosa,*" he said with satisfaction as he un-capped his camera lens. "Bog Orchids. Very early on. Won't flower for another month or so. This species is special because the edges of the leaves put out tiny bulblets that eventually grow into new plants. It's an unusual form of vegetative propagation. Bog Orchids are rare. I've only ever seen them once before, around Le Bugue."

At that point, Jazz trotted up, muddy and looking pleased with himself.

"I don't get it," Mara mused wearily as Julian knelt to photograph his find.

"Get what? Look, Mara, d'you mind moving? You're throwing a shadow."

She stepped aside. "People like you. Bedie. This—this *thing* with plant life." Her tone, she knew, was brittle.

He edged around crabwise for a close-up from another angle. She took in his avid, soiled presence and turned away.

"What thing? Anyway," he said blandly, moving back for a final shot, "without 'people like me' you wouldn't have a hope of tracking your sister. Do you have any idea how many hours of collective field observation—mine and Géraud's, not that he's been much bloody use—you're drawing on?"

He stood up and took a reading on his compass. Then he dug into his rucksack for a notebook, in which he recorded his find, its precise location, and the date. "I'll come back in a few weeks to check on how they're doing," he said. "I'll be able to get them in flower then." He seemed to expect her to be as cheered as himself at the prospect.

"Speaking of your sister," Julian said as he packed his notebook away. "I've been meaning to ask you. How did she get going? On wild orchids, I mean?"

"Oh," said Mara, ruefully aware that Julian had yet to show as much curiosity about her. So much for Prudence's speculations. "It started one summer when she got a job with the Ontario

Ministry of the Environment. They sent her up to map orchids on the Bruce Peninsula."

"Ah." He looked interested. "Did you know that you have something like five species of Lady's Slipper in Ontario?"

"Whatever. Anyway, Bedie spent three months wandering around in the woods, sleeping in a tent, and living on peanut butter. She got eaten alive by blackflies and lost some of her gear to a bear—our woods aren't as tame as here—but she came out with fifty rolls of film and happier than a tick in an armpit."

He studied her critically for a moment. "Different from you."

True, Mara acknowledged. For the first time in her life, she had an inkling of her sister's mind, the passion that ruled true amateurs, motivating them to spend countless hours bending at the waist, as Julian had said, all for the sake of discovering and documenting the existence of a single flower or the breeding ground of a particular species. There was an avaricious, competitive side to it, too, she decided, remembering Géraud's possessiveness as well as Julian's recent expression of gloating, which caused them to hoard, like gold, the sighting of a rare plant.

"We only look alike," she replied dryly, and it occurred to her how much more Julian would have had in common with Bedie than with her. Together they could have tramped the length and breadth of the Dordogne, delighting over the discovery of a *Platanthera* this or an *Ophrys* that. As Patsy had put it in one of their e-mail exchanges, *Whaddya have to do to make it with this guy? Speak Latin?* Unreasonably, Mara was suddenly made uneasy by a stab of jealousy directed at her missing but darkly present twin.

"I see," Julian said, and applied himself to capping his camera. They walked on in silence.

The remaining dot proved to be a disappointing pile of rubble. Mara looked at it briefly, taking in the dimensions of the foundations, and shook her head. Julian concurred.

It was past four by the time they returned to the road where they had left the van. Julian was pleased with his find of Bog Orchids. Mara was footsore, filthy, and stumbling with exhaustion.

·

> . . . *the thing is, Patsy, he was behind some bushes all along, and he must have heard me shouting. Honestly, for a moment I thought he'd been trying to lose me. Of course, right away I saw how ridiculous it was. He was merely gloating over some orchids, and when he's like that, I think a bomb could go off without him even noticing.* <

Patsy e-mailed back:

> *Orchids shmorchids. If he heard you yelling, why the heck didn't he come looking? Just how much do you know about this Julian character anyway?* <

10

The following day, Mara had business in Bergerac, so Julian offered to go alone to Doissat to check out the first of his own Bird's-nest sightings, dating from 1988. Secretly, Mara was relieved. It was her hunt, she knew, but she had blisters on both heels, and her experience in the swamp had deflated her enthusiasm considerably.

He called her that evening to report.

"Well, it's no longer there."

Admittedly, the stand as he remembered it had been patchy. Now he expressed his dismay that not only the *Neottia* but also much of the shady woodland that had once bordered a little watercourse no longer existed.

"The trees have all been cut down," he told her, sounding seriously aggrieved. "There's nothing left but rotting stumps and soggy fields full of cows and flies. And the dots you circled as *pigeonniers* were a cottage and a ruined shed."

There remained only Julian's final sighting in the Bessède Forest.

Julian was not free again until Thursday. He suggested they meet at four at the Intermarché in Siorac-en-Périgord. The supermarket parking lot, when Mara pulled in, was full of shoppers trundling grocery carts. Many had the pale look of English summer residents just arrived to open up holiday cottages. Behind the parking lot, the grounds of the Camping Municipal showed a sprinkling of tents and *roulottes*—the early phase of the tourist invasion. The day had turned cool and overcast, threatening rain.

Julian bumped up in his old Peugeot a few minutes later. He climbed out of his van, looking tired and dusty. In addition to trying to complete Prudence's courtyard before her party deadline, he complained, he was putting in a rockery at the back of her house.

"Does that have to be finished in time for the party, too?" Mara asked.

"No," he said grumpily, "but it involves shifting about a hundred tons of Mediterranean stone."

They went in Mara's car this time. Jazz, relegated to the backseat, once again made his presence felt by driving his chin painfully into Julian's shoulder. Julian was too knackered to push him away. He directed them west out of the town on the D25 and then south. En route, they viewed three out of five dots circled on the map by Mara, none of which were *pigeonniers*.

"We'd better leave the rest and go after the Bird's-nest," Julian said, squinting pessimistically up at the sky, "while the light lasts." He was beginning to feel the pressure behind his eyes that preceded a headache.

A few kilometers past the village of Urval, he pointed her onto a logging road that cut straight into the heart of the Bessède Forest.

"Look, Mara," Julian warned as they lurched along, "I don't want you to get your hopes up. This stand of Bird's-nests dates from quite a few years back. There's been a lot of logging in this area. Chances are it's been totally wiped out."

"It's the only sighting we have left," she said, unnecessarily and a little desperately.

He made no reply.

"Stop here," he ordered eventually. He got out and peered up and down the road. Tall trees rose up around them, admitting a fitful, livid light. He got back in the car and slammed the door. "This isn't it. Keep going."

A few minutes later, he said again, "Stop here."

He got out once more and this time walked a little way forward. He returned and spoke to her through the car window.

"Pull up a bit. There's more space to park farther ahead. I think this might be it."

The way was so narrow that Mara had to nose the Renault into a ditch. She wondered if they would ever get out again.

From there, they went on foot. Twenty meters or so down the road, they found a trail opening to their right.

"Is this what you were looking for?" Mara asked.

"Yes," said Julian dully.

He's fed up with this, Mara concluded to herself. *With me. I'm making him look for something we both know we'll never find. It's hopeless.*

She followed him dispiritedly along a scree-covered path that wound uphill through tall pines. At one point Jazz routed a badger. The animal held its ground, snarling ferociously and showing jagged yellow teeth. Julian prevented a bloody scene only by a timely grab at Jazz's collar.

"Look, can't you leash him?" he roared, hauling at her lunging dog while the badger disappeared into the bushes. "And for pity's sake, Mara, mind where you walk." He freed a hand to gesture irritably at a couple of pale sprigs poking up through the grass.

"Well, excuse me!" Angrily she secured Jazz. "What rare species did I nearly tread on?"

"*Listera ovata.* Common Twayblade," he informed her sulkily. "Better get a move on. This weather's not going to hold."

And then there's my dog, she went on to herself. *But really, the man's impossible. He lives, thinks, and breathes orchids.* Seconds later, she realized that it was why she had come to him in the first place.

•

"It ought to be right around here somewhere," said Julian, scanning the forest floor. He pivoted slowly around. "Damn!"

"How can you be sure this is the place?" Mara gazed about her at the dense, undifferentiated wall of trees and bushes. "It must all look the same, and after so many years."

"I would have sworn this was the spot. The problem is, my notes weren't terribly exact in those days. I was less systematic, didn't take compass bearings."

"Oh. Then what?"

"We'll have to keep searching, won't we? If the stand survived, it's got to be around here somewhere. As I recall, it was a thin, extensive scattering that I thought might have been the remnants of a bigger stand. We'd had a series of dry years, and I figured a lot of the plants had probably died off."

He gazed glumly into the middle distance. "Look, we have to be systematic. We'll take this beech as our reference point." He indicated a tall, smooth-barked tree. "Imagine a guide line running north and south of it. What we'll do is walk out together along the line ten paces to the south. Come on." He led them the required distance. "Okay. Now we split up. You go ten steps to your right, then right again twenty, so you're heading back in the direction you came, and right again another ten. That'll bring you back to the guide line, ten paces to the north of the beech. I'll do the same on the left, so that we each pace out half a twenty-by-twenty square. Scan for the Bird's-nests on either side of you as you go— you know what they look like from the photos. If they're still here, you won't miss them. We'll meet up at the top of the square."

They did it.

"Okay. We'll have to expand the square. Out another ten, and this time you go to your left twenty paces, thirty back down the way you came, and twenty in again. Are you with me?"

She was.

"That's the problem with orchids," he complained after they had completed a second, more lengthy interval of scrambling through the bush. "They're among the most highly evolved and specialized of all flowering plants but bloody temperamental. They can bloom in strength one year and put out only a few straggling plants the next. *Neottia* are the worst. They're sporadic. Sometimes they even flower underground, in which case we won't see anything." He looked deeply offended.

Something on the run shot suddenly across their path. Jazz, off leash again, gave a single, sharp "gruff" and set off in immediate pursuit. There ensued a diminuendo of barks and crashing sounds followed by ominous silence.

"Jazz!" Mara yelled. "Here!"

The dog did not return. "It's all right," Mara said, avoiding Julian's accusing eye. "He always comes back."

Julian looked about to say something, but didn't. Instead, he pinched the bridge of his nose between finger and thumb. The throbbing in his skull was starting. He cursed himself for not bringing his pills with him. But, then, his headaches usually gave him a couple of days' warning. This one, dammit, was moving in fast and promised to be a thumper.

"Try again?" she asked, with a false brightness that irritated him beyond bearing.

"Of course we'll try again!" His voice came out hoarse in his effort not to shout at her. *Stupid cow. Stating the obvious.*

He saw her startled reaction and muttered, "Another ten, and this time thirty, forty, and thirty."

"Are you all right?" Mara asked, but he was already striding away.

Mara pushed off through the brush, pacing out her segment of the square, scanning from side to side as she had been instructed. Julian, she thought, looked appalling. His face was drawn, and he had ugly dark shadows under his eyes. Or maybe it was the light in this damned forest. Everything had a dead, greenish cast. Once or twice she thought she heard Jazz. She called and whistled. The dog did not come.

At the point where she expected to meet up with Julian, she found herself in a small, gloomy dell, hip-deep in bracken. She waited. The air was muggy. Clouds of gnats began to swarm about her head. In the distance she heard a faint rumble of thunder. Julian was taking his time getting there.

A noise in the bushes alerted her.

"Jazz!"

No dog appeared. Only the gentle rustle of a quickening breeze, bringing with it the smell of rain, broke the stillness. She gazed about her. She was surrounded by a wall of trees, towering, ancient, and faintly ominous. Was this the kind of place Bedie had gotten to? she wondered. And then what?

A twig snapped. She swung around sharply.

"Jazz? Come, boy!"

Silence.

"Julian? Is that you?"

If it was, he made no reply. A slight prickling of alarm tickled her scalp. There was another soft movement in the undergrowth, off to the right this time. Slowly Mara turned her head in the direction of the sound. She saw nothing but leaves and branches. Pushing down her growing fear, she began to walk very quickly out of the dell. The sounds of something stepping quietly through the undergrowth followed her.

"Who's there?" she demanded, turning to stand her ground. Then, as her gaze swept the dark understory of the forest, she saw a pale blur, there one moment, gone the next. It took only a split second for her to realize what it was—a face, featureless except for a pair of glittering eyes. The shock of it left her momentarily paralyzed. Then her lips parted in a thin cry. She wheeled about and ran.

Whatever it was ran with her, unseen but keeping pace easily, tracking her as she zigzagged through the trees. With no sense of direction, she clawed her way through the tangled brush, dodging trees, tripping over roots. A large fallen pine blocked her path. She veered, running around the great upheaval of roots at its base. In that moment, a dark shape stepped out suddenly before her. She screamed. Hands grabbed at her as she stumbled and pitched forward. She went on screaming.

"Calmez-vous, madame," a deep voice addressed her. "I have you."

She found herself being lifted and steadied just as Julian broke into sight a little way behind her.

"Mara, are you all right?" he demanded, out of breath. "What's going on?"

The man who held her was tall and strongly built. He had sandy-brown hair, and his eyes were a blue so dark they seemed almost black. As he stared intently at Mara, reading her fear, an odd expression came over his face. Slowly he raised his gaze, to address Julian in fluent if slightly accented English. "I could ask the same thing of you, monsieur." And to Mara, "Are you all right, madame?"

"Yes." She was shaking but standing unsupported now, and she moved a little away from both men. "I'm all right."

"I heard you shouting," Julian said. He looked pale and agitated. "What—what happened?"

She stared at him, breathing hard. "There was someone back there," she spoke finally. "Watching me through the trees."

Julian peered about him. "I don't see anyone."

The sandy-haired man asked more helpfully, "What do you mean, madame, when you say someone was watching you?"

"A—a face. I saw a face."

"For pity's sake, Mara," Julian cried impatiently, "this place is riddled with public footpaths. Look." He pointed to a break in the trees that she had not noticed. "There's one right over there. You saw someone on the path. People come and go in the woods all the time." He came forward and drew her toward him. She resisted at first, but finally let him put his arm around her. Her body, however, was stiff, unyielding. Julian spoke over her head to the man, who watched them curiously.

"Look—er—everything's fine. Thought she was lost. Got panicked. It's happened before."

The man looked unconvinced. "But perhaps madame requires some assistance?" He regarded Julian with slightly narrowed eyes.

"Oh—no." Mara gulped. "I—I'm fine. Thank you."

"Not at all. As long as you're sure you really are all right." The man spoke with careful insistence. He waited for a moment before raising a hand to them in a gesture of parting and moved off through the trees and down the trail. However, he glanced back once, his expression doubtful.

Mara pushed roughly away from Julian. "I did *not* think I was lost," she said through gritted teeth. "And there was someone— or some*thing*"—she waved her hand angrily—"following me."

He shrugged. "Probably a deer. Their tracks are everywhere. Get hold of yourself, Mara. You're letting your imagination run away with you."

"I suppose so," she relented. "I'm sorry. I feel quite stupid."

Julian was leading Mara back in the direction they had come when she clutched his arm.

"Listen."

"What?"

"Barking. Over there." She pulled him toward the sound.

"That dog's a bloody nuisance," Julian grumbled. Hurrying in her wake was making his head worse. He was about to add something sarcastic about the protection of wildlife when Mara stopped so suddenly that he bumped into her, knocking his mouth sharply on the back of her head.

"Shh," she warned. "He's got something cornered."

They found Jazz whining frantically at the base of a tall oak while an enraged marten hissed furiously from the safety of a branch. At that point, Julian forgot his headache and forgave the dog everything, even his rapidly swelling lower lip, for carpeting the forest floor around the tree was a splendid stand of Bird's-nest Orchids, proof that, if left alone, nature went about its procreative business as it should.

"Amazing," he marveled. The swarm of fleshy flowers was almost ghostly in the gloom. Each plant rose from an erect stem, the upper half of which bore an elongated cluster of brownish-yellow blooms. "This is it. This is really it. I thought this colony was a goner. It's come back triple the size! And a lot denser. This is bloody magnificent!"

"Do you think it's the same one Bedie photographed?" Mara, ever practical, asked.

"What? Oh, right." Julian scratched his beard. "Well, it's hard to say. She didn't give us much of the surroundings. Otherwise I'd have been able to place it straightaway. And, of course, the stand as I originally saw it was a mere shadow of what she found and certainly bears no resemblance to what it is now. But is it the same?" He puffed out his cheeks. "Based on the law of probability, I'd say yes. Almost certainly yes. A stand this big is rare, Mara. *Neottia* propagate slowly. Something this extensive would have taken years to establish, and the chances of there being two like it are low."

Carefully he paced out the immense length and breadth of the colony, shaking his head in disbelief. "Another one up on old Géraud."

He took several close-ups, cursing the fading light, and more mid- to long-range shots to capture the extensiveness of the growth. In the last photograph, he positioned Mara in the foreground.

"Just to get a sense of the scale," he said, managing to grin for the first time.

"Great," she said dryly. "I'm a marker. Thank you very much."

"Smile."

She smiled for him, her left cheek dimpling. Framing her in his viewfinder, Julian had a momentary desire to fix her there indefinitely.

"Come on," he cried, energized. "We've got our *Neottia*. Now all we need is a *pigeonnier*."

There remained two isolated dots. Both were situated at the forest's edge, adjacent to farmland. One proved to be a byre. As they drove toward the final dot, Mara was acutely aware that a match on the dovecote, combined with the Bird's-nests, would give her proof that Bedie had come this way, that she was now treading the path that her sister had walked nineteen years ago. Julian's thoughts were entirely on his *Cypripedium*.

They came upon it in the twilight, just as a light rain began to fall: a tall tower rising out of the shadows at the far side of a meadow. Wider at the base and tapering upward to a broken cupola, it leaned drunkenly to one side, as if the land on which it stood had shrugged. They both studied it carefully through Julian's binoculars. But even with the naked eye, they could tell that it was all wrong.

11

Edith was missing. Julian heard about it the following morning through Madame Léon when he went for his eggs.

Shortly after, old Hilaire himself, gnarled and weathered, turned up on Julian's doorstep, belligerently demanding his dog back. His bald, wrinkled head always reminded Julian of a pickled walnut. He was missing most of his front teeth, and he smelled strongly of goat.

"But I don't have your dog," objected Julian. "I haven't seen her for days."

"Then you should have told me, monsieur," said old Hilaire reproachfully and unreasonably, but somehow Julian knew what he meant. The farmer always addressed Julian as "monsieur," just as Julian always referred to him as "old Hilaire." Edith and cheese were the sole things they had in common, their only interaction being the exchange of money for excellent-quality *fromage pur chèvre*.

The long and the short of it was that Edith had not been seen for several days, not by any of the neighbors, including Julian, or by old Hilaire himself. The goat farmer was extremely worried.

"She's a valuable animal, monsieur," Hilaire whistled through the gap in his dentition. "There are thieves about who'd steal a good dog like that, use her in experiments. Besides," he lowered his voice, "she's *in that way*."

That, to the old man, was the worst of it. She needed care, regular meals. In that way or not, Julian was not inclined to be overly anxious about the wayward bitch. She did occasionally go walk-about, and he knew she would eventually turn up. To placate his neighbor, however, he agreed to keep an eye out for Edith and to inform him if he saw her.

·

Julian told Paul and Mado about Edith, and they in turn told Gaston. The postman also promised to keep an eye open for the pointer on his rounds. That made two things he had to look for—the *pigeonnier* and Edith.

In fact, he was on his way now to Les Colombes to have a word with the de Sauvignacs about the dog. He had no mail for them and didn't really expect them to have seen her. The château lay at the eastern end of his route. Little chance Edith would have wandered that far. But it was a hot day, the kind of weather that Gaston believed to be particularly trying for men of his physique. He saw himself as heavily built as opposed to fat, and it was people like him who suffered most from heat. He looked forward to the *coup de blanc* that Monsieur de Sauvignac would certainly offer him. It was a point of honor with such people. Real gentry, not like some.

His minivan had been giving him trouble again. The motor was dying for no reason. Gaston suspected it had something to do with the battery or maybe the alternator. He sighed. He would have to fill out yet another maintenance request at the end of the day. He bumped down the muddy lane past La Binette. As usual, there was nothing for them, either, especially (he was relieved) nothing requiring a signature. He began the rough, steep climb out of the valley bottom toward Les Colombes. He was about three-quarters of the way there when the engine coughed. He downshifted quickly. The engine died completely.

Merde! Why did these things always happen to him? He set the hand brake and considered his options. He was almost through his route, but this meant he'd have to call in to the depot for help. This would make the fourth time in a month, and his boss was giving him sour looks for running up maintenance costs and late deliveries. As if it were his fault. These tin-pot PTT vans, couldn't hold up to the roads.

Well, he could walk up the rest of the way to the château and phone from there. He got out, glumly studying the steep incline before him. Really, it would be simplest to wheel the van around, get it pointed downhill the way he'd come, jump in, and kick-start it on the run. So much for his *coup de blanc*, but, provided he didn't stall, he'd probably make it back to the main road, maybe even all the way to the depot.

He opened the driver's-side door and was setting his shoulder to the frame when it occurred to him that before releasing the brake he'd better do something about preventing the car from rolling backward. He went to the opposite verge to gather some rocks. As he did, his eye caught something below him through the screen of trees. He walked farther up the road to get a better view. He was now looking down at a corner of La Binette, a perspective he normally did not have of the farm. It was a peaceful scene, a low, hummocky field dotted with grazing sheep, old poplars in a line, and a stream heavily overgrown with willow brush at the bottom. Gaston stood very still, a huge grin spreading over his features.

"*C'est vachement fort, ça!*" he exclaimed softly. Really, it was too rich. Luck landed in your very hand when you least expected it.

He hurried back to the van, maneuvered it around—it was infernally hard work because he had to push it uphill a bit first in order to turn it downhill—jumped in, and let it roll. The engine caught on the first kick, and he was away, joyfully bucketing at speed back down the steep, rocky lane, past trees and hedges, approaching the grassy track winding off to La Binette. It was a fairly straight run down, except for the curve at the bottom, one he'd done thousands of times. As he entered the bend, he never really saw, much less had a chance of avoiding, the log lying in the middle of the road, only felt the tremendous shock as his front tires hit it. The van sailed through the air and came down on its side in a long, gouging slide of gravel, shattered glass, and grating metal. Gaston lay stupidly in its wreckage, bleeding profusely from the nose and mouth. His last view of the world, before the darkness gathered in, was of the day's mail littering the grass like confetti and a swollen, one-eyed face hanging upside down above him like a bilious moon.

·

It was *la canadienne* that he called for, her name that he muttered insistently. When Mara arrived, the tall female doctor said disapprovingly that she could stay for a couple of minutes, no more. Gaston's fat wife and seven daughters, huddled together like chickens at one end of the waiting room, glared at her with tear-filled, hating eyes. They now knew her to be the mistress whom slow, fat Gaston had cunningly concealed from them all these years. That's what came of letting foreigners live among you. They included Mara's companions, grouped at the other end of the room, in their outrage. Mado paced like a caged animal, smoking furiously despite a *défense de fumer* notice. Paul huddled massively in a plastic chair that threatened to give way beneath his weight. Julian sat next to Paul, long legs outstretched, gazing at the opposite wall.

Mara followed the doctor's straight white back through the swinging doors and down the long pale-green corridor leading to the intensive-care ward. She returned shortly. Everyone's eyes were on her.

"He's in very bad shape," she said unnecessarily. "He could barely talk. He's full of tubes. I think—I think he was trying to tell me something about the *pigeonnier.*" And she burst out crying.

·

The village of Malpech perched atop a rise and consisted of two dozen dwellings. Mara and Julian approached it along a narrow, winding road. As they entered the village, the first thing they saw was an empty, dusty square flanked at one end by a small, mossy church and at the other by a newish community hall. It was noon, and there was no one about, not even, to Jazz's disappointment, a dog. The houses had a hot, closed look. The only movement centered on a public notice board where badly tacked posters flapped lazily in the breeze.

Beyond Malpech, the road took them down into a leafy valley, over a humpbacked bridge spanning a stream and continued past a thin scattering of farms, with not a pigeon house in sight. Several kilometers farther on, they drew up at the bend in the road where they were told the accident had occurred. Julian braked the van. They got out. Apart from a few shards of glass and plastic, the rutted, gravel road showed no sign of violence.

From where they stood, they were in a kind of bowl with wooded hills rising up around them. The sound of cicadas, sawing drowsily, filled the air. A light, sere wind rustled the foliage, but otherwise the landscape was very still, as if everything were caught in a kind of hot, midday enchantment. Only Jazz was animated, following his nose avidly along the grassy verge. Back and forth he ran, tongue lolling, now loping ahead, now stopping to investigate a smell long and lovingly. Wordlessly, his human companions trudged after him, past a rough field grazed by a few sheep, the only sign of agricultural activity in the immediate vicinity, and past stacks of logs cut from fallen trees and left at the roadside by the work crew after the last windstorm.

From there the road led straight up. Slowly they took the steep ascent.

"You don't suppose Gaston was delirious, do you?" Julian hazarded. As far as they could see, an unbroken canopy of treetops spread away beneath them. The only visible man-made structure was much higher up, where the roofline and chimneystacks of an imposing house could barely be made out through a screen of greenery.

"I don't know. He seemed to think he'd found something. He was very insistent, especially about the money."

"Well, if he did, it wasn't here. In fact, odds are it was somewhere else. His route takes him all over the place."

Mara made no reply.

"It would be simple enough to check it out," Julian offered a moment later. "His route, I mean."

"I suppose we could," she said without conviction. Since the *facteur*'s accident, she had little stomach for pursuing her quest. Gaston had suffered a concussion, a broken arm, four fractured ribs, a broken nose, internal injuries, and facial lacerations. His condition was serious, and he remained heavily drugged, lapsing in and out of consciousness. She had not been able to question him further. For the sake of the family, the doctor had ordered Mara to keep away. She, too, believed that Mara was Gaston's secret companion of joy.

"I'm thinking of giving it up, Julian," she told him finally.

He stopped short. "You're not serious?"

"Very." Her small face was pale, the dark, straight brows knit together.

"But why?"

"I feel responsible. It's pretty obvious Gaston's accident was somehow tied up with that damned *pigeonnier*."

"Oh, come on, Mara, you're not to blame for what happened."

"All the same, he's been badly injured, probably because of a thousand euros and my need to know. Bedie's been missing for nineteen years, is probably dead. I think the time has come for me to let it go."

She called for Jazz. "Well, we've been, we've looked, and now I'd like to go home."

"Of course, it's up to you," Julian conceded as they turned back down the hill. Why did he feel so disappointed when really he should feel relieved? The search for Bedie Dunn was something he had entered into with the greatest reluctance. He was now free to continue looking for the Lady's Slipper alone, without impediment, without the nagging worry of what Mara's presence might mean in his life, of what ultimately he might have to do with her. Her and that dog of hers. But deep down he knew that her withdrawal took the heart out of the chase, and the chase, after all, was what had been driving them—him—from the beginning.

For her part, Mara was convinced of the rightness of her decision. The time really had come to say good-bye to Bedie. A sudden sense of lightness flooded her, as if, having put down the weight of her sister, she could now stand straighter, move without encumbrance. Savoring the relief of the moment, she raised her eyes and saw her surroundings clearly as if for the first time. A dusty country road, shimmering with heat. Below them a peaceful wooded valley. Through the trees, a meadow running down to a stream, thickly bordered by willows and poplars. Her eye rested there, picking out the occasional flash of the watercourse. Then she saw something that made her heart lurch.

"Julian," she cried sharply.

"What?"

Dragging him back uphill to a point where they both could

get a better view, she pointed frantically. There in the distance below them, rising from the meadow and still largely obscured by foliage, was a *pigeonnier*. Craning their necks and leaning this way and that, they put together enough glimpses of it to make it out: a tall, round tower built of local limestone with numerous entry holes for the birds. The steeply pitched roof, what they could see of it, was conical and covered in *lauzes*. From where they stood, part of a shuttered window and a door were visible. They stared at it wordlessly, as if by speaking they feared to dispel an illusion.

At last Mara stirred. "This was not," she said with conviction, "on the Série bleue."

Julian was actively scanning the panorama of forested hills and valleys around them. Eventually, he pointed to his left. "My stand of Bird's-nests can't be more than three to five kilometers northwest of here." He paused for Mara to take in his meaning. "Easily within walking distance. So we know which direction she came from."

"And all we have to do," Mara finished, "is work out where she went."

They walked quickly down the hill. At the bottom, they passed an iron box placed on a small cairn of stones at the side of the road. Speculatively they paused before it. The name BINETTE was crudely lettered on the front. In several places the paint, once red, now weathered almost black, had run, so that the words had a ghastly, dripping look. At right angles to the road, an overgrown, rutted track led across a rough sheep pasture and down toward a heavily wooded combe. The tip of a chimney showing through the treetops indicated a house.

"At a guess," said Julian, "I'd say the *pigeonnier* belongs to this farm."

Something was moving on the track—a large man on a small

bicycle, coming toward them not in haste but steadily. As the bicyclist approached, they could hear the faint rattling of the frame on the uneven ground and the soft, regular squeaking of the crank set with each revolution of the pedals. *Grinch. Grinch. Grinch.* The scene had such a dreamlike quality to it that Mara and Julian stood transfixed, watching it unfold. Now the bicyclist was nearing the point where the track met the road. The rider made the turn in their direction. As he drew even with them, he slowed but did not stop. Nor did he greet them, only fixed them with one bulging eye—the other was covered by a dark lens—craning his neck slowly around as he rode past to keep them, particularly Mara, in view as long as possible. Jazz gave a low growl. Mara retained a vision of pale, ragged hair standing on end and a large, misshapen face resembling an oversized, semi-cooked hunk of engorged goose liver.

"Dear Lord," whispered Mara once she could find her voice, "what was that?"

"Eh bien," said Loulou La Pouge, "you have found a pigeon house."

"The pigeon house," Mara said firmly. Once again they were in the ex-policeman's parlor, perched on overstuffed chairs, being served Monbazillac and nuts. "So that's proof, isn't it?"

Loulou shrugged and threw up both hands. "Proof of what? That it exists? *Soyez raisonable,* Mara, you still have not definitely connected the photographs to your sister, and until you can do that, what is your case?"

"But the photos were taken with her camera," Mara cried impatiently. "Her initials are on the case. How much more do you want?"

"Ah." The old fellow cocked his head at her with a knowing

look. "Always we return to the initials. I'm afraid, *mon amie,* you did not help your own cause there."

She paled. "What do you mean?"

"*B.D.* Presumably for 'Beatrice Dunn'?"

"Well of course!"

"But written *over* the accumulated deposit of dirt and mold. A more recent addition, don't you think?"

Julian started. "A more recent addition? Are you saying someone added those initials at a later time?" He turned to stare unbelievingly at Mara, who flushed a deep red.

"You knew all along!" she burst out furiously at Loulou. "All right. You caught me out. I wrote them myself." Unrepentantly, she glared at Julian, whose eyebrows were hovering near his hairline. "Don't you see? It was the only way I could make the police take me seriously."

"*Au contraire,*" Loulou said gravely. "I can tell you that those of us, myself included, who still remember the case would have liked nothing better than to take you seriously. After all, we still have the unsolved murder of the Tenhagen woman and several disappearances on the books. But we needed more than supposition and—*pardonnez-moi*—flimsy chicanery! It doesn't do"—he wagged a fat forefinger in her face—"no, it doesn't do at all to try to trick the police!"

"So you're saying this camera could have belonged to someone else?" Julian asked.

"No, it did not," Mara almost shouted. "Forget the initials. That camera was Bedie's. I'd know it anywhere. Oh, why won't anyone believe me?"

The two men regarded her in silence. She looked near to tears.

Julian drew a deep breath. "Okay." He turned to Loulou. "It

seems to me you do have proof of a sort. First, Mara recognized the camera as her sister's, even if she did falsify the initials. That ought to count for something. Second, whoever took those photos knew orchids, how to identify and film them. According to Mara, Bedie was an experienced documenter of orchids. Taken together, I'd say these things argue strongly in favor of the camera's provenance."

Heartened, Mara persisted. "And there's something else. We told you the pigeon house is on a farm called La Binette. What we didn't tell you is that it's also just up the road from the spot where the *facteur,* Gaston, had his accident. He was asking around about the *pigeonnier,* you know, showing the photocopy to everyone on his route. Don't you find it odd that he crashed just there? Besides, we got a look at the farmer. He's . . ." She hesitated. How could she say that he was the embodiment of the nameless terror of her nightmares? "There's something horrible about him—brutal, ugly. Maybe you won't be convinced by gut feeling, but I tell you, I *know* he had something to do with my sister's disappearance. Can't you persuade the police at least to question him?"

Loulou shook his head, clicking his tongue softly against his teeth. "Mara, you must understand that your credibility with the lads in Périgueux is not—how shall we say—particularly famous. They see you as someone who has already tried to doctor evidence and who is quite capable of doing so again. Moreover, you bring me nothing more than highly circumstantial information, an argument based, as you put it, on a reaction of the viscera. A *pigeonnier* and an ugly farmer do not make a case. Supposing this man is questioned and denies all knowledge of your sister, as he most certainly will. What then?"

"Ask questions. Make people talk. The police can do that. Someone is bound to know something, to remember something."

Loulou smiled indulgently. "For you it seems so simple. But you don't understand how the rural mind works. Make people talk. *Ma foi!* The locals will simply close ranks. This man is one of them, and the tendency is always to cover for one's own, regardless. Besides, what you need is something much more concrete than local gossip, Mara. A solid link tying this man to your sister. That's what you must establish, don't you see?"

Mara rose, chin set firm. "Loulou, all I can see is that the only thing that will convince you is finding Bedie's body on that farm. Well, if that's what it takes, that's what we'll do!"

Julian, who found himself hurrying out the door after her, wished, not for the first time, that she would be more sparing in her use of the first person plural.

12

Gaston felt like his hero, Marshal Ney. Or, rather, what he imagined Marshal Ney must have felt like as he planned and directed the victorious battles of Friedland, Smolensk, and Borodino. The son of a barrel-maker from Saarlouis, Ney had risen to fame and glory in the days of the Empire. Gaston was also from a line of barrel-makers, from Bordeaux.

First, there was the triumphant moment when Mara had presented him with a check for one thousand euros. This had been in the recovery ward in the presence of his wife and daughters. Now that they understood the situation, they had forgiven him and embraced Mara enthusiastically. Even the once-disapproving doctor shook Mara's hand. The other ward patients thought Gaston had won the lottery. Although his eyes were bruised and bloodshot, tubes still ran out of nearly every orifice, and most parts of his body, including his nose, were heavily bandaged, it had been the best day of his life.

Then followed a deeply gratifying conference with Mara and Julian, both of them hanging on his lips, as it were.

"So you see," Mara appealed to him, "what we need is a way of getting information on those La Binette people without arousing suspicion."

"It's more than that," said Julian. "We need to be able to get onto their land."

"Hrrr," Gaston spoke with difficulty around his tubes. "You ha' to be ca'ful. I heard sub preddy fuddy stories aboud dem."

Mara and Julian nodded. Their sighting of Vrac—the man on the bicycle could have been none other—made them alive to this advice.

In the end, Gaston advised them to talk with the people in the château on the hill, Monsieur and Madame de Sauvignac. He knew them personally, having delivered their mail for nearly thirty years. If there was anything to be gotten on those La Binette folk, the de Sauvignacs would have it. He then gave Mara and Julian a barely intelligible version of the history of the de Sauvignacs as he knew it: the early death of one son, the estrangement of the other, the mother gone right off her head. He finished by describing the present melancholy state of affairs in which the old couple lived out their days alone, rattling about in a great cave of a mansion.

The nurse came in to warn Julian and Mara not to tire her patient.

"Good lug," Gaston gurgled happily after them as they departed. "Leb be doe wha' habbens." And he touched the side of his bandaged nose knowingly with his good hand.

·

When Mara telephoned Henri de Sauvignac, she mentioned only her interest in the *pigeonnier*. The old gentleman was courteous but wary and surprisingly evasive. From this she judged that Gaston must have, at some previous time, given the de Sauvignacs his undoubtedly gruesome version of *la canadienne disparue*. To them, she was only a stranger with unpleasant questions to ask. Henri de Sauvignac made the excuse that his wife was not well, apologized, and said they could not possibly receive her at the moment. However, if she would be good enough to leave her number . . . She did so.

She was extremely surprised when, the following morning, Henri de Sauvignac telephoned and suggested that she come out to the château at four o'clock that afternoon.

Les Colombes stood high on its prominence, surveying a great
sweep of rumpled hills and valleys. As Mara drove up the steep,
winding approach, she could barely make out the dimensions of
the château, so overgrown was it with shrubberies. Then she
rounded a bend and found herself in an empty, dusty forecourt
giving onto a broad, ivy-covered facade. Once grand, no doubt,
Les Colombes now had a shabby, forlorn air. The roof looked in
bad condition. Many of the tall upper-story windows were shuttered. The broad front of the château was dominated by a central
portal above a balustraded terrace. A crumbling pair of Baroque
staircases curved down from either end of the terrace.

Mara parked in the shade. Jazz looked hopeful and then disappointed at being left. As usual, he hung his head out the window and moaned disapprovingly at Mara's retreating back.

Henri de Sauvignac must have been watching for her, for as
she climbed the weed-choked steps the great front door swung
back. He stood in the opening, tall and gaunt.

"Madame Dunn?" His voice was suave, like old velvet, his
deeply lined face still handsome. He wore a tired but well-made
suit of an old-fashioned cut, a shirt of dubious whiteness, and a
paisley cravat.

"Monsieur de Sauvignac?"

Gallantly, he stooped to brush the back of her hand with lips
as dry as autumn leaves.

"How good of you to come at such short notice." His practiced regard, wandering covertly over her body, revealed a liber-
tine beneath the gentleman. "And how clever of you to find us.
Rather out of the way, I'm afraid."

"Your directions were excellent."

Her host stepped back to admit her into an echoing vestibule.
An impressive stone staircase rose at the back of it to the upper

reaches of the house. Passing near him, Mara caught a whiff of eau de cologne, suggestive of a still-potent sexuality but underlain by a faint smell of decay that he seemed to share with the house itself. It was an odor that Mara recognized from her own work in restoring dank places long uninhabited.

"I think the library will be most comfortable." He ushered her through a pair of handsomely paneled doors opening off to the right. "Please. Sit down. May I offer you something? An apéritif?"

Mara preferred tea but accepted vermouth because she thought it would be easier for him. She somehow doubted that the de Sauvignacs kept domestic help. With a small bow, he withdrew.

She had been invited to sit, but Mara remained standing, glancing curiously about her. The library, he had called it. Certainly it contained books, but it looked more like a furniture warehouse—Louis XVI armchairs pushed against the walls, an antique armoire, a dainty Restoration console, an eighteenth-century ebony escritoire. There were little touches of domesticity, too, suggesting that the de Sauvignacs spent much of their time there: a pair of worn velvet settees drawn up to an oil heater; a small television on a scarred mahogany stand; a sewing basket full of scraps of material. The back of the room was entirely taken up by a baronial dining table, set about with sixteen chairs (Mara counted them). It was stacked with papers and bric-a-brac, but a telltale litter of crumbs at one end told her that this was where the couple took their meals.

The paneled doors creaked. Mara turned. It was not Henri de Sauvignac; instead, a tall elderly woman clad in a dress that hung unevenly at the hem, a voluminous green, fringed shawl, and dressy high-heeled shoes.

"Ah," said the woman, fixing Mara with vague kindliness before wobbling toward her in a clattering, jerky gait, like a marionette in the hands of an inexpert puppeteer.

"You must be Madame Dunn? I am Jeanne de Sauvignac. How very kind of you to call." Her rusty voice was pleasant, and she spoke with almost childish pride, as if she had initiated the meeting. She extended her hand to touch Mara's with formal courtesy. "Do sit down." Up close, she emitted the same musty odor as her husband.

Mara seated herself on one of the velvet settees, Jeanne on the other, drawing her shawl about her with care, smoothing its shiny nap with the palm of her hand. Mara studied her with interest. The old woman's clothing was like the room, a gathering of oddments from better times, the dress of fine but much-worn gray silk jersey, the scuffed satin pumps dating from another era and too big now for the bony feet. The grayish-yellow hair was swept up at the sides and held haphazardly in place by two tortoiseshell combs, giving the woman's head a flyaway look. The shawl struck a curious note. Mara realized with a mild sense of shock that it was in fact one of those souvenir tablecloths that one bought at seaside resorts; the word "Biarritz" was emblazoned down one side.

Jeanne was also staring at her, not just curiously but with a hungry interest that made Mara uncomfortable.

A slight, wondering crease crumpled the old woman's brow. "You look so much—" she began eagerly and then broke off.

So much what? Mara wondered, but at that point the husband returned with a small tray bearing glasses and a bottle of Martini & Rossi. He seemed momentarily surprised to see his wife in the room, but merely said as he handed Mara her drink, "Ah, my dear, here is Madame Dunn, who has come to see us." He served his wife and then himself before sitting down beside Mara.

He raised his glass. *"À votre santé, madame."*

"La vôtre aussi," Mara toasted them both in return.

"How nice to have a visitor." Jeanne de Sauvignac favored her with a crooked smile of naive and vacant sweetness. "We often used to have visitors in the afternoon. For tea, you know. I always liked to take afternoon tea, in the English manner, is that not so, Henri?"

"Of course, my dear," murmured her husband. He delved in his pocket and drew out a thin black marocain case, snapping it open with a thumbnail. "Do you smoke, madame?" When Mara declined, he said, "I hope you will permit?" and applied himself to removing a cigarette, striking a match, lighting up, and placing the burnt matchstick in a plastic Cinzano ashtray, each movement carried out with fastidious care. His smoking fascinated her: both greedy and precise, as if he hungered for the taste and smell of the tobacco but apportioned each drag sparingly. With every inhalation, he tapped the ash carefully into the ashtray.

They were clearly waiting for her to begin. For the moment, Mara really had no idea how to go about it. Gaston had not prepared her for such penurious eccentricity. In the end, de Sauvignac saved her the trouble.

Clearing his throat, he said, "You expressed an interest in the *pigeonnier*, I believe?"

"Yes, of course." It was her ostensible reason for coming.

"Unfortunately, I don't know how much I can tell you." He tapped the cigarette. "It was built sometime after this house, probably in the late 1600s, and at one time stood on land that belonged to my family." Momentarily, his voice took on a ring of pride. "In times past, the Seigneurie of Les Colombes extended some ten leagues east to west, farther than a man could walk in a day. In fact, until the last century, Les Colombes was one of the most important holdings in the region. Of course, things are now—how should I put it—much reduced."

"I see." She did not know what else to say.

"However, to return to the *pigeonnier*. But perhaps you are not aware of the historical importance of pigeons in France?" Once more he sucked deeply on the cigarette. Twin trails of smoke streamed thinly from his nostrils. "For centuries they were valued for meat, eggs, and fertilizer, especially here in our southwest, where we have little livestock. In my grandfather's, even in my father's day, pigeon dung was so precious that it was given as dowries and passed down from generation to generation.

"It's not surprising, therefore"—a wave of the hand—"that there are thousands of such structures scattered throughout the Dordogne. However, ours is one of the largest." Again the note of pride. He craned around to frown at the bookshelves. "I believe somewhere there is an architectural drawing showing it in cross section so that you can see the niches set into the interior wall for the birds to nest. At one time we may have had over one thousand nesting pairs. I remember there was a tall, pivoting ladder in the middle for the keeper to climb up. In my father's time, however, the bottom nests were blocked off to reduce the number of birds. Pigeons"—he gave a sardonic smile—"eat a lot of grain."

He paused reflectively. "It no longer belongs to us, of course. The land was sold a long time ago, the *pigeonnier* with it." His gaze traveled to the windows and beyond. "You know, I haven't set eyes on that dovecote in years. I didn't even recognize it when Gaston showed us the picture." His eyes returned to Mara. "Is this sufficient information? I'm really not sure how much more I can tell you."

"Yes. At least where the *pigeonnier* is concerned." Mara hesitated, then plunged. "Monsieur de Sauvignac, I haven't been exactly open with you. It's not so much the *pigeonnier* that I want to talk to you about, although that does come into it. I expect

Gaston has already told you something about me . . ." She drew breath. De Sauvignac waited for her to go on.

"My real reason for being here, as you've probably already guessed, is—I've come for my sister." She was putting it awkwardly, yet she *was* there for Bedie, because of her and on her behalf.

If Henri regarded her impassively, the effect on his wife was electrical. The smile slipped completely from her face. Jeanne gaped at Mara in acute alarm, bordering on panic, as if Mara were a madwoman accusing them of body snatching. "But she's not here!" she cried, appalled.

"I mean," Mara corrected, feeling her cheeks go hot, "it's *about* my sister that I've come."

Quickly, to cover her gaffe, she gave them her version of Bedie's disappearance and the link, through the photograph, with the dovecote. Throughout the telling, the deepening crease in Madame's brow hung like a question mark in the air. When Mara finished, wife and husband were silent for a long moment.

De Sauvignac ground out his cigarette. "Terrible for you, of course, but I don't quite see how we can help you."

Mara explained. "I'd like to approach the people who own the farm below you, where the *pigeonnier* stands. The woman known as la Binette and her son, Vrac. I'd be extremely grateful if you could assist me in this regard."

He frowned. "La Binette and Vrac?"

"I understood from Gaston that you have some influence with them."

"Influence?" De Sauvignac gave a dry laugh, like a cough. "Only in the sense that we are, how should I put it, long acquaintances. I'm afraid those two keep very much to themselves. They don't like strangers, and one has to respect their privacy."

"Could you at least tell me something about them?"

He considered this, then shrugged. "What is it you want to know?"

"Well, how long have they been here? What kind of people are they?"

"They're from these parts, of course. La Binette's father, old Rocher, was a day laborer. Took on odd jobs round about—woodcutting, harvesting. La Binette and her mother did the rough washing for the house. When I was a lad Madame Rocher and little Binette used to wheel their wooden cart up here once a week to collect the dirty things, which they'd take to the stream down below because the communal *lavoire* in Malpech was too far away. La Binette's boy, Armand—the one they call Vrac—grew up simple."

Mara found it curious that he referred to the creature she had seen on the bicycle as a boy.

"I don't like nicknames, do you?" Jeanne de Sauvignac interjected suddenly, pulling the tablecloth tightly around her. "They can be so cruel. Poor Binette had a perfectly proper name once. I can't remember it. Can you, Henri? Oh yes, that's right, Marie-Claire. Such a pretty name. And to call her a thing like that. All because she had that dreadful *tache* on her face. She was born with it, madame, a purple birthmark over one eye. When she was a girl, she always used to try to hide it with her hand, as if she were shading her eyes from the sun."

The old woman leaned forward, addressing Mara with gentle indignation. "Do you know what *binette* means, madame? Of course, most people nowadays think it merely means a hoe, the thing you use in the garden. But in the old days, it meant "ugly mug," and also one of those big old-fashioned wigs, because of course poor Marie-Claire lost all her hair after she had her baby and had to wear that ugly old horsehair thing. I remember well when Vrac was born. Two days she was in labor. When her baby came out his head was badly deformed, and he never was right as a result, poor thing. It affected his brain. Everything shook loose. That's why they called him Vrac."

"I've seen him," Mara ventured. "Frankly, he looks quite terrifying."

"Oh," the wife said softly, "you mustn't be put off by appearances. He's perfectly harmless, one of God's creatures. If you tell him to go away, shoo, like that"—she waved her hand as if she were scattering chickens—"he just fades into the trees. He never bothers anyone."

"Nevertheless," Mara persisted, "Gaston mentioned . . . certain rumors."

"Rumors?" The couple glanced quickly at each other.

"Odd behavior. I'm sorry to ask this, but I have to know. Would he have—has there ever been any history of incidents with Vrac?"

Henri, reaching for another cigarette, paused. "Incidents? I'm not sure I understand what you intend, madame."

"Violence, attacks on people, that kind of thing."

"Ah." Her host was silent for some time, studying her speculatively. Finally, he asked simply, "Are you suggesting that Vrac had something to do with your sister's disappearance?"

Mara chose her words with care. "The photo shows that Bedie was on their land. It may not be that he was involved, but he might have seen her, or else he or his mother might know something that can help me."

"Madame . . ." De Sauvignac's voice was controlled. He replaced the cigarette unlit, snapping the marocain case shut. Mara noted that his hands trembled slightly. "This affair of your sister happened many years ago. You must comprehend that Vrac can't remember things from one month to the next. I doubt he would be able to tell you anything. In any case, as my wife said, he's quite harmless, but simple, you see. It would be . . . entirely inappropriate for you to question him."

"Monsieur de Sauvignac," Mara appealed to him, "having come this far, I'm afraid I can't just leave it. The *pigeonnier* is the first concrete lead I've had in nineteen years."

"Indeed. All the same, I must ask you to avoid upsetting him." His tone grew emphatic. "When all is said and done, Vrac is one of us. I would feel required to intervene if I thought he or his mother was being harassed."

"I don't want to harass anyone," Mara insisted, "but you must understand I have to find out the truth. You see, I have reason to believe my sister came to harm on la Binette's farm."

"You have proof of this?" Henri inquired sharply.

"No," she admitted. "Only the photo of the *pigeonnier*."

He regarded her stonily.

"I don't want to involve the police." It was Mara's only trump, a weak one. "But if I have no other choice . . ."

A dark stain spread slowly over de Sauvignac's face. He spoke with cold dignity. "You must do as you see fit, madame. However, I assure you that neither you nor the police will find anything of interest in these parts." He rose stiffly. "Now, I fear my wife is growing tired. You must excuse us if we bid you good-day."

She had no choice but to rise, too, and follow him out. As she passed from the room, Jeanne's voice wavered after her uncertainly: "Au revoir, madame. Do come again. For tea next time."

The massive front door closed behind her with heavy finality. Bleakly, Mara descended the stone steps. Well, the de Sauvignacs had received her. She'd asked her questions, and they had told her nothing. She knew the house would not be open to her again. She crossed the forecourt dejectedly, making for her car. Just before she reached it, a tall figure came striding around the corner of the house. She had to swerve to avoid a collision.

"You!" Mara exclaimed.

The man stopped short with a look of startled recognition. "Ah, of course. Bonjour, madame. We meet again. I hope in calmer circumstances?" He peered doubtfully down at her and extended a large sunburned hand. "Alain de Sauvignac."

"Oh," she said, taking in the significance of his name. "Mara Dunn."

They shook hands, he holding hers fractionally longer than Mara thought necessary. He had his father's handsome face, only more square-cut and deeply weathered. His sandy-colored hair was shot through with gray. A curious light came into his dark-blue eyes. "If I may ask, how is it that you're here? When last we met you were the frightened rabbit in the woods." It might have been teasingly said, but his look was serious.

"I came . . ." She paused, uncertainly.

"Of course!" he declared, remembering. "To see my parents. Papa said something about a visitor."

She asked a question of her own. "Then you live here?"

"Not at all. I work abroad. I'm only back for the moment, visiting the old ones."

Mara made up her mind swiftly. "Monsieur de Sauvignac, I know it's awfully forward of me, but I wonder if I could impose on you . . . ?"

"At your service," he smiled gallantly. "What can I do?"

"It's rather complicated. You see, I—I would very much appreciate the chance to talk to you. It would mean a lot to me. But I'm afraid it would have to be in confidence."

"In confidence?" He frowned. "What about?"

She shook her head, dug in her bag and gave him her card.

"Not here. This is my number. Can you call me? This evening, if possible? And please, will you say nothing of this to anyone?"

He looked perplexed. "Is it so important? But why the mystery?"

She had no time for more. The massive front door was swinging open.

"Until tonight, then," she said and hurried to her car.

As she backed out, she saw that Henri de Sauvignac had emerged from the house. He made no move to join his son, only stood on the terrace, like a frozen sentinel, overseeing her departure. She caught a final glimpse of him in her rearview mirror as she pulled away. His expression gave her quite a shock. His face was white, his eyes staring, his lips pulled back in a rictus of fear.

13

The bead curtain flew apart noisily. Mara strode into the bistro. Jazz's entry was more sedate, snout first, a quick survey of the room, then a rambling approach to Julian, who was sipping a pastis while watching Paul do accounts at the bar. Julian looked up.

"Well? What happened?"

"They're hiding something," she cried, and hopped onto a stool beside him.

"Eh? Like what?" Paul slapped down his pencil.

She threw her hands up in frustration. "That's just it. I don't know. But it has to do with Vrac, and they won't tell me because *Vrac is one of them*. The husband is especially secretive. He doesn't want me anywhere near La Binette. Virtually warned me off."

"What about the wife?" asked Mado, coming out from the back of the bistro, where she had been setting tables in preparation for the evening crowd.

"She seems sympathetic," Mara ventured doubtfully, "but I don't think she's altogether there."

"D'you mean gaga?" Paul produced glasses and a bottle.

Mara considered the possibility. "No. Just somehow slightly out of focus—or absent. I mean, as if she weren't quite in the room with you, but listening at the door." And she told them in detail about her conversation with Henri and Jeanne de Sauvignac, as well as her encounter with the son.

"The man we met in the woods was Alain de Sauvignac?" Julian queried. Finding Jazz's head within reach, he scratched it.

They all fell silent as Paul filled three glasses with white Bordeaux and topped up Julian's pastis. Mado lit a cigarette. Finally, through a screen of smoke, she said:

"It'll have to be you, Julian."

"Eh?"

"You'll have to go there and snoop around."

He gaped at her, incredulous. "What? Search the château?"

"Not the château. La Binette. The farm holds the clue to everything."

"Why me?"

"Well, *you're* the orchid expert."

"Oh, thank you very much."

"Mado's right," Mara pressed him earnestly. "Don't you see, Julian, if we can identify even some of the orchid sequence on La Binette land, it'll prove Bedie was actually there."

"I thought the *pigeonnier* already did that."

"Not good enough. From the angle of the photo, she could have taken it from the road."

"You can't *see* it from the road," Julian objected.

"Nineteen years ago, there may have been less tree cover. We need to prove that she was actually on that farm."

"I wish you wouldn't keep saying *we*, when what you really mean is *me*."

Mara stared into her wine and made no offer to accompany him.

"So you want *me* to search the whole bloody farm?" Julian glared at each of them in turn. They avoided his eye. He drained his pastis and banged the glass down in disgust. "*Par pitié*, make me a sensible suggestion for a change."

"Take a shotgun with you," Paul advised with a spark of malice.

In the end, Julian gave in. It was true that reconstructing Bedie's path would give Mara something concrete to take to the police. Let the gendarmes do the digging, he thought grimly, and then focused on the more cheerful, if faint, possibility that, if his quest were *really* successful, he would have his Lady's Slipper.

Alain de Sauvignac's phone call came at ten o'clock that evening. Mara snatched eagerly at the receiver.

"Yes, hello?"

"Madame Dunn?" His deep voice had a seductive quality to it. "Perhaps now you will be kind enough to tell me what this is all about?"

Mara took a lungful of air, exhaled slowly and told him as much as she thought he needed to know.

His terms were simple: information conditional on lunch. He came directly to the point. "I'd like to see you again. Under more conducive circumstances."

So now they were sitting on the terrace of La Vieille Guinguette, a little waterside restaurant upriver from the town of Maussac. Jazz dozed at Mara's feet. The day was sunny and the fare simple, mainly traditional dishes like braised sheep's tongues and tripe cooked with leeks. They ordered *chabrol*, bread-thickened soup heavy with garlic and duck fat, a meal in itself. By the time they were adding red wine to the dregs *à la Périgourdine*, they were on a first-name basis and speaking French.

"I admit I was intrigued by you," Alain said, pushing his empty bowl aside. "Who wouldn't be?" He gave her a glance that was half admiring, half speculative, then retreated onto safer ground. "You speak French well. But your accent is unusual. I can't place it."

"Montreal," she grinned, "and absolutely unique. We slur and drawl, flatten our vowels, and compress our sibilants. The point is, can you get us—Julian—onto La Binette land?"

"Your orchidologist friend?" Alain drew down the corners of his mouth. "I wouldn't like to do so *à la dérobée,* as they say. I don't hold much with sneaking. And what you're asking is trespassing, after all. You also have to realize that, if you've already approached Papa and he refused to help you, you're putting me in a damned difficult position."

She shifted uncomfortably. "I suppose you think me deceitful."

He flipped a hand in the air. *"Oui—et non.* If you truly believe Vrac had something to do with your sister's disappearance, I can understand that your desire to know might override all—well, all scruples. However, you must also comprehend my father's reticence. It might sound terribly old-fashioned to you, but Papa has a strong sense of noblesse oblige toward the people of the *territoire,* particularly la Binette and her son. The family worked on the estate, you know. La Binette and Vrac still do the occasional odd job. Local loyalties run deep."

"Even to the extent of protecting a possible murderer? Other women have gone missing, too, you know."

Alain shook his head. "No one's protecting a murderer. Oh, I agree that Vrac and la Binette sometimes get up to things they oughtn't, but Vrac's not a killer. You demonize him because he's ugly and mentally—shall we say incomplete? When really he only represents the dark side of all of us. Look, I've known him all my life. When my brother, Patrice, and I were little and Vrac a few years older, he used to jump out of the bushes at us, screaming and making horrible faces. He'd chase us through the woods, threatening to bash our heads in. I admit, we were terrified. However, I suppose, like most boys, there was also a side of us that relished the gruesomeness of it. I suppose you might say we turned it into a kind of game. We ran, he hunted us down. A variation of *cache-cache*."

"Hide-and-seek? A rather nasty form of it."

Alain grinned ruefully. "We took care not to let Vrac find us, let me tell you. The consequences could be pretty dire. In fact, it became a rule of the game. The hunter could do anything he wanted to you if he caught you."

"Such as what?" Mara asked faintly.

"Oh, mainly shoves and punches. Vrac didn't have the imagination to be very refined in his punishments. But far worse than that were his seizures. It was really frightening, watching him flail around and foam at the mouth. La Binette would have to hold him down him until he grew calm again. Otherwise, he'd break things or hurt himself. But I can assure you, he never did us or anyone else any real harm. Everyone around here knows that."

Mara leaned earnestly across the table. "Alain, that was Vrac as a child. Nineteen years ago, Vrac would have been a man of—what?—thirty? thirty-five? If he found my sister on his land, what do you think he would have done?"

Alain went silent, his gaze drifting unhappily out over the water. Restlessly, he shoved his shirtsleeves up, exposing tanned, muscular arms lightly furred with golden hairs. "In my opinion, Mara, apart from a few threats and obscenities, nothing."

She fixed him somberly.

"And if he came across me alone in the forest? It wasn't my imagination, you know. Someone was stalking me that day. Purposely trying to frighten me. Or worse. I find it hard to believe that a chance passerby simply happened to decide to chase me through the trees."

Alain tossed a heel of bread to the ground for Jazz. "So do I.

But only because there were no passersby." And when she looked puzzled, he went on to explain. "You see, you'd strayed onto Saint-Hubert terrain, the grounds of our local hunting association. My father is the association president. That day, it so happened that he asked me to do a routine check of the area, the posting of hunting-reserve and parking signs and so forth. I was on that footpath and in that stretch of forest for over two hours, Mara. During all that time I saw no one, apart from you and your botanical friend."

Alain's eyes met hers. In the sunlight, the dark-blue centers were surrounded by aquamarine. She held his gaze. At last, he sighed, slumping back in a gesture of defeat.

"All right. I suppose it could have been Vrac. He wanders around a lot, and the woods where you were aren't that far from his land. But if it was he, I can assure you he would have only wanted to frighten you. I doubt he intended you any harm."

Mara smiled tightly. "Another game of *cache-cache*? You don't," she challenged him, "really expect me to believe that?"

Julian's first consideration was how to implement the search. He made it clear that this would not be so easy, since no public footpath or *randonnée* gave legitimate access to La Binette terrain. Going under cover of darkness was impossible for obvious reasons—he needed light to see and photograph the orchids that Mara required as evidence. The search would have to be conducted in broad daylight and at risk of Julian's neck.

It was Gaston who came up with the only feasible strategy. However, he played up shamefully, refusing to talk on the telephone and insisting that all of them come to "consult" with him at his house in Le Coux. He was out of the hospital by then and being assiduously nursed by his wife and seven daughters, who treated him as if he really were a battle hero. Which was only right. He had, after all, been in something very like the wars. And still was because his boss was giving him trouble, sloughing responsibility for the accident onto Gaston in order to cover up his own track record of shoddy vehicle maintenance. But if Gaston's engine hadn't given out, he wouldn't have been freewheeling down the road in the first place.

The four of them drove out on Monday evening, when the bistro was closed. They found Gaston in the garden, eating a roll of *petit-suisse* mashed up with sugar, like a schoolboy. White flecks of the creamy cheese stuck to his teeth. The bruising around his eyes had faded to an unattractive yellowish-green. His nose, no longer bandaged, was the color of an underripe aubergine. Paul and Mado gave him chocolates. Julian, who carried the flowers that Mara had brought as a get-well present, dumped them unceremoniously in the *facteur*'s lap.

Gaston dragged it out as long as he could. First he commanded his daughters to bring chairs. The guests were then served apéritifs and a tasty homemade pâté spread on little slices of grilled bread. After that he and his family had to hear in detail about Mara and Julian's encounter with Vrac and her visit to the château. Gaston was particularly fascinated by Mara's description of the interior of the house, for he had never been farther than the kitchen. He was dismayed that the de Sauvignacs had refused to help her.

"Hmm," he said judiciously. "More to this than meets the eye. But why would they cover up for Vrac? It doesn't make sense."

"They tried to make him out as simple but harmless," Mara said. "Alain, too. But I don't believe it for a moment. I'm sure he had something to do with Bedie's disappearance. We've got to find some way of searching the farm without their knowledge."

"She means me," Julian pointed out unnecessarily.

Gaston rubbed his chin.

Finally, what he told them was this: Vrac fished, and la Binette went sometimes to market to sell cheese. That was their opportunity, when the two of them were away from the farm.

"And when exactly would this be?" Julian inquired sarcastically.

"Well . . ." Gaston pushed his fat lips out and considered. "The old woman sometimes goes to the market in Le Bugue, which is on Tuesdays. Or sometimes she sells her *brebis* over in Montignac, which has its market day on Wednesdays. However, she doesn't go every week. Only when she has cheese to sell. But since it's May, you're probably in luck because the ewes are milking. Now, if it were winter, that would be a different story."

"What about Vrac?" asked Julian. "He's the one I'm worried about."

"I'm getting there. Don't rush me. Vrac, on the other hand, comes and goes like a wild animal. Why, I've seen him standing still as a heron, up to his hips in the lower reaches of the Nauze one day, and prowling around the north shore of the Dordogne the next. The trick, as I said, is to hit on the very day when both of them are away together."

"How?" they all wanted to know.

"It'll take some planning," Gaston admitted. "However, if you just give me a little moment, I think I can come up with *une stratégie* that'll work."

He then went deep into thought. Mara stared at him in frustration. Paul slumped in his chair. Gaston's wife and daughters sat forward in theirs, goggling. Mado paced at the edge of the group, blowing smoke in the direction of the rosebushes. Damaged though Gaston was, Julian had to resist an urge to shake him until his neck snapped.

"What I suggest you do," Gaston said slowly, coming up and

squinting into the middle distance, "is go out early on a Tuesday or Wednesday morning. There's a copse above the farm, just below where the road winds up to Les Colombes. Hide your car in the trees, walk down, and find a spot where you have a good view of the farm. But you'll have to keep a sharp eye out for the people in the château, too. That's important because Madame walks in the woods every day and Monsieur still likes to shoot the occasional rabbit. You don't want them to see you. It would give everything away. Monsieur de Sauvignac would be perfectly in his right to order you off since all of the uphill land around there still belongs to him."

"What about the son?" Julian wanted to know. "He might be wandering around."

"Hmm. You'll have to take your chances there. Anyway, wait until you see la Binette and Vrac go off. The old woman drives the truck. Sometimes she takes Vrac with her and drops him somewhere along the way. Other times he goes off on that bicycle of his. That's the chance you want to watch for. But be careful. The mother's usually back before noon. Her *brebis* sells out fast. With him, it's hard to say. Sometimes he can be away for days. People say he sleeps in the woods."

Julian thought it a hit and miss plan and said so, but no one had anything better to suggest. He sulked in the car all the way back to Grissac. The following day was Tuesday, and he had been prevailed upon by the others to go out to La Binette at the crack of dawn. He pictured himself in the misty chill, crouching in wet grass, peering through leaves, while others slept. He liked to start his day out slowly, with several cups of well-sweetened tea, which he sometimes shared with Edith on the occasions that she chose to drop in. Except that Edith was still missing. Old Hilaire was beside himself, and the entire population of Grissac was worried and on the lookout for her.

"*Courage, mon vieux,*" sniggered Paul. "If you're not back by the end of the day, I'll send in the gendarmes."

"It'll come off fine, *chouchou,*" Mado assured him. "Afterward we'll all have a big lunch at Chez Nous. I'll make you something absolutely to bring water to the mouth."

His own susceptibilities got the better of him, but just. *Chouchou* was what she called dogs and cats. Rabbits, too, before she slaughtered them.

•

So it was agreed that Julian would set out at first light the following day, armed not with a shotgun but with his camera and binoculars. He was to take photographs of anything that could be used as evidence linking Bedie to the farm. He was expected to report back at Chez Nous by noon.

Mara turned up at the bistro at a little before twelve to find it doing unusual business, owing to the car-crash death of France's legendary soccer goalie, Jimmy Bartholème, otherwise known as le Mur, the Wall. Patrons sat at the tables, talking in hushed tones. The newsvendor portion of Chez Nous had sold out of papers early; indeed, Paul said that every copy of *Sud Ouest* in the region had been snapped up by eleven that morning.

By one o'clock, there was still no sign of Julian. Paul, in his multiple role as garçon, barman, and *caisse,* repeatedly went to the door to scan the road leading into the village. Mara brought periodic reports to Mado in the kitchen.

"No sign of him yet."

"But it's nearly two!"

"I hope he hasn't run into Vrac."

"*Dieu l'en garde!*"

The afternoon slid by. Mara, as an alternative to nervous collapse, lent a hand clearing off the tables. Jazz slept unconcernedly in the doorway, where everyone had to step over him.

It was not until half past three that Julian's battered van finally pulled up. He had scarcely pushed his way through the beaded curtain before they jerked him out of the hearing of a last, lingering pair of customers and cornered him at the far end of the restaurant. No one seemed to notice that he was tired, muddy, and scratched.

"Well? Did you—"

"What happened? I was worried—"

"What the hell took you so long?"

Julian avenged his lost morning by refusing to tell them anything until he had been allowed to wash up and was seated with a beer. Even so, he doled it out slowly with each course. By then they had the restaurant to themselves. Over a white bean soup, he informed them that he had left his car in the spot Gaston had described and walked down through the woods in the direction of the farm. He had found a place where he could watch the farmhouse from a safe distance and had seen la Binette drive off at around six-thirty, backfiring through a cloud of smoke.

"I got a good look at her through my binoculars," he told them. "She's about six feet tall, wears rubber boots, and has a face that would stop a clock."

Over a next course of *foie gras en croûte,* he informed them that Vrac had not appeared until much later.

"Mado, this smells terrific." He broke off to fork open a steaming dome of light, flaky crust and allowed himself the luxury of a slowly savored mouthful of baked goose liver before continuing. "Then he spent the morning sticking sheep."

Paul ceased chewing, nudged Jazz away with his knee, and glared at Julian in disbelief.

"By the way, he has two good eyes. I saw him without those sunglasses of his. Anyhow, he had this long pole with a sharpened end, and he went down to the pasture and poked sheep. He wasn't rounding them up or anything, just chasing and sticking them for the hell of it. He seems to be the type who enjoys random acts of violence."

Mara moaned and put down her fork.

Julian went on in a pastry-thickened voice: "I was about to give up, thinking he'd be at it for the rest of the day, when suddenly he went back to the house and came out again with a shotgun. Then he stalked off through the trees. I sat tight, I tell you. The last thing I wanted was to run into him and have to explain my presence on his land. If he even gave me the chance to explain."

He paused while Mado brought out the principal dish, a *ballottine* of pork braised in wine and served in a cream sauce. It came accompanied by asparagus and his favorite, *pommes de terre sarladaises*, potatoes richly browned in goose fat and dressed with parsley and garlic.

Breathing deeply, he resumed. "I waited for what seemed like forever. Eventually, when he didn't come back, I figured he'd gone hunting for the day. It seemed too risky to approach the house, but I was able to check the *pigeonnier* out. It's the same one all right. I photographed it from roughly the same angle as in Bedie's photo and had a quick look inside. It was full of junk, old farm implements, empty bottles. No pigeons, though, because the nest holes are all blocked up. And nothing suggestive."

"Such as what?" asked Mado.

"Er—signs of digging. Of course," he added lamely, "there wouldn't be by now, would there? Anyway, by then it was nearly ten. I figured I had a couple of hours tops before the old woman got back. But I was less worried about her than him, roaming around with that shotgun. However, since he'd gone off in one direction, I did the only thing that made sense. Went off in the other, which took me east along the stream at the bottom of their land. It was very soggy going and fairly open in parts, so I was at a disadvantage from the viewpoint of my personal safety. That is, I expected at any moment to get a backside of shot or manual strangulation, if Vrac spotted me groping around on his property. Not that any of you would care, of course." His sarcasm was lost in a mouthful of hot, succulent pork.

"Did you find any orchids?" Mara demanded, watching him enjoy his food with barely concealed impatience.

He swallowed. "I'm coming to it. I floundered on like that for a bit until I came to a footpath that veered off through the trees. And suddenly I found myself in a water meadow, up to my knees in *Dactylorhiza incarnata*. Early Marsh Orchids to you. The lay of the land looked damned similar to Bedie's photo. Naturally I took pictures for comparison. Now, I assume you all see the importance of the Marsh Orchids . . ."

He paused for another mouthful and also to let them take this in. Since no one offered any comment, he explained: "The point is, they were the next photo in sequence after the *pigeonnier*. So, if it was the same spot, this clearly established that Bedie had come in from the west, which is where the Bird's-nests are, through the forest, along the bottom of la Binette's farm, past the pigeon house, and onto the footpath leading into the water meadow. It's also possible that Bedie did this in a single walk, which answers our question about continuity. It's no more than four or five kilometers between the Bird's-nests and the Marsh Orchids—nothing for a seasoned hiker like Mara's sister."

"*Parbleu!*" uttered Paul.

Julian fell to plying his fork and knife, giving them more time to admire his deductive skills.

"What remained, of course," he mumbled, coming up after a

bit for air, "was to figure out where she went from there. If you remember, Mara, the final sequence of orchids all needed higher, open ground. But I had three problems."

"What?" The others watched as he mopped up a pool of sauce with bread and chewed lengthily.

"First, the water meadow was low-lying and enclosed by forest, so I couldn't get a clear view of the surrounding area. Second, the trail branched off in three different directions. And, third, I was beginning to feel a little nervous because by that time I really had no idea where Vrac was." Pushing away from the table, he leaned back with a sigh.

"So?" Paul inquired, rising to clear away the plates.

"So there was nothing for it but to follow my nose. I assumed Bedie would have stayed on a path, so I picked the first branch and followed it for a couple of kilometers. It went through the woods and then into some fields, and for a while things looked promising, scatterings of Butterfly and Bee and Man Orchids, but then it led down into big pine forest with lots of ferns. I knew the soil there would be too acid for most of the orchids I was looking for, so I turned back and tried the second path."

He paused to help himself to cheese, which Paul had set out. "This one took me up to a hanging meadow. I saw lots of Pyramidals mixed in with sage and daisies, tons of Twayblade, and a nice pair of Monkey Orchids along the way, but nothing indicative. So I went back and tried the third path, which I must admit seemed the least likely of the three because it led straight down into wetland. But then it wound up along the face of a hill. Things started looking promising when I found some Lizard Orchids. Then a scattering of Bees and Flies intermixed with lots of Man Orchids with a few dried out Ladies here and there. Then I came to a beautiful big stand of *Serapias lingua*, Tongue Orchid. Of course, you realize what this means, Mara."

And while she was working it out, he cried, "Well, dammit, don't you see, those were all the orchids in the photographs, in order of appearance. I'd pretty much reconstructed the forward part of Bedie's path!"

"Mais, c'est incroyable!" breathed Mado.

Paul whistled appreciatively.

"And the Lady's Slipper?" Mara asked eagerly.

"Ah. Yes." Julian scratched his beard. "The *Cypripedium.* Well, obviously, I knew if I could find that, it would be the clincher. I also knew the most likely place for it to grow would be on elevated, cooler ground. Now, I'd spotted a long, high, wooded ridge off to my left, just the kind of habitat I was looking for. So I made for it. At one point, I was surprised to realize the path I was on had actually taken me in a wide arc running below Les Colombes. By the way, what's for dessert?"

"Apple-and-prune upside-down cake with crème fraîche," said Mado, placing the handsome confection before him.

"My favorite! Mado," Julian declared, "you're a twenty-first-century Brillat-Savarin. Curnonsky would have devoted chapters to you alone." He leaned over and gave her a greasy and, since Paul was looking, chaste kiss on the cheek.

"Get on with it," growled the husband.

"Okay. Okay. It was quite a rocky climb, pretty much straight up. En route I found a great patch of gentians. Quite a few Butterfly Orchids as well. It's a splendid view from up there, by the way. I could make out Géraud's house on the road beyond Malpech quite clearly."

"The Lady's Slipper?" Mara reminded him exasperatedly. "Did you find it?"

He paused to pick his teeth. "Er . . . no."

Their collective letdown was palpable. Julian was especially sensitive to the disappointment on Mara's face.

"Look," he burst out defensively, all of his accumulated griev-ances surfacing. "You didn't really think—I mean, I was possibly looking for a single flower, for pity's sake. I want to find it as much as you, Mara, but it was hopeless doing it like that. The only way is to go back and do a proper search, square off the area, and this time all of you can get off your backsides and help." He threw down his napkin in disgust.

Mara was immediately contrite. "I'm so sorry, Julian. I didn't mean to sound ungrateful."

"Well, that's how it came across."

"I think you did very well," soothed Mado.

An awkward silence persisted through to coffee. Julian dumped more sugar in his cup than he really needed and stirred angrily. Mado lit a cigarette and sat leg over knee, dangling a backless sandal. Mara stared bleakly at the floor.

Paul, after some inner struggle, heaved himself away from the table, disappeared momentarily, and returned with a dusty bottle of very fine old cognac, possibly by way of amends. Reverently, he served out four small glasses. They had by then been over two hours at table. The afternoon was drawing to a golden finish. A soft breeze stirred the curtains at the open windows of Chez Nous. They sipped in meditative silence.

Eventually, mollified by the cognac, Julian said, "While I was out there, I did a lot of thinking."

"*Parbleu!*" intoned Paul.

"I mean, I'd established to my own satisfaction that part of Bedie's trail cut across La Binette land. But what I started won-dering was how she'd got there in the first place. I don't mean to La Binette. I mean to the *beginning of her path*, which was off a logging road in the middle of the Bessède Forest. If her last stop was Beynac, she couldn't have walked there. It's nearly thirty kilometers away."

"Someone gave her a ride." Mado shrugged.

"But why there?"

Paul suggested, "If she was hitchhiking, she could have been on her way someplace else and simply got put down there."

"But in the middle of the forest, Paul," objected Julian. "It just doesn't make sense."

Mara shook her head impatiently. "How or why she got there isn't as important as what happened to her afterward. We've always thought the Lady's Slipper was the key to everything, Julian. Unfortunately, it's the one flower you couldn't find."

"Oh, look, don't rub it in, will you?" he snapped.

14

Julian put all of his other contracts on hold so that he could concentrate on Prudence's courtyard. With luck, everything would be ready for her party that weekend. It wasn't the kind of work he particularly liked, but he had to admit that the effect he'd created was nothing short of a marvel of container landscaping. She had wanted a tropical look. The walls dripped with hanging baskets of fuchsia and bougainvillea. The pièce de résistance, on which he was still working, was a kind of botanical tour de force built up in the middle of the courtyard, a temporary jungle of potted palms, lacy umbrella plants, flame coleus, and even orchids (rented from Géraud at exorbitant cost) in beds of sphagnum moss. He had not yet presented Prudence with his bill, but she was looking so pleased with everything that he hoped she wouldn't care.

"You should make a business of it," she advised, ever with an eye to the market. "Theme landscaping. Its time has come. Even here. You'll be at my do, of course," she added by way of invitation. "It'll be chock-full of Americans with dollars to burn who'll all want your services, once they see what you can do. Besides, I need people who can *parler français* with the French. And by the way," she added, "Mara's coming. The two of you should get together. I think she's interested in you."

He called Mara, got her answering machine, and left a message: "Look, Mara, there's this thing on at Prudence's on Saturday. I know you've been asked, too. Why don't I pick you up? Or, if that won't work, we could meet up there and go on someplace after."

Mara didn't reply. Too busy, he suspected. He knew she'd been working on Prudence's kitchen, whipping it into shape, with the same deadline as he.

On Saturday evening, the narrow country lane running past Prudence's house was clogged with cars. Among them Julian spotted the Chez Nous van. Guests from Bergerac to Brive filled the courtyard. Mado and Paul, who were catering the affair, moved among them, pouring champagne and replenishing trays of hot and cold hors d'oeuvres.

On entering, Julian was immediately press-ganged by Paul into helping to shift more champagne from the van. Staggering under the weight of a crate of bottles, he spotted Mara through the crowd. She wore a long black dress that made her look as lean as a knife and provocatively dangerous. Her only splash of color was a large, red silk flower pinned to the shoulder.

"Fancy meeting you," he called out as he deposited his load. A moment later, he sidled up and presented her with a refill of champagne. "Let me guess. You are a mysterious double agent posing as an interior designer."

"Clever of you." Mara smiled, tossed her head, and exchanged her empty glass for the full one he offered. She waved at the courtyard. "Very impressive. I didn't know you were so good."

"Oh, I'm very good. What are you doing for afters?" he whispered into her ear in a way he hoped was suggestive.

"Looking after my date," she told him archly and ruined his evening by introducing him to someone whom Julian had difficulty for a moment placing, and then recognized as the sandy-haired man from the forest.

They shook hands. So this was Alain de Sauvignac. He was bigger than Julian remembered, no taller than Julian but more solidly built in that muscular, athletic way that Julian loathed. Attractive, too, he supposed, if you liked the tanned, tourist-brochure look. Instinctively, Julian distrusted him.

Prudence arrived to sweep Mara away, leaving the two men together.

"So you're the orchid expert," Alain said, studying him with an assessing eye. He opted to speak English, which was another thing Julian held against him. As if his own French weren't good enough.

"Amateur," Julian corrected with the false ha-ha voice he used when he was not enjoying himself.

"Nevertheless, Mara tells me you've managed to locate the entire orchid sequence between the Bessède Forest and Les Colombes. Quite a botanical feat."

"The full sequence but one," Julian corrected again. "She might have mentioned that we're missing a *Cypripedium*." He wondered how much Mara had told Alain about her sister and their search for Bedie's trail.

"Ah. Yes, come to think of it, she did say that."

"You work abroad, I hear."

"Right. Gabon, Ivory Coast, Senegal. Most recently Cameroon. I'm a civil engineer. Government-to-government projects. Back on home leave. In between contracts for the moment, actually."

It was Julian's turn to say, "Ah."

The conversation languished. Unhappily, Julian wandered off to do his French bit with the locals and chat up his hostess's wealthy compatriots. That was what he was there for. Over a bumper of champagne, he covertly observed Mara returning to Alain's side, saw him slip his arm around her waist, and felt another headache coming on.

He had drunk too much, eaten too little, and needed air. On his way out to the courtyard, he snagged a couple of *escargots en brioche,* one of Paul's specialties, waved off a compliment or two on his handiwork, and found himself alone in the lane. The evening was filled with distant laughter. An early moon rose through the trees. Sourly, Julian pictured the after-party scene. Alain and Mara would go back to her place. He couldn't see them sitting on her impossible chairs. That left her bed or the Aubusson rug. He scowled and viciously ground a patch of nettles to shreds under his heel.

A low moan caught his attention. It came from Mara's Renault. Jazz was in the car, head thrust through the open window. A slow, malicious smile crept over Julian's face. If there was a God, he thought, Jazz ought to be counted on to take Alain de Sauvignac's head off at the very least.

As it turned out, Jazz did not have a chance to do his work because Alain and Mara had come separately to Prudence's party, Alain arriving in his father's old Citroën.

"It's good to get the old *guimbarde* out on the road," he had explained to Mara. "Papa drives it so little nowadays. But also it's easier this way. I think you realize Papa would be very upset if you turned up for me at the door after he sent you packing."

More than upset, Mara thought, remembering the expression on the elder de Sauvignac's face. The father had been frightened—no, terrified—of something. What? There was something Alain was not telling her. One way or another, she intended to find out.

The existence of Alain in Mara's life was a new dynamic that had been thrown, clanging like a spanner, into Julian's consciousness. He knew she had the right to see whomever she damned well pleased. Nevertheless, after all the effort he had put into helping her with her damnable orchids, he felt that she might have shown him a bit more consideration. It was always like that, it seemed. Just as you got interested in someone, they turned on you, kicked you in the balls.

He confessed all this to Paul and Mado a few evenings later, over a solitary dinner at Chez Nous.

"He *was* very good-looking," Mado affirmed.

It was not what Julian wanted to hear.

"What I mean," he said plaintively, shoving new peas about his plate with his fork, "is that to her I'm just a means of tracing her sister. I doubt she even sees me as a person. Frankly, I feel used."

"Hah!" Mado contrived to look sympathetic and intensely gratified at the same time. Paul merely gave an exasperated snort and demanded what the hell Julian expected.

"Well, not a lot," said Julian defensively.

"What you need," Paul began and stopped. *Bigre!* He didn't quite know how to tell Julian that what he needed was to cash in his chips and settle down. Put crudely, he needed a combination of mothering and regular sex, which he clearly wasn't getting; otherwise, he wouldn't be going around looking like he was holding in a belch and a sour taste in his mouth.

Julian and Mado were regarding him expectantly. Paul shook his head and retreated to the bar.

"What you need," he repeated, fetching back a bottle, "is something for the digestion."

•

That night, Paul was restless as he lay in bed beside Mado. He had been having a spell of *nuits blanches* recently: white nights, in which, although his body was numbed by the desire to sleep, his inner eye stared dry and lidless at a moving jumble of worries, the detritus of the day-to-day thrown onto the conveyor belt of his mind. The transmission of the van needed attention. Last

month's restaurant receipts were down. Julian's face, disembod-
ied, slid by, came past again. Paul exhaled noisily.

"What's wrong?" Mado murmured thickly, turning to curl
against him.

"Nothing," he grunted. Her breathing was slow and soft.
"Except . . ."

"Mmmm?"

"I was just thinking. About Julian."

She said sleepily, "What about him?"

"Oh, I don't know. There's something funny about him. I
mean, have you noticed how none of his relationships seem to
last?"

"He's shy. Besides, he always hooks up with the wrong sort of
person." Mado was fully awake now. "Domineering types who
like to push him around."

Paul wondered if his wife meant Mara. He didn't think she
was domineering. Strong-minded, maybe, but nothing a real
man couldn't handle. He folded his arms behind his head, staring up into darkness. Anyway, it wasn't that Julian was shy so
much as inept. Of the few relationships he'd known his friend to
have, it had always been the woman going off Julian rather than
the other way around. And go off she did, because she never
showed her face around these parts again. Like that skinny
anglaise, Coco Somebody, a few years back. Julian had been very
offhand about her departure. "Oh, she went back to England," he
had said in passing one day and had not referred to her again.

"Well, he's not getting any younger," Paul went on. "Time he
settled down. Got married."

"He was married once," Mado reminded him, raising herself
up on one elbow. She trailed her fingertips over her husband's
chest. "I don't think he liked the experience. Anyway, why are you
worrying about Julian at this time of night?"

"He's a pal," said Paul. The stroking was creating a pleasant, tickling sensation.

"He's a big boy." Tenderly Mado seized his right nipple between her teeth.

"Oh, what the hell," said Paul, dismissing his friend and giving himself over to a certain way of getting a good night's sleep.

•

> *I tell you, Patsy, it's as if I don't really exist for him except*
> *as a botanical exercise. Honestly, if it weren't for that damned*
> *Lady's Slipper, I think he'd be very happy to forget he ever*
> *met me. But you should have seen his face at Prudence's party*
> *when I introduced him to Alain—very attractive, by the*
> *way. You'd like him. I could tell it had never crossed Julian's*
> *mind that I might have a life!*

Mara sighed, reached down to scratch Jazz's ear, and went on typing.

> *The problem with Julian is that he's terribly private. He*
> *never really talks about himself. It's like there's some part of*
> *him that he's afraid of revealing, that he wants to conceal.* <

Patsy wrote back:

> *What do you mean? Like he's some kind of a Bluebeard*
> *hiding a closet full of dead brides? Ease up, kid. He sounds to*
> *me more like a disaster victim, someone who's survived rather*
> *than murdered past relationships.* <

> *What I'm trying to say is, he invites no intimacy, and I'm*
> *not even talking sexually. The truth is, the only really*
> *personal thing we've ever discussed is Bedie. In fact, he seems*

far more interested in her than me. Otherwise, he talks about flowers. And he's so damned pedantic. I mean, why does a snapdragon have to be an Antirrhinum *and everything belong to the buttercup family? And you should hear him on the sex life of the orchid.* <

> Hey, I'd like to! But, you know, it can cut two ways. Have you ever considered that maybe Julian knows as little about you as you do of him? Or that what he sees is too much of Bedie and too little of Mara? I mean, shackled to your leg like she is, figuratively speaking, she does tend to dominate the scene. <

It was true, Mara reflected, and Patsy had said things like this before. However, try as she might, she could not give up her dead. Less now than ever, with the discovery of the *pigeonnier*. Or was it Bedie who would not give her up? For she was always there, standing in shadow at her side, mute but heavy with appeal, asking for—what? Life? Whose life? Mara shuddered.

•

This time lunch was on her. Except that Mara made it dinner at her favorite bistro in Trémolat. On the day, she left her work site early, something she rarely did, and drove home not by the country roads but by the shortest route. Instead of a quick shower, she allowed herself a long soak in a hot tub. She rose from it and stood streaming and naked before her bathroom mirror, careless of puddling the floor, staring at her body. Her flesh gleamed back at her. She was conscious of a sag here or there, but, standing straight and sucking in her stomach, she saw that she was still firm, still attractive. Her dark, wet hair clung to the oval of her face, her chin, as ever, giving a strong finish to her own particular kind of beauty.

That evening Alain did not meet her at the restaurant but instead let her pick him up, although not at the house. He walked down from the château and met her at the roadside.

"Better this way," he said as he got in her car.

Mara wore an off-the-shoulder dress of sapphire blue. She had made up her eyes to accentuate their boldness, outlined her lips in vivid red. She was aware that his cheek-to-cheek greeting lingered like a caress, that he seemed to take her in appreciatively, that his eyes stayed on her the entire time she drove.

At the bistro they took a table inside because the evening was cool. Alain continued to gaze at her steadily over their drinks.

"*Très belle,*" he said finally, but with meaning. He was not, it seemed, a man to use words unnecessarily. In him, his father's suave courtliness and covert sexuality had been distilled to a more direct, casual virility. He had inherited a more rugged version of his father's aristocratic good looks. Unlike his parent, Mara was glad to note, Alain did not evoke the moldy reminder of damp places. He gave off instead a musky scent of aftershave. He wore light-gray slacks, a charcoal silk shirt under a loose-fitting cream-colored linen jacket, a gold Rolex. Building things in Africa must pay well, Mara thought.

"Have you made any further progress?" he asked as they tucked into a platter of steaks served very rare with frites.

Mara shook her head. "Things are rather at a standstill."

"But you have your orchids. Or all but one of them, according to your friend."

"The police, I'm afraid, weren't sufficiently impressed. Circumstantial evidence, they called it."

"I see. So they're not pursuing the matter?"

"No."

"Then what will you do?"

She looked at him lengthily. "That, I think, depends a lot on you."

"Me?" he put down his fork with surprise. "How so?"

She had come prepared to challenge him. "There's something you're not telling me, Alain. Something that you know or suspect but don't want me to know. I assume it has to do with your father . . . or Vrac."

He toyed with his food for a moment before meeting her gaze. In the dimness of the restaurant, his pupils were very dark, reflecting no light. "I take the matter of your sister seriously, Mara," he said at length. "I also lost my brother, Patrice, although at a much earlier age. So you see, in a way, we're alike. Please believe me when I say that, if I could help you in this regard, I would."

She urged, "Then tell me what your father is afraid of. What does he think I'm going to stir up?"

He shrugged. "It's very simple, really. Papa believes you're victimizing Vrac by accusing him unfairly. Despite appearances, Vrac is vulnerable, like a dumb beast. Papa feels obliged to stand between him and the forces you could, with your questions, unleash against him."

He stopped. She waited, unconvinced, forcing him with her silence to continue. Reluctantly, he gave ground.

"Also, perhaps, in disturbing the waters, you could cause my father a certain amount of public discomfort, and he is a man who has much to feel uncomfortable about. Oh, nothing really serious, I assure you. It's just that Papa has always been a man of, shall we say, appetite." He shrugged. "Some men are made that way. From my earliest boyhood, I remember the locals making sly remarks, off-color jokes. Thing-in-his-pocket, they called him, the stallion *en rut*. Of course, it was only when I was older that I came to understand what those things meant. In short, my father's excesses have caused my family much embarrassment . . . and expense. It's also been a source of anger and bitterness between Papa and me, largely because of the pain it has caused my mother. So now you see, Mara, there is no great mystery to unravel. Merely a rather sorry story of seigniorial misconduct."

Alain's mouth went momentarily tight with distaste. "To be quite frank," he resumed, "although Papa's main concern is the de Sauvignac name, as far as I'm concerned, that's his lookout. Old sins cast long shadows, as they say, and he's sinned enough for five men. Let him take what's coming to him. However, your questions, if they probe too deeply, could cause considerable unhappiness to Maman, who, quite frankly, doesn't deserve to have old scandals raked up."

They both fell silent.

At length, he spoke again. "If you don't mind, I'd like to change the subject. I want to know about you." He reached across and took her hand, turning it palm up and studying the crisscrossed lines on its surface "You have," he observed, "very delicate fingers. And"—he frowned slightly—"a very short life line."

"I think that's my heart line you're looking at," Mara corrected, but she allowed her hand, with its fingers, which she had never thought of as delicate, to continue resting where it was. "And it's not short, just broken. Look, Alain, I'm grateful for your honesty. I'm sorry. I had no idea . . ."

"Then be candid with me in your turn," he proposed with a smile.

"What?" She drew her hand back.

"Your friend Julian. Is he an important part of your life?"

"No," Mara answered simply.

"Then let me ask you something else. How much do you trust him?"

"Julian?" She thought about it. "I don't know. Why do you ask?"

"Because"—Alain was watching her closely, judging her reaction—"I'm starting to wonder if *he* wasn't the person who was stalking you that day in the forest."

Mara laughed. "But that's crazy! It was Vrac. You said so yourself."

Alain shook his head vigorously. "I said it could have been. I now realize that was impossible."

"What do you mean?"

"Mara, on the afternoon you were in the woods, Vrac was in Saint-Cyprien, picking up a new motor for a water pump. Our pump, in fact. I can show you the printed invoice for it, with date and time, together with Vrac's scrawl. And he spent the rest of the day at the château installing it."

"I don't believe it," Mara declared. But the words were scarcely out of her mouth when she was reliving her panicked flight, her encounter with Alain, and Julian *coming up behind*, crashing through the bushes only seconds later.

"But why?" she whispered, horrified. "Why would he do that?"

"To frighten you? To put you off the hunt? Mara, are you sure this Lady's Slipper is Julian's only reason for helping you?"

"Oh yes. He's desperate to find it, of that I'm sure."

Alain thought for a moment. "Look, let's approach this logically. You believe that someone was responsible for your sister's disappearance. You don't know who this person is. Your only clue is a set of orchid photographs. But maybe the answer has been in front of your nose all along: Julian. He's an orchidologist. Your sister was an orchid amateur. Supposing she met him by chance, went with him?" He paused, raking his fingers through his hair, leaving it pushed back and tousled.

Mara stared at him. Loulou had said something like that: Bedie would have been easily approachable by anyone who shared her interest. She would have gone trustingly with Julian into the forest.

"And you," Alain went on, "you could have come as a nasty shock to him when you turned up, the spitting image of your sister, asking him to help you find a woman he might have killed nineteen years ago!"

Again, had not Loulou warned her of exactly the same thing? *Your face, Mara. Your face.* She recalled Julian's look of shock when he had first opened his door to her.

And yet something did not fit.

"No. It doesn't make sense," she cried. "I swear Julian was genuinely amazed at the photo of the Lady's Slipper. If he'd been with my sister at the time she took it, wouldn't he have seen it, too? Why would he need her pictures to trace it? He'd already know its exact location."

Alain frowned. "What if," he said slowly, "she took the photos before she met him?"

"But even so, why would Julian try to help me? He's known all along that the whole point of reconstructing my sister's trail was to find out what had happened to her. Why would he want to lead me to himself?"

"Maybe," Alain suggested grimly, "that's part of the kick."

Mara's eyes widened. Her experiences in the forest and in the bog came rushing back to her. "Are you saying this is all part of some kind of sick game?"

"Maybe. Or perhaps," Alain added after a moment's reflection, "it's simpler than that. You see, it really hangs on the camera. You're convinced it belonged to Bedie. But don't you think her assailant—Julian—would have destroyed such a vital piece of evidence? Especially the film it contained? But he didn't. So it really argues the case that the camera you found *can't* have been your sister's. *And the only person to know that would be Julian.* In which case, there would be absolutely no risk to him in searching for an interesting sequence of plants that some other, totally unrelated person had photographed. Particularly if it led to a rare orchid that he very much wanted to find."

In fact, Mara realized, she'd virtually blackmailed Julian into it. No help, no photos. Those were her terms.

Then reason asserted itself. Julian had behaved oddly, even inexplicably, at times. She knew very little about him; he gave nothing away. He was every bit as irascible and botanically obsessive as Géraud. But none of this made him a psychopath or a killer.

"I don't buy it," she told Alain.

He said gently, "I'm sure what I've said comes as a bit of a shock, Mara. But I'd like you at least to consider it. You can't afford to ignore the possibility that Julian may be the very person you're looking for."

She turned away, glancing through the restaurant window at the gathering darkness outside. "I don't know what to think," she murmured dully.

"Then don't. For now, at least." He took her hand again. This time he did not examine her palm, but cradled it in his own. "Let me tell you instead," he said quietly, "about dawn in the Cameroon highlands."

•

Mara drove Alain back to Les Colombes. He let her take him all the way up the narrow lane leading to the rear courtyard. It was late, the old ones would be asleep, and there would be no risk of awkward questions from his father.

The dark mass of the château rose above them as she cut her headlights before pulling up. She keyed off the engine and turned to him.

"You know," she said, "there's no way of proving if your suspicions about Julian are true."

"I agree. You need hard evidence."

"Such as what?"

"Something tying him to your sister? Or any of the other women. If he's responsible for their disappearances, maybe he kept something of theirs. I don't imagine it will be easy to find. Julian seems to have covered his tracks well." Alain sat facing her in the car. Moonlight glinted on his brow, the strong profile of his nose. The rest of his face was cast in shadow.

"Whatever you do, Mara, I don't want to you take any stupid risks. Remember, I'm here if you need me."

He leaned across, cupping her face in both his hands. "This is for luck," he whispered. And he kissed her, long and hard.

Mara watched him slip away from her. His form was quickly swallowed in darkness. There had been something of hunger in his kiss, almost of ferocity. The feeling of his mouth on hers stayed with her, his smell, a faint musky odor, filled her nostrils. In that kiss something indefinable had sprung up, a brief frisson, like electricity arcing momentarily between them. Mara was shaken to acknowledge the depth of attraction she felt for Alain de Sauvignac. It expressed itself in a lurch of the heart, a yearning she had not felt for years. In fact, not since Hal. The realization disturbed her. She put her car in gear and circled about, tires crunching quietly on gravel until they met the rough surface of the lane. A warning sounded in her brain. Hal had been a bastard.

15

Mara chose a morning when Prudence could confirm that Julian was working in her garden.

"He's digging more of those trenches, he and that brawny helper of his," Prudence informed her when she phoned. "Don't ask for what. Why do you want me to call you on your cell phone if he leaves?"

"Too complicated to explain. Just do it the minute he goes, will you? And thanks, Prudence."

"Whatever helps, sweetie."

Julian's front door was locked. His back door, as usual, was not. Mara opened it and stuck her head inside.

"Hello?" she called, just in case.

No response.

She made rapid work of the kitchen, ignoring the clutter of pots and pans, the dirty dishes in the sink. His shelves were stocked with cans of cassoulet and beef ragout, packets of dry soups, rice, sugar, instant coffee, a canister of tea. A lower shelf was taken up with large tins labeled *Borax, Silica Gel, Glycerine.* For drying plants, she assumed. What exactly she was looking for she did not know. Something to tie him to Bedie, Alain had suggested, or to any of the other women. A part of her was equally interested in any intimate information on Julian. Family photographs, love letters, birthday cards, anything to give him a past, dimension. She was torn between wanting to condemn him and to prove Alain wrong, to find nothing more incriminating than the sundry silly, embarrassingly personal desiderata that clutter any normal person's life. She would have been dissatisfied and yet relieved to walk away empty-handed, allowing Julian to continue undisturbed with his earthy if eccentric pursuits.

The scarred dining table at one end of the front room displayed the remains of past meals and a bilingual clutter of old newspapers: *La Presse, The Observer,* and the monthly *News,* serving the local English-speaking community. There was an old desk, its surface covered in bills. A glance informed her that Julian was none too prompt about paying his accounts. The drawers stuck. She pulled them out with difficulty: more bills, bank statements, string, a dried-out bottle of glue, paper clips, a hunk of beeswax, leaky pens, a broken watch, loose batteries, nursery catalogues, letters. This man was a hoarder. The letters were all business correspondence: queries from interested customers, confirmations of landscaping projects. One was a complaint regarding plants that had lifted the coping around a swimming pool. Mara wondered that there should be so little clue to Julian himself. Or perhaps that was how he wanted it.

The shelves sagged with books. Texts on wildflowers, orchids, and plant physiology. She spotted a field manual: *Wildflowers of the Dordogne/Fleurs sauvages de la Dordogne,* by Julian Wood. She pulled it out. It had been published in 1983 and bore the dedication: "To lovers of wildflowers everywhere." The biographical information on the back cover described the author as an authority on local flora, living in Grissac, and showed a photograph of a younger Julian, smiling, with slightly fuller features and no facial hair. It made Mara realize that she rarely saw Julian smile.

Mara flipped through the book. It was filled with photographs of all kinds of wildflowers, taken, as Bedie had done, close up and at a distance and annotated with details on plant structure, habitat, and flowering season. Many were orchids that she recognized. Pyramidals, Bees, and Lizards. Lady and Man Orchids. She saw a portrait of a Bird's-nest Orchid with an accompanying view of a thin scattering of the plants. There was no doubt that it was the same location she and Julian had found in the Bessède Forest. The oak in which Jazz had treed the marten was just visible in the background. *Neottia nidus-avis* was described as thick-stemmed, fleshy, yellowish-brown, with sepals and petals curving into a hood, and labellum pendant. It flowered between May and late June, liked shade, and was partial to beech and coniferous woodlands. These plants, Julian had noted, were possibly representative of a much larger stand, which, owing to several years of dry conditions, was either in decline or semi-dormant. Both photographs were dated 1980.

Suddenly the kitchen door banged. Mara dived down behind the sofa.

"Allo?" cried a woman's voice. *"Julian? C'est moi, Francine Léon. Vous avez oublié vos oeufs."* There was a silence as Madame Léon waited, with the eggs that Julian had forgotten, for a response.

"Bon," Madame Léon called, even though it was apparent that Julian wasn't there. *"Je les mets dans le frigo."*

Mara heard the refrigerator door open and close, and then the clack of the kitchen door as Madame Léon left. Raising her head, Mara saw Madame Léon cut across Julian's back garden on her way to her own, adjoining property.

Mara let her breath out and moved to the bathroom. The medicine cabinet was full of bottles and tubes, including a vial of prescription tablets and a jar of something that, as best she could make out, was a preparation for hives.

In another room she found a dented metal cabinet crammed with cardboard boxes stacked precariously one atop another. The boxes were filled with prints and slides of not only flowers but plants of every description. The backs of many of the prints were inscribed in Julian's untidy script, providing cryptic details on identification, date, and place.

She had only the bedroom to go. The bed was unmade. Clothes trailed over every piece of furniture. One leather slipper, trodden down at the heel, had been kicked under a scarred walnut armoire; the other lay by the door. She checked out Julian's bedside table, stirring around in the contents of the single, shallow drawer: reading glasses, nail clippers, throat lozenges, buttons. Her cell phone went off.

"Hello?" she answered tensely.

"Mara? That you? You sound funny. It's Prudence. Look, I know you wanted me to ring you if Julian left. Well, he took off just around twelve."

"But it's nearly twenty past," Mara exclaimed, with a glance at her watch. "Why didn't you call me straightaway?"

"Couldn't, sweetie," returned Prudence's voice. She seemed to be blowing on something. "He went right in the middle of me doing my nails. Takes an age for them to dry. Matter of fact, they're tacky even as we speak."

Mara cursed as she disconnected. If Julian were returning for lunch, he could be walking through the door at any moment. So far she had come up with nothing.

She rammed the drawer shut and hurried back into the front room. Julian's wildflower book still lay on the floor behind the sofa where she had left it. She scooped it up and shoved it back on the shelf, not where it had been, but at the end of a row of books, wedging it upright with a small plastic box. Her hand hesitated over the box. She took it down and flipped back the hinged lid. It was filled, as she had expected, with personal and business cards. She riffled through them quickly, spotting her own among them, and then another card that caused her to catch her breath. She pulled it out and studied it with narrowed eyes, puzzling over it, and then coming to a conclusion. She did not know if she was sorry or exultant as she slipped it into her pocket.

A volley of barks at the front of the house alerted her. Through a window she glimpsed Jazz, head thrust out of her car, happily greeting Julian's arrival. By the time Julian walked in the back door, Mara was seated at his kitchen table, reading a crumpled newspaper. The kettle was heating on the gas burner.

"Hi," she said, affecting casualness although her hands were shaking. She had to force herself to look at him. "Hope you don't mind me making myself at home. I just dropped by and was about to leave when Prudence called." She gestured at her cell phone. "She happened to say you might be on your way here, so I thought I'd wait. I—er—I'm making some tea."

"You're a stranger," he said coolly. He seemed on edge, suspicious of her presence in his house. Nevertheless, he must have thought tea was a good idea because he took down a couple of mugs and rinsed out the teapot. "What did you want to see me about?"

"Oh." She stopped. What *did* she want to see him about? She glanced nervously at the newspaper which she had found on the kitchen counter, hoping for inspiration. A front page photograph of le Mur's mangled Ferrari, in all its graphic detail, saved the moment. "I just wondered if you'd gotten the film developed. The one you shot at La Binette."

If it occurred to Julian that she could have as easily phoned for the information, he didn't show it. In fact, he looked evasive. "Er, no. Not yet." He stuck his head in the fridge and pulled it out again. "Haven't had time. Have you had lunch?"

"Who, me? Oh, don't worry about me. I can't stay."

Figuratively she kicked herself. That was stupid. She had just said she'd been prepared to wait. "That is, just the tea. Then I have to run."

"Close call," she told Jazz as she drove off ten minutes later. She reached the intersection with the main road and turned onto it, trying to collect her thoughts. The card pointed her in an unexpected direction. However, she still lacked anything tying Julian directly to Bedie.

Or did she? Alain had suggested that Bedie had met Julian by chance, gone with him because of her interest in orchids. An idea began to form in her mind. *Wildflowers of the Dordogne/Fleurs sauvages de la Dordogne,* 1983, which included many species of wild orchids. Bedie could have seen Julian's book in any bookstore and bought a copy. In fact, hadn't Scott said that Bedie had taken some kind of book on flowers with her? Given her keen interest, she would not have hesitated to seek Julian out—he was described in the biographical blurb as "an authority on local flora living in Grissac." And it would have been easy—she could have simply looked him up in the phone book, just as Mara herself had done. The more Mara thought about it, the more plausible her idea seemed. It could be the very link she needed. But was it enough?

An oncoming truck bearing a load of chickens rumbled past, crowding her onto the verge of the narrow road. Then she remembered the Bird's-nest Orchids. She threw her head back in mirthless laughter.

"Damn it, Jazz," she cried. "It's been staring me in the face all along."

Julian had pronounced Bedie's photo to be an almost certain match with his colony in the Bessède Forest, based on the law of probability. *A stand this big is rare,* he had said. *The chances of there being two like it are low.* By the same argument, if the colony was as exceptional as Julian claimed, what were the odds that Bedie had simply stumbled on it by herself? Mara had seen the spot. It was in the middle of nowhere. Julian himself had raised the question of how Bedie had come to be there. The only reasonable answer was that someone who had known about the colony had led her to it.

"And that person," she addressed her dog with grim finality, "could only have been Julian."

He had been clever, initially feigning astonishment at Bedie's photograph, carrying out the charade of consulting Géraud, pointing out that the stand as he had originally seen it was scarcely recognizable as the one Bedie had captured on film. But he had guessed that the colony was representative of a much larger growth—his own words in print gave him away—and as the expert he should have made the connection. Finally, Julian's photo was dated 1980. This meant that, when Bedie had turned up in 1984, he had already discovered the plants and would have been able, and for his purposes more than willing, to guide her to them.

Yet Mara was still nagged by a troubling point. She did not accept Alain's idea that the camera had belonged to some unknown third person. Her sister had taken those photos, she was sure of it. The Bird's-nest Orchids clearly placed Julian with Bedie near the beginning of her trail, so Julian must have known that Bedie had a camera with her and that she was photographing orchids. Maybe he had even helped her set up some of her shots. So how was it that he did not know about the *Cypripedium*? And why, as Alain had asked, didn't he destroy the camera? The only conclusion she could draw was that Julian must have left Bedie before she found the Lady's Slipper. But why would he have done that?

A sickening picture began to form in Mara's head. Bedie

alone in the forest. Something, perhaps a sound, alerts her. She looks back, listens. Uncertain, she moves on. Other sounds, soft, persistent, follow in her wake. Looking over her shoulder, she begins to have her first intimation of real danger. Her pace quickens to a rapid walk. Now, as she realizes the full nature of her peril, she begins to run, fleeing in terror, throwing off her backpack, her camera, all encumbering gear, to speed her flight.

A car honked frantically as it swept past, missing the Renault by centimeters. Mara careened wildly, downshifted, and pulled to a lurching stop onto the verge of the road. She pressed her face into her hands, trying to get her breathing under control.

It wasn't good enough for Julian to attack and kill. The predator needed to stalk his prey. Just as he had "lost" her in the bog and directed her to pace off squares in the forest in order to afford himself the pleasure of the chase, so must he have sent Bedie on her way and then, cruelly and at his leisure, hunted her down. Orchid freak though he was, his focus would have been entirely on his victim, not on what she was photographing. He never thought about the camera she had been carrying. He never knew about the flower that he now coveted so greatly. And the irony of it was that she, Mara, had put the evidence of Bedie's remarkable discovery right into his hands!

Then something else occurred to her that further underscored Julian's capacity for duplicity. The cheapness, the gratuitousness of it almost made her cry with rage. The newspaper she had been pretending to read in Julian's house had been a copy of last Tuesday's *Sud Ouest*. Every paper in the region covering le Mur's fatal accident had been sold before midday, according to Paul. So how had Julian, who was supposed to have been at La Binette from the crack of dawn until late afternoon on Tuesday, gotten a copy?

"The bastard," she fumed to Jazz, putting the car in gear and shooting forward in a spurt of gravel. "It was a lie. He never went there at all." The whole thing had been a fabrication from start to finish.

•

"Mara was around yesterday," Mado called out from the back of the bistro. "She was asking questions about you."

Julian paused, thumbtack in hand. He had stopped by to post a notice on the Chez Nous bulletin board for old Hilaire. In fact, he had helped the farmer to compose it: *Perdue. Chienne pointer blanche et truitée noir. Très gentille.* Lost. White-and-black-spotted pointer bitch. Very gentle. Julian had wanted to add *très gourmande,* but had held his tongue.

"Oh? Like what?"

"Oh," the redhead said evasively, coming up to peer at his hand-lettered sign, "your background."

"My background? What d'you mean, my landscaping qualifications?"

"Of course not," said Mado, giving him a shove. "Your romantic background, *abruti.*"

"Cut a long story short," broke in Paul from the bar, "I think she's making moves on you. She was asking me about your love life, former girlfriends, names, dates, the lot."

"Names—?" Julian was extremely alarmed.

"Don't worry," Paul grinned. "I didn't tell her much. Anyway, she already knew about your ex. I just said that since then you've had a couple of girlfriends, nothing serious. Oh, and she wanted to know if any of them were still in the area."

Julian looked aghast. "What did you tell her, for Christ's sake?"

Paul shrugged. "Well, what could I say? I mean, I've never seen any of them since, have I?"

"She's got a bloody nerve!" Julian fumed. "It's a damned invasion of privacy." And it wasn't the only one he had experienced of late. Someone—he now knew exactly who—had been in his house, rummaging about in his mess. Nothing had been taken, but the telltale signs of disturbance were everywhere.

"Take it from me, *mon vieux*," Paul advised, enjoying his friend's discomfiture, "when a woman starts checking up on you like that, it's a serious sign. They only ever ask those kinds of questions if they're planning on moving in."

The card was slightly soiled, printed on heavy buff stock in Garamond type. Alain studied it carefully, holding it between thumb and forefinger.

"It was the very last place I looked," Mara exclaimed. "I could so easily have missed it."

"Things happen for a reason," Alain said softly.

"You see what it could mean, don't you?"

"Yes."

Then she told him what she wanted them to do.

He thought about it for a moment. "All right," he said. "I'm game."

Later that night, Mara dialed a number and spoke with a woman named Ingrid. Swedish, Mara judged, from her up-and-down accent.

The property, situated outside of Souillac, was set into a hillside well off the road. A modern wing—mostly glass, from what Mara could see—had been added to the original stone structure, giving the house the appearance of being at odds with itself. The result, Mara thought, of a combination of money and bad taste.

Ingrid, or so Mara guessed, answered their knock. She was

tall, white-blonde, friendly, and wore a bikini that left most of her buoyant breasts and buttocks bare.

"Bonjour. Yes? *Ah, c'est vous.* You must be the one who called last night," she said, mixing singsong English and French.

They introduced themselves. She smiled broadly and shook their hands. Mara was amused to note that Alain seemed to regard Ingrid, and at the moment he was regarding quite a lot of her, with a look of stern disapproval.

"*Entrez.* Jackie is on the phone, but I can show you around, if you want." She took them through a large room furnished in glass and chrome and out to a rear terrace.

The garden, Mara had to admit, was magnificent, built on several levels to accommodate the uneven lay of the land. Steps led down past beds of perennials to a free-form pool bordered by bamboo and fed by a fall of water running over deeply pitted boulders, giving it the air of a secret grotto. A winding path led the eye away to a line of cypress standing like sentinels against a clear blue sky. The sloping side of the garden was built out as an extensive rockery.

At that point, Jackie appeared, cell phone clamped to his ear. He was a short, square man in his fifties, dressed in swimming trunks and a pool robe, which was open at the front, exposing a hairy chest and a creased belly. His skin was tanned to a deep mahogany, his lips were full, and his eyes took in Mara appraisingly as he ended his conversation and switched off.

They introduced themselves and raised the matter they had ostensibly come about:

"We're thinking of landscaping our property," Alain lied with surprising fluency. "This fellow Julian Wood gave us your name. Said he'd done work for you. Must say I'm pretty impressed with what I see. I take it you'd recommend him?"

"Sure," said Jackie. "Mind you, he's not cheap. And he took his own sweet time finishing."

"How long ago was this?" asked Mara.

Jackie shrugged. "*Parbleu!* Fifteen—no, fourteen years ago. Eighty-nine, it was."

Yes, Mara thought, the timing fit.

"Do you"—Alain looked around him—"still use him?" Someone had to maintain the place.

"*Pas question!* Not at his prices. I have a gardener come in from the town."

Jackie showed them out, leading the way with Mara. Alain lingered behind with Ingrid. Together they paused to inspect a flowering bush.

"So," Jackie said, taking Mara's left elbow to steer her unnecessarily along the walkway, "you're interested in gardening?"

"Oh," she extemporized, "it's really more my husband."

Jackie let his large, square fingers slide lightly down her arm. He raised her hand. "No ring? Pretty woman like you needs a ring. People might get the wrong impression."

"These visible signs of ownership, rather passé, don't you think?" Mara parried, rather smoothly, she thought, and freed herself from his grasp. At the same time, she seized the opening he had provided. "Speaking of that, Monsieur Ménard, I think I used to know your wife."

He stopped to study her carefully. "Which one?" he asked bluntly.

"Which—? Oh. Julie. You were married to Julie Ménard, weren't you? Or have I made a mistake?"

Jackie Ménard's stare was now coldly assessing. "No mistake," he said after a moment. "But you couldn't have known her very well or you'd have heard. She took off. Left me. Years ago."

"Oh dear." Mara contrived to look genuinely flustered. "I'm terribly sorry."

"I'm not. Quite frankly, she was a bitch in heat." He turned on his heel and walked on.

Bingo. Mara turned to shoot a triumphant glance over her shoulder. She was in time to see Ingrid jump as Alain slid a hand casually over her protuberant and inviting bum. Men, Mara thought, only partly amused. So much for disapproval.

•

> . . . *So you see, Patsy, the evidence is stacking up against Julian. He worked for the Ménards at the critical time, and he said nothing about it when Loulou mentioned that Julie was one of the missing women. For that matter, he had to be pushed before he'd admit that he'd even heard about Bedie and Valérie Rules. But Valérie lived just down the road from him. She probably walked past his house to and from school every day. He could have given her a ride, and then, who knows what happened. As for Bedie, I suspect she bought his wildflower book and contacted him from the information on the cover. He's a local orchid expert. It's also unlikely that she found the Bird's-nest Orchids on her own. Much more probable that Julian took her there.*

There are other things, too. He really did look pretty rattled when I turned up, as Alain said, like a face out of the grave, asking him to help me find a woman he might have murdered. His past is pretty cloudy. Paul told me that all of the women in his life seem to have dropped out of sight. And although I'm sure Julian genuinely wants to find his mystery Lady's Slipper, I think he faked the orchid hunt to throw suspicion on Vrac and the de Sauvignacs. It's true that the pigeonnier is on La Binette land, but apart from that, we only have his word that he actually reconstructed Bedie's trail leading from there to Les Colombes. And, finally, I'm now convinced that he purposely "lost" me in the swamp and stalked me in the forest. His version of fun and games. Oh, and by the way, do you remember what you said about psychos going off their medications? When I was searching his house, I checked his bathroom cabinet. I found some pills, something something acétaminophène. *Does this mean anything to you?* <

Patsy wrote back:

> *For Pete's sake, Mara, what have you got by the tail? Look, you need to understand that you could be dealing with a seriously sick and dangerous person. Corner him and he becomes a land mine. Hidden but highly explosive. Be sensible and turn this over to the* flics!
> *P.S. To answer your question, the something* acétaminophène *is probably the French version of prescription-strength Tylenol. Maybe our boy suffers from bad headaches. Not surprising if what you're telling me is true.* <

> *Don't worry, Patsy. I intend to hand this over to the cops. And I don't plan on taking any stupid risks. According to Loulou, this predator has always chosen his victims so that he can't be linked to them. That's why he's never been caught. I figure too many people have seen me in Julian's company and know about Bedie for him to try anything. Nothing more serious than his sick games of cat-and-mouse, that is.* <

> *Mara, don't count on it. Moreover, being careful also means not jumping to conclusions. Above all not trusting anyone.*

And while we're on the subject, there's something I think you're overlooking. Julian isn't your only candidate for stalker. Alain de Sauvignac was also there in the woods. I know you think you fell into his arms. Or did he lunge out and grab you? <

16

Mara was sitting very upright on the same hard wooden chair she had occupied two months ago in Commissaire Boutot's office at Périgueux Police Headquarters. This time she was there at the Commissaire's invitation. He sat facing Mara across his desk. With his baggy eyes and wilting mustache, he looked more melancholy than ever. Nevertheless, he had been listening to her with evident interest for thirty minutes. While she spoke, he rolled a blue pencil between his palms. His hands were dry, and the friction of the rolling made a scratchy, rhythmical sound. Loulou, who had set up the interview, was strolling about the office, chuckling softly at framed photographs of former *commissaires*, as if sharing a private joke with each of them. He paused to squint at a book on a shelf. It proved to be a biography of master thief-catcher Eugène François Vidocq—Boutot was something of a classicist when it came to crime.

"Alors, madame, your information is interesting," the *commissaire* said when she had finished. "As long, of course, as it is sans spurious embellishments."

Mara blushed at his reference to the faked initials. "Did you check Scott's statement to find out if Bedie had a copy of Julian's wildflower book?"

Boutot was cautious. "In his *déclaration* Monsieur Barrow did state that your sister had taken with her a Michelin guide to Périgord-Quercy and a book on wildflowers in the Dordogne."

"I knew it!" Mara exclaimed.

Boutot shook his head. "We can conclude nothing from this. Even if she had a copy of the book, it doesn't follow that she met up with Monsieur Wood. Indeed, I must point out that much of your so-called evidence against him is circumstantial."

"Maybe." She was undaunted. "But when so many things come together, as they do here, I think the coincidences stop being mere chance."

Boutot considered this, temporarily ceasing his pencil rolling. He dipped his head from side to side. "In fact, we have begun inquiries. Loulou has forwarded a rather interesting theory."

"Landscaping," pronounced the chubby ex-*flic*, bustling over. "You see, at first I thought our perpetrator chose his victims at random along major roads. I now think the link is landscaping. Julian is a landscape gardener. What better than to use his jobs to size up potential victims? Moreover, the distribution of the disappearances suggests the perpetrator was someone who moved around a lot. Julian's work—*mon dieu*—it takes him all over the region. He also has a van. Handy for transporting bodies."

Loulou plopped himself down on a chair next to her. "Look at it this way. Landscaping lets him get near his victims, observe their habits in situ, as it were. Picture that he's trimming the hedges around the house." He pumped his arms together in an enthusiastic hedge-clipping motion. "The target gets used to seeing him about. He's just the nice English fellow who tends the garden. That meets the criterion of trust. Child's play for him to get to know her routine, follow her somewhere, or even make an assignation, and *paf*!" Loulou slammed his right fist into his left palm with a look of shining satisfaction. The *commissaire* winced.

"Of course," Loulou conceded, "we still need to find out if our man also worked for Valérie Rules's parents and the Charlebois woman." He looked at his former colleague. "Any feedback on that, Antoine?"

Boutot sighed. The pencil started up again. "Monsieur and Madame Rules are now divorced, but one of my men spoke with the wife, who says they never employed a gardener and she's never heard of Monsieur Wood."

"Ah," said Loulou with a vigorous wag of a forefinger, "but in that instance perhaps he didn't need to work for them. He only lived a couple of kilometers away. He would have had ample opportunity to approach the kid."

"To the mother's knowledge, Valérie didn't know him, either. But maybe, as you say, he noticed the girl and events proceeded from that. As to the other, old Madame Charlebois died a couple of years ago. So there's no way of knowing if she or her daughter, Mariette, employed our suspect. However, I have someone questioning the neighbors."

"But in any case, Julian's link to the Ménards is solid," declared Mara. "He worked for them the same year Julie Ménard disappeared. We've established that."

"*Bien sûr*, we are also reexamining the Ménard affair," the *commissaire* assured her. "All the same"—he thrust his chin in Loulou's direction—"I have a little problem with your landscaping theory."

"What problem?" demanded Loulou.

"It doesn't explain Madame Dunn's sister or the Dutch tourist whose body we found in the Quercy woods. Neither of those two had any connection with landscaping. Your idea, moreover, implies a certain amount of planning. Yet the Tenhagen woman was probably hitchhiking, suggesting a random encounter. Mademoiselle Bedie was probably a chance meeting, too. Valérie Rules?" He shrugged. "And Mariette Charlebois, who knows?"

"In Bedie's case the link was orchids," Mara said. "Maybe

Hanneke Tenhagen had an interest in orchids as well. Have you looked into that?"

The *commissaire's* hands paused again. His mournful gaze fixed on her. "No. We didn't know about the orchids at the time. But it's an interesting angle to pursue. However, what about the other missing women? Were they also interested in orchids?"

"Pooh," said Loulou with an explosive breath. "I think we're making it more complicated than it needs to be."

Boutot cast a weary look at the chubby ex-lieutenant. "And your idea is?"

"Why, simply that, in addition to using his landscaping contracts to size up his victims, our man also seized his openings as they came, whether his victims were clients or strangers, as in the cases of Mara's sister, who might have approached him; the Tenhagen woman, who was hitchhiking; or *la petite* Valérie on her way home from school. As for Mariette Charlebois, maybe he did work for them."

The *commissaire* shook his head. "I still don't like it. It's too messy. In my experience, *mon vieux*, serial killers almost always adopt a consistent approach. That's not the case here. It's almost as if"—this time Boutot put the pencil down; his baggy eyes were unhappy—"we're looking for two different people."

•

Patsy e-mailed Mara:

> *Well, I'm glad you've quit playing cops-and-robbers and turned this over to the professionals. But listen, kid, if landscaping really is a thread running through all this, and if we're looking at a four- or five-year cycle of events, then I'd say your killer is overdue for another victim. I think you'd better forget about Bedie for the moment and concentrate on Julian's client list and who could be his next target.* <

My god, Mara thought when she read Patsy's message. *Prudence.* Julian had been digging around her property for the last three weeks. And hadn't he said something about a rockery? Where else had she seen rockeries? Was Julie Ménard buried beneath a hundred tons of Mediterranean stone?

Mara keyed in Prudence's number. Come on, come on, she whispered as the phone at the other end rang. And went on ringing.

•

Mara pulled up in front of Prudence's house with a screech of brakes. She raced to the front door and hammered on it with both fists.

Prudence took her time opening. She was wearing another of her Quimper-style smocks, and her hair and nails, as usual, were perfect.

"Oh," said Mara, taken aback. "Are you okay?"

"Fine. Why shouldn't I be? *Entrez.* Or do you just want to stay out there and beat down my woodwork?"

"I called you." Mara followed her inside. "You didn't answer."

"I must have been out in the back. Inspecting the trenches."

Mara said, "Prudence, about those trenches. I—I need to speak to you. Do you have any idea why Julian is digging them?"

"Something to do with drainage for my rockery. But if you're really that turned on by technical details, why not ask the expert?" In a lower voice, she added, "Lover Boy is here."

"Here?"

"Hullo, Mara," said Julian quietly, stepping into view. "Why should that surprise you?"

"It doesn't," said Mara. She took a deep breath and faced him squarely. "That is, I came to have a word with Prudence. Privately, if you don't mind."

"Oh?" He glanced at Prudence, who only shrugged. Then he

smiled. "No problem. I can always come back another time. I'll leave you to it, shall I?

·

At the town of Le Buisson, the D25 swings away from the river, to run south through fields and forests. In May, traffic along it is sparse.

Along this stretch, a green Peugeot was coming to a coughing halt. The driver nosed the car as far as possible onto the grassy verge. The engine gave a final sputter and quit. In dismay, the driver, a prim, pretty woman named Arlette, stared at her fuel gauge and realized that she was out of gas. Only then did she remember that she had meant to fill up after leaving Toulouse. How stupid to have forgotten. But with so much on her mind . . . Her neatly packed suitcase lay on the backseat, silent witness to her flight.

Anxiously she checked the car clock against her watch. The car clock said six-thirty, her watch six-thirty-five. She always set her watch five minutes fast. But here she was, already an hour late because she'd missed a turnoff, and only *le bon dieu* knew how long it would take to get gassed up again. *Merde!* She couldn't have that much farther to go, but with an empty tank, it might as well have been the other end of the earth. *Calm down,* she thought, and fumbled in her purse for her glasses and her cell phone.

Merde again! Her phone card had expired. She yanked her glasses off, jerking loose a strand of blond hair from the tight little bun perched on the top of her head. Where was this godforsaken place she had gotten to? She could not remember the name of the last village she had passed. Everything here was trees. Trees and fields. She got out of the car, slammed the door in frustration, and gazed angrily up and down the road in either direction. She recalled passing a farm not too far back. Perhaps someone there could help her. She locked the car, hooked her purse over her shoulder, and set out on foot in the direction she had come. The rough verge made walking difficult, especially in wedge sandals. The shoes were new. She cursed as she stumbled more than once. Why in heaven's name could she not have worn more sensible footwear?

But then, what she was doing was not sensible. Of course, she acknowledged as she trudged along, sense was what had kept her locked up within herself all these years, mutely complying with the expectations of family, friends, associates. Like a bad actor, she had gone through the motions of a role she had long ago ceased to want to play. Well, that was over now. All but the shouting. Suddenly she felt glad, despite running out of gas and her treacherous shoes, glad she'd thrown convention aside, glad of her leap into the void.

A car with foreign plates swung around a bend, coming rapidly toward her. She waved frantically, but it whizzed by. Another, but this one, too, passed in a gust of wind. Once again the road lay empty. Futilely, she tried her cell phone once more. Dead.

A vehicle appeared ahead of her on the horizon. Momentarily, she lost it behind a bank of trees. Then it broke into sight again, moving at a leisurely pace. Standing as far into the road as she dared, Arlette semaphored her distress with outstretched arms. The vehicle rumbled past, and she thought that it, too, would continue on. However, to her great relief, and with a grinding of gears, it slowed, stopped, and began to back up. When it was even with her, the driver rolled down the window.

"Bonjour," said Julian, sticking his head out. "Problems? Can I help?"

17

They were back at La Vieille Guinguette, eating an excellent confit of duck. Alain had listened gravely as she told him what she had learned from Commissaire Boutot. Now he leaned forward.

"*Ecoute,* Mara, I have to be away for a few days this week. While I'm gone, I want you to be very careful. Do nothing until I get back. Do you understand me? Landscaping and orchids tie Julian in with Bedie and Julie Ménard. He could be a very dangerous man. I want you to promise that you'll wait until I return before taking further action."

Reluctantly, she agreed. "But where are you going? How long will you be away?"

His mouth turned down. "Paris. To negotiate another contract. I'm taking the TGV up on Wednesday. I'll be back Sunday."

"Another contract?" she echoed.

Alain nodded. "It's a multiyear stint in Mauritius, starting in September." He broke off to look earnestly at her. "I want to be honest with you, Mara. If I'm offered the job, I'll have to take it. I've worked abroad for the past twenty years because—well, partly because it pays better than anything I can get in France, and Les Colombes requires a lot of upkeep. But I make you this commitment. I won't go until this matter of your sister is resolved."

September, she thought with an unexpected feeling of impending loss. Three and a half months. So little time.

He reached out to cover her hand with both of his, blue eyes serious. "And when it is, when this is all over . . ." He paused, took a deep breath, and said huskily, "I want you to consider coming out to join me. No, don't answer now. Think about it. It needn't be right away. Just when you're ready. You'll like the scent of frangipani on the sea wind. I promise you."

On Tuesday, Mara drove to Limeuil to pick up an order from the three elderly sisters who did all her custom-sewing commissions. The women had names, but were referred to by everyone as l'Aînée (elder sister), la Cadette (next in line), and la Benjamine (baby of the family).

As usual when she called, the trio seated her in their tiny parlor and treated her to a small but potent glass of la Cadette's plum wine. They huddled around her, wispy and gray and smelling of mothballs, reminding her of a triplicate version of Jeanne de Sauvignac.

"Leslie Caron," exclaimed l'Aînée, who was always comparing Mara to one or another film actress. Last month it was Audrey Tautou, whom they'd seen in *Amélie*. This time she drew inspiration from a rerun of an old American film they'd watched on television. "My dear, you look so much like Leslie Caron. You know, in *Gigi*. *Très gamine*. Don't you agree, sisters?"

La Cadette and la Benjamine did.

On the return journey to Ecoute-la-Pluie, Mara's mind strayed laterally to Jeanne de Sauvignac. The memory of her lopsided smile and gentle, kindly air of derangement unsettled Mara almost as much as the husband's secretiveness and fear. Or was it something more concrete than that? Yes, Mara decided, sifting through her impressions of their meeting. In fact, it was something the old woman had said, words that at the time had been lost in her general oddity but that now plucked at Mara's consciousness with a vaguely troubling resonance. Because one of the sewing sisters had said it, too. Or something like it.

That night she e-mailed Patsy Reicher.

•

On Wednesday, as Alain was taking his train to Paris, Mara drove to Toulouse to negotiate an order of tiles from Pablo. Instead of her usual quick *croque-monsieur*, she ended up having lunch with her supplier at the Brasserie des Beaux-Arts, overlooking the muddy waters of the Garonne. They opened with an apéritif of light, fruity muscat on ice. Pablo had an intense way of leaning his fat body across their little table when speaking. She half expected him to turn amorous, but his ardor proved to be reserved for food alone.

"Shall we say a half-dozen each of the number six?" he murmured huskily, referring to the oysters.

•

An hour later and an ocean away, as Mara watched Pablo climax on a dessert of *mousse au chocolat,* Patsy opened her morning and her electronic mail.

> *Patsy, it's me again. You remember my telling you about my visit to Les Colombes a couple of weeks ago? Well, there was something I forgot to mention that struck me as odd at the time, and I still can't make it out. See what you can do with it. When she first met me, Madame didn't say "enchantée" or "comment allez-vous" or any of the usual chitchat. Instead, she goggled at me in that nutty way of hers, and then she said, or started to say, "You look so much . . ." The actual words she used were: "Vous paraissez tellement . . ." She didn't finish because her husband came into the room at that point. All the same, I had the feeling that she was about to*

·

*make some kind of personal remark, which I find extremely
peculiar because French women of her class and generation
simply don't make personal remarks. At least, not right away.
So much what?* <

In her uptown office, Patsy popped a tablet of gum into her
mouth and chewed thoughtfully. She pushed away from her
desk, leaning back in her chair and glancing through the window
at an ugly Manhattan sky. The light outside had taken on a peculiar greenish tinge. A sudden clap of thunder shook the building.

So much what? Patsy sat motionless. The phone purred on her
desk. She ignored it. Rain began to slash against the windowpanes. Yes, Patsy thought, that's got to be it. She tapped out:

> *Mara, try "so much like your sister." I think Madame has
seen Bedie, at least once. The question is, alive or dead?* <

Parts of the puzzle were beginning to interlock, but the full picture was still incomplete, critical pieces missing here and there.
Although Commissaire Boutot had talked of two separate per-
petrators, Mara felt in her bones that one person—Julian—was
responsible for the death of Hanneke Tenhagen and the disappearances of the other women. Yet the de Sauvignacs were also
somehow involved. Madame had seen Bedie before; the expression of fear on Henri's face was enough to tell Mara that the man
was covering up much more than past sexual excesses; Alain had
to know more than he was telling. And where did Vrac and la
Binette fit in?

Confusedly, Mara grappled with the necessity of making
some connection between Julian and the de Sauvignacs. Land-

scaping? She doubted it. Then she remembered something Gaston had said: "Madame walks in the woods every day, and Monsieur still likes to shoot the occasional rabbit." Had Jeanne or Henri witnessed the attack on Bedie? But why hadn't they reported it? Perhaps the woman was so far gone she hadn't realized what she had seen. Or, Mara pondered, reflecting on the lack of funds so evident at Les Colombes, perhaps Henri had been using the knowledge to blackmail Julian. It couldn't have been for much. Julian was not a wealthy man. Unless, she concluded, a steady bleeding year after year was the reason.

If this was so, Mara knew that Henri would never talk. It was down to Jeanne, the link in the chain of lies and duplicity most likely to give. Mara's plan, therefore, was simple: return to Les Colombes and ransack Madame's knowledge for the missing puzzle pieces. To do that, Mara had to get her alone.

•

Thursday morning found Mara crouched in a thicket with a view of the rear courtyard of the château. Gaston had no idea when, between dawn and dusk, Madame's walk in the woods took place. Mara came prepared for a long stakeout. The problem was which door to watch. Châteaux of the style of Les Colombes had many doors, most connecting directly with interior staircases linking the various levels of the house. She counted on Jeanne's using the scullery door. In any case, Mara could not be in more than one place at a time.

By noon, Mara concluded that the worst of the exercise, not that she had any experience to go by, was the boredom. Apart from the listless waving of a rag on a sagging clothesline and the PTT—Gaston's substitute was a young, dark-haired fellow who left the mail on the scullery-door stoop—Les Colombes seemed devoid of life. Only a series of dormer windows, serving to light and ventilate the high loft of the château, seemed wakeful, peering down at her like quizzical, deep-set eyes. One of them, she noticed, had been blocked off at the bottom.

By three o'clock, Mara was cramped and stiff from sitting on the hard ground. Her sandwiches had long ago been eaten, her thermos of tea drained. In the valley below, a cuckoo voiced its lonely, intermittent call. The utter stillness of the place made her wonder if the de Sauvignacs were even there. She decided to risk a reconnoiter. As she pushed through wilderness that had once been formal garden, a tall, shadowy form suddenly barred her way, arm outstretched accusingly. She choked back a sharp yell of fear as she realized that she had come upon a small park of statuary, lost in the shrubbery.

Late-afternoon shadows were filling the courtyard when Henri de Sauvignac emerged from the scullery door. He carried a shotgun, broken at the barrel—off to bag his rabbit, no doubt. Mara held her breath as the old man paused, gazed up at the sky, and finally stepped off the stoop. With a stiff gait, he crossed the courtyard, walked down the lane running past the back of the château, and disappeared into the forest.

Swiftly, she darted from her hideout. She had anticipated intercepting the wife away from the house. With Alain in Paris, this would do as well. The scullery door opened into a vast kitchen where old and new mixed oddly: a massive hearth, big enough to roast an ox; a white enamel stove where a simmering pot of soup gave off an aroma of celery and onions; a deep stone sink; a portable dishwasher; and, near the old-fashioned larder, a small refrigerator, gurgling faintly, like a hunchbacked and displaced dwarf.

She made a quick search of the pantry and the ancient *lavoir,* the wash area. No one was there. Stone steps, concave with use, led her up to the main floor. She passed through a progression of vast, empty chambers, each giving onto another. In one salon, where the smell of mold was particularly strong, the walls were covered in stained, yellow brocade that hung in tatters, like the ruined finery of a dead queen. Eventually, she found herself at the library where she had interviewed the de Sauvignacs. It was unoccupied.

Mara took the steps of the great central staircase two at a time. The first-floor landing gave onto a wide, windowed gallery that ran the entire width of the building. At the near end of the gallery was a narrow archway. A quick look told Mara that it accessed a dimly lit spiral stairway that wound up to the loft and down to the lower story of the château. The servants' staircase, no doubt.

Rooms, most of them empty, opened off the north side of the gallery. Everywhere was the same complexity of smells—damp stone, old wood, the odor of decay, of things closed off. She paused before a partly opened door, listened, gave the door a push, and stepped inside.

Jeanne de Sauvignac was standing just to the right of the door, gripping a large pair of tailoring shears.

"Is it you, then, my dear?" Jeanne de Sauvignac was clothed this time in a soiled blue dress, a shapeless cardigan, and grubby carpet slippers. Her hair had the same flyaway look, and the lower half of her face gawped in the same silly smile. She crossed the distance dividing them, eyeing Mara avidly. Involuntarily Mara took a step back.

"Madame de Sauvignac," she broke out jerkily, "forgive me. I had to talk to you. There seemed no other way."

"Of course." The other seemed to regard Mara's presence as natural. She waved a hand. "Do sit down."

Apart from a chair drawn up to a little table by the window, there was nothing to sit on. In fact, the large room contained no other furniture than a high matrimonial bed, an armoire, and a chiffonier cluttered with photographs—a wedding picture, the groom distinguished by a bred-in-the-bone arrogance apparent even today; the slim, pretty bride, swathed in such quantities of white tulle as to render her somehow inconsequential. Portraits of two small boys, the older wide-eyed and serious, the younger grinning a lopsided grin that reminded Mara of the mother.

Madame crossed the room and seated herself in the chair before the table.

Mara followed. "I came," she began awkwardly, "I came to talk to you about my sister. Beatrice Dunn."

If Jeanne de Sauvignac heard her, she gave no sign. Taking up a man's shirt, she began to hack it into random pieces with the shears, an aimless act of minor destruction that only strengthened Mara's impression that the woman was barking mad. What was it Gaston had said? She had lost a child and had never been right since. The glinting blades made a sharp, bright, and, to Mara's ears, awful sound.

Mara positioned herself squarely before the table. "Please listen to me, madame. I believe that nineteen years ago a man named Julian Wood brought my sister to the forest below your château. Something happened there. I think you were a witness."

The shears paused over the ravaged shirt.

Mara gripped the table's edge. "Madame, I need to know what happened."

Unwillingly, Jeanne raised a troubled face, eyelids fluttering like withered petals in a faint stirring of air. Her gaze fixed on Mara. Then she said it: *"You look so much like her."*

Mara's heart lurched. "Yes," she breathed. "You saw the likeness the moment you met me. And the only way you could have known is if you'd already seen my sister." Gently but firmly Mara removed the shears from the other's grip and set them aside. "You were there, weren't you? You saw it all. What did he do to her?"

"Oh, my dear." Jeanne recoiled, looking genuinely shocked, as if Mara were broaching a socially embarrassing subject. "One doesn't speak of such things. *Ce . . . ce n'est pas convenable.*"

Pas convenable. Not seemly. The arid gentility of the old woman's choice of words made Mara want to shake her. She gripped Jeanne's arm. "Madame de Sauvignac, I have to know. *Tell me what happened to my sister!*"

"As to that," a voice spoke harshly at her back, "it's a question you would have been much better not to ask."

Mara whirled around to face Henri de Sauvignac. He stood in the doorway, breathing heavily and white with fury. Under his arm he still carried his gun. It was pointed at the floor, but this time the barrel was not broken. "You should be more careful where you park your car, madame."

Mara confronted him accusingly. "You! You know, don't you!"

"Enough!" Henri cried in a choking voice. "Why couldn't you let it be? Go away from here. Go now, before it is too late!" He brought the gun up sharply so that the barrel pointed at her breast. His eyes burned darkly in their sockets. He was old, but not without force or malice.

In desperation, Mara swung back to the wife, grasping at the slender thread that held her to Bedie. "Madame, for the love of God, tell me! What happened to my sister?"

"Jeanne!" The husband strode across the room. "Jeanne, I forbid—"

But Madame, hands fluttering up like frightened birds, cried out before he could stop her mouth. "It was her head," she moaned, rocking as if with pain. "Her poor, poor head!"

That evening, Julian, carrying an envelope of slides, arrived at the monthly meeting of the Société Jeannette. It was held in the Sainte-Anne community hall, which had once been a primary school. The words *garçons* and *filles* were cut into the stone lintels above the doorways of the separate boys' and girls' entrances. It was a good turnout—some thirty members. Iris and Géraud were there, Géraud looking smug, Iris cheerful and heavy with wooden beads.

"Come sit with us, Julian." Iris patted the empty chair next to her.

"I give you fair warning," she confided in a mock whisper as Julian settled himself. "Géraud's full of himself. Wait till the members' bit."

"Just let *him* wait," Julian grinned. "I've got something that'll knock his socks off."

The meeting started off with general business. Julian took the opportunity to alert the gathering to Edith's disappearance. They then moved on to nominations for the Prix Vénus. This was a prize awarded annually to the member who had contributed most to furthering the society's botanical knowledge or to the protection and public appreciation of flora in the region. In practice, this meant whoever had provided the best Bring and Brags. Inevitably, Julian and Géraud were nominated. Julian, who had joined the society only half a dozen years ago, was regarded as the upstart contender against Géraud, who won the prize with boring regularity. Julian was damned if he was going to be beaten out again.

The last part of the meeting was always reserved for the Bring and Brag. Here, there was usually a slight tussle as to order. Because Julian and Géraud almost always had something to show, it was understood that any other members wishing to make presentations (invariably inferior in point of botanical interest) had right of way. The issue of contention between Julian and Géraud was not which of them went next, but who went last, claiming the honor of rounding off the evening with the main spectacle, so to speak. The two men generally engaged in a species of wrangling, disguised as polite deference, each urging the other to precede him.

This time a resident German, Wilhelm Schroeder, led off with a nice series of slides of mountain wildflowers he'd snapped while hiking in the Ariège. When he stood down, there was a ripple of appreciation followed by a pause. Heads turned expectantly to Julian and Géraud. Julian sat back, knowing that what he had to show was well worth waiting for. To his surprise, Géraud did not demur but edged past him to the slide projector without ceremony.

"Just *un petit amuse-gueule*," he snickered at the gathering, "to whet the palate for the undoubtedly splendid botanical pièce de résistance that I'm sure my colleague Julian Wood has prepared for us." And he projected a close-up which caused Julian to sit forward agog.

"Saprophytes, as some of you may know, live on decomposing matter and are relatively rare. This fine example of the sapro-phytic *Neottia nidus-avis*, popularly known as Bird's-nest Or-chid, is not at all common in the region. In fact, in all my years of spotting, I've come across very few examples—"

"*Voyou!*" Julian choked, outraged, to the consternation of those who sat within hearing.

Géraud continued unperturbed. "—and certainly nothing to match this magnificent colony, which I just happened to come upon recently." Julian's stand, in all its dense, brownish-yellow glory, flashed on, covering the screen.

"The immense size of this colony," Géraud went on, "is an ex-cellent example of successful vegetative propagation. As you know, orchids, in addition to dropping seeds, spread underground through rhizomes or tubers, which clone off more plants, and so on. This way, quite massive carpets of a species like the *Neottia* here can grow up over time . . ."

Amid the murmurs of admiration, Iris turned to Julian. "What did I tell you?"

There was loud applause as Géraud wound up his presentation and sat down.

"*Pirate!*" Julian spat out as the other sidled past. "*Voleur!*"

Géraud smirked. "No such thing, *mon ami*. Believe me, your directions were more of a setback than a help. But don't keep us waiting. *Allez*, the show is all yours."

Julian glared. "Bugger the show!"

18

A scampering sound brought Mara to her senses. Rats. Or more probably a *fouine,* a stone marten, she figured once she realized where she was; for she could make out a paleness that resolved itself into a dormer window. She was somewhere in the loft of the château. Judging from the quality of the light, it was early evening. Her head throbbed terribly. She tried to move and found that her hands and feet were bound. She rolled over on her stomach and attempted to push herself into a kneeling position. The effort made her sick and dizzy. With a moan, Mara collapsed onto a hard, filthy mattress that bore traces of her own blood.

The pain was mostly concentrated on the left side of her head. That was where Henri de Sauvignac had struck her, hard, with the butt of his shotgun. She remembered now his look of desperation and fury as he crashed the weapon, held like a club, into her skull. Her last conscious thought had been that he intended to kill her.

She tried again to raise herself up to a half-reclining position against the wall. Another rush of nausea and dizziness. When her vision cleared, she saw that she was in a small garret containing only the bed she lay on. The space, which had been walled off from the rest of the loft, had an air of long abandonment. The floor was thick with dust.

She sensed movement. A small door at the far end of the garret opened. Jeanne de Sauvignac stepped into focus, carefully balancing a basin of liquid before her. Reaching Mara's side, she stooped worriedly over her.

"How are you, my dear?" She seated herself on the bed. Dipping a cloth into the basin, she began to dab very gently at the side of Mara's face. The pungent smell of vinegar hit Mara with such force that she recoiled.

"Lie still," the old woman murmured, pausing in her ministrations. "This will do you good. You've had a very nasty fall."

"Fall!" Mara gasped hoarsely. "Your husband tried to kill me. Surely you must realize that?"

"Ah." The other thought for a moment. "But *then* you fell."

With a sinking feeling, Mara recognized that Jeanne de Sauvignac was either crazier or more cynically sane than she had thought.

"Untie me. You can't keep me here. I'm hurt. I need a doctor."

"Hush," said Jeanne, studying her patient with interest. "I'll take very good care of you. I know a great deal about head injuries."

It occurred to Mara that Jeanne herself might be the product of a head injury. Then she remembered Bedie.

"What happened to my sister?" she croaked. "Did someone hit her on the head?"

Jeanne's regard shifted to the basin. She fingered the wet cloth. Mara waited, her own temples throbbing, willing the other to talk. At last, the older woman spoke. "He was born that way. He couldn't help the things he did." She said it simply, as if of some beast shaped by nature to violence, and with a compassion that sounded somehow out of place.

Was the woman talking about Julian? Fighting against an overwhelming drowsiness, Mara forced herself to concentrate. Her blackmail theory seemed insufficient reason for the violence of Henri's reaction. Surely the de Sauvignacs would not go to the extent of attacking and tying her up just to protect their hold over Julian and what had to be a meager source of money. Unless, of course, it was their own complicity they were desperate to hide. Then her thinking cleared, and she realized there was a simpler explanation. She turned to the woman at her side, who was now gazing distractedly into the basin as if seeking something in its cloudy depths. Jeanne had not been referring to Julian at all, probably had no inkling of who he was.

"Vrac," Mara said with a long release of breath. "It was Vrac all along, wasn't it? You knew, but you did nothing. Because he and his mother are 'your people' you kept silent. *Mon dieu,* you probably even helped them dispose of her body! But why?" She pulled away in revulsion from the other's touch. "Why did you cover up for him? Why did you risk so much to protect someone who's probably a psychopathic killer?"

Mara had her answer even before she finished her question, guessed it from Jeanne's quickly averted face, heard it in her silence. Henri's sense of noblesse oblige. The games of *cache-cache.* There was only one reason why children of the château would have been allowed to play with a common washerwoman's spawn.

"The blood tie," she concluded. "That's what binds you to him, isn't it? Vrac is your husband's bastard."

"Let me go," Mara cried. "People will be looking for me. They know I'm here. Your son—" an uneasy thought crossed her mind—"does Alain know about my sister?"

Jeanne sighed, a soft, sad rush of air. "My boy was away. In Africa. Building roads and bridges. His father won't let him live here. That's why he works abroad."

"Well, your boy is going to be back on Sunday," Mara challenged. "How will you explain me?" Then doubt edged in. Would they tell him? Would he even know she was up there in the garret? Would he help her if he knew?

She had no idea what the de Sauvignacs intended to do with her, only that she was one against many. A half-mad woman. Henri, arrogant, desperate, and armed. Behind him, the lurking specter of Vrac. And la Binette. Mara balked a little at the thought of Henri taking his pleasure with someone whom she had heard Gaston describe as big as a tree, ugly as a troll. But perhaps, when young, the woman had offered a brief attraction. Where had it happened? Mara wondered. At the stream where she routinely took the washing? Had the young milord taken her from behind, like an animal? She did the rough, the old man had said with fine distinction. How many couplings had it required to produce her misbegotten son?

Finally, there was Alain. Was he really ignorant of what his parents had done? Could they have kept something so monstrous from him? She wanted desperately for him to have no taint of collusion. Because if Alain had known, then his silence made him as guilty as they.

Later that night, Jeanne returned with a blanket and a bowl of soup. Mara caught the disheartening whiff of celery and onions. The soup was greasy, oversalted, and thickened with bread. The woman seemed to take pleasure in helping Mara to eat, cradling her torso against her own bony, stale-smelling body, lips moving in sympathetic movement with each mouthful that Mara took. Despite her revulsion at the physical contact, Mara ate it all. She needed her strength to fight against them. The light from a single, naked bulb suspended from the ceiling threw their shadows against the wall in a slow, wavering duet of motion.

When Mara said she needed to relieve herself, Jeanne offered her the use of a dusty chamber pot that she pulled from under the bed. Mara refused and insisted on being taken to a proper toilet. Jeanne untied her legs and escorted her out of the garret, down the spiral stairs to the floor below. Any thought Mara had of making her escape faded when she realized how weak and dizzy she was. She could hardly walk, let alone run. The water closet, situated off the gallery, was none too clean. Since Mara's hands were still bound, Jeanne had to help her. Mara recoiled from the intimate physical contact, but at least the woman was quick about it, pulling down her jeans, wiping her as efficiently as a nurse. Also surprisingly strong. Then Jeanne brought her back and tied her legs again, but not as tightly as before. With a murmured *"bonsoir,"* she clicked off the light. Mara heard the grating of the key in the lock.

She waited breathlessly in the dark. The great house was absolutely still. Awkwardly she dropped her legs over the side of the bed and slid to the floor. It was a painful process, rolling over the hard floorboards, and she had to stop many times to let her swimming head stabilize. When she reached the door, she pushed herself up to a standing position. She slid her cheek against the wall until she found the old-fashioned switch and flipped it on with her chin. Once again the single bulb came to life, filling the garret with a weak light.

Her exploration of the garret told her a few things. The door was made of solid timber with no knob or handle, only a metal plate housing a deadbolt lock, an unusual fitting for a garret. No hope of escape there. The dormer window was boarded off at the bottom. That was enough to tell her it was the one she had noticed from the rear courtyard during her stakeout. She stored up this precious piece of information. At some point the PTT van would drive up the rear lane and park by the scullery door. If there was some way she could open the window, she could shout for help when the dark-haired *rouleur* arrived with the next mail delivery.

But how to do it? The window was set high in the wall, and the boarding made it impossible for her even to see out of it. There was no chair or table in the garret, nothing to climb on. She would have to shift the bed over to the window somehow. She tried moving it the only way she could, by rolling onto her back and shoving it with her feet, using the power of her legs. It was extremely heavy. She managed to slide one end of the bed a small distance from the wall before a sudden wave of nausea overcame her. She rolled onto her side and vomited a pale-yellow liquid in which gobbets of undigested bread floated. Exhausted, she closed her eyes. She slept.

•

The following morning broke cool and overcast. Julian was standing sleepily in his kitchen, pouring himself a first mug of tea. He took it well sweetened, with a dash of milk. The back door was open, admitting a moist breeze. The phone rang.

"Julian?" It was Iris.

"Yes?" he inquired coldly, the memory of Géraud's scoop making him uncivil.

"Look, I've been stewing about this since last night. I felt I simply had to call you."

"About what?"

"Géraud, of course!" Iris's indignation crackled in his ear. "He told me what he did to you. He was laughing about it all the way home from the Société meeting. For what it's worth, I think it was a perfectly filthy trick."

"Oh that. Finder's rights." Behind feigned indifference, Julian was still furious. The only thing that had saved the evening for him was the fact that he had arranged a double billing: the

Neottia, which he did not show—what was the point?—and his slides of *Hammarbya paludosa*, the Bog Orchids he had discovered on his first day out with Mara. The effect, however, had been much discounted by the fact that they were not yet in flower.

"But you don't know the worst of it," Iris went on.

"There's worse?" He pulled up a chair and sat down heavily.

"Géraud purposely misled you to buy time for himself. He *made up* that Bird's-nest colony outside Le Double! Meantime, he checked out your locations, which, of course, were genuine."

Julian swore. The thought had crossed his mind, but he had been unable to believe that Géraud would stoop so low.

"Listen, Julian, I think it's too bad, what he did. I want you to know I had no part in it."

"No, of course not."

"However, to be fair to Géraud, you're always trying to one-up him, too, and he feels the pressure. Everything's so competitive nowadays. In fact, it's perfectly disgusting, the tricks some Société members play to outdo each other. In old Henri de Sauvignac's time, such things would never have happened. All the same, I think Géraud needs to be taught a lesson. The only way to punish him is to hit him where it hurts."

"Where's that?" Julian asked with interest.

"The Prix Vénus. He's won it seven years running. Beat him out for it."

Julian snorted. "How, if he's prepared to cheat?" All the same, he was gratified by Iris's blatant betrayal of her lover.

"Well, *I* don't know. You're the botanist."

Something Iris had said earlier only now registered with him. "Wait a minute, Iris. *Who* did you say?"

"Géraud, of course."

"No, before that."

"Henri de Sauvignac? He founded the society, didn't you know? But, of course, that was well before your time. Lovely old gent. Absolutely gaga about wildflowers. You'd have liked him."

"Are you talking about the de Sauvignac of Les Colombes?"

"Well, not the present *châtelain*, of course. Henri de Sauvignac *père*. Avid orchidologist. Both of them."

"Both of who?"

"He and his daughter-in-law. The two of them used to prowl the countryside collecting specimens for their plantations. Had them dotted all over the estate. He named the society for her, you know. 'Jeannette' is a *jeu de mots*, the diminutive for 'Jeanne,' which is her name. It also stands for *jeannette jaune*, yellow daffodil. He died years ago, god rest his gentle soul, but Jeanne de Sauvignac is still around, flitting through the woods."

"And her husband, the present Henri de Sauvignac, does he share this interest in botany?"

Iris gave a peal of laughter. "More interested in *les jeunes filles en fleur*, budding young women, than daisies, if you get my meaning. A real lady-killer in his day, with a penchant for rough sex, or sex in the rough."

"What do you mean?"

"Well, he had a liking for village wenches and he took it where he could get it, in field and forest. They say his youngest son drowned in a pond because the maid who was supposed to be looking after him was otherwise occupied in the tall grass with her employer. It destroyed his wife, which was very sad, especially as it's poor Jeanne de Sauvignac who's had to pay out all these years to hush up her husband's sexual indiscretions. She's the one with the money, you see. Or was. They're poor as church mice now, but he refuses to sell that barn of a place they live in. Family pride. Still, give the devil his due, after the old man died, Henri *fils* did his bit as Société president for many years, made pretty speeches at the annual assembly, handed out the Prix Vénus, which his father also founded, that kind of thing. Neither the present Henri nor Jeanne has come to meetings for donkey's years, of course."

Julian's mind was racing. "The Prix Vénus . . . That wouldn't happen to have been named after the Sabot de Vénus, would it?"

"Why, now that you mention it, I believe it was. Yes, I'm sure of it, because I remember that Henri senior and Jeanne once tried to grow Sabot de Vénus on the grounds of their château."

Julian was on his feet and gaping. "Are you saying they tried to breed *Cypripedium calceolus* here?"

"What?"

"*Cypripedium calceolus.* Sabot de Vénus. Lady's Slipper."

"Ah. I forgot that's what you experts call it. Well, yes, come to think of it, I believe they did. From rootstock they took from, mmm, I can't remember where."

"Look, I'm not just talking about one or two show plants, Iris. I mean, do you know if they actually tried to establish a viable plantation of them?"

"Might have." He could almost see her shrug. "Although, if they did, I doubt it came to very much."

"However, you don't know for certain that they failed, do you?" Julian was breathing hard.

"Oh," Iris murmured vaguely, "I rather think that if old Henri had succeeded we'd all have heard about it."

"And does Géraud know about this attempt to grow *Cypripedium?*"

"Bound to. But you know Géraud, vain as a peacock, scoffs at anything anyone else tries. Doubt he ever believed in it."

Until, of course, Julian thought sourly, *I turned up with that photo.* Aloud, he said, "Thanks for telling me this, Iris. You're a real treasure."

She chuckled conspiratorially. "Just give the old devil what's coming to him, all right?"

"You're on," he assured her.

Julian hung up with two thoughts driving everything else from his mind. First and foremost, if *Cypripedium calceolus* had been established at Les Colombes, then the plant could have mutated and the resulting flower could have been the one Bedie had photographed nineteen years ago. Second, Géraud, nobody's fool, was, like himself, on the hunt for the Lady's Slipper, probably closing in on it at that very moment.

A panicky urge to rush back to Les Colombes seized him, but he restrained himself. Les Colombes and the surrounding forest encompassed a large area, and he might be looking for a single plant. *If* it had survived. The logical approach would be to find out from Jeanne de Sauvignac where she and her late father-in-law had tried to establish the *Cypripedium* rootstock. That at least would narrow the search. Assuming the woman could remember. She sounded barmy, from Mara's description.

He took it for granted that he could count on Mara's cooperation. She wanted to find the *Cypripedium* as much as he—for different reasons, of course. However, he was aware that a coolness had set in between them ever since that damned Alain had happened along. Julian was quite certain that she looked at him differently of late, almost as if— Well, it was past thinking. All the same, it gave him a stab of uneasiness.

He drove straight out to Ecoute-la-Pluie. There he found Mara's front door open and the cleaning woman, a bony person named Madame Audebert, on hands and knees in the main room, vigorously waxing the floor. The smell of encaustic hung sweetly in the air. She looked up at Julian with eyes like olive pits. He asked if Mara was in.

"But her bed has not been slept in, monsieur," Madame

Audebert told him sardonically, as if to imply that, if he did not know why, then it was none of his business.

Alain, Julian, concluded wrathfully.

The *femme de ménage* added that she came at nine twice a week and let herself in with her own key. Sometimes Madame Dunn was there when she arrived and sometimes not. This time not. Regardless, she got on with her work. She gave him an acid look.

"Oh, right—" He was about to leave her to it when he was startled by a deep bark. "Wait a minute. Is Jazz here?"

By way of answer, Madame Audebert jabbed her hairy chin in the direction of the back of the house. Julian strode across the room. Through the glass panels of the double doors, he could see the dog straining at the end of a chain, looking anxious amid the Patsy Reicher statuary.

"He hates the vacuum," Madame Audebert muttered at his back, "so I put him in the garden. He barks a lot because he doesn't like being tied up." She seemed to imply that Julian should do something about it.

"Look," Julian said, "I want to leave Mara—Madame Dunn—a message." He peered about for something to write on. The woman was unhelpful. He settled for the back of a bill he found in his pocket. Hastily he scrawled: *Mara—where the hell are you? Call me. Urgent. Julian.*

"I'll put it here, shall I?" He placed it conspicuously on one of the Louis Something consoles.

"Comme vous voulez, monsieur." From the floor, Madame Audebert pursed her lips, as the French picturesquely called it, *en cul de poule*. It was a fitting description, Julian thought nastily. Her puckered mouth really did resemble a chicken's arse.

No sooner had he returned to his van than he regretted leaving a message at all. What was the point of waiting for Mara to take her sweet time getting back just to tell her about his discovery? Now that she was so thick with Alain, he wouldn't put it past her to cut him out, use the son to get the information from Jeanne de Sauvignac, and try to find the *Cypripedium* herself. Just to spite him. And the damnable thing was, the bloody woman might succeed. After all, her sister had stumbled on it. His anger and his resentment mounted.

He was considering retrieving his note when another volley of barks, desperate this time, sounded from the garden. Julian hesitated, then walked around to the back of the house. Jazz, frantic with delight, lunged and scrabbled on his tether.

"Oh, all right," Julian gave in grumpily. "But just this once."

"Tell Madame Dunn," he called to the *femme de ménage* through the front door, "I've taken Jazz."

She gave him a look that said he could go to the devil for all she cared, the dog with him.

•

"Count yourself lucky," Julian snarled at Jazz as he started the engine and roared out of Ecoute-la-Pluie in the direction of Les Colombes. For want of information from Jeanne de Sauvignac, he had to make assumptions. He had already guessed that the ridge on which the château stood offered the kind of soil and the cool, wooded environment that *Cypripedium* liked. That's where he would have chosen to establish a plantation of Lady's Slippers if it had been up to him.

He had come away without any of his usual hiking paraphernalia, but at least he had his compass and maps, which he normally carried in his van. Using a Série bleue, he found a road that allowed him to approach the estate from the east. That way he could avoid crossing La Binette land, which lay to the west of Les Colombes. He had no desire to be caught trespassing by Vrac or his hulk of a mother.

He parked at the roadside near a scattering of tiny Burnt-tip Orchids. The high tree canopy offered him no view of his destination, so the first thing he did was to set a westerly bearing on his compass that would orient him roughly in the direction of the château and the ridge. Since there was no path, he would have to break his own trail, and he estimated that he had a good hour's hike ahead of him.

He set out. Jazz vanished immediately (Julian had also not thought to bring a leash). Slightly alarmed, Julian called him back. The dog took his time coming but eventually returned. This happened repeatedly. Finally, Julian got tired of calling and left the animal to his own devices. When he came across a mass of pink Heath Orchids growing in a clearing, he forgot entirely about the dog. Later he found a fine stand of *Limodorum abortivum*. The tall, handsome plants were in peak condition, with their mauve blossoms spiraling up each individual stem. He made a mental note of their location.

After about twenty minutes, Julian stumbled on a path that seemed to be trending in the right direction. He followed it. It took him past a crudely fenced pasture where a nervous huddle of ewes and lambs broke apart at his approach, skittering away before wheeling around from a safe distance to stare at him sideways with stupid, squarish eyes. At this point, he had no idea whose land he was on. The pasture sloped down to a stream so heavily overgrown with willow brush that although he heard the sound of water he could not see it until he nearly fell into a narrow, deeply cut rivulet that rushed away at his feet.

His path ended there. A network of faint tracks led off in several directions. Referring again to his compass, he chose one that snaked along the water's course. He had not gone far when a shrill, inhuman scream brought him to a startled halt.

"Bloody hell!" he uttered. "What was that?" His first thought was that Jazz had seized on some poor, unwary animal. The sound had come from farther along the watercourse. He ran forward, breaking through a heavy screen of willows. What he saw caused him to pull up in sheer terror. Vrac stood below him on the other side of the stream, bare arms spattered in blood. In one hand he grasped a knife, in the other the thing he had just slaughtered. It was a lamb, which he secured by the hind legs while he disemboweled it. Bluish intestines spilled onto the mud. The water of the stream ran a ghastly shade of red.

For a moment Vrac stared stupidly up at Julian. The monolens sunglasses blanked out one eye, but the look in the other turned quickly ugly. Julian took two involuntary steps backward, spun about, and fled.

Counting on speed he did not really have, Julian crashed through the trees. Behind him he heard a fearsome bellow and the thud of heavy footsteps. The realization that Vrac had been merely poaching someone's livestock, probably for his evening chops, did not make Julian less inclined to put distance between him and his pursuer. Poaching was a serious offense in those parts, and Vrac clearly resented being caught at it. Julian did not like to think what Vrac could do with that knife of his.

Dodging branches, Julian found himself at another section of the stream, where it curved off in a wide, shallow bend. He flailed across it. The splatter of water in his wake told him that Vrac was not far behind. Gasping for breath, Julian scrambled up the steep, wooded embankment on the other side. Small avalanches of scree rattled down behind him as he surged over the top of the rise. The land fell away precipitously before him. He galloped down recklessly.

A root caught his foot. He spun sideways, rolled wildly, and came up hard against the base of a tree. The impact knocked the wind out of him. He lay fighting for air. Painfully he dragged himself on his elbows into the cover of a dense bed of ferns. Pressing himself flat against the ground, he listened. The only sound he heard was the hammering of his own heart.

Cautiously, Julian raised his head. Small white butterflies danced over a gray-green sea of bracken that spilled thickly down the slope. Light filtered lazily through the treetops. All about him the woods were quiet. He lay still for a few moments longer, then congratulated himself on a close escape. Vrac appeared to have abandoned the chase and was probably going back for his lamb. Julian judged that he would finish gutting it and make for home as fast as possible.

Julian pushed himself upright, reoriented himself, and set off again, scrambling along the steep side of the embankment. A break in the trees gave him his first, distant glimpse of Les Colombes, or, rather, its chimneystacks. It stood high on its prominence across a broad, wooded valley. He took another compass reading and headed down into the valley floor, pushing his way, often with difficulty, through the tangled undergrowth. When he came across another network of trails, he chose one trending in a westerly direction. It took him through a gloomy pine forest.

Now the land began to rise before him. Pines gave way to beeches, old-growth chestnuts, and oaks. After another fifteen minutes, he found himself in a hornbeam grove at the base of the ridge. The château stood high above him to his left. The trail veered off toward it. To his right, the ridge continued on for a kilometer or so before coming to an abrupt end in a spectacular hanging cliff.

He decided to begin his search by working diagonally up the slope face, away from the château and toward the cliff, sticking to tree cover as much as possible until he was out of sight of the château. There was no path, and large boulders frequently blocked his way. One, as big as a house, rose up before him. He was edging around it when the ground suddenly gave way beneath him. With a startled cry, he found himself dropping into a void and managed only just in time to catch himself with his out-flung arms. Panicked, he kicked about to find some purchase with his feet, which only caused him to slip farther. A shower of earth and stones struck bottom somewhere ominously far below him. He now dangled over nothingness, supported only by his hands and forearms. Gradually, as the friable soil crumbled beneath his weight, he lost even this precious hold. In a minor avalanche, he plunged down into a pit of darkness. It was as if the earth itself had swallowed him up.

•

Mara awoke to daylight. She was on the floor, where she had collapsed the night before. She felt cold and clammy. Then the sour smell of her own mess hit her. Miserably she rolled away from it and found herself staring into the dim, dusty space beneath the bed. Something shiny was wedged in a gap between the floorboards just by one of the legs of the bed. Frowning, she scooted forward and picked it out with her teeth, dropping it out in the open where she could study it better. It was a plain, narrow metal band, slightly pitted with rust and bent tightly in upon itself. A hair clip of some kind, too flimsy to be of use to her. Disappointed, she rolled away. Then faint recognition stirred. She closed her eyes and struggled to visualize. Hair. Bedie's hair, pinned back at the temples. *This was a woman's hair clip such as Mara had seen in every one of her nightmares for nineteen years:* Bedie's barrette.

Her brain in turmoil, Mara struggled to understand how it came to be there. She fought to concentrate, staring at this terrible and yet precious token of her sister. Her mind went back to the knobless door, the deadbolt lock, the dormer window that had been altered to let light in but blocked any view of the outside world. The garret was fitted out like a prison.

I know a lot about head injuries, the old woman had said. Bedie—who had been struck on the head, but who had not died, at least not right away—Bedie had been there once. Mara was sure of it. The bed bore the impression of her body; the walls, the enclosed space of the garret held her presence like a bottled ghost.

She struggled to rise, ignoring the pounding in her head. Hobbling on her knees to the barrier of the door, she fell against it, pivoted around, and hammered at it with her feet, shouting with all the force she could muster.

"Get up here, you monsters! Get up here and tell me what you've done with my sister!"

•

Julian landed heavily. Instinct told him not to move. In the dimness, he saw that he was on a limestone shelf only slightly wider than himself. It was, in fact, what had saved him, for it projected out over a chasm, the depth of which he could only guess at by the rattle of debris still on its way down. He was in an *edze,* a typical geological feature of the region, where rifts in the calcareous mantle of the earth, dissolved by rain, opened out into deep pits underlain by subterranean rivers. He sat up carefully. Apart from being stunned and shaken, he did not seem to have broken anything. Above him, he saw a ragged patch of daylight, the hole through which he had fallen.

Julian's horror and revulsion at encountering Vrac at the stream were now replaced by a strong desire to see the man again, for there was no way he could climb out without help. The mouth of the *edze* was perhaps five meters up, more than twice his own height. The shaly sides offered no hand- or foothold. To make things worse, the pit interior was wider at the bottom, sloping inward at the top. Despite his belief that Vrac was capable of slitting him open like a hogget, Julian got to his feet and began to shout.

He shouted until he was hoarse. Exhausted, he slumped down against the wall of his prison. *Get a grip*, he ordered himself and set about studying his situation. Although the *edze* was vase-shaped, he saw that it narrowed at one end. By bracing his back and feet against the opposing faces, Julian thought he might just be able to work his way to the top. However, he was also aware that the ledge he was on extended only partway across the gap. Between it and the far wall lay a maw of blackness. The rocky projection had saved him once. If he slipped, would it catch him a second time?

He rolled over onto his stomach and peered down into the darkness below. As his eyes adjusted, he discovered to his relief that the fissure, although undoubtedly deep, was not as sheer as he had thought, for the opposite wall sloped outward, forming another shelf not far below him. All kinds of rubble had accumulated on it. He made out a dark jumble of shapes. Maybe there was even something down there he could use.

Carefully, he lowered the top half of his body over the side of the ledge, extending one arm down in a sweeping motion. His fingertips brushed something. He wriggled as far forward as he dared to go and closed his hand on a hard, rough object. He brought it up, a wedge-shaped thing that he flung away immediately, for it was horrific, studded with teeth and trailing stiff shreds of woolly hide: the lower jaw of a sheep.

Julian sat back, shaken. For the first time in his life, he earnestly wished he had a cell phone.

19

"Vrac hit her on the head!" Mara screamed at Henri, who stood in the doorway. Behind him, fluttering in her shawls, was Jeanne. Mara struggled to her knees to confront them. "But she was alive, wasn't she, when you brought her here! Was it was your wife, who isn't competent to care for a dog, who finished her off?"

"Shut up," Henri de Sauvignac ordered curtly, seizing her under the arms and dragging her roughly back to the bed.

"The police will come looking for me." Mara fought against him as he lifted her and shoved her facedown on the mattress. "What story will you concoct for them? It'll have to be good because they'll find evidence of me everywhere—hair, blood, vomit—it's all over the floor. Or will you simply tell them that, having covered up the murder of one sister, you thought you'd finish off the other?"

"Stop that." Jeanne hurried forward to aid in holding her still while Henri checked her bonds. "No one is going to finish you off. We just want to help you, make you better."

"Like you did my sister?"

The other woman cried indignantly, "I gave her the best of care!"

"Jeanne, *tais-toi!*" the husband ordered sharply, but the words were out.

It was like a boulder dropped from a great height into a deep pool. Mara lay still as the admission sank and lodged in the depths of her consciousness. She rolled over to stare up at Jeanne.

"And how was that, madame?" she began softly, but her voice became quickly shrill. "How exactly did you care for her? By tying her up here and refusing her medical attention? Because you wouldn't have wanted to risk a doctor, would you? By feeding her stale bread dipped in slop? How long did she last before she choked on her own vomit or died of a hemorrhage of the brain?"

"Since you insist," said Henri, with a savage jerk at her knots, "fourteen years."

Mara went limp beneath his hand. It was as if her known world had suddenly shattered like glass, sending jagged shards flying in all directions, exposing a void in which nothing made sense.

"Fourteen years? In this garret? You locked my sister up here for fourteen years?"

"You must understand, my dear," Jeanne's voice wavered apologetically above her, "it was necessary. She was terribly damaged. She couldn't speak, she couldn't care for herself. I had to do everything for her, feeding, baths, cleaning up her messes."

"You kept her caged like an animal!"

"Not at all!" The woman sounded deeply offended. "I nursed her like my own child. I used to put her head on my lap and brush her hair. I always had to pin her hair back, out of her eyes, you see. She became very agitated if her hair was in her eyes."

"And then what? At what point did you get tired of playing jailer? Were people starting to ask questions? Or were Alain's home leaves getting too much for you to manage?" Mara rolled away from them and propped herself up on her elbows, the better to see their faces as she worked out the truth for herself. "That's why you couldn't let him live here, isn't it? Why your 'poor boy' has to work abroad. You were terrified he'd learn your secret. Or was he becoming suspicious? Was that when you decided to get rid of her? How did you do it? Hold a pillow over her face? Or did you simply let her starve to death up here?"

"No, no!" Jeanne wailed, her hands flying up around her face as if warding off Mara's accusations. "It wasn't like that at all. I did my best to make her comfortable. And happy. She was happy here with me. Until"—the old woman's voice cracked, and Mara realized that she was crying—"one day, one morning, I brought her coffee up to her. She was lying on her stomach. I couldn't wake her. I rolled her over. Then I saw that she was dead. She had simply died in the night, you see."

"It took her long enough," Henri cut in brutally.

Fourteen years. Dully Mara's mind began to compute. For at least two of those years, she had lived and worked in the Dordogne, not more than twenty kilometers from the place where her twin had been held a mindless captive. For fourteen years her nightmares had been not of a sister dead but of a sister living, feebly signaling for rescue from a twilight existence. And then, like a light exhausted, all signals had ceased. A wrenching sadness filled Mara as she realized that Bedie Dunn had slipped away, had dropped her end of the string that bound sister to sister, while she, Mara, had been unable to pull her back from the brink.

"But why?" The question rose again to her lips, for the improbability of the de Sauvignacs' motive weighed once more on her. Why would a family like the de Sauvignacs take such risks to shield a bastard? And how had Bedie come to Les Colombes? For, if Julian had really reconstructed her path, then it had brought her right onto the grounds of the château. She could not have been dragged there struggling because she had stopped to take photographs along the way. Would she have willingly gone with a monster like Vrac? Or, more likely, have accompanied someone comme il faut, as Loulou had suggested, someone presentable? Not Julian, she knew that now. Someone else. Someone who was able to move about the region with ease and for whom places like Limoges, Bordeaux, and Biarritz, where other women had gone missing, were within striking distance. A man whose wife wore a souvenir of Biarritz as a shawl. Thing-in-his-pocket. The stallion in rut.

"It was the other way around, wasn't it," Mara hissed at Henri in a slow release of breath. "Not Vrac. But you. *You* hit my sister on the head."

Nineteen years ago, Henri would have been a vigorous man in his fifties. Had it begun as a simple grope that escalated into a struggle and accidental death? Or a vicious, planned attack? Just as he had struck Mara herself down, had he also smashed the butt of his gun into Bedie's skull? How many others had de Sauvignac disposed of in his need to assert his seigniorial rights? The noble rot applied to more than grapes.

"And you caught him in the act, didn't you." Mara twisted about to accuse the wife. "That's why he didn't finish her off and simply bury her in your woods. Why you had to keep her here. Not to shield Vrac, but to protect your husband's precious skin."

Jeanne was staring at her haggardly, wordless, not denying. Mara now realized that there was no limit to what Henri would do to save himself. She also realized that her own danger was made more acute by Alain's planned return. Henri would make sure his son did not find her there.

"Leave us, my dear." Henri turned to his wife and ushered her quickly from the room.

"Let me go," Mara bargained desperately when he returned to stand over her. "I won't make trouble. Even if I went to the police, what can I prove? If I haven't been able to make a case against Vrac—and I've tried, believe me—who will credit that Henri de Sauvignac, *seigneur* of Les Colombes, is a serial killer?"

"Fool!" Henri spat furiously.

"I may be a fool, but you are a monster." Mara's anger surged as she saw that all pleading was futile. "Your victims trusted you, didn't they. You, with your aristocratic air, your fine courtesy. How did you lure my sister onto your land? With orchids? With promises to show her a place where rare species grew?"

Henri laughed outright. "Madame, I have never been particularly knowledgeable about orchids and would not, if given the opportunity with a young woman, have ever wasted time talking about flowers."

"Who else, if not you?" Mara challenged, galled by his sneering indifference.

He regarded her cynically, as if assessing how much information to divulge. Finally, he spoke, with an upward curling of the lip: "My wife."

She stared at him, speechless.

"It was she, you see," he said, as he turned to leave, "who met your sister in the woods."

Young Carlos, the *rouleur* filling in for Gaston, swung by the house in Le Coux at the end of his Saturday-morning round of deliveries.

"How's it going, old man?"

"Hmm." Gaston pulled a face and flipped his good hand back and forth to indicate so-so. "You? What's new?"

"Didn't you hear? The patron's made a dog's breakfast out of everything. He's split your route between René and me. So now I have to do your half in the morning and somehow finish up old Geneste's in the afternoon." Carlos ran a hand through his thick, black hair. "Worst fucking roads in the region. No wonder your van kept breaking down."

"Tell me," said Gaston, highly gratified.

"Oh, by the way, looks like those old birds of yours got themselves a new car."

"What old birds?"

"Them. In Les Colombes."

"Monsieur and Madame de Sauvignac to you," said Gaston severely, offended to hear his favorites treated so offhandedly. But he was curious. "What kind of car?"

"Renault Clio. Green. Well, not new, exactly. Used, by the look of it. Saw it parked around the side the other day when I made my delivery. Finally traded in that old thing of theirs, I guess."

Gaston sniffed. "That 'old thing' of theirs was a genuine antique. Probably fetched a few sous. I tell you, Carlos, you treat the de Sauvignacs right and they'll treat you right. Always good for a *coup*. Quality shows."

.

With the first light of day, Julian began again to try to work his way out of his prison. In between unsuccessful attempts, he shouted for help. Although his body ached and he was hungry and thirsty, his head had remained surprisingly pain-free. It was the only upside to his horrible predicament.

At the moment he was stretched horizontally across the *edze*, back and shoulders pushing against one face of it, feet against the other. It was, it seemed, his thousandth attempt. *Come on,* he urged himself as he squirmed his way upward, gasping with the effort. On each of his previous tries, his progress had been checked by crumbling shale that had given way beneath his weight, causing him to slither painfully, sometimes head-first, back down onto the ledge. Each time, the small avalanche of rock and soil loosened by his efforts ricocheted off the rift walls below him, ending at some greater depth in a series of faint splashes.

He was doing better this time, had managed to work his way more than halfway up his prison wall. Already he could see the ragged edge of the pit mouth clearly above him, full of brilliant light.

Back and shoulders. Feet. Centimeter by centimeter. Then he slipped. He fell amid a shower of dirt and stones, landing heavily on his side. His legs flopped over the edge of the ledge, and the rest of his body, driven by the momentum, followed, tipping him into a void. He tried to save himself by throwing out his arms but was unable to prevent himself from tumbling down onto the lower shelf.

Julian lay still, feeling sick at the thought of how much farther he could have fallen if this second outcropping had not caught him. He was lying on top of a pile of wool and bones. The sheep's jaw no longer held any terrors for him. He realized that it was the sheep's carcass that had broken his fall.

He sat up gingerly, rubbing a painful shoulder, thankful that he was still in one piece. He judged that, with a certain amount of scrambling, he would be able to hoist himself back onto the upper ledge. As he pushed himself unsteadily to his legs, his fingers touched something. Fur? Some other kind of animal pelt? It came away in his hand. A pale hank of longish fibers. Hair. And then he saw it: wedged up against the *edze* wall and overlaid by the jumble of sheep bones, the rounded cranium with its blank eye sockets. Pushing the sheep's carcass aside, he uncovered first the entire skull, then the rib cage and long bones of a human skeleton.

•

Back and shoulders, hands clawing behind him at the sharp layers of shale. Feet. Digging the heels of his boots in, scrabbling for any niche, any irregularity in the damp, slippery rock that would gain him one more centimeter. Julian concentrated on the spot, higher up, where the *edze* narrowed. Once he passed that point, it would be easier. His best attempts so far had taken him only slightly more than halfway up before he had lost his hold and fallen in a shower of debris. This time he would not fall. He did not like what was waiting for him at the bottom.

Inevitably he fell, sliding down the interior rock face of his prison, crashing onto the top ledge, barely managing to keep from tumbling off it a second time. He lay stunned and shattered. The bright mouth of the *edze* might have been a galaxy away. He closed his eyes. Exhausted and weak, he slid into unconsciousness.

He dreamed that he was lying on an island of bones. A blood-red tide roared over him in waves of deep, rhythmical sound. The roaring was accompanied by a dribble of soil that fell into his open mouth. A pebble, striking him hard on the nose, brought him to. A shower of pebbles. The *edze* was collapsing, and he was being buried alive. He groaned and rolled over. The hail of stones and earth accelerated, bouncing off his hair and neck. Something was tearing at the mouth of the pit. A cacophony of noise echoed in his ears. He began to make sense of it: loud, anxious barking resonating all around him.

Julian staggered up, steadying himself against the rift wall.

"Jazz!" he yelled with all the force he had remaining. "Jazz!"

Back and shoulders. Brace with arms and hands. Now feet, sliding them upward one at a time, heels digging in. The dog's vociferous presence overhead gave him renewed strength. Back and shoulders. Feet. He was two-thirds of the way to the top. Already he felt the greater purchase afforded by the smaller space his body had to bridge. He could drive now with all the strength remaining in his legs and back, progressing a hand's breadth at a time. Soon he was able to make out in clear detail the trailing roots of plants dislodged by his original fall. Above him, barking a frantic encouragement, Jazz raced around and set up a powerful digging with both front paws. Earth and vegetation flew, showered down on Julian, blinding, choking him, destroying the very handholds he needed in order to surface.

"Jazz!" he bellowed. "Get off it! Down, dammit, down!"

The dog obeyed, whimpering perplexedly somewhere over Julian's right ear. Back and shoulders. Feet. The pit perimeter was just above eye level. He could make out individual blades of grass, trembling in the breeze. His head emerged into blinding sunlight. He wanted to shout aloud with joy. Then something beneath his heel gave way. Wildly, Julian threw up an arm as his left leg lost purchase and his right threatened to follow. Just as he slipped, a powerful clamp closed down on his collar. Jazz had taken hold and was pulling mightily, as only a dog of his size and strength could pull, dragging Julian up the remaining distance until he lay, half in, half out, and was able at last to crawl to safety. He sprawled, Jazz panting by his side, in warm sunshine on the sweet surface of the earth.

•

"Get up."

Julian breathed deeply. Never had the soil and its vegetation smelled so good to him.

"Get up."

A large, booted foot dug at his ribs. Jazz whimpered and moved away. Julian raised his head, too weak to defend himself. La Binette, in her straw-colored wig, her face congested by its disfiguring stain, towered over him. Next to her stood Vrac. Mother and son regarded him impassively. Jazz, a little off to one side, looked on but was not inclined to come to Julian's aid.

Between the two of them they dragged him. He made no resistance, merely allowed them to seize him under the arms and pull him along. At one point, as they crossed a source flowing from the hillside, he begged for water. They dumped him into it. He drank greedily. After that he was able to croak, "Where are you taking me?"

La Binette's basilisk eye, set in a creased and leathery face, fixed him stonily. She jerked her head over her shoulder. "To him. You're on his land." She turned to her son. "Where is he?"

"Pond," Vrac grunted and with one hand hauled Julian up again.

●

The pond lay in the forested valley bottom. Reeds grew thickly at its margin, except where, here and there, they had been broken down by the passage of water rats. In the middle of the pond was an island where irises still showed their withered yellow flags.

Henri stood at the muddy edge, staring into the still surface of the water. He carried his shotgun under his arm. A freshly killed rabbit lay in the grass at his feet. He turned as two people, dragging a third and followed by a dog, broke through the trees. Mother and son dumped Julian unceremoniously at the *seigneur's* feet.

"Caught him trespassing," said la Binette.

With an effort, Julian heaved himself up on his elbows. He said with all the aplomb he could muster, "Which undoubtedly gives you the right to order me from your grounds. Call these two off"—he jerked his head in the direction of la Binette and Vrac—"and I'll go quietly."

De Sauvignac studied Julian's crumpled form suspiciously. "Who are you? What were you doing on my land?"

"Nosing around, he was," Vrac said gutturally. "They came together the other time. Saw them. Him and her."

Julian took in the tall, stooping man. Alain resembled his father, he thought. "Your son knows about my interest in orchids," he lied. "He said his mother and grandfather had planted some unusual species around the estate and told me to have a look around anytime I liked. So I'm not here uninvited."

"He was with her, you say?" Henri asked.

Vrac confirmed this with a growl.

"I see." Henri considered the man on the ground with an expression of distaste. "Vrac, m'boy," he said at last, "help me take care of him, will you?"

Once again Julian was hoisted roughly to his feet.

"And Binette, get rid of that cur."

The woman did so by the mere expediency of looping her finger through Jazz's collar and leading him off in the direction they had come. If Julian had been hoping for some display of canine heroics, he was disappointed. Except for a strong territoriality with respect to cars, Jazz was a remarkably easygoing dog.

Mara came to with a start. Jeanne de Sauvignac was hovering over her.

"Ah," murmured the old woman. "You're awake. I looked in several times, but you were always sleeping." She lifted Mara to a sitting position, propping her against the wall.

Once more Mara was aware of Jeanne's strength. This time she noticed how large the woman's hands were.

"I brought you some medicine, my dear."

Mara glared suspiciously at a glass of murky liquid. Was this it? Were they planning to drug and dispose of her while she lay senseless? *Dear Lord,* she prayed, *don't let them bury me alive. They're both crazy enough to do it.* Henri's last words came back to her, setting off a deafening internal alarm. *What exactly had happened when Jeanne de Sauvignac met Bedie in the woods?* Mara clenched her jaws and turned her head away.

The other looked disappointed. "It's not really medicine," she admitted. She sat down on the edge of the bed and put the glass on the floor beside her. "Only sugared water. I used to give it to her. The other one. It was a game we played. I would say, Now, *poupoule,* drink this, it will make you well again. She liked sugar, you see. Sometimes I gave her lumps of sugar soaked in brandy. She loved that. It made her smile. Your smile, my dear, is just like hers."

Mara was stunned and sickened by the woman's maudlin need to nurture coupled with her total disregard of the larger issues of good and evil. She had lost a son. Was she like some demented beast, driven endlessly to find substitutes for her dead child? Between the husband and the wife, Mara did not know whose guilt was greater. But here at least was a weakness that she thought she could exploit.

"You nursed her well, madame."

The rumpled face brightened. "Like my own child."

"And yet you let her die."

The brightness faded.

"There was another death, too, wasn't there? Patrice," Mara drove the name at her cruelly. "Your little boy. My sister. And now me. I'll be dead, too, if you try to keep me here, you know. This house doesn't have a very good track record, does it? One way or the other, people die here. Do you want that? Do you really want another death?"

"Oh, my dear." Jeanne's hands flew up about her face in a characteristic fluttering.

"You know your husband intends to kill me."

"Don't be silly." Jeanne's head came up sharply. "Henri would never do such a thing."

"He will. He has to. Don't you see? He can't afford to let Alain find me here."

The other stared at her, stricken.

Mara whispered urgently, "Untie me. All you have to do is let me get away from here without your husband knowing."

The ragged head swung from side to side. "I can't. Henri wouldn't like it."

"Damn Henri," Mara nearly shrieked. "Can't you understand? *He's going to kill me.* Madame, you have to help me, or be an accomplice to murder!"

The faded blue eyes fixed on Mara with a look of vague unease. For a second, Mara hoped as she felt the light touch of fingers on her arm. Then hope died. Jeanne's expression crystallized into a smile of almost cloying indulgence.

"It's impossible," Jeanne laughed softly. "You're far too ill to leave here, my dear. You need to rest. I'm afraid you'll be staying with me for a very long time."

There were noises on the stairs. Mara could have wept with desperation. The garret door flew open. Henri entered first, Vrac followed, hunched and burdened with something large that he threw roughly to the floor. A body. Julian's body.

20

Grissac lost to Le Buisson five to zero on Saturday. It was a hotly contested match, for revenge hung in the balance, Le Buisson having beaten Grissac badly the year before. Paul and the entire team were furious. Not only had Julian not turned up, he had not even bothered to let them know he wasn't coming. The *anglais* wasn't the most brilliant fullback, but at least he offered a damned sight more body than that weed of a José whom they'd had to drag in at the last minute. Paul swore violently all the way back to Chez Nous, where Mado, for once sympathetic to his rugby woes, made soothing noises while massaging his shoulders with a penetrating salve.

"We could have beaten that canaille if that calf's head had bothered to show up."

"Hmmm. Still, it's not like Julian. You don't suppose he's sick?"

"He'll be sicker when I squeeze his neck."

"No. I mean really sick. Too ill to call."

Paul craned around to squint up at her through a wave of mentholated fumes. The kneading of his muscles was having a relaxing effect. "How d'you mean? Dying?"

She chewed a provocative lower lip and bent forward, showing deep cleavage. "At least you could check up on him."

Paul rolled himself over on the bed, displaying a vast expanse of hairy chest and formidable-looking nether parts. He pulled Mado to him. "First things first," he growled.

Later he did drive round to Julian's cottage. The back door, as usual, was not locked. Paul stuck his head inside and bellowed, "D'you know you cost us a loss, you *voyou!*" There was no answer, not even a scuttling sound that might have told him that Julian was trying to hide. He left, slamming the door.

However, when Madame Léon, whom he happened to encounter in the lane, mentioned that Julian had not been by for his weekly dozen eggs, Paul began to wonder. Back at Chez Nous, he rang Mara, only to get her *répondeur.*

"That'll be it," he told Mado. "The two of them have done a bolt. Probably having it away in Spain."

•

"You two have created quite a problem for me." De Sauvignac stood alone in the center of the garret, cradling his shotgun over his arm. He had dismissed his wife. Vrac, after trussing Julian up by the simple expedient of slipping a noose over his head, jerking it tight, and winding the long end around his ankles and the remaining length around his wrists, had also gone.

"You've done that for yourself," said Mara. She turned a pale face to Julian. "He attacked my sister and left her brain-damaged. He and Jeanne kept Bedie in this garret for fourteen years. They claim they found her dead one morning, but I think they simply finished her off when she became too inconvenient to explain."

"That explains the skeleton I found," said Julian. At Mara's startled exclamation, he went on to describe his gruesome discovery in the *edze.* He turned back to their captor. "That's where you dumped her body, isn't it. In the *edze.* Is that what you plan to do with us?"

Henri inclined his head slightly. "That of course is the question. What to do with you. No doubt you would like your freedom. On the other hand, to let you go would create considerable trouble for me. You must understand that I feel compelled to protect my interests. A dilemma, don't you agree?"

He raised the gun. Mara and Julian braced themselves. Henri noted their reaction with a bitter twisting of the lips. To their astonishment, he merely broke the barrel and tucked the weapon under his arm.

"Don't worry," he assured them cynically. "It won't be anything as crude as that." Over his shoulder, he gave them a mocking smile, "You see, at heart I am not a sufficiently evil man."

He left, locking the door behind him.

•

Mara told Julian about her stakeout of Les Colombes and its consequences; her conclusions about Vrac's parentage; and her fear that Henri would be forced to dispose of them before Alain's return.

"When does he get back?" Julian asked.

"Sunday. What's today? I've lost track of time."

"Saturday. I think."

"If we could just hang on until tomorrow."

"That assumes Alain will help us. Henri is his father, after all."

"I don't think he'd stand by and watch us be murdered," Mara countered. She added less optimistically, "Provided he knew."

"I wouldn't trust him as far as I could toss him," Julian muttered.

Julian described his encounter with Vrac and his ordeal in the *edze*. When he got to the point where Jazz had dragged him out of the pit, Mara cried, "Jazz? Here? What's happened to him?"

"La Binette took him away, I'm afraid. I'm sorry, Mara. I shouldn't have brought him. I never thought anything like this would happen."

"Poor Jazz," she moaned, and closed her eyes.

They fell silent—Julian because he was occupied trying to work his wrists free, Mara because the revelation of Henri's guilt now made her suspicions of Julian acutely embarrassing.

"Julian, I . . . I have something to confess," she said at last.

He swiveled around on the floor to peer up at her. "What's that?"

"I . . ." Where to begin? "I searched your house."

"Oh. That. I know."

"You know?"

"Well, I guessed. For Christ's sake, Mara, what the hell did you think you were playing at?"

"I wasn't playing," she began indignantly, and then stopped, sure that if she told him the full extent of her suspicions he would never speak to her again. "It's just that certain things made me think . . . Why, even the newspaper on your kitchen table . . ." She trailed off lamely.

"What newspaper?"

"The one headlining le Mur's death. You see, there was no way you could have gotten a copy of that edition if you'd really been in the woods looking for orchids at La Binette that day. It made me think you'd faked the search."

"Faked the search?" Julian was deeply offended. He propped himself up awkwardly on an elbow and said, with all the dignity he could muster from his position on the floor, "Mara, I would *never* fake an orchid search."

A moment later he said, "It was probably Madame Léon."

"Madame Léon?"

"She always wraps my eggs in newspaper."

"Oh," Mara said faintly and decided she had made enough damning admissions for the time being.

•

"That chamber pot," cried Julian with sudden inspiration.

Mara blinked at him. "What about it?"

"Break it. We'll use the shards to cut ourselves free."

It was a beautiful piece, eighteenth-century, in flawless condition, with a blue-and-green acanthus motif on a cream ground. Mara's clients would have paid good money for it. Probably use it as a planter, she thought ironically. Nevertheless, she slid off the bed and seized it between her feet, bringing it down hard on the wooden floor. It took three tries, but the pot eventually shattered into several pieces. She chose the one with the best cutting edge and scooted across to Julian. Positioning herself back to back with him, she sawed away at the rope binding his wrists. It was slow work, but once his hands were loose, Julian was able to free himself and Mara in minutes.

Their next concern was a means of escape.

"It's too bad the post won't come around again until Monday," Mara said, rubbing feeling back into her arms. "That dormer looks out on the back of the house. If there's mail, the van will drive right into the rear courtyard. We could smash the window and yell down. Except we probably won't be alive by then."

Julian rose rather shakily to his feet and looked around him. "What are the odds of breaking through that door?"

"Not good. It's as thick as a brick and fitted out with a dead bolt."

"Well, then, Jeanne. Do you think we can persuade her to help us?"

Mara shook her head. "I've tried. Although she acts as nutty as a fruit bar, she's been covering for Henri all these years. And, Julian, I found out it was she who met my sister in the woods."

"Jeanne?" Julian broke off his inspection of the garret to turn back to her. "What are you saying? You don't think *she* hit your sister?"

"I don't know. I really can't make her out." Mara paused, troubled. After a moment, she said, "There's only one possibility. Until Henri decides how to dispose of us, she'll probably keep on bringing us food. That might be our chance. We could jump her as soon as she comes in with her tray."

"Speaking of food," Julian murmured, "I could do with some." When was the last time he had eaten? Two days ago? "Does she come alone?"

"So far. Although I have a feeling he's never far away. With his gun."

•

Henri stood on the top step of the scullery stoop, surveying the empty courtyard of the château. Above him rose the bulk of Les Colombes, where generations of de Sauvignacs had come into the world, lived, and died. Clouds scudded across a darkening afternoon sky. There would be no sunset. A storm was building up, the song of its approach strong on the wind.

A moment later, Jeanne joined him on the stoop. The wind whipped her shawls about her so that it seemed she would really fly away.

"Henri?"

"Yes, my dear?"

"I've nothing for the soup." Her voice was thin and plaintive.

Her husband turned his gaze from the panorama of the valley, where trees huddled like beasts in anticipation of rain. "Not to worry, my dear. I think we can forgo our supper tonight." He gave his wife a bleak smile, took her elbow and turned her gently into the house. "Go back in now, Jeanne. I have some things to take care of."

Alone again, he descended the stoop steps, crossed the courtyard, and stood looking down the lane. The wind brought with it a dusty smell. He felt rather than heard the muffled thunder bulging in the air. Eventually, Vrac materialized from the trees.

"Ah. Vrac, m'boy." Henri paused. He was a long time gazing

at his bastard son, as if seeking to relate the clumsy body, the heavy, swollen features to himself. Vrac bore the inspection impassively, hands dangling loosely at his sides, mouth slack. Pale stubble, like stalks on a winter field, sprouted from his large, misshapen jaw. In the fading light his expression was unreadable.

"Give your mother a message, will you?" Henri said. "Tell her there are things I need her to do for me."

•

Their plan was simple: wait for Henri or Jeanne to return and make the most of what would probably be their only opportunity to fight their way to freedom.

Mara said, "If we stand on either side of the door, we can be ready to tackle whoever comes through it. If it's Jeanne, and if she's alone, the important thing is to prevent her from warning her husband. We'll have to knock her out or something. And we'll have to be quick about it. There can't be any struggling or crying out. He'll have to think she's feeding us as normal."

Julian assumed it was up to him to do the knocking out. He was not sure he was equal to it. For one thing, he was weak from lack of food. For another, the only weapon he had was the chamber-pot shard, and he couldn't see any way of silencing Jeanne apart from slitting her throat. The last thing he wanted to do was kill the woman. She was the only real lead he had to the mystery *Cypripedium*.

"If he comes in with her," Mara went on, "you tackle him, I'll deal with her. If we can get his gun away from him, everything should be easy."

"Unless, of course, the pair from hell are hanging around at the bottom of the stairs."

Mara stirred fretfully. "I can't think what's keeping her. So far she's been coming up every three or four hours to check up on me. I don't like it. Something's happened."

Rain began to patter softly on the roof, growing heavier until it drummed overhead in a steady tattoo. Night fell. Jeanne de Sauvignac did not come.

By Mara's watch, it was approaching ten. They sat in darkness in order not to alert their captors. The rain had slowed to a steady drizzle. Still Jeanne de Sauvignac did not come. This made them almost more uneasy than the thought of the husband bursting in on them suddenly and blowing them to pieces with his shotgun.

"You don't suppose they've decided to let us starve to death?" Julian speculated anxiously. Food, or the lack of it, was becoming a serious issue for him.

"He might, but I don't see her doing it. The feeding instinct is very strong with her. You should have seen her, spooning slop into me like a surrogate baby."

Julian was silent for a moment. "I wonder how long it would take."

"What?"

"Dying of starvation. I've heard of people surviving for weeks without food."

"I think it's the dehydration that gets you first," offered Mara.

A few minutes later Julian observed, "Things are awfully quiet."

"The château is solid stone throughout. You wouldn't hear a bomb go off."

"I was thinking maybe they've done a run."

Mara frowned. Then she added hopefully, "Julian, if they've really gone, all we have to do is hang on until Alain returns and shout for help."

"Don't forget, la Binette and Vrac are still around. Oh, my Christ," Julian burst out as an unpleasant thought struck him. "What if he's left them to finish us off?"

The possibility—which quickly took hold in their minds as a strong likelihood—made them both go cold. It stood to reason that Henri would employ Vrac and his mother to do his dirty work. Both realized how vain their plans were for escape. It was no longer a matter of overpowering two elderly people, one armed with a shotgun. At the appointed time, la Binette and Vrac would mount the stairs. The door would open. Against those two, they had no chance.

Forgetting caution, Julian turned on the light and, using a piece of the chamber pot, began to dig frantically at the wood around the lock fitting in the door. After a long time, he saw that he had managed to gouge out only a small trough along the edge of the metal plate. The wood, seasoned oak, was extremely hard. At the rate he was going, the job would take him days.

They sat on the floor, one on either side of the door, anticipating their fate. They both expected it to happen sometime that night. Now Julian knew the heightened awareness achieved by people awaiting execution. Every sensation was magnified tenfold, the pumping of his heart as loud as thunder. He imagined that Vrac could break his neck with a single, effective blow.

While Mara slept, Julian forced himself to stay awake. He preferred to meet death ready rather than have it take him unawares. At last, he, too, slipped into unconsciousness. He dreamed that he was standing on a windy ridge. The *Cypripedium*, enormous and grotesque, rose beckoningly before him. As he reached his hand out to it, he saw that the plant was broken just below the flower head. A poisonous blue exudate dripped from the damaged stem.

21

"Julian."

"Hmm?"

"Wake up." Mara was kneeling by his side, shaking him. He opened his eyes. She looked pale and frightened. A somber morning light slanted into the garret.

"Something's happening."

Lightheaded and disoriented, he struggled to sit up. His entire body hurt.

"What?"

"I don't know. But I can sense it."

She was right. Something had occurred or was about to occur. The atmosphere, the very stillness of the place, held a kind of dreadful expectancy, of breathless waiting, as if past events had collected there and were waiting for their final resolution. He rose unsteadily to his feet.

Then he heard it. A sound at the bottom of the stairs. Two sets of heavy footfalls, their cadence unhurried, fateful as the knell of doom. This was it. The unholy pair were coming to finish off what Henri de Sauvignac had started. Heart pounding, Julian gestured Mara to the other side of the door. They stood, backs pressed against the wall, listening. The footsteps stopped. The key turned in the lock. The door swung open.

Julian brought la Binette down with a flying tackle that would have done his team proud. The woman crashed to the ground, but, with the agility and strength of a wrestler, slipped from his hold, overturned him, and pinned him with her full weight. He beheld the frightening spectacle of one deep-set eye glaring balefully at him out of a vivid splash of purple. At that point Mara fell on la Binette's back. The woman struck out, sending Mara crashing against the wall. Julian seized the moment to drive her off with his knees, but she grabbed him by the throat. He was on his back, crushed beneath her big, unwholesome body. He clawed at her face. She slammed his head against the floor so hard that he saw stars, punched him until blood spurted from his nose. He choked on his own blood. Someone was shouting. Another body moved across his line of sight. He managed to roll free, but the woman was on him again, slamming and punching. The walls and ceiling of the garret spun before his eyes.

"*Assez!* Enough!" bellowed Loulou, struggling to separate the two. His normally cheerful face was red, and the tail of his shirt trailed out of his trousers.

La Binette stood up and dragged Julian to his feet. He hung limply in her grip. With a grunt of disdain, she dropped him. He fell heavily to the floor.

"*Sacré,* you two are prepared to sell your lives dearly," Loulou panted. He helped Mara up and then bent over Julian. "*Ça va, mon vieux?* That was quite a welcome you provided. Didn't think you had it in you."

•

Julian attended to his bleeding nose at the kitchen sink while la Binette stood grimly by, arms folded, watching his every move.

"I'm not going to pinch the silver, if that's what you think," Julian snapped.

La Binette thrust her jaw out, but Loulou stepped in quickly to prevent another eruption of violence. "*Doucement.* Madame is only carrying out instructions."

"What, to break my head?"

"You did go for her first," interceded Mara, who seemed to have a better grasp of the state of things than he.

"Wait a minute," Julian objected. "I thought that was the idea. And what the hell are you doing here?" he demanded of the ex-*flic*.

"Ah," said Loulou, looking pleased with himself. "I was sent to collect you."

"Collect—!" Julian stopped trying to staunch his bleeding nose and stared warily about him.

"That's right, *connard*," snarled la Binette, hurling two sets of bright, metallic objects at them. They fell noisily to the stone floor. Their car keys. "Your dog's outside. Now get lost."

"It's all right," said Mara. "We're free. We can go."

"Exactly," crowed Loulou. "My friends, Henri de Sauvignac is in custody at Périgueux Police Headquarters right now. He has confessed."

•

For the third time in as many months, Mara was in the *commissaire's* office, sitting on a hard chair, watching Boutot roll a pencil between his palms. As before, Loulou strolled about the room. Julian was elsewhere, being interviewed by Boutot's second-in-command.

"You're saying he simply turned himself in?" Mara was incredulous.

The *commissaire* nodded gravely. His mustache drooped. The pouches under his eyes were blue. He looked as if he hadn't slept the night before. "He had no choice. You had learned the truth about your sister, his son was about to return, and Monsieur Wood had found a skeleton on his estate."

"Just walked in and handed across a written statement," declared Loulou from his position behind her at the bookshelves.

"However," continued Boutot, "he claims it was an accident."

"He's lying!" Mara cried.

"According to him, nineteen years ago, your sister found herself in the forest adjacent to Les Colombes—"

"Courtesy of la Binette's taxi," snickered Loulou, coming into view.

Mara was uncomprehending. "La Binette's taxi?"

"That's right," Loulou grinned. "De Sauvignac said Bedie had been hitchhiking and the Rocher woman had given her a ride. However, reading between the lines, this ties in with complaints we've received over the years about a pair resembling Madame Rocher and her son who like to pick up hitchhikers, drive them to inconvenient places, demand a fee, and leave them to find their way back."

"In any case," resumed Boutot wearily, "Mademoiselle Beatrice was in the forest, and that is where she met Madame de Sauvignac. We assume your sister's interest in orchids was strong enough to offset any inconvenience she had suffered at the hands of the Rochers. Madame, who is herself a serious amateur, recognized a fellow enthusiast. She directed your sister onto the estate, telling her about an orchid walk, created by Madame and her late father-in-law, that runs along their land." The *commissaire* put down his pencil. "I'm given to understand that it was old Monsieur de Sauvignac's ambition to plant Les Colombes with every wild orchid native not only to the Dordogne but to all of Europe."

"I see," murmured Mara, a piece of the puzzle slipping into place.

"Henri de Sauvignac happened to be out hunting that day. He says he ran into Mademoiselle Beatrice, fell into conversation with her, made a pass, and she resisted."

"Always looking for a bit of *frou-frou*," elaborated Loulou. "A real skirt-chaser in his day."

"Quite," the *commissaire* murmured dryly. "He says there was a struggle, she stumbled, fell backward, struck her head on a stone—"

"No," Mara cut in hotly. "I think it was an intentional, brutal assault."

"Hmm. De Sauvignac's version might be difficult to disprove after so much time."

"Not if you have a body," said Mara. "Don't forget Julian's skeleton."

"She's right," Loulou contributed. "Forensics can check the skull for injuries consistent with a fall as opposed to, say, a crushing blow to the head."

"Possibly," Boutot conceded. "At any rate, Henri claims he was horrified at what had happened. He says he brought your sister to the château."

"Why didn't he call a doctor?" demanded Mara.

Boutot nodded. "Indeed. This is where the man accepts full blame. He admits he made no attempt to get your sister medical attention. First, because he didn't realize at the time how badly she was injured. Second, because she was a foreigner and he was afraid that it would not be so easy to buy her family off, as apparently he was accustomed to doing whenever his sexual excesses caused a local scandal. He hoped instead that he and his wife could nurse Mademoiselle Beatrice back to health themselves."

"But fourteen years!" Mara cried. "And his son? Where does—where was Alain when all of this was going on?"

"In Abidjan. Working on a water-containment project. That, of course, can be checked. Alain knew nothing of your sister's injury or incarceration. In fact, Monsieur de Sauvignac said that he had to forbid him access to the château, except for brief visits home, while your sister was alive, for fear that he would discover her presence."

Mara let her breath out softly.

"Even now Monsieur Alain has no idea of what has transpired." Commissaire Boutot referred to a note on his desk. "He's returning from Paris this evening. Two of my men will meet his train. He'll be informed, and we'll need to take a statement from him as well. His mother, unfortunately, is in a state of collapse and can't be questioned. The Rocher woman is caring for her."

Mara shook her head. "Jeanne de Sauvignac is tougher than she looks, believe me. And Julian?" She thought tardily of the man she had so recently denounced. "I take it Henri's confession clears Julian?"

"Ah," said the *commissaire*. Something in his voice caused Mara to sit up.

"That one's not so simple," pronounced Loulou, pulling up a chair and plumping his fat bottom onto it. His expression was bland, but his complexion had gone pink with suppressed excitement. "De Sauvignac's confession clears Julian of involvement with Mademoiselle Beatrice, certainly. But there's still the little matter of Julie Ménard."

"But surely Henri—"

Loulou wagged a finger back and forth. "Nothing sure about it. De Sauvignac claims to have no knowledge of any of the other missing women. And we have no evidence linking him to them."

"What have you said to Monsieur Wood about your suspicions?" asked Boutot.

"Well, very little," replied Mara uncomfortably. "I mean, it's not the kind of thing one wants to talk about."

"Just as well," chuckled Loulou. "Because there's more. Tell her, Antoine."

Boutot sighed and blinked lugubriously at Mara. "One of my men just took a statement from a neighbor of the late Madame Charlebois. It seems that this person remembers a gardener who used to work for the old woman. She thinks it might have been around the time Mariette disappeared, and she had the impression that he only came a few times and then stopped. Described him as a foreign chap, English, she thought. Her description of this man fits Monsieur Wood almost exactly."

"Julian?" Mara murmured, all her old doubts reviving.

"But the final straw"—Loulou jumped up, no longer able to contain himself—"is that another woman's gone missing!"

Mara gaped at him.

"Arlette Cousty," Boutot informed her. "Legal secretary, forty-five years old, married, no children, resident of Toulouse. Her husband reported her missing last week. She hasn't been seen or heard of since. Her car was gone, some of her clothes as well. The husband admits to their having marital difficulties but believes that even if she had left him something must have happened to her subsequently because she would not have failed to contact him. She was a very responsible type, you see."

Mara shook her head. "But Toulouse is in the south. It's a hundred and fifty kilometers away. How can this tie in?"

"Hear me out. The interesting thing is that Madame Cousty's credit card was used to purchase gas on the evening of the day she went missing. Can you guess, Mara, where this purchase was made?"

Beynac, Carennac, Souillac, La Bique. The place names came back to Mara.

"Somewhere along the D703 or D25?" she hazarded.

"Exactly. At a station just outside of Beaumont. Shortly after seven on the evening in question, somebody purchased thirty-seven liters of gas at a Total station. Unfortunately, the cashier was one of these young cretins with earphones plugged into his head. Couldn't recognize his own nose, let alone identify a photograph of Madame Cousty as the bearer of the card. Nevertheless, you see what this signifies, don't you? Beaumont puts Arlette Cousty's last known location right within our zone of interest!"

Mara stared first at one man and then the other. "What's being done about it?" she asked at last.

Boutot fingered his pencil. "It's being treated it as a case of domiciliary abandonment. So far."

"Ha!" barked Loulou. "But you realize what all this means for Julian? He already has some explaining to do regarding Julie Ménard. Now, supposing he's identified as the man who worked for Madame Charlebois, *and* if he just happened to be cruising the area around Beaumont on the night in question, I'd say *he's still very much in the frame!*"

22

Mara wrote to Patsy.

> They've made a positive identification of the skeleton based on old dental records. So that lays Bedie to rest. Although I'd always hoped somehow to find her alive, at least this gives me closure, me and everyone who loved her—Mum, Dad, and especially Scott, who's suffered as much as any of us from all these years of not knowing. Henri's sticking to his story that it was an accident, but I don't believe him. He insists that Bedie's eventual death was "natural." Since there seems to be no evidence to the contrary, I guess I can at least be grateful that Henri and Jeanne let Bedie die in her own time.

The police have reopened investigations on Julie Ménard and Mariette Charlebois, and they're checking into the latest woman to go missing, Arlette Cousty. So far, they haven't questioned Julian directly. Loulou says they're purposely playing their fish until—tac!—they have enough evidence to pull him in. Meantime, Commissaire Boutot has asked me to stay clear of Julian and take basic precautions, although I think he's less concerned about my safety than worried that I'll give something away. At any rate, it hasn't occurred to him to offer me any armed protection. For the rest, I'm just getting on with my work and trying to put Bedie behind me . . . <

Mara glanced out the window at trees, a blue sky, and sunshine. There seemed nothing more to say. She signed off, got up, and wandered restlessly about her studio. The unfinished plans for a kitchen renovation (another of Prudence's referrals) lay on her workbench. In a corner stood a recently acquired nineteenth-century cheval glass mounted in a beautifully carved walnut frame. She had bought it quite reasonably from a *brocante* in Monpazier with another client in mind. Now she wasn't sure she wanted to part with it. She stood before it, staring at her slightly tarnished reflection. Her eyes met those in the mirror. My face, she thought sadly. Bedie's face. Hesitantly, she reached out to trace the contours of her image with a fingertip that met only the flat, cold hardness of glass.

My god! she whispered as the realization hit her.

Rushing back to the computer, she logged on again.

> *Patsy, I've just thought of something. It's a minor detail, but if it means what I think it means, it could turn everything upside down . . .* <

A shadow fell into the room.

"Hello." Julian stood in the open doorway.

"Oh," said Mara and sat very still.

Jazz, who had been snoring on the floor, gave a grunt, heaved himself up, and ambled over to greet their visitor. Julian scratched the dog's ear. He did not come farther into the studio but spoke from where he stood.

"We have unfinished business, Mara."

"What—what do you mean?" She snapped her fingers for Jazz to return to her side. The dog ignored her.

"The *Cypripedium.*" Julian seemed exasperated at having to spell it out. "I mean, you've got what you—that is . . ." He trailed off awkwardly.

"I've found my sister but you still haven't found your orchid. Is that what you're trying to say?"

"Well, I wouldn't have put it quite like that. But we did have a deal."

"So?"

He looked a little surprised at her ungraciousness. "Look, I'm not asking you to hike the forest with me. Unless, of course, you want to. But I need your help."

"How do you mean?"

"Jeanne de Sauvignac and her late father-in-law tried to establish a plantation of *Cypripedium calceolus* at Les Colombes. I think the mystery Lady's Slipper was a mutant of this attempt. There's a slim chance that it continued to propagate. I have to find this plantation. Jeanne is the only person who can tell me where it is. I understand she's pretty incoherent right now, but time is running out fast. I mean, the flowering season, and without a flower, I haven't a prayer of proving my theory. I thought if you could ask Alain to get some sense of the location from his mother, even generally, it would narrow down my search tremendously. I happen to know that Géraud is also on the hunt, and I'm damned if I'm going to let that *voyou* beat me out again."

She nodded. Julian had told her of Géraud's scoop at the Société Jeannette meeting.

"All right," she said. "I think I can do that for you."

•

"Of course you realize it's risky?" Loulou warned when Mara called him later.

"I do, but I think it's the only way. Certainly you can see how what I've just told you puts things in a different light? It could be one of them, or both."

"Hmm," said the ex-cop. "I'll talk with Boutot. He might just agree that your idea has some interesting possibilities."

"Are you sure?" Julian adjusted his glasses and scratched his head.

They stood in the forecourt of Les Colombes, peering at a hand-drawn map held by Alain. It was the second time Julian had spoken with the son, and he liked him no better, even though the man had obviously gone to some trouble to get the information Julian needed.

"It's the best Maman could do, I'm afraid," said Alain. "She's in a state of shock, and her memory never was very good at the best of times. I could ask her again, if you think it would help."

Julian considered this.

Mara, dressed in a baggy sweatshirt despite the warm day, said, "We may as well check the spot out first. If we don't turn up anything, maybe you could talk to her again, Alain."

He nodded. "Yes. That would be better. She's still in a pretty bad way at the moment. I hadn't realized how dependent she's become on my father over the years. She's frantic with anxiety. Binette and I had to restrain her physically from trying to go to Papa last evening. Speaking of which, I'd better return to the house. We're sitting with her in turns, and Binette needs to get back to her cheesemaking."

He left them.

"It doesn't make sense," Julian grumbled as they walked down the road leading away from the château.

"Why not?" asked Mara. This time she had left Jazz at home.

"Well," he scowled at the map. "This puts it in low, wet land, under pine-forest cover. If I'm not mistaken, there's a lot of bracken, which suggests acid soil, and"—he struggled to recall his first meeting with Henri de Sauvignac—"a big pond nearby. Lady's Slippers like semi-shade and drier, alkaline soil." Julian directed them onto a path snaking down in the direction of the valley he had crossed the day he fell into the *edze*. "If Jeanne and her father-in-law knew anything about orchids, and we have to assume they did, they'd never have tried to establish the rootstock there."

"Watch where you're going," warned Mara, scrambling after him down the steep slope. "You don't want to fall into another pit."

They descended to the valley floor. It was hot and windless there. The woods at noon were very quiet.

"This should be the spot," said Julian after another twenty minutes or so. Deciduous trees had given way to conifers and ferns. "Really," he muttered after a few minutes of pacing the ground, "this is damned odd. You don't suppose she'd purposely try to mislead us, do you?"

"Why would she do that?"

"Because, from the sound of it, she's round the twist." He stopped and turned back to Mara. "Or because there's something she doesn't want us to find. Quite honestly, I don't know about you, but I never really bought Henri de Sauvignac's confession." He shook his head. "It's too convenient, somehow. Almost as if—as if he were protecting someone."

Mara looked up sharply. "What do you mean?"

"Well, you said it was Jeanne who met your sister in the woods. I asked you before if you thought it could have been her and not Henri who attacked Bedie. She sounds crazy enough to have done it, you know. What if she has a sick need to find substitutes for her dead child? Or maybe she's driven to punish young women because of the maid who let her little boy drown."

It was a troubling hypothesis that called forth some of Mara's own doubts about Jeanne de Sauvignac. She remembered the woman's surprising strength, and the thought crossed her mind once again that behind Jeanne's goggling appearance there was a purposeful intelligence, albeit functioning fitfully, like a faulty switch.

"Are you saying she's setting us up for something?"

"Who knows," muttered Julian. He resumed his pacing. "Anyway, I don't see anything here that faintly resembles an orchid. Dammit, the habitat's all wrong. Still, I suppose we ought to make a thorough search." He sought a landmark and selected a tall pine tree standing in a small clearing. "We'll take this as our point of reference. You remember how we squared off the ground when we were looking for the *Neottia*? Well, this time we'll do it a little differently, and we'll have to cut it finer. We're no longer looking for an extensive colony of plants but possibly a single plant. You know what it looks like—dark-pink slipper, two long, spiraled petals springing out from the sides, blackish-purple sepals, fifty to sixty centimeters high. In case it's past its flowering, keep your eye out for anything with three to five broad oval leaves, deeply veined, coming out of a single stem."

He indicated two imaginary lines extending due east and west of the pine. "These will be our guide lines. We'll start out back to back at the tree. I'll go north twenty paces, you go south the same amount. Be sure to look to either side of you as you go. When you've done your twenty, go five to your right, then right again, and return twenty paces, which should bring you back to the pine but in your case five paces farther west along your guide line. I'll be five paces farther east. Then we repeat the procedure, each time ending up five paces farther away from the pine. After four repetitions, we'll have each walked a twenty-by-twenty square. If we haven't found anything, we'll meet back at the pine, set the guide lines running north and south, and pace to east and west. At the end, together we'll have walked a forty-by-forty square. It's slow going, but it's the only way to handle the search in such heavily overgrown terrain. Are you with me?"

Mara said she was.

"Good," said Julian. "And—er—Mara, if anything happens, remember I'll never be very far away."

She glanced uneasily at him. "What can happen?"

"Oh, if you should get lost or something," he said casually.

Yes, she thought. *Or something.*

They set off.

After two turns, Mara lost sight and sound of Julian entirely. She went carefully, poking at the undergrowth with a stick and stopping from time to time to listen to the forest. The profound silence made her nervous. After her fourth turn, she followed her line back to the pine tree. Julian was waiting for her.

"No luck?" she asked.

He shook his head. "A nice crop of cèpes, but I'm not very interested in mushrooms at the moment."

They reset the guide lines along a north-south axis and resumed their pacing, Julian going west and Mara east. Her way was frequently barred by tangled undergrowth that she had to beat aside with her stick. At one point, through the trees she saw the glint of water. The pond Julian had mentioned. She completed her square without seeing anything of interest and again followed her line back to the tree. This time Julian was not there. She sat down on a log to wait. Time passed, but he still did not appear. She, who had been on the alert for something to happen at any moment, was frankly puzzled. Had he found something, or was he at that very moment moving up silently behind her? The thought made her glance uneasily over her shoulder. A cuckoo called. It was the first birdsong she had heard since they had been in the forest.

"Hello, Mara."

The voice behind her made her jump.

"Oh," she said, turning, a lead weight sitting on her heart. "It's you. I was wondering if you'd show up."

"Could you doubt it?"

"I suppose you've decided to join the hunt?"

"I've been looking forward to it."

"Who's with your mother, then?"

Alain smiled. "Drugged to the eyeballs. I doubt she'll know I've gone. Have you found your orchid?"

"I haven't. I don't know about Julian. We've been pacing off the area in opposite directions. He should be meeting me back here any minute."

Alain shook his head. "He won't be coming."

Mara frowned. "What do you mean?"

"I mean he's *hors de combat*. Out cold."

Mara stood up, giving a nervous tug at her sweatshirt.

"In any case," Alain assured her, "for what we are about to do, we don't need him."

Mara felt herself go clammy. "What are we about to do, Alain?" she asked quietly.

"I think you know," he said, moving close enough so that she could see a flicker of excitement burning in his dark-blue eyes. He was breathing hard. "*Cache-cache*. You run, I chase. You see, I'm giving you a fair chance."

"Like the game you used to play with Vrac? You're not a child anymore, Alain."

He smiled. "I know. I've learned to reverse the roles."

"Is that"—Mara stepped back—"how it happened with my sister? She ran, and you hunted her down like an animal?"

"Does it surprise you?"

Mara took a deep breath. "No. I knew it had to be one of you. I admit, you did everything to make me believe it was Julian. Very plausible. But you made one small mistake."

"Oh?"

"You said that Julian would have been shaken to see me because I was the spitting image of a woman he'd killed."

"And what was wrong with that?"

"I told you Bedie and I were twins, Alain. *But I never showed you her photograph and I never said we were identical.* Unfortunately, I didn't get the significance of this until just the other day, and even then I couldn't be sure if it was just an assumption on your part, or if it meant only that you'd seen my sister in the garret, or if it was really you and not your father who had met her in the forest."

He laughed harshly. "And do you have your answer?"

"Yes," said Mara, watching him closely. "I think I do. There's one thing I don't understand, though. Why didn't you finish Bedie off at the time? In some ways it would have been better for her if you had."

Alain shrugged. "Vrac caught me at it. The stupid fool took her back to the château, slung over his shoulder like a gutted sheep. You can imagine the state Papa was in."

"But he did nothing?"

"How could he? There was the precious family name to protect and Maman to deal with. She'd already lost one son, you know, because of him. If he hadn't been rolling that fat slut of a nursemaid in the grass, we wouldn't have played the game that day. Patrice wouldn't have gone down to the pond. He was always very good at hiding, you see, and he thought he could fool me by crouching in the reeds. But he didn't think about his footprints in the mud. After all, he was only seven. I was ten. All I had to do was track him down."

Mara stared at him speechlessly. At last she asked in a faint voice, "How exactly did your brother drown, Alain?"

He looked at her inquiringly. "Patrice?" His gaze shifted momentarily. "The rules of the game. And the water in that pond is very deep. But we were talking about your sister. I told Papa I'd swear it was Vrac who had attacked her. If she died—and at the time I didn't think she'd last out the hour—it would have been the word of an idiot against mine. They didn't have the means of DNA testing in those days. No one would have believed him over me. That stopped Papa cold."

"Of course," agreed Mara acidly. "Vrac is also your father's son."

"His by-blow!" Alain sneered. "In the end, Papa and I struck a deal. I stayed away, paid their upkeep, and he kept silent. Voilà, all nicely arranged and the family name untarnished."

"Except that you were free to go on murdering women," Mara cried. "Because I'm sure that's what happened. In Africa and here. Women went missing every time you returned on home leave, didn't they? The periodic cycle. Surely your father saw the connection. And yet he protected you—goes on protecting you."

"Of course. I am the last of the de Sauvignacs. Besides, what proof had he? Women go missing all the time. I don't have a monopoly on evil."

"On the contrary. You are a monster. You know, when I was in that garret, I thought the deadbolt lock was put on the door to keep my sister in. But I'm not so sure now. She was a vegetable. She couldn't have escaped. I'll bet it was there to keep you *out*."

"You're very good at this," said Alain, a note of mocking admiration in his voice. "But enough teasers. We must move on to the principal course, which is where the main enjoyment is to be had. Shall I give you a minute's head start? Don't worry. I won't rape you. One has to be careful about evidence nowadays. Or perhaps two minutes? You'll have to run for your life. Literally. I know these woods like the back of my hand."

Mara held her ground. "I'm not running, Alain." She turned

away. With a sudden movement, she whirled around, clutching her stick with both hands and using the momentum of her body to smash it with all her strength across his face. He reeled from the blow. Then she ran, screaming.

He was on her in seconds, throwing her to the ground, was now on top of her, gripping her wrists, while she fought against him with all her strength. When he felt the hardness below her breasts, he yanked her sweatshirt up, revealing a small tape recorder strapped to her torso and a tracking device clipped to her belt. He hesitated, taking in the significance of these things, just long enough for her to drive her knee up as hard as she could into his groin. With a roar of pain he rolled off.

"Putain!" he howled. "Filthy whore!"

She scrambled up, but he seized her leg. She fought him, kicking, clawing, screaming, as he dragged her to him. His hands were on her throat, squeezing. She felt her eyes bulge, thought her brain would burst. Her tongue was thrusting from her mouth when Alain released her abruptly. She was now in danger of being trampled under the heavy feet of two desperately struggling men. Her vision cleared in time to see Julian land Alain a mighty clout in the face that sent a pinwheel spray of scarlet spinning through the air.

Then the area was all at once busy with running uniforms as gendarmes surged out of the trees. Commissaire Boutot appeared from a different direction. Two agents fought Alain to the ground and handcuffed him. Last but not least, Loulou came trotting up, puffing with exertion.

"What took you so bloody long?" Mara tried to yell at them, but the best she could manage was a broken croak.

23

June came on the Dordogne, with sunshine and tourists. The spring flowers had finished, except for a remnant poppy here and there, showing scarlet among the young wheat. Many of the orchids had reached the end of their blooming, but roses and honeysuckle garlanded every wall.

They were gathered at Chez Nous, eleven end to end. Mado and Paul had pushed the tables together to form a banqueting board running the length of the bistro. The windows stood open to catch the cool night breeze. Julian, with bruised face and a splinted ankle—he had sprained it badly in his struggle with Alain—and Mara, her neck in a brace, sat at one end; Loulou and Gaston at the other. In between were Prudence, Gaston's wife, Géraud, and Iris. Julian had included Géraud only because of Iris, who had given him his lead on the mystery *Cypripedium*.

Next to Mara lounged a large, long-legged body in a green pants suit—Patsy Reicher, arrived the day before from Manhattan. Her broad face with its topping of iodine hair turned from side to side as she followed the story told piecemeal by everyone. Places were set for Paul and Mado, but they occupied them only in between sallies to the kitchen. They were assisted by Bernard Léon, Julian's erstwhile bulldozer, who performed the tasks of underwaiter with surprising aptitude. Jazz moved down the company, thrusting his head hopefully into everyone's lap.

At this point in the meal they were eating scallops in cream sauce, accompanied by a chilled dry Bergerac.

"You see," Loulou addressed the gathering at large as he waved a forkful of scallop, its bright-orange comma of roe attached, in the air, "Henri de Sauvignac was not just protecting the family name. He was trying to make up to his wife for the loss of one son by salvaging the other."

"Guilt and atonement," murmured Patsy, ignoring her food.

Mara said, "The irony of it is that I think Alain killed his own brother. I think he hunted him down at the pond and pushed him in. Or held his face underwater."

"*Mon dieu,*" shuddered Gaston's wife.

"They've moved Jeanne to hospital, you know," Iris said. "They say the poor woman may never recover."

Loulou wagged his head. "Nevertheless, both she and her husband will be charged as accessories after the fact, although in her case there will probably be a plea of reduced responsibility. The evidence Mara got on tape makes a strong case against Alain, despite his story that it was a casual sexual fling that went wrong."

"Lying bastard," muttered Mara to no one in particular. "I can't believe I trusted him."

"But it wasn't just Mara's sister," Mado called from her end of the table. She was slightly flushed with all the rushing back and forth from the kitchen, which perhaps accounted for the inner glow that lit her face. "What about those other women?"

Loulou raised a hand. "Denies any involvement with them. However, the lads have established that Alain was in France at the time of Hanneke Tenhagen's murder. And Valérie Rules and Mariette Charlebois's disappearances both coincided with later visits home. By the way, they plan to drag the pond in the forest. Who knows what they'll find?"

"*Mon dieu,*" repeated Gaston's wife, clutching her throat.

"And while we're on the subject, reports are coming in from

Abidjan, Dakar, Yaoundé, and Douala. Seems there's quite a trail of missing and dead women everywhere our Monsieur Alain was known to have worked."

"I had a mass murderer at my party," murmured Prudence wonderingly. "How can someone so sick look so good? I mean, he was a damned sexy man. *Incroyable!*"

"Serial killers are often extremely persuasive and charming," said Patsy. "It's a skill they develop to get close to their victims."

Mara touched her neck brace and shifted unhappily in her chair.

"Well, I still think Julian owes us an explanation about that Ménard woman," roared Géraud. "What's this about you trying to hide the fact that you'd worked for her, eh?"

"I didn't," Julian said hotly. "Try to hide anything, I mean. I never met her. It was her husband who hired me, he paid cash, and I only ever knew him as Jackie. How was I supposed to connect?"

"There. You see?" said Iris, jabbing her paramour in the side with her elbow.

"Hmph," grunted Géraud, unconvinced. "And la Charlebois?"

"The neighbor had it wrong," Loulou declared, mopping up sauce with a bit of bread. "Turns out the fellow in question was Portuguese and not a gardener at all but a man come to fix the fence. As for Julie Ménard, the lads are also digging up Monsieur Jackie's rock garden in Souillac."

"At my suggestion," Mara murmured dryly.

"Bloody hell," Julian exclaimed, more upset by Loulou's news than he was at Géraud's insinuations. "I built that rockery. In the days before Bernard." He jabbed his chin in the direction of the underwaiter, who had stopped in his tracks sometime ago, mouth agape. "Are you telling me they think she's buried under it?

Damned shame. I planted some unusual varieties of dwarf rhododendron in that rock garden, as I recall."

"Maybe you ought to rethink the rockery Julian's putting in for you," Paul addressed Prudence with a malicious glint in his eye. "All those trenches."

"I get these headaches," Julian confided to Patsy, shifting topics. "Thumpers. When I'm tired or stressed. Now, the funny thing is, while I was in that *edze* and then in the garret, I was fine. I mean, my head was. In fact, I haven't had a headache since."

"You were concentrating on more important things," Patsy said, amused. "Like survival."

"What happened to the woman, Arlette Cousty?" Mado asked, rising to clear the course and giving Bernard a sharp shove in the direction of the kitchen.

"Ah," said Loulou. "That one. She turned up. Yes indeed. She turned up. Apparently ran off with her lover, but couldn't bring herself to tell her husband about it because, *tenez*, the lover is a woman. She thought he wouldn't be able to handle it. Turns out he's been having a same-sex relationship on the side himself. Both are greatly and mutually consoled."

Paul, getting up as well, called over his shoulder, "So nothing happened to her?"

"Nothing apart from running out of gas," affirmed Loulou. "She said a kind monsieur stopped and gave her a couple of liters, just enough to get her to a station outside Beaumont."

"Oh." Julian looked startled and choked on his wine. "That was Arlette Cousty?"

"Mais oui," said Loulou, glancing at him curiously.

"Did I tell you the police are also looking more closely at my accident?" Gaston announced. "They found a log near where I had my accident that had bits of glass and plastic embedded in it that match the parts broken off my van. The suspicious thing is that it was piled back in with a stack of cut wood at the side of the road. They've had a conversation with Vrac about it, but he put on his idiot act, so they couldn't get much out of him, and all la Binette would say was, *Allez-vous en foutre.*"

"Speaking of them," Loulou broke in, "you might be interested to know that a German hitchhiker made a complaint a month or so back about a pair answering the description of la Binette and Vrac. Said they picked him up and tried to extort money from him."

"Something needs to be done," said Gaston's wife angrily. "That pair are a menace to society. My husband could have been killed."

"For Alain it was the thrill of the chase as much as bludgeoning his victims to death," Mara was telling people at her end of the table. "A sick perversion of a childhood game."

"Hoo boy," marveled Patsy. "This one should make psychoanalytical annals."

"And he would have hunted you down and left Julian to take the blame?" cried Mado, back from the kitchen. *"Quel salaud!"*

Mara went on, "It was simple for him to fake the map and then slip down to the forest to wait his chance. But Julian knew something was wrong from the start."

"Hah!" snorted Géraud.

"And if it hadn't been for Julian," Mara went on with a severe look for both Géraud and Loulou, "Alain would have killed me. So much for the lads."

"Nonsense," Loulou called down to her, "they had you covered every centimeter of the way."

"Well, they took their damned sweet time getting there."

Julian shook his head at Mara. "I can't believe you actually suspected me of doing away with your sister. And a string of other women as well!"

She blushed into her plate.

He leaned meaningfully across the table. "You owe me, Mara."

Her dark eyes flashed. "I already apologized."

Julian shook his head. "Not good enough. Jeanne de Sauvignac can't remember where they planted the rootstock. It could be anywhere." He lowered his voice. "With my ankle, I'm going to need help if I'm to beat out that *chameau*"—he jerked his head in the direction of Géraud—"for the Prix Vénus."

"Oh, now wait a minute. If it's that bloody *Cypripedium* again—"

Géraud, whose ears had caught the mention, sneered, "Figment of your imagination, *mon vieux*. It never existed."

Julian ignored him and reached for Mara's hand. "A friend in need?" His look was appealing.

Her face softened. Laugh lines reasserted themselves over the frown. "Okay," she gave in. "You're on, damn you."

"Watch out, kid," warned Patsy over the rim of her wineglass. "He'll have you speaking Latin."

"*Cypripedium?* Greek, actually," announced Julian. "From *kypris*, which relates to Aphrodite or Venus, and—er—*podion*, little foot."

"Rubbish," snapped Géraud. "It's from the Latin *pedium*, for 'shoe.' "

"Whatever," Julian sighed.

"*C'est très ironique*," Prudence remarked to the company at large. "All this interest in *pigeonniers*, and no one ever thought about Les Colombes. I mean, *colombe* means 'dove,' doesn't it, which is a kind of pigeon?"

"Ah, ça." Loulou cocked his head, impressed. *"C'est très bon, ça!"*

Mado and Paul came from the kitchen to announce the *plat principal:* tender, juicy squabs, studded with truffles and simmered in a rich wine sauce. The birds were presented in individual lidded clay casseroles. Bernard helped with the serving up. When the covers were lifted, a heady aroma wafted out, causing an ecstatic ripple of approval. There were also platters of asparagus and Julian's favorite, pan-fried Sarladaise potatoes, dressed in garlic and parsley. Paul moved swiftly from glass to glass, pouring out a fine chilled Chablis.

Julian hobbled to his feet and rapped for attention. "Friends, I think we should all toast the culinary artistry we've been privileged to experience tonight." He raised his glass. The others did the same. "I name this superb dish *Suprème de pigeonneau à la Mado.*" There was laughter and loud applause.

Paul leaned over the head of the table to give another thunderous rap. "Listen up, everyone. Important announcement. Mado's given up smoking."

"I don't believe it," cried Julian. "What brought this on?"

"Has to, doesn't she?" said Paul in a choking voice. He went the color of raw beef. "Got a bun in the oven!"

Loud cheers and general pandemonium. Everyone kissed Mado, who was immediately made to sit. Gaston's wife and Iris would have had her recumbent if she had not protested.

In the middle of all this, Bernard hissed in Julian's ear, "Old Hilaire's here. He wants to see you."

"What? Now?"

The young bulldozer grinned and gave a massive shrug. Old Hilaire pushed through the bead curtain. He looked as he always did, like a pickled walnut, and, as usual, brought with him a whiff of goat.

"I found her!" he bellowed over the noisy company. His face

was wreathed in triumph and delight. "*Ma petite* Edith. She turned up at the animal shelter in Bergerac."

More cheers. Everyone who knew Edith had great affection for her. Those who didn't shared in the general enthusiasm all the same.

The farmer went around, shaking everyone's hand. When he got to Julian, he stopped, looking self-conscious.

"Monsieur," he spoke with a kind of awkward ceremony. He fished around in one of his capacious pockets. "Voilà, monsieur. For you."

It was small, round, and fawn-colored, with a snub muzzle, bright eyes, black-tipped ears, and chubby white paws. A diminutive white blaze was just discernible on its chest. Julian received the pup, thinking that he really didn't want a dog. Edith, now that she was back, was enough for him. But the pup made small murmuring noises as he held it and nibbled his ear with painfully sharp little teeth. It was warm, and its fur smelled of straw. Jazz saw it and, with a sharp bark, came up to investigate. Carefully and gently he sniffed the tiny body.

"Oh, the darling!" cooed Mara, reaching out.

Julian handed the pup across to her. She nuzzled it.

"Nine of them." Hilaire was prouder even than Paul. "This one's the pick of the litter. With Maman Edith's compliments."

"Hilaire, I'm honored." Julian rose and shook the farmer warmly by the hand.

Jazz stood by, amiably wagging his tail.

Julian looked down at him. "Why, you old son of a bitch," he growled fondly at the dog, who cocked at him a smug and knowing eye.

MARY
HIGGINS
CLARK

I've Got You Under My Skin

Simon & Schuster

New York   London   Toronto   Sydney   New Delhi

Simon & Schuster
1230 Avenue of the Americas
New York, NY 10020

First Simon & Schuster hardcover edition April 2014

SIMON & SCHUSTER and colophon are registered trademarks of Simon & Schuster, Inc.

For information about special discounts for bulk purchases, please contact Simon & Schuster Special Sales at 1-866-506-1949 or business@simonandschuster.com.

The Simon & Schuster Speakers Bureau can bring authors to your live event. For more information or to book an event, contact the Simon & Schuster Speakers Bureau at 1-866-248-3049 or visit our website at www.simonspeakers.com.

Interior design by Jill Putorti

Manufactured in the United States of America

10 9 8 7 6 5 4 3 2 1

Library of Congress Cataloging-in-Publication Data is available.

ISBN 978-1-4767-4906-8
ISBN 978-1-4767-4910-5 (ebook)

Fic.

Acknowledgments

And so once again, the tale has been told. Last night, I wrote the last words and then slept for twelve hours.

This morning I woke up with the joyous understanding that all the dates with friends that I have cancelled can be reinstated.

But it is so satisfying to tell another tale, to share another journey with characters I have created and come to care deeply about—or not.

As always, for the last forty years, Michael V. Korda, my editor, has been the captain of my ship. I send him twenty or twenty-five pages at a time. His phone call "The pages are fine," is music to my ears. Let me repeat even more fervently, Michael, it's been grand working with you.

Marysue Rucci, the new editor in chief at Simon & Schuster, has been a marvelous friend and mentor. It is a joy working with her.

The home team starts with my right hand, Nadine Petry, my daughter Patty and my son Dave, Agnes Newton and Irene Clark. And of course, John Conheeney, spouse extraordinaire, and all of my family.

Abiding thanks to copy editor, Gypsy da Silva and to art director, Jackie Seow. Her covers make me look so good. Thanks as well to Elizabeth Breeden.

It is time to start to think about what comes next. But I will put that off just a little while. After all, tomorrow is another day.

For John
And our Clark and Conheeney children and grandchildren
with love

Prologue

❦

Dr. Greg Moran was pushing three-year-old Timmy on the swing in the playground on East Fifteenth Street in Manhattan, not far from the apartment.

"Two-minute warning," he laughed as he gave another push, just strong enough to satisfy his daredevil son, but not strong enough to risk having the seat flip over the top of the swing. A long time ago he had witnessed that scene. No one was hurt, because it was a child safety seat. Even so, with the long arms that went with his six-foot-three frame, Greg was always super careful when Timmy was on these swings. As an emergency room doctor, he was all too familiar with freak accidents.

It was half past six, and the evening sun was sending long shadows across the playground. Now there was even a slight chill in the air, a reminder that Labor Day was next weekend. "One-minute warning," Greg called firmly. Before bringing Timmy to the playground, Greg had been on duty for twelve hours, and the always busy emergency room had been absolutely chaotic. Two cars filled with teenagers racing each other on First Avenue had collided and crashed. Incredibly, no one had been killed, but there were three kids with very serious injuries.

Greg took his hands off the swing. It was time to let it slow down and stop. The fact that Timmy didn't attempt a futile protest meant that he must be ready to go home, too. Anyhow, they were now the last ones in the playground.

"Doctor!"

Greg turned to face a powerfully built man of average height with a scarf covering his face. The gun he was holding was aimed at Greg's head. In an instinctive movement Greg took a long step to the side to get as far away from Timmy as possible. "Look, my wallet is in my pocket," he said quietly. "You're welcome to it."

"Daddy." Timmy's tone was frightened. He had twisted in the seat and was staring into the eyes of the gunman.

In his final moment on earth, Greg Moran, age thirty-four, distinguished physician, dearly loved husband and father, tried to throw himself on his attacker but had no chance to escape the fatal shot that hit with deadly accuracy the center of his forehead.

"DADDYYYYYYYY!" Timmy wailed.

The assailant ran to the street, then stopped and turned. "Timmy, tell your mother that she's next," he shouted. "Then it's your turn."

The gunshot and the shouted threat were heard by Margy Bless, an elderly woman on her way home from her part-time job in the local bakery. She stood for long seconds absorbing the nightmarish event: the fleeing figure turning the corner, the gun dangling from his hand, the screaming child on the swing, the crumpled figure on the ground.

Her fingers trembled so badly it took three tries before she was able to punch in 911.

When the operator answered, Margy could only moan, "Hurry! Hurry! He may come back! He shot a man, then he threatened the child!"

Her voice trailed off as Timmy shrieked, "Blue Eyes shot my daddy . . . Blue Eyes shot my daddy!"

1

Laurie Moran looked out the window of her office on the twenty-fifth floor of 15 Rockefeller Center. Her view was of the skating rink in the middle of that famous Manhattan complex. It was a sunny but cold March day, and from her vantage point she could see beginners there, wobbling unsteadily on their skates, and in sharp contrast others who moved across the ice with the grace of ballet dancers.

Timmy, her eight-year-old son, loved ice hockey and planned to be good enough to play with the New York Rangers by the time he was twenty-one. Laurie smiled as her mind filled with the image of Timmy's face, his expressive brown eyes sparkling with delight as he imagined himself in the position of goalie in future Rangers games. He'll be the image of Greg by then, Laurie thought, but quickly gave herself a mental shake and turned her attention to the file on her desk.

Thirty-six years old, with shoulder-length hair the color of honey, hazel eyes more green than brown, a slim build, and classic features untouched by makeup, Laurie was the kind of woman people turned to take a second look at when she passed by. "Classy and good-looking" was a typical description of her.

An award-winning producer at Fisher Blake Studios, Laurie was about to launch a new cable series, one that she had had in mind even before Greg died. Then she had put it away—she felt people might think she had conceived it because of his unsolved murder.

The premise involved reenacting unsolved crimes, but instead of using actors, gathering the friends and relatives of the victims to hear from their lips *their* version of what had happened when the crime occurred. Whenever possible, the actual setting of the crime would be used. It was a risky venture—with great potential for success and also for chaos.

She had just come from a meeting with her boss, Brett Young, who had reminded her that she'd sworn she would never touch another reality show. "Your last two were expensive flops, Laurie," he said. "We can't afford another one." Then he pointedly added, "Neither can you."

Now as Laurie sipped the coffee she had carried in with her from the two o'clock meeting, she thought of the passionate argument she had used to persuade him. "Brett, before you remind me again how sick you are of reality series, I promise you this one will be different. We'll call it *Under Suspicion*. On page two of the folder I gave you is a long list of unsolved criminal cases and others *supposedly* solved where there is a real possibility the wrong person went to prison."

Laurie glanced around her office. The glance reinforced her determination not to lose it. It was large enough to have a couch under the windows and a long bookcase that showcased memorabilia, awards she had won, and family pictures, mostly of Timmy and her father. She had long ago decided that her pictures of Greg belonged at home in her bedroom, not here where they would inevitably bring to everyone's mind the fact that she was a widow, and her husband's murder had never been solved.

"The Lindbergh kidnapping is the first on your list. That happened about eighty years ago. You're not planning to reenact *that*, are you?" Brett had asked.

Laurie told him it was an example of a crime that people talked about for generations because of its horror, but also because there were still so many lingering questions about the case. Bruno Hauptmann, an immigrant from Germany who was executed for kidnapping the Lindbergh baby, was almost certainly the one who made the ladder that went to the baby's bedroom. But how did he know the nanny went to dinner every night and left the baby alone for forty-five minutes at exactly that time? How did Hauptmann know that—or who told him?

Then she told Brett about the unsolved murder of one of the identical twin daughters of Senator Charles H. Percy. It happened at the beginning of his first campaign for the Senate in 1966. He was elected, but the crime was never solved, and the questions remained: was the sister who was murdered the intended victim? And why didn't the dog bark if a stranger had entered the house?

Now Laurie leaned back in her chair. She had told Brett the point is that when you start to mention cases like this, everyone has a theory about it. "We'll do a reality show about crimes that are anywhere from twenty to thirty years old, where we can get the point of view of the people who were closest to the victim, and I have the perfect case for the first show: the Graduation Gala," she'd said.

That's when Brett really got interested, Laurie thought. Living in Westchester County, he knew all about it: Twenty years ago, four young women who grew up together in Salem Ridge graduated from four different colleges. The stepfather of one of them, Robert Nicholas Powell, gave what he called a "Graduation Gala" to honor all four girls. Three hundred guests, black tie, champagne and caviar, fireworks, you name it. After the party, his stepdaughter and the other three graduates stayed overnight. In the morning, Powell's wife, Betsy Bonner Powell, a popular, glamorous forty-two-year-old socialite, was found suffocated in her bed. The crime was never solved. Rob, as Powell was known, was now seventy-eight years old, in excellent physical and mental shape, and still living in the house.

Powell never remarried, Laurie thought. He had recently given an interview on *The O'Reilly Factor* in which he said he would do anything to clear up the mystery of his wife's death, and he knew that his stepdaughter and her friends all felt the same way. They all believed that until the truth came out, people would wonder if one of *them* was the murderer who took Betsy's life.

That's when I got the go-ahead from Brett to contact Powell and the four graduates to see if they would participate, Laurie thought exultantly.

It was time to share the good news with Grace and Jerry. She picked up her phone and told her two assistants to come in. A moment later the door of her office flew open.

Grace Garcia, her twenty-five-year-old administrative assistant, was wearing a short red wool dress over cotton leggings and high-button boots. Her waist-length black hair was twisted up and clamped with a comb. Tendrils that had escaped from the comb framed her heart-shaped face. Heavy but expertly applied mascara accentuated her lively dark eyes.

Jerry Klein was one step behind Grace. Long and lanky, he settled into one of the chairs at Laurie's desk. As usual, he was wearing a turtleneck and a cardigan sweater. It was his claim that he intended to make his one dark blue suit and his one tuxedo last for twenty years. Laurie had no doubt that he would succeed. Now twenty-six, he had joined the company as a summer intern three years earlier. He had turned out to be an indispensable production assistant.

"I won't keep you in suspense," Laurie announced. "Brett gave us the go-ahead."

"I knew he would!" Grace exclaimed.

"I knew he had from the expression on your face when you got off the elevator," Jerry insisted.

"No you didn't. I have a poker face," Laurie told him. "All right, the first order of business is for me to contact Robert Powell. If I get the go-ahead from him, from what I saw in that interview he gave, his stepdaughter and her three friends will very likely go along with us."

"Especially since they'll get paid very well to cooperate, and not one of them has any real money," Jerry said, his voice thoughtful as he recalled the background information he had gathered for the potential series. "Betsy's daughter, Claire Bonner, is a social worker in Chicago. She never married. Nina Craig is divorced, lives in Hollywood, makes a living as an extra in films. Alison Schaefer is a pharmacist in a small drugstore in Cleveland. Her husband is on crutches. He was the victim of a hit-and-run driver twenty years ago. Regina Callari moved to St. Augustine, Florida. She has a small real estate agency. Divorced, one child in college."

"The stakes are high," Laurie cautioned. "Brett has already reminded me that the last two series were flops."

"Did he mention that your first two are still running?" Grace asked, indignant.

"No, he didn't, and he won't. And I feel in my bones that we have a potential winner with this one. If Robert Powell goes along with us, I almost bet the others will as well," Laurie said, then added fervently, "At least I hope and pray that they will."

2

First Deputy Commissioner Leo Farley of the New York Police Department had been rumored to be appointed the next police commissioner when he unexpectedly put in his retirement papers the day after his son-in-law's funeral. Now, more than five years later, Leo had never looked back at that decision. At sixty-three, he was a cop to his fingertips. He'd always planned to be one until he hit mandatory retirement, but something more important had changed his plans.

The shocking, cold-blooded murder of Greg and the threat that the elderly witness had overheard—"Timmy, tell your mother that she's next, then it's your turn"—had been sufficient reason to decide to dedicate his life to protecting his daughter and grandson. Ramrod straight, average height, with a full head of iron-gray hair and a wiry, disciplined body, Leo Farley spent his waking hours on constant alert.

He knew that there was only so much he could do for Laurie. She had a job she both needed and loved. She took public transportation, went for long jogs in Central Park, and in warm weather often ate lunch in one of the pocket parks near her office.

Timmy was another matter. In Leo's mind there was nothing to prevent Greg's killer from deciding to go after Timmy first, so he appointed himself as his guardian. It was Leo who walked Timmy to Saint David's School every morning, and it was Leo who was waiting for him at dismissal time. If Timmy had activities after school, Leo unobtrusively stood guard beside the skating rink or the playground.

To Leo, Greg Moran was the son he would have created for himself, if that had been possible. It was now ten years since they had met in the emergency room at Lenox Hill Hospital. He and Eileen had frantically rushed there after they received the call that their twenty-six-year-old daughter, Laurie, had been hit by a cab on Park Avenue and was unconscious.

Greg, tall and impressive even in his green hospital togs, had greeted them with the firm assurance, "She's come to, and she'll be fine. A broken ankle and a concussion. We will observe her, but she'll be fine."

At those words, Eileen, desperate with worry about her only child, had fainted, and Greg had another patient on his hands. He grabbed Eileen quickly before she fell. He never left our lives again, Leo thought. He and Laurie were engaged three months later. He was our rock when Eileen died, only a year after that.

How could anyone have shot him? The exhaustive investigation had left no stone unturned to find someone who might have had a grudge against Greg, unthinkable as that was to anyone who knew him. After they had quickly eliminated friends and classmates from consideration, the records had been scoured in the two hospitals where Greg had worked as a resident and staff director to see if any patient or a family member had ever accused him of a mistaken diagnosis or treatment that had resulted in a permanent injury or death. Nothing had come to light.

In the DA's office the case was known as the "Blue Eyes Murder." Sometimes an expression of alarm would come over Timmy's face if he happened to suddenly turn and look directly into Leo's face. Leo's eyes were a light china-blue shade. He was sure, and both Laurie and the psychologist agreed, that Greg's killer must have had large, intense blue eyes.

Laurie had discussed with him her concept for a new series, leading with the Graduation Gala murder. Leo kept his dismay to himself. The idea of his daughter gathering together a group of people, one of whom was probably a murderer, was alarming. Someone had hated Betsy Bonner Powell enough to hold a pillow over her head until the last breath had been squeezed from her body. That same person probably had a passion for self-preservation. Leo knew that twenty years ago all four young women, and Betsy's husband, had been interrogated by the best-of-the-best homicide detectives. Unless someone had managed to make his or her way into the house undetected, if the series was given the green light, the murderer and suspects would all be together again—a dangerous proposition.

All this was in Leo's mind as he and Timmy walked home from Saint David's on Eighty-ninth Street off Fifth Avenue to the apartment, eight blocks away on Lexington Avenue and Ninety-fourth Street. After Greg's death Laurie had moved immediately, unable to bear the sight of the playground where Greg had been shot.

A passing police cruiser slowed as it drove by. The officer in the passenger seat saluted Leo.

"I like it when they do that to you, Grandpa," Timmy announced. "It makes me feel safe," he added matter-of-factly.

Be careful, Leo warned himself. I've always told Timmy that if I wasn't around and he or his friends had a problem they should run to a police officer and ask for help. Unconsciously, he tightened his grip on Timmy's hand.

"Well, you haven't had any problems that I couldn't solve for you." Then he added carefully, "At least as far as I know."

They were walking north on Lexington Avenue. The wind had shifted and felt raw against their faces. Leo stopped and firmly pulled Timmy's woolen cap down over his forehead and ears.

"One of the guys in the eighth grade was walking to school this morning and some guy on a bike tried to grab his cell phone out of his hand. A policeman saw it and pulled the guy over," Timmy said.

It hadn't been an incident involving someone with blue eyes. Leo was ashamed to admit to himself how relieved that made him. Until Greg's killer was apprehended, he needed to know that Timmy and Laurie were safe.

Someday justice will be served, he vowed to himself.

This morning, as she hurried out to work seconds after he arrived, Laurie had said that she was going to hear the verdict on the reality show she was proposing. Leo's mind moved restlessly to that concern. He knew he would have to wait for the news until tonight. Over their second cup of coffee, when Timmy had finished dinner and was curled up in the big chair with a book, she would discuss it with him. Then he would leave for his own apartment a block away. At the end of the day, he wanted Laurie and Timmy to have their own space, and he was satisfied that no one would get past the doorman in their building without a phone call to the resident they claimed to be visiting.

If she got the go-ahead to do that series, it's going to be bad news, Leo thought.

A man with a hooded sweatshirt, dark sunglasses, and a canvas bag on his shoulder, seeming to come out of nowhere, darted past him on roller skates, almost knocking over Timmy, then brushing a very pregnant young woman who was about ten feet ahead of them.

"Get off the sidewalk," Leo shouted as the skater turned the corner and disappeared.

Behind the dark sunglasses, bright blue eyes glittered, and the skater laughed aloud.

Such encounters fed his need for the sense of power he felt when he literally touched Timmy and knew that on any given day he could carry out his threat.

3

Robert Nicholas Powell was seventy-eight years old but looked and moved like a man ten years younger. A full head of white hair framed his handsome face. His posture was still erect, although he was no longer over six feet tall. He had an air of authority that was instantly apparent to anyone in his presence. Except for Fridays, he still put in a full day at his Wall Street office, chauffeured back and forth by his longtime employee, Josh Damiano.

Today, Tuesday, March 16, Rob had made the decision to stay home and meet television producer Laurie Moran here in Salem Ridge instead of in his office. She had told him the reason for her visit and had couched it in an intriguing premise: "Mr. Powell, I believe that if you, your stepdaughter, and her friends agree to re-create the events of the Graduation Gala, the public will understand how incredible it is that any one of you could have been responsible for your wife's death. You had a happy marriage. Everyone who knew you knew that. Your stepdaughter and her mother were very close. The other three graduates had been in and out of Betsy's home from the time they were in high school, and then, when you and Betsy were married, you made them always feel welcome. You have a very large house, and with so many people at the party, there is every possibility that an intruder went undetected. Your wife was known to have beautiful and expensive jewelry. She was wearing her emerald earrings and necklace and ring that night."

"The tabloids turned a tragedy into a scandal." Robert Powell remembered his bitter retort to Laurie Moran. Well, she'll be here soon, he thought. So be it.

He was sitting at the desk in his spacious downstairs office. Large windows looked out over the back gardens of the estate. A beautiful sight in spring and summer and early fall, Rob thought. When it was snowing, that bare and naked view was softened and sometimes magical but on a damp, cold, sunless winter day in March, when the trees were bare and the pool covered and the pool house was shuttered, no amount of expensive planting could soften the stark reality of the winter landscape.

His padded desk chair was very comfortable, and Rob, smiling to himself, pondered the secret that he did not share with anyone. He was sure that sitting behind the impressive antique mahogany desk with the elaborate carvings on the sides and legs lent even more prestige to the image he had so carefully cultivated. It was an image that began the day he left Detroit at age seventeen to begin his freshman year as a scholarship student at Harvard. There, he referred to his mother as a college professor and his father as an engineer; in fact she was a kitchen worker at the University of Michigan and he was a mechanic at the Ford plant.

Rob smiled, remembering how in his sophomore year he had bought a book on table manners, purchased a box of battered silver-plated table settings, and practiced using unfamiliar utensils such as a fish knife until he was sure he was comfortable with them. Following graduation, an internship at Merrill Lynch began his career in the financial world. Now, despite a few rocky years along the way, the R. N. Powell Hedge Fund was considered one of the best and safest investments on Wall Street.

At precisely eleven o'clock the sound of the chimes at the front door announced the arrival of Laurie Moran. Rob straightened his shoulders. Of course he would get up when she was escorted into his office, but not until she had seen him seated at his desk. He realized how curious he was to meet her. It was hard to tell her age from her voice over the phone. There was a crisp, matter-of-fact note in the way she had introduced herself, but then her tone had become sympathetic when she spoke about Betsy's death.

After their conversation he had googled her. The fact that she was the widow of the doctor who had been shot in the playground and that she had an impressive background as a producer intrigued him. Her picture showed her to be a very attractive woman. I'm not too old to appreciate that, Rob thought.

There was a tap on the door, and Jane, who had been his housekeeper from the time he married Betsy, opened it and stepped into the room, followed by Laurie Moran.

"Thank you, Jane," Rob said, and waited until Jane had left, closing the door behind her, before he got up. "Ms. Moran," he said courteously. He extended his hand to Laurie and indicated the chair on the other side of the desk.

Robert Powell could not know that Laurie was thinking, Well, this is it, as with a warm smile she settled in the chair. The housekeeper had taken her coat when she arrived. She was wearing a navy pin-striped pantsuit, white shell blouse, and navy leather boots. Her only jewelry was a pair of small pearl earrings and her gold wedding band. She had pulled her hair back and pinned it into a French knot, a style that made her feel more efficient.

Within five minutes she was sure that Robert Powell had already decided to go ahead with the program, but it took him ten minutes before he confirmed that fact.

"Mr. Powell, I'm thrilled that you are willing to let us re-create the night of the Graduation Gala. Now, of course, we will need the cooperation of your stepdaughter and her friends. Will you help me persuade them to participate?"

"I'm happy to do that, although obviously I can't speak for any of them."

"Have you stayed close to your stepdaughter since your wife died?"

"No. Not that I haven't wanted to stay close. I was and am very fond of Claire. She lived here from the time she was thirteen until she was twenty-one. Her mother's death was a terrible shock for her. I don't know how much you studied her background, but her mother and father were never married. He took off when Betsy became pregnant with Claire. Betsy was doing bit parts on Broadway and when she wasn't acting she worked as an usher there. It was hardscrabble for her and Claire until I came along."

Then he added, "Betsy was beautiful. I'm sure she could have easily married someone along the way, but after her experience with Claire's father, I know she was gun-shy."

"I can understand that," Laurie said, nodding.

"I can, too. Never having had children, I thought of Claire as my own daughter. It hurt when she moved out so quickly after Betsy's death. But I think that between us there was too much grief to hold under one roof, and she sensed it immediately. As I'm sure you know, she lives in Chicago and is a social worker there. She never married."

"She never came back here?"

"No, and never accepted my offer of generous financial help. She returned my letters torn up."

"Why do you think she did that?" Laurie asked.

"She was fiercely jealous of my relationship with her mother. Don't forget, it was just the two of them for thirteen years."

"Then do you think she'll refuse to take part in the program?"

"No, I don't. Every so often an enterprising reporter has written about the case, and some of them have quoted Claire or one of the other girls. What they have said has been uniform. They all feel as though people look at them with questions in their eyes, and they'd all like an end to it."

"We're planning to offer each of them $50,000 for being on the program," Laurie told him.

"I've kept track of all of them. There isn't one who couldn't use financial help. In order to ensure that they accept, I authorize you to say that I am prepared to pay each one of them a quarter of a million dollars for their cooperation."

"You would do that?" Laurie exclaimed.

"Yes, and tell me anyone else you will want to interview on your program."

Laurie said, "Of course, I will want to interview your housekeeper."

"Give her the $50,000 you're giving the others and I'll give her another $50,000. I'll make sure she does it. It is not necessary that she be paid the same as the others. I am seventy-eight years old and have three stents in the arteries leading to my heart. I know that, like the girls, I am under suspicion—or do you call it a 'person of interest' these days? Before I die, I want to sit in a courtroom and see Betsy's murderer sentenced to prison."

"You never heard any sound from her room?"

"No. As I'm sure you're aware, we shared a suite. The sitting room was in the middle, our bedrooms on either side. I confess I am a heavy sleeper and snore very loudly. When we said good night, I went to my bedroom."

That evening Laurie waited until Timmy was deep in his Harry Potter book before she told her father about her meeting with Powell.

"I know I shouldn't make any judgment yet, but I heard the ring of truth in Powell's voice when he was talking," Laurie said. "And his offer to pay the girls a quarter of a million dollars is wonderful."

"A quarter of a million dollars plus what you pay them," Leo repeated. "You say that Powell knows all four women could use the money?"

"Yes, that's what he said." Laurie realized that she sounded defensive.

"Has Powell helped any of them out along the way, including his stepdaughter?"

"He indicated that he didn't."

"I think it's a question you should look into. Who knows what his real motive may be to hand out all that money." Leo couldn't help but question these people's intentions. It was the cop in him. And the father. And grandfather.

With that, he decided to finish his coffee and go home. I'm getting too jumpy, he thought, and that won't do either Laurie or Timmy any good. Even the way I shouted at that guy on skates. I was right, he could have hurt someone; but it was the fact that he actually brushed against Timmy that scared me. If he'd had a gun or a knife, even with my hand in Timmy's, I couldn't have protected him from an attack fast enough.

Leo knew the grim reality that if a murderer had a grudge against someone, no order of protection or vigilance could keep them from satisfying his need to kill his target.

4

Claire Bonner settled at a table in the Seafood Bar of The Breakers Hotel in Palm Beach. She was facing the ocean and watched with detached interest as the waves crashed against the retaining wall directly below the Bar. The sun was shining but the winds were stronger than she had expected in Florida on an early spring day.

She was wearing a newly purchased zippered jacket in a light shade of blue. She had bought it when she noticed that it carried the name of THE BREAKERS on the breast pocket. It was part of the fantasy of spending this long weekend here. Her short ash-blond hair framed a face that was half-hidden by oversized sunglasses. The glasses were seldom off, but when they were, Claire's beautiful features were revealed, as well as the tranquil expression that had taken her years to achieve. In fact, a discerning observer might have realized that the expression was caused by the acceptance of reality rather than peace of mind. Her slender frame had an aura of fragility as though she had been recently ill. The same observer might have guessed her to be in her mid-thirties. In that case he would have been wrong. She was forty-one.

In the past four days she had had the same polite young waiter and now was greeted by name as he approached her table. "Let me guess, Ms. Bonner," he said. "Seafood chowder and two large stone crabs."

"You have it," Claire said as a brief smile touched the corner of her lips.

"And the usual glass of chardonnay," he added as he jotted down the order.

You do something for a few days in a row and it becomes the usual, she thought wryly.

Almost instantly the chardonnay was placed on the table before her. She picked up the glass and looked around the room as she sipped.

All of the diners were dressed in designer casual clothes. The Breakers was an expensive hotel, a retreat for the well-heeled. It was the Easter holiday week, and, nationwide, schools were closed. At breakfast in the dining room she had observed that families with children were usually accompanied by a nanny who skillfully removed a restless toddler so that the parents could enjoy the lavish buffet in peace.

The lunchtime crowd in the bar was composed almost totally of adults. In walking around she had noticed that the younger families gravitated to the restaurants by the pool, where the choice of casual fare was greater.

What would it have been like to vacation here every year from childhood? Claire wondered. Then she tried to brush away the memories of falling asleep each night in a half-empty theatre where her mother was working as an usher. That was before they met Robert Powell, of course. But by then Claire's childhood was almost over.

As those thoughts went through her head, two couples, still in travel clothes, took the table next to hers. She heard one of the women sigh happily, "It's so good to be back."

I'll pretend I'm coming back, she thought. I'll pretend that every year I have the same oceanfront room and look forward to long walks on the beach before breakfast.

The waiter arrived with the chowder. "Really hot, the way you like it, Ms. Bonner," he said.

The first day, she had asked for the chowder to be very hot and the crabs to be served as the second course. The waiter had also committed that request to memory.

The first sip of the chowder almost burned the roof of her mouth and she stirred the rest of it inside the soup bowl that was a scooped-out loaf of bread to cool it a bit. Then she reached for her glass and took a long sip of the chardonnay. As she had expected, it was crisp and dry, exactly as it had tasted for the last few days.

Outside an even stronger wind was churning the breaking waves into clouds of cascading foam.

Claire realized that she felt like one of those surges of water, trying to reach shore but at the mercy of the powerful wind. It was still her decision. She could always say no. She'd said no to returning to her stepfather's house for years. And she passionately didn't want to go now. No one could force her to go on a national cable television show and take part in reenacting the party and sleepover twenty years ago when the four of them, best friends, had celebrated their graduation from college.

But if she did take part in the show, the production company would give her fifty thousand dollars, and Rob would give her two hundred fifty thousand dollars.

Three hundred thousand dollars. It would mean that she could take a leave of absence from her job in Chicago's youth and family services. The bout of pneumonia she had survived in January had come close to killing her, and she knew her body was still weak and tired. She had never accepted Powell's offer of money. Not a single cent. She had torn up his letters and returned them to him. After what he did.

They wanted to call it the "Graduation Gala." It had been a beautiful party, a wonderful party, Claire thought. Then Alison and

Regina and Nina had stayed overnight. And sometime during that night, my mother had been murdered. Betsy Bonner Powell, beautiful, vivacious, generous, funny, beloved Betsy.

I thoroughly despised her, Claire thought quietly.

I absolutely hated my mother, and I loathed her beloved husband, even though he kept trying to send me money.

5

Regina Callari was sorry she had gone to the post office and picked up the registered letter from Laurie Moran, a producer at Fisher Blake Studios. Take part in a reality program that would re-enact the night of the Graduation Gala! she thought, dismayed — and, frankly, shocked.

The letter upset her so much that she knew she had lost a sale. She had to fumble for the features of the house she was show-ing, and in the middle of the walk-through the prospective client said, abruptly, "I think I've seen enough; this is not the house I'm looking for."

Then, after she got back to the office, she had to phone the owner, seventy-six-year-old Bridget Whiting, and tell her that she had been wrong. "I was sure we had a good prospect but it just didn't happen," she apologized.

Bridget's disappointment was palpably evident in her voice. "I don't know how long they'll keep that apartment for me in the assisted-living home, and it's *exactly* what I want. Oh dear! Regina, maybe I built up my hopes too much. It's not your fault."

But it is my fault, Regina thought, trying to keep raw anger out of her voice as she swore to Bridget that she was going to find her a buyer and fast, and then, knowing how difficult that would be in this market, said good-bye.

Her office, a one-room former garage, had once been part of a private residence on the main street in St. Augustine, Florida. The bleak housing market had improved, but not sufficiently for Regina to do more than eke out a living. Now she put her elbows on her desk and pressed her fingers to the sides of her forehead. Wisps of curly hair reminded her that her midnight-black hair was growing with its usual annoying rapidity. She knew she would have to make an appointment for a trim. The fact that the hairdresser always insisted on talking a blue streak was what had kept her from making the appointment—that, and the cost.

That silly fact made Regina annoyed at herself and her own always present impatience. So what, she told herself, if for twenty minutes Lena yak-yak-yakked away? She's the only one who knows how to make this unruly mop look decent.

Regina's dark brown eyes traveled to the picture on her desk. Zach, her nineteen-year-old son, smiled back at her from it. He was just completing his sophomore year at the University of Pennsylvania, an education fully paid for by his father, her ex-husband. Zach had phoned last night. Hesitantly, he had asked if she would mind if he went backpacking through Europe and the Middle East this summer. He had planned to come home and get a job in St. Augustine, but jobs were hard to find there. It wouldn't cost all that much, and his father would finance him.

"I'll be back in time to spend ten days with you before the term starts, Mom," he had assured her, his tone pleading.

Regina had told him that it was a wonderful opportunity and that he should jump at it. She hadn't let the keen disappointment she felt sound in her voice. She missed Zach. She missed the sweet little boy who used to come bounding into the office from the school bus, eager to share every single moment of his day with her. She missed the tall, shy adolescent who would have dinner waiting if she was out late with a client.

Since the divorce, Earl had been skillfully carving out ways to separate her from Zach. It had begun when, at age ten, Zach went to sailing camp in Cape Cod for the summer. The camp was followed by the shared holidays when Earl and his new wife took Zach skiing in Switzerland or to the South of France.

She knew Zach loved her, but a small house and a tight budget could hardly compete with life with his wildly rich father. Now he'd be gone for most of the summer.

Slowly, Regina reached for the letter from Moran and reread it. "She'll pay fifty thousand, and the mighty Robert Nicholas Powell will pay each of us two hundred fifty thousand," she murmured aloud. "Mr. Benevolence himself."

She thought of her friends and former co-hosts of the Graduation Gala. Claire Bonner. She was beautiful, but always so quiet, like a faded shadow next to her mother. Alison Schaefer, so smart she put the rest of us to shame. I thought she'd end up the next Madame Curie. She got married the October after Betsy died, and then Rod, her husband, was in an accident. From what I understand, he's been on crutches all these years. Nina Craig. We called her "the flaming redhead." I remember even as a freshman if she got mad at you, watch out. She would even tell a teacher off if she thought she didn't get a good enough mark on an essay.

And then there was me, Regina thought. When I was fifteen I opened the door of the garage to put my bike away and found my father swinging from a rope. His eyes were bulging and his tongue was lapping over his chin. If he had to hang himself, why didn't he do it in his office? He knew that I'd be the one to find him in the garage. I loved him so much! How could he have done that to me? The nightmares have never stopped. They always started with her getting off her bike.

Before she called the police, and the neighbor's house where her mother was playing bridge, she had taken the suicide note her father had pinned to his shirt and hidden it. When the police came they said that most suicide victims leave a note for the family. Sobbing, her mother had searched the house for it, while Regina pretended to help.

The girls were my lifeline after that, Regina thought. We were such close friends. After the Gala and Betsy's death, Claire and Nina and I were Alison's bridesmaids. That had been such a stupid move. It was so soon after Betsy died; the tabloids had made a spectacle of the wedding. The headlines were all a rehashing of the Graduation Gala murder. That was when we realized that all four of us would continue to be under suspicion; maybe for the rest of our lives.

We never got together again, Regina lamented. After the wedding we all went out of our way to avoid any contact with each other. We all moved to different cities.

What would it be like to see them again, to be under the same roof? We were all so young then, so shocked and frightened when Betsy's body was discovered. And the way the police questioned us, together, then separately. It's a miracle one of us didn't break down and confess to smothering her, the way they hammered at us. *"We know it was somebody inside that house. Which one of you did it? If it wasn't you, maybe it was one of your friends. Protect yourself. Tell us what you know."*

Regina thought of how the police had wondered if Betsy's emeralds might have been the motive. She left them on the glass tray on her dressing table when she went to bed. They suggested that she woke up while she was being robbed and whoever was there panicked. One of her earrings was on the floor. Had Betsy dropped it when she took it off, or had someone, wearing gloves, panicked and dropped it when she woke up?

Regina got up slowly and looked around. She tried to visualize having three hundred thousand dollars in the bank. Almost half of that would go to income tax, she warned herself. But even so, it would be an unimaginable windfall. Or maybe it would bring back the days when her father had been so successful, and they, as well as Robert and Betsy Powell, had the big house in Salem Ridge with all the trimmings, housekeeper, a cook, a landscaper, a chauffeur, a top New York caterer for their frequent parties . . .

Regina looked around her one-room real estate office. Even with the Sheetrock walls painted light blue to coordinate with her white desk and the white armchairs with blue cushions for potential clients, the room looked like what it was: a brave effort to hide a thin budget. A garage is a garage is a garage, she thought, except for the one luxury I installed when I bought this property after the divorce.

The luxury was down the hall past the unisex restroom. Unmarked and always locked, it was a private bathroom with a Jacuzzi, steam shower, vanity sink, and wardrobe closet. It was here that sometimes, at the end of the day, she would shower, change, and then meet her friends or go out to a solitary dinner followed by a movie.

Earl had left her ten years ago, when Zach was going on nine. He hadn't been able to put up with her bouts of depression. "Get help, Regina. I'm sick of the moods. I'm sick of the nightmares. It's not good for our son, just in case you haven't noticed."

After the divorce, Earl, a computer salesman at the time, whose hobby had been writing songs, had finally sold a collection of his music to a major recording artist. His next step had been to marry budding rock singer Sonya Miles. When Sonya hit the charts with the album he wrote for her, Earl became a celebrity in the world he coveted. He took to that life as a duck takes to water, Regina thought as she walked over to the row of files on the far side of the room.

She took an unmarked package from the bottom of the locked

file. Buried under miscellaneous real estate advertisements, it was a cardboard box that contained all the newspaper coverage of the Graduation Gala murder.

I haven't looked at it in years, Regina thought as she carried the box back to her desk, laid it down, and opened it. Some of the newspapers had begun to crumble at the edges, but she found what she was looking for. It was the picture of Betsy and Robert Powell toasting the four graduates—Claire, Alison, Nina, and herself.

We were all so pretty, Regina thought. I remember how we went shopping for dresses together. We all had done well in college. We had our plans and hopes for the future. And they were all destroyed that night.

She put the newspapers back in the box, carried it over to the file, and dropped it in the bottom drawer, carefully concealing it below the ads. I'm going to take his damn money, she thought. And that producer's as well. Maybe if I do, I can take hold of my life. I do know I can use some of the money to take Zach on a fun vacation, before he goes back to school.

She slammed the drawer, put the CLOSED sign in the window of the office, turned out the lights, locked the door, and went back to her private bath. In it, as the water ran in the Jacuzzi, she stripped and looked at herself in the full-length mirror on the door. I've got two months before the show and I need to lose twenty pounds, she thought. I want to look good when I get there and tell what I remember. I want Zach to be proud of me.

An unwanted thought crept into her mind. I know Earl always wondered if I was the one who killed Betsy. Did he ever plant that suspicion in Zach's mind?

Regina knew she didn't love Earl anymore, didn't want him anymore, but even more than that, she didn't want to have any more nightmares.

The Jacuzzi was filled with water. She stepped into it, leaned back, and closed her eyes.

As her curly black hair became straight and sleek around her face, she thought, This is my chance to convince everyone that *I* wasn't the one who killed that rotten slut.

6

Rod Kimball signed for the certified letter and opened it while his wife, Alison, was busy filling a prescription. When the customer left she hurried over to take it from him.

"Who's sending a registered letter?" she asked, her tone worried, as without breaking stride she took it from him, turned, and went back to the pharmacy area of their drugstore, giving him no chance to warn her of the contents. Dismayed, he watched as her face flushed, then paled as she read the two-page missive. Then she dropped it on the counter. "I can't go through that again," she cried, her voice trembling. "My God, do they think I'm *crazy*?"

"Take it easy, love," Rod cautioned. Trying not to grimace with pain, he slid off the stool behind the checkout counter and reached for his crutches. Twenty years after the hit-and-run accident that had crippled him, pain was always a fact of life for him. Yet some days, like this one, cold and wet in late March in Cleveland, Ohio, it was more severe than others. Pain was etched into the lines around his eyes and the resolute set of his jaw. His dark brown hair had turned almost completely gray. He knew he looked older than his forty-two years. He hobbled over to Alison. Across the counter from her, his six-foot body towering over her petite frame, he felt an overwhelming need to protect her. "You don't have to do anything you don't want to do," he said firmly. "Tear up that letter."

"No." Shaking her head, Alison opened the drawer beneath the counter and shoved the letter into it. "I can't talk about it now, Rod," she said.

At that point the jingling sound that signaled the opening of the door told them that a customer was coming into the store, and Rod made his way back to the checkout counter.

He had been a rookie quarterback for the New York Giants when he and Alison were married. He was raised by a single mother who worked as a caretaker for an invalid to support him. His father, a hopeless alcoholic, died when he was two. The sportswriters were unanimous that a brilliant career was ahead of him when he had signed his first big contract. He and Alison were both twenty-two then, and he had been crazy about her since kindergarten. In fact, when they were in kindergarten together he had announced to the class that he was going to marry her someday.

Alison's family had never had any money. Her father was the produce manager in a grocery store. Alison went to college on a mix of student loans and working part time. She had lived in a modest section of Salem Ridge, not far from where Rod Kimball had lived. She had missed out on a scholarship to graduate school.

He officially proposed the day he was offered the big contract with the New York Giants. That was two months after Betsy Powell's murder. An important part of the proposal was that he knew Alison wanted to go to medical school and then into research. He promised to pay for her education, to tiptoe around the house when she was studying, and to delay having children until she obtained the degree she wanted so badly.

Instead, three weeks after the wedding, he had been in the accident, and Alison had spent the better part of the next four years at his bedside helping him to heal. The money he had saved from his one season with the Giants was soon exhausted.

At that point Alison had taken out more loans and gone back to school to become a pharmacist. Her first job came about because her elderly childless cousin had hired her to work with him in his drugstore in Cleveland. "Rod, there's a job for you as well," he had said. "My assistant is leaving. She does the ordering of everything except for the drugs, and she handles the cash register."

They had both been glad to get out of the New York area, where they always seemed to encounter speculation over Betsy Powell's death. A few years after they moved to Cleveland, the cousin retired and they took over the store. Now they had a wide circle of friends, and no one ever asked them about the Graduation Gala murder.

The nickname "Rod" had come about because in his college years on the football field, a sportswriter had commented that he moved as fast as a lightning rod. After the accident, Thomas "Rod" Kimball had managed not to let that nickname become a source of bitter irony.

The morning was fairly quiet, but in the afternoon business was brisk. They had two part-time assistants, a semiretired pharmacist and a clerk who stocked the shelves and helped at the cash register. Even with their help it was an exceptionally busy day, and by the time they closed at 8 P.M., he and Alison were both bone tired.

By then it was raining hard, a cold driving rain. Alison insisted that he use the wheelchair to get out to the car. "We'll both be drowned if you try to use the crutches," she said, an edge in her voice.

Many times over the years he had sought the courage to insist that she leave him, that she meet someone else and have a normal life. But he had never been able to bring himself to utter those words. He could not visualize a life without her now, any more than he could have visualized it all through his growing years.

He sometimes thought of an observation his grandmother had made long ago. "In most marriages, one of the couple is more in love than the other, and it's best if it's the man. The marriage will have a better chance of going the whole way."

Rod did not need to be told that with Alison, he was the one who loved the most. He was almost sure that she would not have accepted his proposal if he had not offered to send her to medical school. And then, after the accident, she was too decent to walk out on him.

Rod didn't let himself drown in that kind of speculation often, but the letter today brought back so much—the Graduation Gala, the pictures of the four girls plastered all over the newspapers, the circus the media had made of their wedding.

When they reached the car, Alison said, "Rod, let me drive. I know you're hurting."

She was shielding him with the umbrella as she opened the door, and without arguing he slid into the passenger seat. It was impossible for her to hold the umbrella and fold the wheelchair at the same time. He watched regretfully as the rain pelted her face and hair until she was finally settled behind the wheel. Then she turned to him. "I'm going to do it," she said. Her tone was defiant, as if she expected him to argue with her.

When he said nothing, she waited for a long minute, then started the engine. "No comment?" Now he detected a slight tremor in her voice.

He was not going to tell her what he was thinking—that with her long brown hair wet on her shoulders, she looked so young and so vulnerable. He knew she was frightened. No, he thought. Make that terrified.

"If the others agree to take part in the program and you don't, it wouldn't be good," he said quietly. "I think you have to go. I think *we* have to go," he corrected himself quickly.

"I was lucky last time. This time I may not be so lucky."

They were both silent for the rest of the trip. Their ranch-style home, designed to accommodate his disabilities, was a twenty-minute drive from the pharmacy. They were spared any further exposure to the downpour because a door from the garage opened into the kitchen. Once inside, shaking off her wet raincoat, Alison sank into a chair and buried her face in her hands. "Rod, I'm so scared. "I never told you but that night when we all went up to bed all I could think of was how much I hated Betsy and Rob Powell." She hesitated and continued haltingly, "I think I was sleepwalking that night and I might have gone into Betsy's room."

"You thought you were in Betsy's room that night!" Rod dropped his crutches as he pulled a chair closer to Alison and eased himself into it. "Do you think there is any possibility that anyone saw you?"

"I don't know."

Alison pulled away from his embrace and turned to face him. Her large, expressive light brown eyes were her dominant feature. Now with tears streaming from them, they looked haunted and defenseless. Then Rod heard a question he never expected to hear from his wife's lips.

"Rod," she asked, "isn't it a fact that you have always believed that I killed Betsy Powell?"

"Are you crazy?" he asked. "Are you absolutely crazy?"

But even to his own ears, he knew that his protest sounded hollow and unconvincing.

7

"Well, have you made up your mind if you're going?"

That was the question Nina Craig heard as she pushed open the door of her condo in West Hollywood. Oh God, she's in one of those moods, Nina thought, and bit her lip to keep from making a sharp reply to her sixty-two-year-old mother. It was five-thirty, and it was clear to her that Muriel Craig had started her private cocktail hour well before her usual five o'clock with a pitcher of apple martinis or a bottle of wine.

Muriel was still in her nightgown and robe, which meant that whatever time she had woken up, it was in the cloud of depression that so often enveloped her. It's going to be a long night, Nina thought resentfully.

"No response from the Academy Award winner?" her mother asked sarcastically as she refilled her glass from the almost empty bottle.

Ten years ago Nina had given up the hope of becoming a successful actress one day and had joined the guild for extras, the background people who worked on a day-by-day basis. Arriving at 5 A.M., she'd spent all day on the set of a film about a revolution and had been one of the hundreds of extras who held up banners. The set was in the desert near Palm Springs, and it had been mercilessly hot.

"I don't know what I'm going to do, Mom," Nina said, trying to keep her tone even.

"Why not go? Three hundred thousand dollars is pretty good money. I'll go with you. I wouldn't mind getting an in-person look at good old Robert Nicholas Powell again."

Nina looked at her mother. The hair that, like her own, had once been a natural deep red was now dyed a bright fire-engine shade and looked harsh against Muriel's face. Years of smoking had left deep lines around her lips and cheeks, and her skin was mottled with brown spots. Her shoulders slumped as she leaned forward on the couch, her two hands encircling the glass.

It was hard to visualize the beautiful woman who at one time had been one of those rarities, an actress who worked steadily. *She* had talent, Nina thought bitterly, not like me. And now look at her!

Don't you go into all that again, Nina warned herself. It's the end of the day, and you're hot and fed up with everything. "Mom, I'm going to shower and get into something comfortable," she said. "I'll join you for a glass of wine when I get dressed."

"Take the three hundred thousand." Her mother spat the words out at her. "Use it to buy me my own condo. You don't want me living with you any more than I want to be here."

Muriel had followed Nina to California after the acting jobs became fewer and fewer in New York. A year earlier, she had barely escaped being burned to death when her carelessly dropped cigarette had ignited the carpet in the living room of her apartment in a two-family house in Los Angeles. The people who owned the house where she had rented had refused to let her return after the damage to the apartment was repaired. "The same thing could happen in the middle of the night," the owner told Nina. "I'm not taking any more chances."

Her mother had been living with Nina for almost a year now.

Now she, too, worked as an extra, but too often did not feel up to responding to a potential job.

I can't take it much longer, Nina thought as she closed and locked the door of her bedroom. In her mother's present frame of mind, it would not be unusual for her to follow Nina in to continue the discussion about the letter from the producer.

The room was cool and inviting. White walls, polished floors with white throw rugs on either side of the bed, narrow apple-green draperies at the windows. The white bedspread was accentuated by apple-green and white pillows. The four-poster bed and matching dresser were left over from her ten-year marriage to a mildly success-ful actor who had turned out to be a serial cheat. It was better that they had not had any children.

They'd been divorced for three years. I'm ready to find someone else, Nina thought. But I can't while I'm stuck with my mother. Who knows? I still look good. If I go on that program I might be able to parlay it into getting back into real acting, or even one of those reality shows. I can be a mad housewife with the best of them.

What would it be like to see Claire and Regina and Alison again? We were such kids, Nina thought. We were all so scared. The cops kept twisting what we were saying. Mom gave the performance of the year when she was asked if it was true that she had been seriously dating Powell before he met Betsy. "I was dating at least three people at that time," she said. "He was one of them."

That's not the way I heard it, Nina thought grimly. Her mother blamed her for introducing Betsy to Powell. She blamed me, and blamed me, and blamed me, Nina thought. It was all I ever heard from her. I ruined her life.

Muriel had turned down the part that would have made her a star because Powell didn't want her to be locked into a contract when they got married. Those were the exact words he used: "When we get married."

She'd thrown them at Nina often enough over the years.

Nina felt the white-hot anger that those memories evoked wash over her. She thought of the night of the Graduation Gala. Her mother had refused to come to the party. "I should be *living* in that house," she had said.

Betsy had made a point of seeking Nina out. "Where is your mother?" she had asked. "Or is she still a sore loser about Rob?"

I'm glad no one heard her ask me that question that night, Nina thought. It wouldn't have looked good when Robert Powell discovered his wife's body the next morning. But at that moment, if I had had that pillow, I would gladly have held it over her face.

I had much too much to drink that night. I don't even remember going to bed. I don't think I showed it, because no one mentioned it, including that nosy housekeeper who said that she thought Alison was drunk.

When she and the others got there Powell was collapsed on the floor, and the housekeeper pulled the pillow from Betsy's face.

Her mother was turning the handle of the door. "I want to talk to you," she called. "I want you to go on that program."

With a supreme effort Nina managed not to show how angry she was as she called back, "Mom, I'm stepping into the shower. It's all right. I *am* going to accept that offer. I'll be able to get you your own place."

Before I kill you, she added silently. And then wondered again what else she hadn't remembered about the night Betsy Powell was suffocated.

8

The agreements to participate in the reenactment of the events of the Graduation Gala had trickled in to Laurie's office one by one. The last of them had taken nearly two weeks, and it was from Nina Craig. The letter stated that she had consulted a lawyer and there were additional conditions she felt were appropriate. Robert Powell should put in escrow two hundred fifty thousand dollars for each of the four graduates, and it should be a net sum to each of them. Fisher Blake Studios must also offer fifty thousand net to the graduates. "Both Mr. Powell and Fisher Blake can well afford to compensate us fairly," Nina had written. "And now that I have contacted my longtime childhood friends, I realize that we have all suffered emotional damage from being in the Powell home the night Betsy Bonner Powell lost her life. I believe by once again exposing ourselves to the glare of publicity, we are surrendering our hard-earned anonymity, for which we should receive appropriate compensation."

Dismayed, Laurie reread the letter. "To net them that much money will mean we'd just about have to double what we're paying them," she said.

"I don't think Brett will go for it." Jerry Klein's flat tone did not match the disappointment that came over his face. He had signed for the certified letter from Ms. Nina Craig and carried it into Laurie's office.

"He's got to go along with it," Laurie said. "And I think he will. He's been talking the series up, and he won't want to pull back now."

"Well he won't be happy about it." The worried expression on Jerry's face deepened. "Laurie, I hope you haven't put yourself out on a limb with this *Under Suspicion* idea."

"I hope not, too." Laurie looked out the window toward the Rockefeller Center skating rink. It was a warm day for early April, and there were few skaters on the ice. Soon the rink would be gone, and the area it covered would be filled with tables and chairs for outside dining.

Once in a while Greg and I used to have dinner out there, she thought as a wave of longing for him swept over her. She knew why it had come at this moment. The show was about closure. Even though she had no intention of revealing her concern to either Jerry or Grace, she knew Jerry was right. After becoming openly enthusiastic about the project, her boss, Brett Young, would probably rather double the price he had agreed to pay the participants than back out.

"What about Robert Powell?" Jerry was asking. "Do you think he'll pony up and pay the taxes so they clear the two hundred and fifty grand?"

"I can only ask," Laurie said. "And I think I'd better do it in person. I'll call and ask if he can see me today."

"Shouldn't you check with Brett first?" Jerry suggested.

"No. There's no use in getting him going if it's a lost cause. If Powell doesn't agree to pay, our next move has to be for me to fly to Los Angeles and see if Nina Craig can be persuaded to accept our offer. The others all agreed to the original terms, but it's obvious she got them stirred up."

"What will you tell her?" Jerry asked.

"The truth. If necessary we'll do it without her, and that wouldn't look good for her. And don't forget that Betsy Bonner Powell was forty-two years old when she died. She'd be only sixty-two or sixty-three now. Today many people live well into their eighties. Betsy was robbed of half of the life she might have enjoyed if someone hadn't held a pillow over her face that night. The person who did that has woken up every morning since then and been able to enjoy a brand-new day while Betsy's body is in a casket in a cemetery."

Laurie knew her voice had become heated and angry and that it wasn't just about Betsy Bonner Powell. It was about Greg and the fact that his killer was a free man. Not only *free*, but a living, breathing threat to her and Timmy. Then she said, "Sorry, Jerry. I know that I have to be careful not to make this sound like a personal crusade."

She picked up the phone. "Time to make another appointment with Robert Nicholas Powell."

9

Rob Powell was on the three-hole golf course on the back lawn of his estate. The warm April day was conducive to getting out his clubs and practicing his swing before he joined a foursome at the Winged Foot Golf Club. Not bad, he thought as a well-struck putt rolled to the bottom of the cup.

Concentrating on his golf game had given him the opportunity to put aside the fact that he had not yet heard from the doctor. The chemo three years ago had seemed to take care of the nodules on his lungs, but he knew there was always a chance they would come back. He had had his semiannual checkup earlier in the week.

"Par for the course," he said aloud as he made his way back to the house, swinging his golf club.

Fifteen minutes until his guest arrived. What did Laurie Moran want? he asked himself. She'd sounded concerned. Is she going to tell me that one of them won't take part in the program? Rob frowned. I need to have them all here, he thought. No matter *what* it takes.

Even if Moran's report was favorable, Rob had a sense of time going by too swiftly. He needed closure, and when Laurie Moran had come to see him in March and proposed her concept of re-enacting the night of the Graduation Gala, it had been the answer to a prayer. Except, Rob thought, I've never been much of one to pray. I left all that to Betsy.

At that thought he laughed, a mirthless sound that came out more like a bark, and was followed by a fit of coughing.

Why hadn't the doctor called with the results?

His housekeeper, Jane Novak, was opening the sliding glass door as he stepped from the cobblestone walk onto the patio. "Hole in one, Mr. Robert?" she asked cheerfully.

"Not quite, but not bad, Jane," Rob said, trying not to be annoyed that Jane always asked that after he had been on the greens. If there was one thing about Jane he wished he could change, it was her total lack of any sense of humor. She meant that question to be a joke.

Jane, a solidly built woman with steel-gray hair and matching eyes, had come to work for him shortly after he married Betsy. He had understood why Betsy was not comfortable with the previous housekeeper, who had been hired by his first wife and who had stayed with him after her death. "Rob, that woman *resents* me," Betsy had said. "I can *feel* it. Tell her it's not working out and give her a healthy severance check. I know just who I want in her place."

The person Betsy wanted was Jane Novak, who had worked backstage when Betsy was ushering in the theatre. "She's a marvelous organizer. She actually keeps the dressing rooms neat. And she's a good cook," Betsy had raved.

Jane was all of that. After entering the country on a green card from Hungary, she was overwhelmed with joy to be put in charge of the mansion, and, as Betsy had promised, she was fully up to the job. Exactly Betsy's age, Jane was now sixty-two. If she had any close friends or family, Rob had never seen them. Her very comfortable apartment was located behind the kitchen, and even on her days off, from what he could see, she seldom left it. Unless he was out of town, he knew that at seven-thirty every morning she would be in the kitchen ready to prepare his breakfast.

Over the years Rob had learned to see the slight nuances in Jane's placid expression that signaled any kind of distress. As he stepped inside the house, he realized he was seeing them now. "You said that Ms. Moran was coming, Mr. Rob," Jane said. "I hope you don't mind if I ask, but does that mean that the program is going to happen?"

"I don't mind you asking, but the answer is I don't know," Rob said. Even as he spoke, he realized that he *did* mind Jane asking, because there was a note of disapproval in her question.

He had just enough time to change into a long-sleeved sport shirt and go back downstairs before the doorbell chimed.

It was exactly four o'clock. He wondered if she had timed her arrival so precisely or if she had arrived a little early and waited in her car before coming up to the house.

It was the kind of totally irrelevant speculation that Rob Powell had found himself indulging in lately. "Woolgathering" is what they used to call it, he thought. He had even gone to the trouble of looking up the word in the dictionary. The definition was "indulging in idle fancies and daydreaming; absentmindedness."

Rob thought to himself, Snap out of it! and got to his feet. He had asked Jane to bring Laurie Moran into the library instead of his office. Betsy had liked the English custom of four o'clock tea. After her death he had gotten away from it, but today it suddenly seemed appropriate.

More woolgathering, he acknowledged as Jane came into the room, followed by Laurie Moran.

He had considered Moran to be an attractive woman when she came to the house last month, but now as she hesitated for a moment and stood framed in the doorway, he realized that she was beautiful. Her hair, a soft honey shade, was loose on her shoulders, and in place of the pin-striped suit she was wearing a long-sleeved print blouse and black-belted skirt that accentuated her small waist. Her black patent leather heels did not have the ridiculous stilts that were the fashion nowadays.

Once again, the seventy-eight-year-old appreciated her lovely looks.

"Come in, Ms. Moran, come in," he said heartily. "I won't bite you."

"I wasn't afraid of that, Mr. Powell," Laurie said, smiling as she crossed the room and sat on the couch opposite the roomy leather armchair where he was settling himself.

"I've asked Jane to prepare tea," he said. "You may serve it now, Jane, thank you."

"How kind of you."

It *was* kind of him, Laurie thought.

She drew a deep breath. Now that she was here, with so much at stake, it was difficult to appear calm. The four women, the stars of the Graduation Gala, would cost this man nearly two million dollars, instead of half that amount, to appear on the program.

Laurie marshaled her pitch to him, but before she started she waited for Jane's somewhat forbidding figure to turn and leave the room.

"I'm going to make this easy for you," Robert Powell said unexpectedly. "A problem has come up. I don't have to be particularly astute or a deep thinker to guess that it's about money. One of the four girls—women now—doesn't think we're paying enough to coax them to expose themselves to public scrutiny."

Laurie hesitated for the length of a few seconds, then said, "That's right."

Powell smiled. "Let me guess which one. It wouldn't be Claire. She has refused to let me help her since Betsy died. When she learns I have left her a substantial amount of money in my will it will not impress her. When the time comes, she might even give the money to charity.

"We were *very* close, but Claire was very close to her mother, too. The fact that Betsy died was overwhelming for Claire. Somehow it became *my* fault, not that she thought I had killed her mother, mind you. Angry as she was, she knew that was impossible, but I think that in her mind, she was begrudging me the time I had alone with Betsy." For a long moment he looked past Laurie.

"My guess," he added slowly, "is that Nina Craig is the one holding us up for more money. In that way she's very much like her mother. I actually dated Muriel Craig for a time. A very attractive woman, but with a touch of ruthlessness in her character. I didn't stop seeing her only because I'd met Betsy. It would have happened anyhow. It was just a coincidence that it happened at approximately the same time."

Jane carried in the tea tray, interrupting his reverie. She set it on the coffee table between the couch and Robert Powell's chair. "Shall I pour, Mr. Powell?" she asked. She was already holding the teapot and pouring it into Laurie's cup.

Robert Powell raised his eyebrows and cast an amused glance at Laurie. After Jane had offered cream or lemon and sugar or sweetener, and then left the room, he said, "As you can see, Jane asked a rhetorical question. She does that all the time."

Laurie realized she had skipped lunch and was starved. She made herself take only a nibble of the quarter-sized crustless salmon sandwich. Her first instinct was to pop it into her mouth whole and reach for another one.

But even as she made herself eat slowly, daintily, she had the feeling that Robert Powell was toying with her. Did he really guess that Nina Craig was the one looking for more money, or had Nina contacted him personally?

And did he know how much she was going to demand?

"Am I right about Nina?" Powell asked as he crossed his legs and began to sip his tea.

"Yes," Laurie said.

"How much does she want for all the graduates?"

"Two hundred fifty thousand dollars net each."

"She's even greedier than I remembered," Powell murmured. "So like her dear mother." The amused tone left his voice. "Tell her I'll pay it."

The abrupt change in his expression and tone shocked Laurie.

"Ms. Moran," he explained, "you need to understand something: like the four girls at the Gala, I have lived with the cloud of suspicion hanging over me for a long time. Today people are living to be one hundred, but many more don't live past eighty or eighty-five. Before I die, I want to have a chance for a wide audience to see the girls and me, and perhaps understand how big this house is, and how many people were in and out that night. How it could have been an intruder. As you know, we have extensive films of the party."

"I do know that," Laurie said. "I think I've read everything written about the case."

"Well, then, you can understand that except for some generous donations to charity and the schools Betsy, Claire, and I attended, I have a great deal of money to spend before I die, so the amount Nina is holding out for is quite insignificant.

"But do me a favor. When you write to say we accept the conditions of their appearance, please tell Nina that I hope her mother is planning to come east with her. It would be a pleasure to see her again."

He anticipated Laurie's protest. "Of course, I don't mean for her to stay as a guest in my home. I will reserve a room for her at the St. Regis."

He's going along with it. Laurie did not expect the tsunami of relief that swept over her. The possibility of the program had unexpectedly gathered momentum, and if Powell had flatly turned down Nina Craig's demand, the show could easily have been doomed, and her job along with it. Two failed series, then a rejected proposal, after intense media interest, would easily have meant her dismissal.

Brett Young did not tolerate failure.

She started to thank Powell, then realized he was looking past her out onto the patio beyond the glass doors of his den. Her eyes followed to see what he was looking at that had caused the sudden expression of disapproval.

She saw a landscaper standing on the patio outside the den, edging the grass around it with a clipper.

Powell looked from the man to Laurie. "Sorry," he said, "but I find it annoying that they're working this late. I've made it clear that I want any work on the property completed by noon. If I have guests coming, I don't want those big trucks in the driveway."

Outside, Blue Eyes saw that Powell was looking at him. He finished clipping the last section around the patio and, without looking, carried his gardening equipment quickly back to the truck. It was his first day on the job for Perfect Estates. If Powell complained about him being there so late, Blue Eyes would say he stayed after hours to impress his new boss.

The Graduation girls won't be the only ones here when they are filming that show, he thought. I'll be here, too.

What a perfect scenario for him to take out Laurie Moran.

He had already prepared the sign he wanted to put on her body.

GOT GREG

GOT YOU

TIMMY'S NEXT

10

⬦

In June, preproduction for the "Graduation Gala" went into high gear. Laurie had already obtained all available film footage taken of the party, but then Robert Powell willingly turned over the extra footage other guests had captured that night.

It was like watching Cinderella's night at the ball. Only there were four Cinderellas, Laurie mused as she ran tape after tape.

After Betsy died, George Curtis, a member of the Winged Foot Golf Club in Mamaroneck, had brought to the police the footage he had taken that evening. But it was mostly a duplicate of what the police already had. The tape was copied and given to Robert Powell, who had requested it. "It's very similar to what I've already given you," he had told the detective in charge of the investigation, "but there are some scenes of Betsy and me that are particularly precious to me." He had pictures made of several of the frames in which he and Betsy had been together—one of them looking at each other, another of them dancing on the patio, another toasting the graduates.

"These films sure give us a look into the party," Laurie commented to Grace and Jerry as she played the copies over and over in the screening room of the office, trying to decide which scenes she wanted to include.

I start with the body being discovered and the cops arriving, she thought. That was at 8 A.M. Powell went in to wake up Betsy. He was carrying a cup of coffee for her. He always brought her wake-up cup at that time, even if she had had a late night.

Jane rushed in, screaming Betsy's name, and yelling for the others to dial 911.

We'll end the first segment with Betsy and Powell toasting the graduates. We'll have the narrator say, "At that moment, beautiful Betsy Bonner Powell had only four hours to live," Laurie decided.

George Curtis knew that he might be caught on security cameras around the Powell estate, but it did not worry him. Half of Salem Ridge is driving past this house, he thought as he followed the stream of cars on the quiet road.

So what if the cops think I'm a voyeur? he thought. Practically everyone else on this road is, too.

He had chosen to drive the SUV rather than his red Porsche convertible. Unless security cameras photographed the license plate, he doubted very much that he would be recognized. Plenty of Salem Ridge residents had top-of-the-line SUVs. He was wearing a cap and dark glasses.

Sixty-three years old, tall, with a full head of gray hair, George Curtis had the trim appearance of a seasoned athlete. Married for thirty-five years and with college-age twins, he had been the scion and sole heir of a big chain of fast-food restaurants. After his father's death, when he was twenty-seven, he had taken over the business. A playboy until then, everyone expected him to sell the chain and live off his wealth. Instead he had married shortly afterward, and over time tripled the number of restaurants both in the United States and abroad until now the company boasted of serving a million meals a day.

Unlike Robert Powell, he had gone to Harvard as a fourth-generation legacy. The welcome mat had been laid out for him, as was his admission to Hasty Pudding, the student theatrical society at Harvard.

The fifteen-year difference in their ages had never interfered with his friendship with Robert Powell, even though, as he turned the car off Evergreen Lane, George thought, If he ever knew, if he ever guessed . . .

But Rob Powell had never suspected. George was sure of that. George had never given him reason to.

The phone rang, an unexpected and abrupt sound. He pressed the answering button on the steering wheel.

"George Curtis," he said.

"George, it's Rob Powell."

My God, was he looking out the window? George felt his face flush. No, he couldn't possibly have read the license plate, and certainly couldn't have recognized me just driving by.

"Rob, how are you, and when are we going to get together for a round of golf? I warn you, I broke eighty two Saturdays in a row."

"That means you'll never do it three weeks in a row! Tee-off time nine o'clock?"

"You're on. I'll make the reservation." George felt a palpable sense of relief as he turned left onto his own street. Rob Powell was not one to stay on the line longer than necessary. That's why when Rob said, "George, I have a favor to ask of you," he was startled.

"Whatever it is, the answer is yes," George said, sounding rattled to his own ears.

"I'll take all your franchises in Europe," Rob joked, then his tone became serious. "George, you can't have missed the news that the anniversary of Betsy's death in June is going to be the basis for a television program."

"No, I didn't miss that," Curtis said quietly.

"The point is that, besides the girls, they'd like to have one of the friends who was there that night to comment on the party between excerpts from the films. I suggested you, and they leaped at the prospect of getting you on camera. Of course I should have asked you first, but you can always say no to them."

Go on camera to talk about that night to a national audience? He could feel his hands turning sweaty on the steering wheel.

George Curtis found his throat constricting, but he kept his voice calm and warm as he said, "Rob, I told you a minute ago that whatever favor you wanted, it was yours. I meant it when I said it, and I mean it now."

"Thanks. It was hard for me to ask, and I'm sure hard for you to agree."

An abrupt click broke the connection. George Curtis realized that he was drenched with perspiration now. Was Rob Powell setting a trap for him? he asked himself as a feeling of dread engulfed him.

Now utterly distracted, he almost drove past his own driveway.

11

From the windows of the ornate and seldom-used living room, Jane Novak watched the stream of cars pass the house.

Today the television crew was upstairs in Betsy's bedroom.

I mean Mrs. Powell's bedroom, Jane thought sarcastically. Betsy had become "Mrs. Powell" to her the day she took over as housekeeper here twenty-nine years ago.

"Mr. Powell is quite traditional, Jane," she had said. "He told me that it was fine with him if I wanted to hire you, but that it was necessary for you to refer to me that way."

At the time, thirty-three-year-old Jane hadn't minded. She'd been thrilled to get the job. Mr. Powell had insisted on meeting her and sent his chauffeur to bring her up for an interview. He explained that because it was such a large house, two maids from a cleaning service came in four hours a day and would work under her supervision. She would prepare the meals. If they had a dinner party, their caterers would handle it. With two maids reporting to her, instead of having to clean dressing rooms after sloppy actors, Jane could spend most of her day cooking—a joy, not a task. She couldn't believe her good fortune.

By the time the first anniversary of working for the Powells had passed, Jane's heartfelt gratitude for the job had evolved.

She'd fallen passionately in love with Rob Powell.

She did not for a minute believe that she would ever have the slightest prospect of his looking at her as a man looked at a woman.

Providing for his comfort, glowing at his praise for the meals she served, hearing his footsteps as he came downstairs in the morning to get Betsy's wake-up coffee was enough. In the twenty years since Betsy's death, Jane had been able to live the fantasy that she was married to Rob.

Whenever he said, "I'm going out to dinner tonight, Jane," she would panic with fear and secretly look at the calendar he kept on his desk.

But women's names appeared only occasionally, and Jane had come to believe that, at his age, there would never be another Mrs. Powell.

One day last year he had been going over his will with his lawyer, who was also his close friend, and didn't put it away when they went outside to play on the golf course.

Jane had flipped to the end of the will and found what she was looking for—the bequest to her: three hundred thousand dollars for a condo in Silver Pines, the fifty-five-plus community where he knew Jane had formed a few friendships with residents she had met at her church. And an income of one thousand dollars a week for the remainder of her life.

Reading that made Jane's worship of Robert Powell even deeper.

But this program would start trouble. She knew it. Let sleeping dogs lie, she thought as she watched rubberneckers pass the house.

Jane shook her head and turned from the window and realized that the producer, Laurie Moran, was standing in the doorway.

"Oh," Jane said, startled out of her usual reserve.

Laurie sensed the housekeeper's resentment at her presence. "Oh, Ms. Novak, I'm sure you must be sick of us being here already, but I don't want to disturb Mr. Powell. I have just one question."

Jane managed to smooth her expression.

"Of course. What is it, Ms. Moran?"

"Mrs. Powell's bedroom is exquisite. Were the drapes and spread and carpet replaced after she died, or were they here the night of the murder?"

"No, Mrs. Powell had just had a decorator redo the room, then didn't like the effect. She said the colors were too bold."

The waste, Jane thought, not allowing herself to shake her head. The absolute waste of money.

"She'd ordered new draperies and a new headboard and a new carpet. After she died, Mr. Powell had them installed to honor her wishes. It's exactly as you see it now."

"It's beautiful," Laurie said sincerely. "Is it ever used?"

"It is *never* used," Jane said. "But it is always kept fresh. You'll never see the silver brush and comb on the dressing table not looking polished. Even the towels in her bathroom are replaced regularly. Mr. Powell wanted her room and bath to always look as if she were about to open the door and come in."

Laurie couldn't resist asking, "Does he spend much time in her room?"

Jane frowned. "I don't think so, but that's the kind of question I think you should ask Mr. Powell."

Now the disapproval was evident in the housekeeper's expression and tone of voice.

Oh boy, Laurie thought. I'd really hate to cross this one. "Thank you, Jane," she said soothingly. "We're all leaving now. We won't be back over the weekend. We'll see you Monday morning. And let me reassure you we will absolutely be finished on Wednesday after lunch."

It was nearly noon, which meant Robert Powell expected the crew from the production company to clear out. It was also a Friday, the day he worked from home. He had been in his office with the door closed since they'd arrived.

Three days, Laurie thought later that day in her office as she went over her notes with Jerry and Grace, who were with her every day of the shoot in Salem Ridge.

It was Grace who voiced what all three of them were thinking. "That place is gorgeous," she said. "In one way it makes me never want to come home to my five-story walk-up apartment that's not big enough to take three steps in without bumping into a wall." She paused, her expressive eyes even more mascaraed than usual, then finished, "On the other hand, it gives me the creeps. My grand-mother used to say that a pigeon flying into the room was a sign of death coming to the house. Laurie, were you in Betsy Powell's bed-room today when a pigeon was flying around outside, trying to find a way to get in?"

"Oh, come on," Jerry said. "Grace, that's a stretch even for you."

Of course it's a stretch, Laurie told herself.

She was not about to admit to Grace and Jerry that the magnifi-cent home where Betsy Powell had died also gave her the creeps.

12

At noon on Sunday Josh picked up the first arrival, Claire, at the Westchester Airport. Although she knew Josh, who had been hired shortly before Betsy's death, she gave him only a brief hello and did not engage in any conversation with him. As he drove her to the Westchester Hilton, she reflected on the plans for the next three days. On Monday they would meet for the first time over breakfast. They would be free for the rest of the day to reacquaint themselves with the house and the grounds. The individual interviews would take place on Tuesday. They had all agreed to sleep at the house Tuesday night in the same rooms they had been in twenty years earlier. Wednesday morning would be Robert Powell's interview, followed by their being photographed at the luncheon table. They would then be driven to their departing flights.

"While we are certainly aware of how painful this will be for all of you, by your willingness to appear on the program, you each are making a forceful statement to clear your names," was the conclusion of Laurie's letter.

Clear our names! Claire Bonner thought bitterly as she checked into the Westchester Hilton.

She was wearing a light-green summer pantsuit she had bought at an expensive boutique in Chicago. In the three months since the first letter had come from Laurie Moran, she had let her hair grow and had lightened it so that now it was a shining mane around her shoulders. But today she had it tied in a ponytail with a scarf over her head. She had also practiced using makeup, but was wearing none today. With makeup and hair combed as her mother had worn it, she knew she bore a startling resemblance to her. She did not want Josh to see that resemblance and tell Powell until she met with him face to face.

"Your suite is ready, Ms. Bonner," the clerk said, and waved to the bellman. Claire caught the long glance he gave her and the hint of excitement in his voice.

Why not? It would be almost impossible to miss all the newspaper articles about the upcoming program. The gossip magazines were having a field day digging up everything they could find about Betsy Bonner Powell. USHERED TO A FATAL NEW LIFESTYLE was a particularly grating one that had appeared on the front page of the *Shocker*, a sensational weekly. The article detailed the first meeting of Betsy Bonner and Robert Powell. Betsy had taken her daughter, Claire, to lunch at a restaurant in Rye for her thirteenth birthday. Robert Powell, a widower, had been seated across the room with Claire's friend Nina and her mother. As Betsy and Claire were leaving, Nina had called to them. They walked over to Powell's table, where Nina introduced Betsy and Claire to the Wall Street hedge fund multimillionaire.

"The rest is, as they say, history," was the trite introduction to the final columns of that story. Robert Powell claimed it was love at first sight. He and Betsy Bonner were married three months later.

"Actress Muriel Craig put up a brave front, but insiders say she was furious and blamed her daughter, Nina, for making it a point to call out to Claire in the restaurant."

I know that's true, Claire thought as she followed the bellman to the elevator. Poor Nina.

The suite consisted of a large bedroom and living room, a full bath, and a powder room furnished in pastel shades. It was both attractive and restful.

Claire tipped the bellman, phoned room service, and unpacked her one suitcase. It contained the three outfits she had selected to bring with her, as well as her supply of new cosmetics.

In one of her e-mails, Laurie Moran had requested Claire's size and height, saying that she would have wardrobe changes available.

Wardrobe changes! Claire had thought when she read the e-mail. Why on earth would I need changes?

But then she had understood. Moran would provide gowns similar but not identical to the ones they had worn twenty years ago at the Gala.

They would reenact a few of the scenes in the films, like the one of the four of them clinking glasses or with arms around one another, posing for the cameras. And individually being questioned by the police.

I know I look good, Claire thought. Now I'm so like my dear mother.

A light tap at the door told her that room service had arrived with the chicken salad and iced tea she had ordered.

But as she nibbled at the salad and sipped the tea, Claire realized that she was not as brave as she had thought.

Something was telling her not to go forward with her plan.

Just nerves, she tried to reassure herself. Just nerves.

But it was more than that.

Like a drumbeat in her head, her inner voice was saying, *Don't do it. Don't do it. It is not worth the risk!*

13

It had been a long trip from Cleveland to Westchester Airport. A heavy rainstorm had caused their plane to sit on the tarmac for two hours, and even though they were flying on a small private jet, there was little space to move around. This made it very difficult for Rod's back. At one point, she suggested they just forget the whole thing.

"Alie, this is your chance to get the degree you always wanted. Between Powell and the production company, you'll net three hundred thousand dollars. It will pay for medical school and all the other expenses, but every cent counts. You know how desperately you have always wanted to be a doctor and then go into medical research," Rod had said in refusal.

Even if I can commute to school, I will have to be studying all the time. Where does that leave Rod? Or if I have to go away to school, does he leave his job at the pharmacy and come with me but then have nothing to do? she wondered. But if that happens, then the pharmacy loses both him and me, and we have to hire two new people. I don't know how that's going to work.

It was three o'clock by her wristwatch when they landed in Westchester. By then Rod's expression was sufficient proof of the pain he was in. After he hobbled on crutches from the cabin to his waiting wheelchair, Alison bent over him and whispered, "Thank you for making this trip."

He managed a smile as he looked up at her.

Mercifully the driver, a ruddy-faced man of about fifty with the build of an ex-boxer, was waiting for them in the terminal. He introduced himself to them. "I'm Josh Damiano, Mr. Powell's chauffeur. He wanted to be sure you had a comfortable ride from the airport to your hotel."

"How kind of Mr. Powell." Alison hoped that the contempt she felt did not show. Now that they were back in New York, a kaleidoscope of memories was flooding her mind. Neither one of them had been in New York in fifteen years. That was when the doctors had told Rod there would be no more operations.

By then their money was gone and Rod's family was taking out loans to support them, but Alison had managed to take the necessary courses at night for a year and get her license as a pharmacist. They had gratefully seized the opportunity to go to Cleveland and work in his cousin's pharmacy.

I loved New York, she thought, but I was happy to get away from it. I always thought that the minute people saw me, they wondered whether I'd killed Betsy Bonner Powell. In Cleveland, for the most part, we have lived quietly.

"There are benches near the doors," Damiano said. "Let me get you settled comfortably and go for the car. I'll try not to be too long."

They watched as he collected the luggage from the pilots. He was back for them within five minutes. "The car's right outside," he said as he helped Rod with his wheelchair.

A shiny black Bentley was waiting at the curb.

When Damiano helped Rod out of the wheelchair and into the backseat, Alison felt her heart wrench.

He's in so much pain, she thought, but he never complains, and he never talks about the football career he would have had . . .

The big car began to move. "The traffic's light," Damiano told them. "We should be at the hotel in about twenty minutes."

They had chosen to stay at the Crowne Plaza in White Plains. The town was near enough to Salem Ridge, but far enough away from the hotels where the other three childhood friends who were on the program were staying. Laurie Moran made sure of that.

"You two okay?" Damiano asked them solicitously.

"I'm very comfortable," Alison assured him as Rod murmured his assent.

But then Rod leaned over and whispered, "Alie, I was thinking, when you're on camera, not a word about sleepwalking and possibly being in Betsy's room that night."

"Oh, Rod I never would," Alison said, horrified.

"And don't volunteer that you're hoping to go to med school unless they ask. It will remind everyone how disappointed you were when you didn't get the scholarship to medical school, and how furious you were that Robert Powell got the dean to throw it to Vivian Fields."

The mention of her heartbreak the day of her graduation from college was enough to make Alison's face contort with pain and rage. "Betsy Powell was trying to get into the Women's Club with the top-of-the-line socialites, and Vivian Fields's mother was the president of it. And of course Powell had leverage—he'd just donated a dormitory to the college! The Fieldses could have afforded to pay Vivian's tuition one hundred times over. Even the dean looked embarrassed when he called out her name. And then he muttered something about Vivian's academic brilliance. Right! She dropped out in her second year. I could have scratched Betsy's eyes out!"

"Which is why if they ask you what you'll do with the money, just say that we're planning to take a round-the-world ocean cruise," Rod counseled.

•   •   •

Glancing into the rearview mirror, Josh Damiano observed Rod whispering something to his wife and watched her shocked reaction and how upset she instantly became. He could not hear what they were saying, but he smiled inwardly.

It doesn't matter whether I can hear them, he thought. The recorder picks up everything that's said in this car.

14

Regina Callari's initial response upon learning that, between Fisher Blake Studios and Robert Powell, she would net three hundred thousand dollars for appearing in the program was one of relief and elation.

The crushing burden of living paycheck to paycheck, which translated to house sale to house sale in a terrible real estate market, had been lifted from her shoulders.

It almost gave her that warm, secure feeling she had felt in early childhood, until the day she found her father's body hanging in the garage.

Over the years she had had the same dream about her early life. In it, she woke up in her big bedroom, with the pretty white bed that had a spray of delicate pink flowers painted on the headboard, the night table, the dresser, the desk, and the bookcase. In the dream she could always vividly see the pink-and-white bedspread, the matching draperies, and the soft pink rug.

After her father's suicide, when her mother realized how little money they had, they had moved to a three-room apartment, where they shared a bedroom.

Her mother, who loved fashion, had gotten a job as a personal shopper at Bergdorf Goodman, where she had once been a valued

customer. Somehow they'd gotten by, and Regina had proudly graduated from college on a financial-aid scholarship.

After Alison's wedding and all the gossip about Betsy's death,
I moved to Florida to escape, Regina thought as she boarded the
plane in St. Augustine. Some escape. Put it aside, she told herself.
Don't keep dwelling or you'll drive yourself crazy.

A few hours earlier she had seen Zach off on his backpacking trip
to Europe. He was meeting his group in Boston, and they were flying to Paris tonight.

Regina settled comfortably in the small private plane and helped
herself to a predeparture glass of wine.

She smiled briefly at the memory of the visit she and Zach had
just shared.

When he had arrived home from college two weeks earlier, she
had put a CLOSED FOR VACATION sign up on the front door of the
office and announced to Zach that they were going on a vacation
together—a cruise through the Caribbean.

The closeness between them that she was so afraid was lost had
been regained—even magnified—on that trip.

Zach purposely said little about his father and stepmother, but
once she asked, he told her everything.

"Mom, I knew when Dad made money, lots of money, he should
have given you more. I think he would have, except he was afraid of
Sonya's reaction. She has a really bad temper."

Zach's father was writing the songs that made him rich when we
were married, but the first one didn't sell until a year after we were
divorced. I couldn't afford a lawyer to prove that he wrote it when he
was married to me, Regina had thought bitterly.

"I think he regrets marrying Sonya," Zach had told her. "When
they have an argument, the decibel level goes through the roof."

"I *love* it," Regina remembered telling Zach.

She warmed at the memory of Zach's compliments about her

twenty-pound weight loss. "Mom, you look so cool," he'd said, more than once.

"I worked out at the gym a lot these past two months," she told him. "I realized that I'd gotten out of the habit of going there regularly."

On the cruise he asked her about her parents. "All you ever really told me was that Grandpa committed suicide because he had made some bad investments and was broke, and that Grandma was planning to live in Florida when she retired, but died in her sleep only a year after you moved here," he said.

"She never got over losing my father."

Zach looks so much like my father, Regina thought now as the plane took off. Tall, blond, and blue-eyed.

The last night they were at dinner on the cruise Zach asked her about the night Betsy died. He had overheard his father telling Sonya all about it and had googled it.

Regina had then told him about the note.

Was I wrong to tell him about it? she wondered now. I needed to talk to someone about it. I was always worried I had made a mistake by *not* showing it to my mother.

Don't dwell on it, Regina thought as she helped herself to a second glass of wine.

It was eight o'clock when she landed at Westchester. The driver who met her introduced himself as Mr. Powell's chauffeur, Josh Damiano. He told her that Mr. Powell wanted to ensure her comfort.

It was hard not to laugh out loud. When he opened the door of the Bentley for her, she could not resist commenting to him, "I guess Mr. Powell has outgrown the Mercedes?"

"Oh no," Damiano answered with a smile. "He has a Mercedes wagon."

"I'm so glad." Shut your mouth, Regina warned herself as she stepped into the car.

They were barely leaving the airport when her cell phone rang.

It was Zach. "We're about to board, Mom. Wanted to be sure you landed safely."

"Oh, Zach, how sweet of you. I miss you already."

Zach's tone changed. "Mom, the note. You told me you were tempted to shove it in Powell's face. Have you got it with you?"

"Yes. I have it, but don't worry. I won't be that crazy. It's in my suitcase. I promise you, no one can find it."

"Mom, tear it up! If anyone found it, you could be in big trouble."

"Zach, if it makes you feel better, I promise I'll tear it up."

No I won't, she thought, but I can't let him get on that plane upset about me.

In the front seat, Josh Damiano had not expected to record Regina because she was traveling alone. When he heard her phone ring, he quickly turned on the recorder. Maybe I'll get lucky, he thought.

You couldn't be too careful when you worked for a man like Mr. Powell.

15

It had been a long day. Sitting in her office with Jerry and Grace, Laurie had gone over a myriad of details to ensure everything was in order for the first day of shooting.

She finally leaned back and said, "That's it, the die is cast, we can't do anything more now. The graduates are all here, and tomorrow we meet them. We start the day at nine A.M. Mr. Powell said that the housekeeper will have coffee and fruit and rolls prepared."

"It's amazing. They claim that not one of them has been in touch with the others all these years," Jerry observed, "but I bet they google each other once in a while. I would if I were one of them. My aunt always googles to see what her ex is up to."

"I would guess this meeting will be awkward for at least the first few minutes," Laurie said, a worried note in her voice. "But they were close friends for years, and they all went through hell being interrogated by the police."

"Nina Craig once told a reporter every one of them was accused of having been part of a plan to murder Betsy, and that the detective told her she'd better turn state's witness to get a lighter sentence," Jerry recalled. "That must have been pretty scary."

"I still don't get why any one of the graduates would have wanted to kill Betsy Powell," Grace said, shaking her head. "They're celebrating their graduation at a lavish party. They have their whole lives in front of them. They all look happy in the films of the party."

"Maybe one of them wasn't as happy as she looked," Laurie suggested.

"This is the way I look at it," Grace declared. "Betsy's daughter, Claire, certainly didn't seem to have any reason to kill her mother. They were always very close. Regina Callari's father lost his money in one of Powell's hedge funds, but even her mother admitted that Powell had repeatedly warned him that while he might make a lot of money, he should not invest more than he could afford to lose. Nina Craig's mother was dating Powell when he met Betsy, but unless you're really crazy you don't suffocate someone for a reason like that. And Alison Schaefer married her boyfriend four months after graduation. He was already a football star with a multimillion-dollar contract. What reason would she have had for putting a pillow over Betsy Powell's face?"

As she was speaking, Grace held up her fingers one by one to illustrate the point she was making. "And that sour-looking housekeeper had been hired by Betsy," she continued. "My guess is it was as simple as a burglary gone wrong. The house is big. There are sliding glass doors all over the place. The alarm wasn't on. One door was unlocked. Anyone could have gotten in. I think it was someone who was after the emerald necklace and earrings. They were worth a fortune. Don't forget, one of the earrings was on the floor of her bedroom."

"Someone in the crowd may have been a party crasher," Laurie agreed. "Some of the guests asked to bring friends, and there are a couple of people in the films that no one could identify positively." She paused. "Well, maybe this program will bring that out. If so, Powell, the housekeeper, and the graduates will certainly be glad they participated."

"I think they're already glad," Jerry observed. "Three hundred thousand dollars net is a pretty nice number to put in your wallet. I wish I had it."

"If I did, I'd treat myself to a new apartment that's only a *four-story walk-up*," Grace said with a sigh.

"But if it turns out that one of them did it, she could always hire Alex Buckley to defend her," Jerry suggested. "With his fees, that three hundred thousand dollars would go up in smoke."

Alex Buckley was the renowned criminal lawyer who would be the host of the program and would conduct separate interviews with Powell, the housekeeper, and the graduates. Thirty-eight years old, he was a frequent guest on television programs discussing major crimes.

He had become famous by defending a mogul accused of murdering his business partner. Against tremendous odds Buckley had secured a not-guilty verdict, which the press had deplored as a miserable miscarriage of justice. Then, ten months later, the business partner's wife committed suicide, leaving a note saying that *she* had murdered her husband.

After watching countless videos of Alex Buckley, Laurie had decided he would be the ideal narrator of the Graduation Gala program.

Then she had to convince him.

She had called his office and made an appointment to see him.

A moment after she was ushered into his office he had taken an urgent phone call, and sitting across from his desk Laurie had had a chance to study him closely.

He had dark hair, blue-green eyes accentuated by black-rimmed glasses, a firm chin, and the tall, lanky build that she knew had made him a basketball star in college.

Observing him on television, she had decided that he was the kind of man people instinctively liked and trusted, and that was the quality she was looking for in a narrator who would also be on camera. That instinct was reinforced as she heard him reassuring the person he was speaking to that there was no reason to worry.

When he finished the phone call, his apologetic smile was warm and genuine. But his first question—"And what can I do for you, Ms. Moran?"—warned her not to waste his time.

Laurie had been prepared, succinct, and passionate.

She thought back to the moment when Alex Buckley leaned back in his chair and said, "I'd be very interested in taking part in the program, Ms. Moran."

"Laurie, I was sure you were going to get turned down flat that day," Jerry said.

"I knew that the money I could offer Buckley for being on the program wasn't enough to compensate him, but my hunch was he might be intrigued by the unsolved Graduation Gala case. Thank heaven it turns out that I was right."

"You were right on," Jerry agreed heartily. "He'll be great."

It was six o'clock. "Let's hope so," Laurie said as she pushed back her chair and got up. "We've labored in the vineyard long enough. Let's call it a day."

Two hours later as they sipped coffee, Laurie said to her father, "As I told Jerry and Grace today, the die is cast."

"What does that mean?" Timmy asked. Tonight he had not asked to be excused after he finished dessert.

"It means that I've done everything possible, and we start filming the people on the program tomorrow morning."

"Will it be a series?" Timmy asked.

"From your mouth to God's ear," Laurie said fervently, then smiled at her son. So like Greg, she thought, not just in looks, but in the expression he gets when he's thinking something through.

He always asked about any project she was working on. This one she had described in the broadest terms as "a reunion of four friends who grew up together but haven't seen each other in twenty years."

Timmy's answer to that was, "*Why* didn't they see each other?"

"Because they lived in different states," Laurie answered honestly.

The last few months have been hard, she thought. It wasn't only the pressure of the enormous amount of preparation for the filming. Timmy had received his First Holy Communion on May 25, and she had not been able to keep the tears from slipping past her dark glasses. *Greg should be here. Greg should be here, but he'll never be here for all the important events in Timmy's life. Not his confirmation or graduations or when he gets married. Not any of them.* Those thoughts had sounded like a drumbeat in her head, repeating themselves over and over as she made a desperate effort to stop crying.

Laurie realized that Timmy was looking at her, a worried expression on his face.

"Mom, you look sad," he said anxiously.

"I didn't mean to." Laurie swallowed over the lump that was forming in her throat and smiled. "Why should I? I have you and Grandpa. Isn't that right, Dad?"

Leo Farley was familiar with the emotion he sensed his daughter was feeling. He often had moments of intense sadness when he thought of the years he and Eileen had been married. And then to lose Greg to some devil incarnate—

Leo stopped that thought. "And I have you two," he said heartily. "Remember, don't stay up too late, either one of you. We all have to get up early tomorrow."

In the morning Timmy was going away to camp for two weeks with some of his friends.

Leo and Laurie had wrestled with their abiding worry that Blue Eyes might somehow find out where Timmy was going, then realized that if they isolated him from activities with his friends, he would grow up nervous and fearful. In the five years since Greg's murder, they'd struggled to make Timmy feel normal—while keeping him safe.

Leo had gone upstate personally to look the camp over, and had spoken with the head counselor and been assured that the boys Timmy's age were under constant supervision, and that they had security guards who would spot a stranger in a heartbeat.

Leo told the counselor the words Timmy had been screaming: "Blue Eyes shot my daddy." Then he repeated the description the elderly witness had given the police. "He had a scarf over his face. He was wearing a cap. He was average height, broad but not fat. He was around the block in seconds, but I don't think he was young. But he could run really fast."

For some reason the image of the guy who had skated past them on the sidewalk in March ran through Leo's mind as he spoke the words "really fast." Maybe it's because he almost knocked over that pregnant lady who was ahead of us, he thought.

"A little more coffee, Dad?"

"No thanks." Leo had made himself stop telling Laurie that getting those people from the Graduation Gala under one roof again was too risky. It was going to happen, and there was no use wasting his breath.

He pushed his chair back from the table, collected the dessert dishes and coffee cups, and brought them into the kitchen. Laurie was already there, about to start loading the dishes into the dishwasher.

"I'll do those," he said. "You double-check Timmy's bag. I think I have everything in it."

"Then everything is in it. I never knew anyone so organized. Dad, what would I do without you?"

"You'd do very well, but I plan to be around for a while." Leo Farley kissed his daughter. As he said that, the words of the elderly woman who had witnessed Greg's death and heard the murderer shout to Timmy, *"Tell your mother that she's next, then it's your turn,"* rang in his head for the millionth time.

At that moment Leo Farley decided that he would quietly drive up to Salem Ridge for the days of the filming. I'm enough of a cop that I can do surveillance without being observed, he thought.

If anything goes wrong, I want to be there, he told himself.

16

Alex Buckley's alarm went off at 6 A.M., only seconds after his interior alarm made him stir in his sleep and open his eyes.

He lay quietly for a few minutes to collect his thoughts.

Today he would be in Salem Ridge for the first day of filming the Graduation Gala.

He pushed off the sheet and got up. Years ago, a client who was out on bail had come to his office. When he stood up to greet her, she had exclaimed, "My God, I never realized there's no end to you!"

Six foot four, Alex had understood the remark and laughed. The woman was only five feet tall, a fact that had not prevented her from fatally stabbing her husband during a domestic quarrel.

The woman's remark ran through his mind as he headed for the shower, but it quickly disappeared as he thought about the day ahead.

He knew why he had decided to accept the offer from Laurie Moran. He had read about the Graduation Gala when he was a sophomore at Fordham University and had followed the case with avid interest, trying to imagine which graduate had committed the crime. He had been sure it was *one* of them.

His apartment was on Beekman Place, by the East River, that

was home to high-ranking UN delegates, as well as quietly wealthy businesspeople.

Two years ago he had happened to visit the apartment, and at the dinner table learned that the hosts were putting it on the market. He instantly decided to buy it. To him, its only downfall was the large, incessantly blinking red PEPSI-COLA sign on a building in Long Island City that marred the view of the East River.

But the apartment had six large rooms, as well as servant quarters. He knew he didn't need so much space, but on the other hand, he rationalized, the full dining room meant he could have dinner parties; he could turn the second bedroom into a den; and it would be handy to have a guestroom. His brother Andrew, a corporate lawyer, lived in Washington, D.C., and came up to Manhattan regularly on business.

"Now you won't need to go to a hotel," he had told Andrew.

"I'm willing to pay the going rate," his brother had joked, then added, "As it happens, I'm sick of hotels, so this will be great."

When he bought the apartment, Alex decided that instead of a biweekly housekeeper it would be better to have one full-time employee who could keep the apartment clean, run errands, and prepare breakfast and dinner when he was home. Through the recommendation of the interior decorator who had furnished his new home with quiet good taste he had hired Ramon, who had been with one of her other clients but had chosen not to move to California with them. Ramon's former employers were an eccentric couple who kept erratic hours, and what they didn't wear they dropped on the floor.

Ramon happily settled in the studio-sized room and bath off the kitchen, which had been designed for a live-in helper. Sixty years old, born in the Philippines, he was long divorced, with a daughter in Syracuse.

Ramon had no interest in Alex's private affairs, and it would never have occurred to him to read anything Alex left on his desk.

Ramon was already in the kitchen when Alex, dressed in his usual business suit, white shirt, and tie, took his seat in the breakfast nook. The morning papers were next to his plate, but after greeting Ramon and skimming the headlines, he pushed them away.

"I'll read them when I get home tonight," he said as Ramon poured coffee into his cup. "Anything exciting in them?"

"You're on Page Six of the *Post*, sir. You escorted Miss Allen to the opening of a film."

"Yes, I did." Alex was still not used to the unwanted publicity that accompanied the celebrity status he had achieved by his frequent television appearances.

"She is a very beautiful woman, sir."

"Yes, she is." That was something else. As an unmarried, prominent lawyer, he could not escort a woman to an event without being linked to her. Elizabeth Allen was a friend, and nothing more.

Alex made short work of the fruit, cereal, and toast Ramon set before him. He realized that he was anxious to get up to the home of Robert Powell and meet both him and the returning graduates.

They'd all be forty-one or forty-two by now, he thought, Claire Bonner, Alison Schaefer, Regina Callari, and Nina Craig. Since he had agreed to be the narrator of the program, he had done extensive research on each, and had read everything that had been in the media at the time of Betsy Powell's murder.

He had been asked to arrive at the Powell estate at nine o'clock. It was time to leave. "Will you be home for dinner tonight, Mr. Alex?" Ramon asked.

"Yes, I will."

"Do you plan to have a guest or guests?"

Alex smiled at the diminutive man who was looking so anxiously at him.

Ramon is a perfectionist, he thought, not for the first time. He did not like to waste food when it could be avoided, and he happily

welcomed being informed when Alex was inviting friends for dinner. Alex shook his head. "No guests," he said.

A few minutes later Alex was in the garage of his building. Ramon
had phoned ahead, so his Lexus convertible was already parked near
the exit ramp with the roof down.

Alex put on his sunglasses, started the car, and headed for the
East River Drive. The questions he would ask the six people who
were known to be in the house on the night that Betsy Bonner Powell had been suffocated in her sleep were already in his head.

17

Leo Farley gave his grandson a bear hug as he prepared to climb aboard the chartered bus from Saint David's School to Camp Mountainside in the Adirondacks. He was careful not to show any sign of his ever-present worry that Blue Eyes might ferret out Timmy's location.

He said, "You're going to have a great time with your pals."

"I know it, Grandpa," Timmy said, but then a frightened expression came over his face.

Glancing around, Leo could see that what was happening to Timmy was the same with all his friends. The moment of saying good-bye to parents or grandparents was causing a flicker of worry over *all* their faces.

"Okay, boys, all aboard," one of the counselors who were accompanying the campers called.

Leo hugged Timmy again. "You're going to have a great time," he repeated as he planted a kiss on Timmy's cheek.

"And you'll take care of Mom, won't you, Grandpa?"

"Of course I will."

Laurie had had breakfast with Timmy at six o'clock before she was picked up by a Fisher Blake Studios car for the drive to Salem Ridge. Their good-bye had been tearful, but blessedly brief.

As Timmy turned and got on line for the coach, Leo could only think that the boy, who now had only an occasional nightmare about Blue Eyes, still retained his awareness of that terrible threat his father's killer had shouted.

And at eight years old, he was also worried that something would happen to his mother.

Not on my watch, Leo thought. After waving good-bye to the parting campers, he headed for the rented black Toyota he had parked a block away on Fifth Avenue. He had not wanted to risk Laurie catching sight of his familiar red Ford sedan. He turned on the engine and headed for Salem Ridge.

Forty-five minutes later he was on Old Farms Road as the limousine bringing the first of the graduates turned and entered the long driveway of the Powell estate.

18

Blue Eyes always followed his instincts. He had known that day five years ago that it was time to begin taking his revenge. He had followed Dr. Greg Moran and Timmy from their home in the Peter Cooper Village apartment complex on Twenty-first Street to the playground on Fifteenth Street that afternoon.

It had given him a rush of power seeing the two of them walking hand in hand to the place of execution. At the busy crossing on First Avenue, the doctor picked up Timmy and carried him. Blue Eyes laughed when he saw Timmy, his arms around his father's neck, a happy smile on his face.

For an instant he had wondered if he should kill both of them, but he decided against it. Then there would only be Laurie left. No, better to wait.

But now it was Laurie's turn. He knew so much about her; where she lived, where she worked, when she jogged along the East River. He had followed her sometimes onto the crosstown bus and sat next to her. *If you only knew, if you only knew!* It was hard not to say it out loud.

Blue Eyes adopted the "Bruno Hoffa" name after he was released from serving his five-year term. *It was really easy to change my name and get phony documents after my parole was completed,* he thought.

Most of the last six months, since he was released from prison for the second time, he'd been doing the kind of jobs where no one cares much about your background, like construction work and day labor.

He didn't mind hard work; in fact, he liked it. He remembered overhearing someone say that he looked and acted like a peasant.

Instead of being angry he had laughed at the remark. He knew he had the squat body and powerful arms people associate with someone who dug ditches, and that's the way he wanted it.

Even at sixty, he knew he could probably outrun any cop who tried to chase him.

In April he had read in the newspapers that Fisher Blake Studios was going to reenact the Graduation Gala murder and that Laurie Moran would be the producer.

That was when he knew he had to get a job somehow on the Powell estate to allow him to be there without arousing suspicion. He drove past Powell's property and observed the oversized truck with the PERFECT ESTATES sign on it. He looked up the company and applied for a job. As a kid he had worked for a landscaper and picked up everything he needed to know about the job. It didn't take a genius to mow a lawn or clip hedges and bushes or to plant flowers in the places pointed out by the boss.

He liked the job. And he knew Laurie Moran would be up there a lot when they started filming.

He had seen Laurie at the estate for the first time right after he got the job. He recognized her when she got out of her car and immediately grabbed a grass clipper to get close to the den, where Powell always met business guests.

He could have taken her out that day as she was walking back to her car, but he had decided to wait. He'd waited so long already, savoring her family's fear. Wouldn't it be better to wait until she was here with her film crew? he asked himself. Wouldn't the media coverage of her death be more dramatic when it was attached to the publicity around the Graduation Gala filming?

Powell had told Blue Eyes' boss, Artie Carter, that the filming would begin June 20th. Blue Eyes' concern had been that Powell would order all the planting and mowing and trimming be completed before the filming began.

That was why Blue Eyes spoke to Artie on the 19th, as they were wrapping up their final trimming and planting.

"Mr. Carter," he said, as he always did, even though the rest of the workers called him Artie. He had explained it was because he had been taught to respect the boss, and he sensed that Carter was pleased by it.

Actually, Artie Carter felt there was something not quite right about Bruno Hoffa. He never joined the other workers for a beer after work. He never entered debates about the baseball season when they were driving from one job to another. He never complained if the weather was lousy. In Artie's opinion, Bruno had one card missing from his deck, but so what? He was the best worker of all his crew.

As Artie finished inspecting the grounds, he was satisfied. Even the pain-in-the-neck client, Mr. Robert Powell, couldn't find anything to complain about.

It was then that Bruno Hoffa approached him.

"Mr. Carter, I have a suggestion to make," he said.

"What is it, Bruno?" It had been a long day, and Artie was ready to go home and have a nice cold beer. Or maybe a couple of nice cold beers.

Now Bruno, his narrow mouth extended into a forced smile, his lidded eyes fixed on Artie's neck, his tone unusually subservient even for him, hesitantly began his planned speech.

"Mr. Powell came out the other day when I was planting flowers around the pool house. He said that the flowers were beautiful, but he was really annoyed because he knew the film crew would crush the grass. He supposed it would be inevitable, but he wished he could do something about it."

"Mr. Powell is a perfectionist," Artie said. "And our biggest customer. From what I understand they'll be photographing outside all week. What are we supposed to do about that?" he asked irritably. "We've been told to stay off the property after today."

Blue Eyes began his carefully prepared pitch. "Mr. Carter, I was thinking. We couldn't have one of the trucks in the driveway, because Mr. Powell would have a fit. But maybe you could suggest I be stationed in the pool house. That way if the film crew tramples on the grass or makes holes with their heavy equipment, I could repair it the minute they leave the area. Also, the people who are in the film might decide to take a walk on the grounds, or maybe have lunch outside and leave litter behind them. I could take care of that, too. If he agrees, I'd have to be dropped off in the morning and picked up when they're finished shooting at the end of the day."

Artie Carter considered. Powell was such a perfectionist that this might appeal to him. And Artie knew that Bruno was so self-effacing that he wouldn't get in the way of anyone in the production company.

"I'll give Mr. Powell a call and suggest that you be around for the shooting. Knowing him, I bet he agrees."

Of course he will, Blue Eyes thought as he struggled to keep a triumphant smile off his face. Laurie, you won't have to grieve much longer for your husband, he told himself. That's my promise to you.

19

Much to Nina Craig's dismay, there was a message for her mother waiting at the desk at the St. Regis when they checked in.

As she had feared, it was from Robert Powell, inviting Muriel to the 9 A.M. breakfast.

Muriel smiled with delight, then waved the note in Nina's face. "You thought he was toying with me," she snapped. "You don't, or won't, understand that Rob and I were deeply in love. The fact that his head was turned by Betsy Bonner doesn't mean he didn't care about me."

Nina realized that Muriel, having drunk a vodka and at least two glasses of wine on the plane, and after their argument in the car when she was screaming how much she hated Betsy, was out of control.

She could see the two desk clerks taking in the tirade. "Mother, *please* . . . ," she began.

"Don't 'please' me. Read the reviews I got. You're nothing but an extra, a nobody. Didn't that woman stop me on the street and tell me how wonderful I was in the remake of *Random Harvest?*"

Muriel's voice was rising and her face was becoming flushed as she spat out the words. "As for you, you couldn't make it to first base as an actress. That's why you're an extra, a member of the crowd scenes."

Nina could see that the clerk had put the keys to the rooms in separate envelopes. She reached out her hand. "I'm Nina Craig," she said quietly. "I apologize for the scene my mother is making."

If Muriel had heard her, she did not indicate it. She was still finishing her sentence. ". . . and you're always trying to put me down."

The clerk was tactful enough not to offer any reply to Nina other than to murmur, "I'll have your bags sent up to your room."

"Thank you. I just have the large black one." Nina pointed to it, then turned and brushed past Muriel, who had finally stopped talking. Furious and embarrassed by the curious eyes of the onlookers who were in line at the desk, she walked rapidly to the elevator and managed to get in as the door was closing.

On the sixth floor she got out, and following the arrow to the odd-numbered rooms, hurried to get into 621 before Muriel arrived and tried to follow her into her room.

Once inside, Nina sat down in the nearest chair with her hands clenched and whispered, "I can't stand any more. I can't stand it any more."

Later she called for room service. It would have been typical of her mother, who was in the room next door, to phone her about dinner. But that didn't happen. Nina would not have agreed to meet with her, but was denied the satisfaction of saying the words that were crowding her throat. *Go ahead. Make a fool of yourself tomorrow. I tried to warn you. You're Muriel Craig, B-actress and a total failure as a mother* and *as a human being.*

Hoping to hear more from them, Josh had arranged the car service so that he was the one who picked them up in the morning and again taped their angry conversation.

That morning, Josh had arrived half an hour early for an eight o'clock pickup. But when he phoned Nina Craig, she had said, "We'll be right down."

Nina had thought that there was nothing else her mother could possibly do to upset her, but she quickly realized she was wrong. Muriel wanted to arrive at the breakfast early so she could have time with Robert Powell before the others arrived. At least this time they rode in silence.

When they arrived at the estate, the door was opened by Powell's longtime housekeeper, Jane. She eyed them up and down, greeted them by name, and said that Mr. Powell would be down at nine, and that the producer, Ms. Moran, was already in the dining room.

Nina watched as her mother hid her disappointment and became Muriel Craig, the actress. Her smile was gracious, her tone warm when she was introduced to Laurie Moran, and she thanked her for being invited to accompany Nina.

"Mr. Powell is your host, Ms. Craig," Laurie said quietly. "I can't take any credit for it. I understand that after the breakfast you'll be driven back to the St. Regis?"

Wonderful, Nina thought with satisfaction. As she extended her hand to Laurie, she realized how surprised she was that the producer of the program was so young. Mid-thirties, Nina thought enviously. Nina's forty-second birthday the previous week had made her keenly aware that her life was going nowhere, and this three-hundred-thousand-dollar windfall would only serve to buy her mother an apartment and get her out of her hair once and for all.

On the set of her last movie, Nina had been an extra in a ballroom scene, and the producer, Grant Richmond, had told her that she danced beautifully. "You put the others in the scene to shame," he had said.

Nina knew he was pushing sixty and recently widowed. Then, the other night, he had invited her to meet him for cocktails. He had taken the trouble to explain that he had promised to have dinner with the producer, but that "we'll make it another time." He sent her home in his car.

I wish my mother was right, that Robert Powell might still be interested in her, she thought. Then, as she accepted the housekeeper's offer of coffee, Nina appraised Muriel carefully. Her mother did look good. She was wearing a white suit—very expensive, and bought with Nina's American Express card—with white high-heeled shoes that showed off her long legs and excellent figure. At the pricey salon, she had accepted the beautician's tactful suggestion that perhaps her fiery red hair could be toned down a bit. Now it was an attractive rust shade and had been cut and shaped so that it was barely touching her shoulders. She had always been skillful at applying her own makeup. In other words, Nina thought, my beloved mother looks great.

How do I look? she wondered. Okay, but it could be better. I want space. I want to be able to go home to a neat, restful apartment that isn't choked with cigarette smoke and have a glass of wine on the deck looking over the pool by myself.

And be able to invite Grant Richmond in for a drink if he *does* invite me out for dinner, she thought.

With a cup of coffee in her hand, Muriel was telling Laurie Moran how vividly she remembered that terrible, tragic night twenty years ago when her dear, dear friend Betsy was viciously murdered. "My heart was broken," she was saying. "We were *such* good friends."

Disgusted, Nina walked to the windows overlooking the pool and, beyond it, the putting green.

The door of the pool house opened, and she could make out the figure of a man emerging onto the lawn.

Did Robert Powell have a guest staying there? she wondered,

then realized something was dangling from the man's hand. As she watched, he began snipping at the bush nearest to the pool house.

Then the doorbell rang, and Nina turned from the window. One of the other suspects in the death of Betsy Bonner Powell had arrived.

20

George Curtis had become increasingly more nervous about why Robert Powell was drawing him into the Graduation Gala filming.

It was bad enough that he had been forced to agree to be on camera at some point, but why was he being invited to this breakfast, where, as Rob put it, "all the suspects will gather"? Then Rob quickly added, "Not that you're one of the suspects, George."

Now, as he parked his red Porsche in the driveway, George pulled out a handkerchief and patted his forehead dry, an unusual gesture for him. The convertible top was down and the air-conditioning was on. There was no reason to be sweating—except anxiety.

But George Curtis, billionaire, constant on the Forbes list, friend of presidents and prime ministers, at that moment acknowledged to himself that by the end of the week it was possible that he would be under arrest, in handcuffs. He dabbed at his forehead with his handkerchief again.

Taking a long minute to steady his nerves, he got out of the car. The June morning was, as one television weatherman was prone to saying, "A gift. A perfect day." And today he'd be right, George thought—blue skies, sun glowing warm, a soft breeze coming from nearby Long Island Sound. But he didn't care.

He started to cross the driveway to the front door, then waited as a limousine rounded the curve. The limo stopped to allow him to walk in front of it.

He did not ring the bell, but waited until the chauffeur opened the back door and the occupants stepped out. Even though it had been twenty years, he immediately recognized Alison Schaefer. She hasn't changed much, was George's immediate impression—tall, slender, the dark hair not quite so long on her shoulders as it used to be. He remembered that on the night of the Gala he had chatted with her for a few moments and had the impression that there was repressed anger in her when she said something about the lavish party. "The money could be put to better use," she said bitterly. Because it was such an unexpected statement coming from one of the honorees, George had never forgotten it.

Now Alison waited by the car until the other occupant got out with painfully slow movements. As George watched, Rod Kimball pulled himself to his feet and adjusted his crutches firmly under his arms.

Of course, George thought. Alison married the rookie football player who was struck by a hit-and-run driver.

He rang the bell as the couple negotiated the one step to the wide entrance. With polite constraint, Alison and George greeted each other, and Alison introduced Rod.

Then Jane was opening the door for them. She greeted the three with what for her was warmth and said, unnecessarily, "Mr. Powell is expecting you."

After Alex Buckley parked in front of the Powell mansion, he took a moment to study the massive stone house before he left his car.

What had Betsy Bonner thought when she saw this house? he wondered. She had been renting a modest condo in Salem Ridge in the hope of meeting someone with money.

She sure struck it rich for a lady born in the Bronx and making a living as an usher in a theatre, Alex thought as he got out of the car and walked to the front door.

He was admitted by Jane, and introduced to the group already in the dining room. He was relieved to see Laurie Moran had arrived before him.

"Well, here we go," she said when he walked over to her.

"Just what I was thinking," he replied, his tone equally low.

Regina knew it was dangerous to carry her father's suicide note with her to the breakfast. If anyone opened her purse and found it, she would become the most logical suspect to have murdered Betsy Powell. They might as well stop filming the show, she thought.

On the other hand, she had an almost paranoid fear that if she left the letter in the safe at the hotel, someone would steal it. It would be just like Robert Powell to pull off something like that, she thought. I should know! At least I can keep my pocketbook with me.

Then she had folded the note so that it fit inside the small bill-fold that held her credit and insurance cards.

As her limo turned into the familiar driveway, she saw the front door being opened and three people going into the house. One of the men was on crutches.

That has to be Alison's husband, she thought. By the time she'd heard about the accident she'd been in Florida.

We were such dopes when we agreed to be her bridesmaids! she thought now. The press had had a field day taking pictures of Claire and Nina and me walking down the aisle in front of Alison. One of the captions read, "The bride and her fellow suspects."

Talk about a low blow!

Regina was so deep in her thoughts that for a moment she did not realize the car had stopped and the driver was holding the door open for her.

Taking a deep breath, she got out of the car and climbed the steps to the door.

How many times have I been in this house? she asked herself as she pressed the bell. She'd been close to Claire in high school.

But why did I keep coming after Daddy killed himself? Was it morbid curiosity to look at Betsy throwing her charm around? Or was it that I always planned to get back at both of them someday?

In the few moments she waited until the door was opened, she nervously reassured herself about her appearance.

She had lost the twenty pounds she vowed to drop when she received that letter asking her to be in the series. She had bought some new clothes for this trip, and she knew that the black-and-white jacket and white slacks flattered her reclaimed figure and complemented her midnight-black hair.

Zach kept telling me how good I look, she thought as the door opened and Jane, a perfunctory welcome on her lips, stepped back to admit her into the house.

Regina's unwelcome thought as she entered the mansion was to remember her promise to Zach to burn the letter before it provided a reason to suspect she had killed Betsy Bonner Powell.

Claire had thought she would be nervous and fearful at the meeting with her stepfather, Robert Powell. It had been years since they'd seen each other. Instead she woke from a troubled sleep alert with icy calm. Her room service order arrived promptly at seven, and she ate her continental breakfast sitting in the chair in front of the television, watching the news.

But instead of seeing the latest report on a series of muggings in Manhattan, she flashed back to the television coverage of her mother's body being carried out of the house.

We were all together, huddled in the den, she thought. We had robes on.

And then the police started to question us . . .

She turned off the television set and carried her second cup of coffee into the bathroom. There she drew a bath, and when the tub was nearly full, dropped the bath salts she had carried with her into it.

Dear Betsy's favorite, she thought. I want to smell just like her when I get there.

She was in no hurry. I want to be sure they're all there when I arrive. She smiled at the thought. Betsy was always late. It drove Rob crazy. He was a stickler for punctuality, no matter what the occasion.

I should know!

The outfit Claire had chosen was a sky-blue Escada cashmere and silk jacket and narrow gray slacks.

Betsy loved this color, she thought as she slipped on the jacket. She thought it brought out the color of her eyes. Well, let it bring out the color of mine.

The one piece of jewelry that she had taken when she left Robert Powell's house for the last time was the simple strand of pearls that had originally belonged to the grandmother whom she only vaguely remembered. But I *do* remember loving her, she thought. Even though I was only three when she died, I remember sitting on her lap while she read books to me.

At eight thirty the driver called to announce that he was downstairs.

"I'll be another half hour," she told him. She had calculated that that would bring her to the house about 9:20. Again she reassured herself that all the others would be gathered there.

Then Betsy Bonner Powell's daughter will make her entrance.

21

Laurie had known that this breakfast would be charged with tension, but had underestimated how electric the atmosphere in the room would become.

It hadn't taken a minute to know that Muriel Craig was a perpetual liar when she rattled on about how dear a friend Betsy Powell had been to her.

Everyone knew that at one time Muriel had been linked to Robert Powell, and that she had issued a statement after his sudden marriage to Betsy claiming that he was only one of three men she was dating.

What is she thinking when she looks around this house and knows it might have been hers? Laurie wondered. The dining room had a portrait of an aristocratic man with a disdainful expression, whom Jane had explained was Mr. Powell's ancestor, a signer of the Declaration of Independence, of course.

I'll check that one out, Laurie thought. She'd always heard Powell was self-made. That said, the dining room was beautiful, with its red walls and Persian carpet and splendid view of the back gardens. She watched as the film equipment was unloaded for the outdoor scene that would be one of the first shots of the program. They had already filmed the mansion from the front. Now Alex Buckley would begin his narrative as those clips were unrolling.

Jane had laid the juice, coffee, rolls, sweet buns, and fruit on the top of the antique sideboard.

The handsome table had been set for ten. The sterling flatware had the mellow glow of antique pieces, as did all the serving platters.

Powell is certainly making sure that this little breakfast get-together is a not-too-subtle reminder of who and what he is, Laurie thought as in quick succession George Curtis, Alison Schaefer and her husband, Rod, and Alex Buckley arrived. They were followed soon after by Regina Callari.

She watched with keen interest as the three friends, who had not seen one another in twenty years, clasped hands and then exchanged spontaneous hugs.

"My God, it's been so long . . . You haven't changed a bit . . . I've missed you guys . . ." were the seemingly genuine expressions from the three graduates, while Muriel Craig, George Curtis, Rod Kimball, and Alex Buckley held themselves back from the reunion.

Promptly at nine o'clock Robert Powell entered the dining room. "Jane has told me that Claire is not here yet," he said. "In that way she is *exactly* like my dear Betsy."

Watching him closely, Laurie was sure that beneath the façade of being amused by Claire's absence, he was furious. He must have wanted to make an entrance with all four of the graduates here, she thought.

She watched as, one by one, Powell embraced each guest with an effusive welcome. He greeted George Curtis with a "Thanks so much for coming, George. We'd both be happier on the golf course." He turned to Rod with a warm "We never did meet, did we?" Finally he approached Muriel Craig.

"I saved you for last," he said tenderly as he put his arms around her and kissed her. "You're as gorgeous as ever. Have you been in a time capsule these twenty years?"

A radiant Muriel returned his embrace, then, as Laurie watched closely, shot a look at her daughter, who shook her head and turned away.

"I see you all have coffee," Rob said. "But you've got to at least sample the muffins Jane has baked for you. I can promise they're delicious. Then please sit down wherever you want, except that Muriel will sit next to me."

My God, he's laying it on, Laurie thought. The next thing, he'll be proposing to her on bended knee. She was surprised he was being so obvious. But of course, she *was* his old flame.

They all sat at the table, Alex Buckley choosing a seat between Nina Craig and Alison. Rod Kimball hobbled over to the chair on Laurie's left. "We're very grateful to you, Ms. Moran, for creating this opportunity for the girls—I guess I should say women—to try to clear themselves from the lingering suspicion that one of them was a murderer," Powell said.

Laurie did not say that there were two other people in the house that night: Robert Powell, Betsy's husband, who had been rushed to the hospital in a total collapse with third degree burns on his hands; and Jane Novak, Betsy's longtime friend and housekeeper.

Jane had arrived in the room seconds after Powell had become hysterical.

It would have seemed to me that he wouldn't want to keep her, but he did, Laurie thought. Since we've been around, it's obvious that her main purpose in life is to anticipate his every wish.

"I can only imagine what it would be like to never know when some journalist will rehash the story," Laurie said now.

"You don't need a journalist," Rod said grimly. "Everyone has a theory. There are wild rumors all over the Internet."

Laurie realized she had liked Alison's husband the minute she met him. His handsome face bore lines of the suffering he had endured after the terrible accident that had left him disabled and ruined his career, but she saw no trace of self-pity in his demeanor. It was obvious he was devoted to his wife. He had stood protectively at her side with his arm around her when she was greeted by Robert Powell. But why was that necessary? Laurie wondered.

"Well, let's hope that the program will give people an understanding that these young women were incidental to the tragedy. I know my two assistants have read everything there is to read about the circumstances, and both are convinced that an intruder, who may have crashed the Gala in evening clothes, slipped in through the unlocked door and was after Betsy's emeralds."

The sound of the doorbell hushed all conversation. Everyone turned to look at the entrance to the dining room.

Robert Powell pushed back his chair and stood up. They heard the sound of footsteps coming down the hall, and then she was there, Claire Bonner, stunning with her blond hair touching her shoulders, her blue eyes accentuated by carefully applied makeup, her slender figure elegant in a couture suit, a warm smile on her face as she looked from one face to the next at the table.

My God, she's the image of her mother, Laurie thought, then heard a strangled moan and the heavy thud of something falling on the floor.

Nina Craig had fainted.

22

Leo Farley drove past Robert Powell's house at a normal speed. In no way did he want to attract attention, although if he were stopped for any reason, he had his NYPD retirement ID in his wallet.

That thought made him smile. *"Dad, every cop in the tristate area recognizes you; for years you were the one who talked to the media when there was a major crime."*

It was true, Leo acknowledged to himself. His boss, the then police commissioner, had preferred to be away from the glare of the media. "You do the talking, Leo," he always said. "You're good at it."

On his last drive-by he had noticed that the driveway next to Powell's had a chain across it to keep unwanted vehicles out. The shades of the mansion did not fully cover the windows, but were drawn very low. There were no cars in the driveway, and in general the entire property had an air of stillness about it that suggested the occupants of the house were away.

The name of the owner, J. J. Adams, was on the mailbox. Leo had googled and then looked him up on Facebook. It was a lucky hunch. A picture of Jonathan Adams and his wife was there, and their message to their friends was that they were in their villa in Nice and having a wonderful time. It was amazing what kind of information people volunteered, Leo thought. If he'd been a criminal, he could have used it to break into this house or worse.

Leo parked his car ten blocks away, near the railroad station, and then began to jog back to Old Farms Road. He had taken up jogging after he dropped Timmy off at school, and it was easy enough for him to get back to the place he had chosen as his observation post.

He was stopped at the corner by a squad car pulling up beside him. A veteran cop was next to the driver. "Inspector Farley, what are you doing here? I didn't know you set foot outside your territory."

It was a genial sergeant, whom Leo recognized as being a member of the bagpipe band that played on special occasions in Manhattan, such as the St. Patrick's Day Parade.

Leo did not believe in happenstance. His immediate question after greeting the sergeant was whether Ed Penn was still the chief of police in Salem Ridge.

"You bet he is," the sergeant confirmed. "He's retiring next year."

Leo considered. He had not planned to talk to the local police, but suddenly it seemed like a good idea. "I'd like to see him," he said.

"Well, hop in. We'll take you to the station house."

Five minutes later, Leo was explaining to Chief Edward Penn why he was jogging on the streets of Salem Ridge.

"You know, of course, that my son-in-law, Greg Moran, was gunned down, and that the killer told my grandson his mother and he were next."

"I remember, Leo," Penn told him quietly.

"Did you know my daughter is the producer of the Graduation Gala program?"

"I did. She's an impressive woman, Leo. You must be proud."

"Call it a hunch, but I have a feeling that this program could be trouble."

"So do I," Penn said crisply. "Don't forget, I was around twenty years ago when we got the call from the housekeeper, screaming that Betsy Powell was dead. We thought it was a heart attack and called for an ambulance. Then we got there and the room was full—not just Robert Powell, but the four graduates and the housekeeper. It was a mess. And of course that meant that the crime scene was contaminated."

"What was Powell's reaction at that point?" Leo asked.

"White as a sheet, heart fibrillations, beyond shock. He always brought her coffee in the morning, so he was the one who found her, but I guess you read that in the papers."

"Yes, I did," Leo agreed, taking in the familiar sights and sounds of the station house. First the squad cars parked outside as he got out of his ride, then the sergeant's desk, and then the hallway that he knew led to the holding cell and jail.

Leo missed being on the force in New York City. He had joined New York's Finest as soon as he graduated from college. It was the only career he ever considered, and he had loved every minute of it.

He also knew that had he not retired, when a new police commissioner was appointed last year, he would probably have gotten the job. But none of that was important compared to preventing Blue Eyes from carrying out his threat.

Ed Penn was saying, "We gave those four girls a pretty tough grilling, but not one of them broke. I always thought that one of them did it, but it is possible that an intruder got in. That was a big party, and someone in formal clothes could have mixed with the crowd. According to the housekeeper, she had locked all the doors before she went to bed, but someone opened the one from the den onto the patio and left it open. Turns out two of the girls, Regina and Nina, had gone out there a couple of times to smoke a cigarette."

It was everything that Leo had read. "You really think it was one of the girls who killed her?"

"They were too calm. Wouldn't you think they'd all be more upset? Even Betsy's daughter was mighty composed. I don't think

I saw a tear shed by any one of them either in that bedroom or the whole next week."

"Would any one of them have had a motive?"

"Well, Betsy and her daughter, Claire, were so close that Claire drove back and forth to Vassar rather than boarding. Regina's dad went bust and hanged himself after investing in Powell's hedge fund. Regina was fifteen, and she found him hanging. But even her mother agreed that Powell had warned him strongly to invest only what he could afford to lose. Nina's mother, the actress Muriel Craig, had been dating Powell, but when she was asked about it, she said they were just friends and both were seeing other people when he met Betsy. That leaves only Alison Schaefer. She was going around with Rod Kimball, the football player, and married him four months later. No motive there. As for Robert Powell, by all accounts he was broken up by her death and he's never been linked to another woman."

"If it wasn't an intruder, that leaves the housekeeper," Leo suggested.

"No motive there, either. Betsy knew her from her ushering days. Knew what a good worker she was and that she was a good cook. Betsy wasn't comfortable with the previous housekeeper Powell had. She had been hired by Powell's ex-wife, so there was no love lost there. Jane went from cleaning dressing rooms in the theatre to living in a three-room apartment in a mansion and commanding a pretty big salary. Betsy was always saying how much she valued her."

"So that leaves an intruder," Leo said.

Chief Penn's expression became somber. "It doesn't mean that having all of those six people together might not bring something to light. If it was one of them, that person is going to make sure she doesn't raise any suspicion now, or that one of the others might know something that didn't come out before. I read in the papers that Alex Buckley, the big-shot defense lawyer, is going to question all of them on camera. The idea is for each of them to convince a national audience that she isn't guilty."

Leo sensed that it was time for him to reveal why he was jogging in Salem Ridge some twenty miles from his home. "I've always thought that getting those people together to, in essence, *relive* that murder was a bad idea. But you know how we cops have hunches."

"Sure I do. We'd be out of luck if we didn't have them."

"I have a hunch—make that a premonition—that my son-in-law's killer, 'Blue Eyes,' as my grandson described him, might think that this is the perfect time for him to try to kill my daughter."

Leo ignored the startled expression on the other man's face. "It's been five years. Laurie has had a lot of publicity about this program. Her picture has been in the media. On Twitter people have been giving their opinions of who might be guilty of Betsy Powell's murder. Wouldn't it make sense for the psychopath who killed Greg and threatened Laurie and Timmy to make his move now? Can you see the headlines if he succeeded?"

"I can. But how do you plan to prevent it, Leo?"

"Have an observation post on the grounds of the house next door. I checked, and the residents are away. I'll watch for someone trying to sneak in over the back fence of the property. From what I've seen, that would be the only way an intruder would get in."

"What if he tried to mingle with the television crew? Is that possible?"

"Laurie runs a tight ship. All the crew is on the lookout for the paparazzi. Any one of them would recognize a stranger in a minute."

"So what happens if you see someone climbing over the fence?"

"I'm there before he gets over it." Leo shrugged. "It's the best I can do. No one is going to get inside the house while they're filming there. Crew members will be guarding to make sure someone doesn't come in and spoil a scene. They wrap up at about six o'clock, and I'll take off. But I can't let Laurie know I'm around her. She'd be furious. This program will either enhance her career or, if it doesn't work, cost her her job." Leo was quiet, then said seriously, "So, Ed, now you know why I'm jogging through your town."

He saw a pensive look cross Penn's face.

"Leo, we're going to work with you. It won't seem unusual for a squad car to drive by the Powell estate every fifteen minutes or so on both the front and back roads. His property goes to the next street. If we see a car parked anywhere around the Powell place, we'll run the license plate. If we see anyone walking, if we don't know him, we'll check who he is."

Leo's heart surged with gratitude, and he stood up. "And of course this may all be unnecessary. My son-in-law's murderer may be on another continent right now."

"And he may not be," Chief Edward Penn said. Then he rose from his chair, reached across his desk, and gripped Leo's hand.

23

Alex Buckley rushed to Nina and knelt over her, checking her heartbeat, making sure she was breathing.

After their initial shocked silence, the others pushed back their chairs. Muriel, genuinely pale, clutched Robert Powell's arm, then leaned over her daughter.

Nina's eyes fluttered.

"She's all right," Alex said. "But give her air."

"Betsy," Nina moaned. "Betsy."

Laurie's eyes turned to look at Claire, who had not moved from the doorway. It seemed to her that there was something of a triumphant expression on her face. Laurie had seen enough pictures of Betsy to guess that Claire had deliberately done everything possible to enhance her startling resemblance to her mother.

Alex picked Nina up, carried her into the den, and laid her on the couch. The others followed him as Jane came running in with a cold towel, which, with expert fingers, she folded on Nina's forehead.

"Someone call a doctor!" Muriel screamed. "Nina, Nina, talk to me."

"Betsy," Nina murmured. "She came back." Then, as Nina looked around, Muriel swooped down and clasped her face with both hands. "Nina, baby, it's all right."

With a sudden, violent motion, Nina pushed her mother away. "Take your hands off me," she snapped, in a voice that was trembling with emotion. "Take your miserable hands off me!" And then she began to sob, "Betsy came back from the dead. She came back from the dead."

24

B lue Eyes watched with avid interest as Laurie Moran, clearly in charge now, directed the sequence of the filming.

She's very efficient, he decided, watching her check the cameras to see if the angle was what she wanted.

At one point she beckoned to him, and Bruno went scurrying over.

She smiled briefly and asked him to remove the extra plants he had put in early this morning.

"They're lovely," she said, "but they weren't here when we photographed last week."

Bruno apologized profusely, even while he felt the thrill of being so near his prey. She's so pretty, he thought. It would be a shame to spoil that beautiful face. He wouldn't do it.

But, as he was standing so close to her, a new and wonderful plan began to form in his mind.

Five months earlier he had hacked into Leo Farley's computer and phone, and since then he had known everything there was to know about his, Laurie's, and Timmy's activities. The computer courses he'd taken online had really paid off, he thought now.

He knew that Timmy was now in Camp Mountainside in the Adirondacks. And that it was only a four-hour drive from here.

Timmy's entire schedule of activities at the camp was on Farley's computer. And what was most interesting was that the hour between

7 and 8 P.M. was free time, when the campers were allowed to make
or receive one phone call.

That meant that after 8 P.M., Laurie would not expect to speak to
Timmy for another twenty-three hours.

How could he get the director of the camp to let him take Timmy
away without arousing suspicion?

Blue Eyes pondered that question as he kept himself in the background, always ready to repair the slightest hint of damage to the
lawn or shrubbery.

He even chatted a bit with the man and woman who were always
close to Laurie.

Jerry and Grace. Young, both of them. The world ahead of them.
He hoped for their sakes that they weren't too near Laurie when her
time to die arrived.

Which it would. Oh, yes.

It was with regret that Blue Eyes watched the equipment be put
away for the day. From the talk around him, he knew that they'd be
back at eight o'clock tomorrow, and at that time they'd start filming
the graduates.

Always anxious to stay under the radar, as instructed, he phoned
the office of Perfect Estates and gave the secretary fifteen minutes'
notice to pick him up.

When the van arrived, Blue Eyes was not pleased to see that
Dave Cappo was behind the wheel. Dave was too nosy. "So, Bruno,
where'd ya come from? Wuz ya always in landscaping? The wife and
I would like to have you over for dinner any night at all. Up to ya." Big
wink from Dave. "You and I know she'll squeeze your brains to hear
everything about those four grads. Which one do you think did it?"

"Why don't we make it a day or so after they wrap up here?" Blue
Eyes suggested.

By then, he thought, with any luck, I'll be gone, and you and
your wife will have *plenty* to chew on.

25

"So other than that, how did the day go?" Leo asked. He and Laurie were having a late dinner together at Neary's, their longtime favorite restaurant on East Fifty-seventh Street. It was half past eight, and Laurie was visibly tired. She had just described the breakfast and Nina Craig's fainting spell to him, then Nina's reactions to her mother.

"It actually went all right," Laurie said wearily.

"Just all right?" Leo tried to sound casual as he reached for his glass and took another sip of wine.

"No, I should say it went well," Laurie said slowly. "We open with a view of the house as though we're coming down the driveway. Alex Buckley was definitely the right choice for narrator. Then we show some tape of the Graduation Gala from twenty years back with the four graduates, none of them looking particularly happy."

"How about Betsy Powell? Do you have much film of her interacting with the graduates?"

"Not that much," Laurie admitted. "Most of the frames with her show her with her husband or talking to other adults—not that the graduates were kids," she added hastily. "They were all twenty-one or twenty-two. But they were hardly ever with Betsy. We ran through the tapes with them today. I think they were all uncomfortable. Tomorrow we film them watching the excerpt we'll use on camera, then Alex starts talking with them about the Gala."

She sighed. "It sure has been a long day, and I'm starved. What about you?"

"I'm ready to eat," Leo admitted.

"What did you do all day now that your buddy is in camp, Dad?"

Leo was prepared for the question. "Nothing much," he said, biting his tongue over the lie. "The gym, picked up a couple of sport shirts at Bloomingdale's, nothing fancy." He hadn't meant to say it but involuntarily he added, "I miss Timmy, and it's only his first day away."

"Me, too," Laurie said fervently, "but I'm glad I let him go. He was looking forward to it so much. And as much as we miss him, he sounded great on the phone an hour ago."

"I don't know why they limit those kids to one phone call a day," Leo grumbled. "Haven't they heard about grandparents?"

Laurie realized that her father suddenly looked drawn and gray.

"Are you all right?" she asked anxiously.

"I'm fine."

"Dad, I should have thought to get home in time to share Timmy's call with you. I promise I will tomorrow."

They both sat thoughtfully, each with their own feelings about Timmy being so far away and without Leo's careful supervision.

Laurie glanced around the room. As usual, virtually every table was filled. The conversations were lively, and everyone looked as if they were having a good time. Are they all as free from stress as they seem to be? she wondered.

Of course they're not, she told herself. Scratch the surface and everyone has some sort of problem.

Then, determined not to voice her fear about Timmy, Laurie said, "I'm having liver and bacon tonight. Timmy doesn't like it, and I love it."

"I'll join you," Leo decided and waved away the menu when a smiling Mary, one of Neary's longtime waitresses, approached them.

"We both know what we want, Mary," he said.

Peace of mind, was Laurie's immediate thought. And that's not in the cards for us now, or maybe ever.

26

They were finally all gone. By the end of the day Jane could tell that Mr. Powell was sick of his "guests."

The minute the last car drove away he walked into the den, and Jane followed to ask if he wanted a cocktail.

"Jane, you read my mind," he said. "A scotch. And make it a strong one."

For dinner she had planned his favorite meal of salmon, asparagus, a green salad, and sherbet with fresh pineapple.

When he was home he liked to eat at eight o'clock in the small dining room. But tonight he did not finish his dinner, nor did he pay his usual compliment about how good it was. Instead he said, "I'm not very hungry, skip dessert." Then he got up and retreated back into the den.

Jane had the table cleared and the kitchen in its usual shining order in just a few minutes.

Then she went upstairs, turned down his bed, adjusted the air conditioner to sixty-five degrees, and placed a carafe of water and a glass on the night table.

Finally she laid out his pajamas, robe, and slippers, her hands moving tenderly over the clothing as she hung it in his bathroom.

Some nights when Mr. Powell was home he sat in the den for a couple of hours, watching television or reading. He enjoyed classic movies, and the next morning would comment to her about them. "Watched two of the Alfred Hitchcocks, Jane. No one could do suspense the way he did."

If he had had a hard day at the office, he would go directly upstairs after dinner, get changed, and read or watch television in the sitting room of his suite.

Other nights he invited six or eight people for cocktails and dinner.

It was a predictable pattern, making Jane's job quite easy.

The evenings that worried her were those when he went out and she saw in his appointment book that he was taking a woman to the club.

But that didn't happen very often, and he seldom saw the same woman more than two or three times.

All this was going through Jane's mind as she completed the nightly ritual.

Jane's final task of the day, when Mr. Powell was home alone, was to look in on him and see if there was anything else he needed before she retired to her apartment.

Tonight he was sitting in the big chair in his den, his feet on the hassock, his elbows on the arms of the chair, his hands folded. The television was not on, and there was no sign of a book or magazine next to him.

"Are you all right, Mr. Powell?" she asked him anxiously.

"Just thinking, Jane," he said as he turned to face her. "I assume all the bedrooms are fresh?"

Jane tried not to bristle with annoyance at the suggestion that any room in the house wasn't in perfect order. "Of course they are, sir," she said.

"Well, just recheck them. As you know, I have asked all of the participants to stay overnight tomorrow night. We will have a celebratory brunch before we send them on their way."

He raised his eyebrows and smiled a secretive smile that he did not share with Jane.

"That should be very interesting, don't you think, Jane?"

27

Josh Damiano lived across town, just fifteen minutes from the Powell estate, but in an entirely different world.

Salem Ridge was a village on Long Island Sound adjacent to the wealthy town of Rye.

It had been settled in the late 1960s by people of medium income, moving into the Cape Cod and split-level houses developers had built.

But the unique location, only twenty-two miles from Manhattan and on Long Island Sound, attracted the interest of Realtors. Property values began to soar. The modest homes were bought and torn down, replaced by replicas of the kind of mansion Robert Powell had built.

A few owners held out. One of them was Margaret Gibney, who liked her house and didn't want to move. After her husband's death, when she was sixty, Margaret renovated the upstairs floor of her Cape Cod into an apartment.

Josh Damiano was her first and only tenant. Now eighty, Margaret thanked heaven every day for the quiet, pleasant man who took out the garbage unasked and even used the snowblower for her if he was home.

For his part, Josh, after a young marriage to his high school sweetheart that had lasted fourteen unpleasant years, was delighted with his living arrangement and his life.

He respected and admired Robert Powell. He loved his job of driving for him. Even more, he loved taping the conversations of executives when Mr. Powell sent him in the Bentley to pick up one or more of them for meetings or luncheons. Even if alone, a passenger's cell phone conversation was often helpful to Powell. When there was a particularly interesting conversation, like talking about insider trading, Josh would play it back for that executive and offer to sell it to him. He didn't do it much, but it proved to be very lucrative.

Over time, instead of listening to the tapes, Mr. Powell would merely ask Josh if there was anything interesting on the tapes. When Josh said "no," as he did with the graduates, Mr. Powell trusted him. "They all just said 'hello' and 'thank you,' sir," was what Josh had told him about his trips to pick up the graduates at the airport. A disappointed Robert Powell had just shaken his head.

At moments like that Josh remembered how he had almost lost his job. He had been working for Mr. Powell for only a few months when Betsy Powell died. His impression of her had been instantly unfavorable. Who does she think she is, the Queen of England? he would think as she waited imperiously for him to extend his hand and help her into the car.

A week before she died, he heard her say to Mr. Powell that she thought Josh was too familiar and lacked the dignity required of a servant. "Haven't you noticed how he slouches when he opens the door for us? He should know enough to stand up straight."

That rattled Josh, who had settled into his new job and liked it. It had been all he could do to act shocked and saddened by Betsy's demise. In fact he had breathed a sigh of relief that she was no longer around to fill Mr. Powell's ears about his supposed lack of dignity.

The day of the breakfast, Mr. Powell had had him pick up Claire Bonner. Maybe I'll be lucky and she'll make a phone call.

That hadn't worked. When he picked Claire up at the hotel, she got into the Bentley and promptly leaned back and closed her eyes—a definite signal that she was not going to be engaged in conversation.

Josh had been shocked to see how much Claire resembled her mother. He remembered her as a mousy-looking kid, young for her twenty-two years at the time.

That first day of filming, Josh had stayed at the mansion all day, helping Jane prepare sandwiches and dessert and serving them on the patio, where the breakfast group retreated between scenes.

When everyone left, Mr. Rob told him to go home and to pick up Claire again in the morning.

"Try to talk to her, Josh," Mr. Rob instructed. "Say how much you liked her mother, even though I know you didn't." At six o'clock Josh drove his own car home.

It was one of the nights when Mrs. Gibney was in a talkative mood and invited him to share the roast chicken that she had prepared.

That happened about once a week, and usually Josh was happy to accept—Mrs. Gibney was a good cook. But tonight he had things on his mind and he thanked her, saying he had had an early dinner. It was a lie, but he wanted to think.

In his pocket he had copies of the tapes he had made in the car of Nina Craig and her mother, Alison Schaefer and her husband, and Regina Callari on the phone with her son.

It was obvious that none of those women would want the tapes to be heard by either Mr. Powell or the police. They had agreed to come here to try to finally clear themselves from being under suspicion in Betsy's death, but each of the tapes revealed a motive for them to have killed Betsy.

They were all getting money for being on the program, a lot of money. Each would be horrified to know their motives were caught on tape, loud and clear. If they didn't trust him to stick to his side of the agreement, he has an answer prepared.

"I'll always have the master tape. You can destroy the copy I give you," he would say. "You don't want to go to Mr. Powell or the police with these tapes. Neither do I. Pay me and nobody will ever hear them."

He had figured out his suggested price—fifty thousand dollars. Only one-sixth of the three hundred thousand they would all be collecting.

It should work. They were all scared. He could sense it while he was serving them on the patio.

Josh wanted to build up his nest egg. He'd taken Mr. Powell to the cancer doctor a number of times. He had a hunch that Mr. Powell was sicker than anyone suspected. If anything happened to him, Josh knew he was in the will for one hundred thousand dollars. But adding $150,000 to that wouldn't hurt.

Now, if he could only get something on Claire!

28

George Curtis drove the four blocks to his home, outwardly composed but inwardly in a state of emotional exhaustion.

Rob Powell was toying with him. Rob knew about him and Betsy, George was sure of it. He thought about Laurie Moran, the producer, discussing the sequence of filming the next day. She had thanked him in particular for participating in the program.

"I know how busy you must be, Mr. Curtis," she said. "Thank you for giving up your day to be with us. I know there was a lot of waiting around while we set up for the shooting. Tomorrow we'll film you standing in front of the backdrop of clips of the Gala, then being interviewed by Alex Buckley about your memories of that night."

Memories, George thought as he turned into his driveway, memories. That was the night Betsy had given him an ultimatum. "Tell Isabelle you want a divorce like you promised, or pay me twenty-five million dollars to stay with Rob and keep my mouth shut. You're a billionaire; you can afford it."

And it was on the way to the Gala that Isabelle, her face radiant, had told him she was four months pregnant with twins.

"I waited to tell you, George," she had said. "After four miscarriages I didn't want to disappoint you again. But four months is a big milestone. After fifteen years of waiting and praying, this time we'll have a family."

"Oh my God," was all he could say. "Oh my God."

I was thrilled and terrified, George thought. I asked myself how I could ever let myself get involved with Betsy, my best friend's wife.

It had all started in London. George was there for a business meeting with the European director of the Curtis fast-food restaurant chain that his father had founded in 1940. Rob and Betsy Powell were in London at the same time, and they, too, were staying at the Stanhope Hotel, in an adjoining suite. Rob flew to Berlin overnight.

I took Betsy to dinner, then back at the hotel she suggested having a nightcap in my suite, George remembered. She never left that night. It was the beginning of a two-year affair.

Isabelle and I were growing apart, George thought as he parked the car in front of the house. She was taken up with volunteering for a number of charities, and I was all over the world opening up new markets. When I was home, I didn't want to go to the charity dinners with her.

Because anytime Rob was away, I met Betsy somewhere.

But after a year it began to wear off. I finally saw her for what she was: a manipulator. And then I couldn't get rid of her. She kept hounding me to get a divorce.

At the Gala, Isabelle was telling her friends that she was pregnant.

When Betsy heard that, she told me she knew I wouldn't get a divorce. Instead she wanted that twenty-five million dollars to keep her mouth shut. "You can afford it, George," she had said, smiling, always aware of the audience around her. "You're a billionaire. You won't even miss it. Otherwise I tell Isabelle about us. Maybe the shock will cause her to miscarry again."

George was sickened. "If you tell Isabelle or anyone else, Rob will divorce you." George could hardly even manage to form the words. "And I know your prenup leaves you with almost nothing."

Betsy had actually smiled. "I know that won't happen, George, because you're going to pay me. And I'll keep living happily with Rob, and you and Isabelle will be in a state of bliss with your twins."

She continued to smile as George heard himself say, "I'll pay you, Betsy, but if you ever say anything to Isabelle or anyone else, I will kill you. I swear it."

"Here's to that agreement," Betsy said as she clinked her glass against his.

Twenty years later, George thought as he unlocked the door of the car. His mind switched to what Laurie Moran had told him about the rest of his part in the filming.

"And then we'll have you and Alex Buckley sitting together, and he'll ask you your overall impressions of the party and of Betsy Powell," Laurie had said. "Maybe you have some stories you could tell about Betsy. From what I understand, you were close friends of the Powells and frequently saw them socially."

I told Moran that I saw Rob more on the golf course at the club than socially, as couples, George thought as he walked up the three steps to the charming brick house that he and Isabelle had built twenty years ago. He remembered how the architect had come in with pretentious renderings of houses in which the entrance hall was big enough for a skating rink and twin staircases led to a balcony "where you could put a full orchestra."

Isabelle's comment was, "We want a home, not a concert hall."

And it *was* homey. Spacious but not overwhelming. Inviting and warm.

He opened the door and headed to the family room. As he had

expected, Isabelle and the twins, Leila and Justin, who were home from college for the summer, were there.

George's heart swelled with love as he looked at the three of them.

And to think I almost lost them, he thought as he remembered his threat to Betsy.

29

When Claire got back to the hotel, the first thing she did was to put a DO NOT DISTURB sign on the door, then rush to wash her face.

All the carefully applied makeup vanished into the soapy washcloth as she checked and rechecked to be sure that every vestige of it was gone. Well, it served its purpose, she thought. I saw the look on all their faces, especially Rob Powell's, when they saw me. I'm not sure whether Nina pulled that faint or if it was genuine. She was a pretty good actress, even if she never did make it big.

But I think she upstaged Daddy Rob. He was just about to faint himself before she beat him to it. Well, didn't he used to brag that in high school he was voted best actor in the senior play? And he's perfected his act since then.

30

Nina could see the look of disappointment on her mother's face when Rob didn't extend an invitation to dinner. But in the car Muriel pointed out that he had referred more than once to the good times they had had together. That much is true, Nina acknowledged to herself.

As they got off the elevator in the hotel, Muriel asked, "Did you see the chandelier? It must be worth forty thousand dollars."

"How do you know?"

"I saw one like it when we were in Venice for background scenes."

Fitting, Nina thought. Now, as an actress, you're in the background again.

"Did you see how that housekeeper acted as if we were a bunch of intruders?"

"Mom, I remember her from the time when we were growing up. Jane always looked as if she disapproved of everyone except Betsy." Nina hesitated, then added sarcastically, "I mean 'Mrs. Powell.' That's what Jane was forced to call her, even though they'd worked together for years."

"Well, I certainly would have made her call me 'Mrs. Powell' instead of Muriel," her mother snapped. "If I had married Rob."

"I'm going to my room. I'll have dinner served there," Nina replied, rolling her eyes to heaven. As she walked rapidly away from

Muriel, she thought, the greatest gift you ever received was that Betsy was out of your way, but even though you called Rob Powell any number of times after she died, he didn't want to see you again. And now it's obvious to me that he's just toying with you.

Will you ever learn?

31

Regina was barely in her hotel when she received a telephone call from Zach from London. He got directly to the point.

"Mom, please be honest, did you bring that letter with you?"

Regina knew there was no use in lying.

"Yes, I did. I'm sorry, Zach. I lied to you because I didn't want you to be upset."

"Then, Mom, I have to tell you. I destroyed the copy you had. I've been wanting to tear that letter up ever since you told me about it. I would have torn up the original, too, but I couldn't find where you put it."

"Zach, it's okay. I know you're right and after this week, I *will* destroy it. Or if you want, I'll let you burn it. That's a promise."

"Awesome, Mom, I'll hold you to that."

They both said, "I love you," then said good-bye.

Regina raced to the dresser where she'd left her pocketbook, opened it, and with trembling fingers reached for her wallet. She had known when she arrived at the Powell estate that she should not have carried the letter with her.

She opened the secret flap in her wallet where she had carefully folded the letter.

It was empty.

Whoever had taken it must have suspected she might be carrying something important, or else had gone through all the pocketbooks that had been left on the patio table for the same reason.

And the letter provided the perfect reason for her to have murdered Betsy.

Frantically she dumped her pocketbook on the table and rummaged through the contents, hoping against hope that somehow she would find it. But it was not there.

32

$\diamond$

Rod woke at four in the morning after hearing a door close. "Alie," he called. He turned on the overhead light. The door to the sitting room was open, and he could see Alison was not there. He bolted up and reached for his crutches. After all these years his arms and shoulders were powerful, and he could move swiftly on them. Was Alison sleepwalking again? He glanced into the bathroom and the dressing room. She was not in either of them. He reached the outer door of the room in seconds and threw it open. There was Alison, walking slowly down the long hallway.

He caught up with her at the top of the staircase to the lobby.

Once there, he reached for her hand and whispered her name. He watched her eyes blinking, and she turned her face to him.

"It's fine," he said soothingly. "It's fine. We're going back to bed."

When they were inside the room she began to cry. "Rod, Rod, I was sleepwalking again, wasn't I?"

"Yes, but it's all right. It's fine."

"Rod, the night of the Gala I was so angry. People were asking me if I was planning to go to medical school. I told them I was going to have to work for a year at least. Whenever I looked at Betsy all I could think was that she had stolen that scholarship from me so that she could get into a fancy club." Her voice a desperate whisper, she said, "I was sleepwalking that night of the Gala. I woke up leaving Betsy's room. I was so grateful she hadn't heard me. Or is it possible I killed her?"

Her words were drowned in sobs.

33

Leo Farley dropped Laurie off in a cab, then instructed her driver to wait until he had seen the doorman open the door into the lobby and close it behind her.

As safe as I can make her, he thought, then leaned back in the cab with a weary sigh. It had been a long day, made even longer by his anxiety about Timmy being away at camp.

He was so deep in thought that he did not notice when the cab pulled up at his apartment building on the next block.

Tony the doorman was there, waiting to open the door. Leo usually bounded out of the cab, but tonight, after he had paid the fare, he moved slowly and even reached for Tony's hand to help get him to his feet.

And then he felt it begin—the rapid pulsing of his heart that meant he was beginning to have an attack of cardiac fibrillation. As Tony waited attentively, Leo started to get out, then remembered that his doctor had warned him that he must not, absolutely *must not* ignore it when his heart began to beat like this—like a locomotive out of control.

"Get to the hospital right away, Leo," he had ordered. "A lot of people have this condition, but yours is much more serious than most. Your heart has to be slowed down immediately."

Leo looked up at Tony. "Just remembered I left something at my daughter's house," he fibbed, then added, "I may stay over with her."

"That's fine, sir. Good night."

Tony closed the door with a decisive click, and Leo reluctantly told the driver to take him to Mount Sinai Hospital.

At least it's only a few blocks way, he thought as he again checked his rapidly accelerating pulse.

34

Alex Buckley pondered the events of the day as he drove home from Salem Ridge to Manhattan. The four girls, now women, had been friends since their freshman year in high school, and it was obvious that their greetings to each other had been guarded, although as the hours wore on they seemed to be warming up.

Their reaction to Robert Powell was unmistakably hostile, even as they kept up a thin veneer of cordiality.

Years of interrogating witnesses had given Alex the ability to cut through the surface of what someone was saying and study their eyes and body language. What he concluded from all four graduates today was that they despised Robert Powell.

The question was, why? Alex would bet the animosity began more than twenty years ago.

Then why did they go along with the Graduation Gala? Even if my best friend wanted to share his graduation party with me, I wouldn't have done it if I hated his father, Alex thought. And that raised another question. How did they feel about Betsy Bonner Powell? If one of the four had killed her, there had to be a compelling motive for her to seize the opportunity to stay overnight at the Powell home.

These questions Alex began to sort in his head as he pulled the car into his garage and went to his apartment.

Ramon was quick to hear his key turn the lock in the door. He appeared in the foyer, a smile on his face. "Good evening, Mr. Alex. I hope you had a good day?"

"Let's call it an *interesting* day," Alex said, returning the smile. "I'm going to change right away. I certainly didn't need to wear a tie and jacket today. It was hot outside."

The apartment was comfortably cool, and as usual his closet was a masterpiece of precision, thanks to Ramon, who hung every jacket and shirt and tie in color groupings. Alex's trousers were placed in the same orderly pattern.

Now Alex changed into a short-sleeved sport shirt and khakis. Then he washed his hands, splashed water on his face, and decided that what he wanted was a cold beer.

As he passed the dining room, he saw that the table was set for two.

"Ramon, who's coming?" he asked as he opened the refrigerator door. "I don't remember inviting anyone."

"I didn't have a chance to tell you, sir," Ramon replied as he prepared a small plate of hors d'oeuvres. "Your brother should be here any minute. He has an appointment in New York in the morning."

"Andrew's coming, that's great," Alex said sincerely, although he had a fleeting moment of disappointment, since he had intended to jot down all his impressions of the day over dinner. But Andrew knew today was the beginning of the filming and would probably have lots of questions. Questions could be useful in drawing out facts. If anyone should know that, it's me, Alex thought.

His first sip of beer coincided with the sound of chimes announcing Andrew's arrival. He had his own key and was letting himself in when Alex walked into the foyer.

For a long time it had been just the two of them. Their mother had died when Alex was a freshman in college, and their father two years later. Alex had just turned twenty-one and had been appointed Andrew's guardian.

Like most brothers, they had had their squabbles growing up. Both were competitive in sports, and a victory over the other in golf or tennis was a source of great joy.

But competition had disappeared when it was just the two of them. They had only distant cousins in their extended family, none of whom lived in New York. They sold their home in Oyster Bay and moved into a four-room apartment in Manhattan on East Sixty-seventh Street, which they shared until Andrew had graduated from Columbia Law School and accepted a job in Washington, D.C.

Alex, by then five years out of NYU Law and a rising star in a litigation firm, had stayed in that apartment until he bought the one on Beekman Place.

Unlike Alex, Andrew had married six years ago and now had three children—a five-year-old boy and twin two-year-old daughters.

"How are Marcy and the kids?" was the first question Alex asked after giving his brother a brief hug.

Andrew, six two to Alex's six four, his hair slightly darker than Alex's, his eyes blue-gray, but with the same disciplined body, laughed.

"Marcy is jealous that I'm getting away overnight. The twins are living the concept of the terrible twos. Their vocabulary consists of one word: 'no.' Johnny, as usual, is a great kid. If he ever was a two-year-old like the girls, I don't remember it."

He looked at the glass in his brother's hand. "How about one of those for me?"

Ramon was already pouring the beer into a chilled glass.

They settled in the den, and Andrew hungrily reached for the plate of hors d'oeuvres. "I'm starving. I skipped lunch today."

"You should have ordered out," Alex suggested.

"That's profound wisdom. If only I had thought of it."

The brothers exchanged a brief grin, then Andrew asked, "And now for the sixty-four-thousand-dollar question. How did it go today?"

"Interesting, of course." Alex began telling him about the breakfast gathering. When he came to the fact that Nina Craig had fainted at the sight of Claire, Andrew interrupted.

"Was it a real faint or was she faking it?"

"What makes you ask that?" Alex said quickly.

"Well, don't forget, Marcy did a lot of acting before we were married. She lived in California for five years after college. When we knew that you were involved with all this and that the journalists were rehashing the case, she told me she had been in a play with Muriel Craig and that every night after the show Muriel would head for a bar, get drunk, and start telling people how she could have married Robert Powell except that her stupid daughter had dragged her friend's mother over to meet him. She'd rant on about how she and Powell were practically engaged and that right now she could be living in a mansion with a handsome, rich husband if it hadn't been for her stupid daughter, Nina. Apparently Nina was there one night, and after Muriel got finished, they almost came to blows!"

"Well, maybe that explains it," Alex said. "I think the faint was genuine, but as she was coming out of it, Nina screamed at her mother to take her miserable hands off her!"

"How long had Betsy been married to Powell when she was murdered?" Andrew asked. "Wasn't it six or seven years?"

"Nine years."

"Do you think there's any chance that Nina Craig took the opportunity to get rid of Betsy by staying over at the house after the Gala and hopefully make Powell available for her mother again? From what Marcy told me, Nina can be a tough cookie."

Alex did not answer for a long minute, then said wryly, "Maybe you're the one who should have been the criminal lawyer."

Ramon was standing in the doorway. "Dinner is served if you are ready, sir."

"I hope we have fish," Alex commented as he stood up. "It's supposed to be brain food, isn't it, Ramon?"

35

Laurie had set the alarm for six o'clock but woke at five-thirty. A glance at the clock on her night table told her that she had the luxury of lying in bed for another half hour.

This was the hour when if Timmy woke up early, he would come into her room and snuggle against her in bed. She loved the feeling of putting her arm around him and having his head tucked under her chin. He was tall for his age, but he still seemed so little and vulnerable that a fierce need to protect him always filled her being. I would *kill* for you, she would think passionately when the threat Blue Eyes had shouted flooded her mind.

But today Timmy had just completed his first overnight away from her or her father since he was born. Whenever she had to go away on business, Leo moved in and stayed with Timmy.

Was Timmy enjoying camp? Was he homesick? That would be natural, she told herself. All first-time campers are bound to feel that way for a day or two.

But I'm homesick for *him,* she thought as she threw back the light covers, knowing that it would be easier to get up than to lie awake worrying about Timmy.

She allowed herself to pick up the framed picture on her dressing table. It had been enlarged from a snapshot someone had taken of Greg, Timmy, and her when they had been with a group of friends at the beach in East Hampton.

It was the last picture of the three of them. Greg had been shot a week later.

Laurie ran the tip of her finger over Greg's face, a gesture that she had made hundreds of times in the last five years. She sometimes fantasized that one day instead of the flat surface of the print she would feel Greg's face, that she would run her finger along the outline of his mouth and feel it curve into a smile.

She thought of how one night a few months after Greg's death, her need for him had been so strong that she fell asleep whispering his name over and over again.

Then she dreamt so vividly of him, his expression troubled and sad, as if he were in distress that she was so aggrieved . . .

Shaking her head, she put the picture back on the dresser. Fifteen minutes later, her hair still wet from the shower, her cotton bathrobe covering her slender body, she went into the kitchen where the coffee had already brewed on the timer.

Jerry and Grace picked her up at 7:45. The rest of the crew would meet them at the Powell estate.

As usual, Grace was trying to pull herself awake. "I went to bed at ten o'clock," she told Laurie, "and then I couldn't sleep. I was trying to figure out which one of them might have killed Betsy Powell."

"What's your conclusion?" Laurie asked.

"Any one of them or all of them banded together—the four graduates, I mean. Like in *Murder on the Orient Express*. They all took turns stabbing the guy who had kidnapped the baby."

"Grace, even for you that's over the top," Jerry said flatly. "I say the housekeeper is guilty. She so obviously wishes we were all on Planet Mars that I think it's more than the fact that her usual routine is interrupted. I think she's worried. What about you, Laurie?"

Laurie was pulling out her cell phone. She had heard the faint sound that indicated she had received a text message.

It was from Brett Young. It read, "Laurie, the financial statements for the quarter indicate another drop in revenue. As I told you, the last two pilots you produced were expensive and disappointing. Make sure this one works."

36

M̲r. Powell had awakened earlier than usual. By seven-fifteen he was finishing his second cup of coffee. From where he sat in the breakfast room he had a full view of the backyard, a sight that usually pleased him. But today, despite the fact that the rosebushes around the patio were in full bloom and the fountain was sending a spray of crystal water into the air and the plants around the pond made a display of color like the palette of an artist, the look on his face was one of displeasure. The film company had left two large vans pulled up to the side of the house in back, and Jane knew that the sight of them was as displeasing to Mr. Rob as it was to her.

Jane knew his moods. Last night he had seemed almost amused by the events of the day, like Nina Craig's fainting and Muriel's obvious and flirtatious reminders about dates they had shared before Betsy entered the picture.

How much did he know about George Curtis and Betsy? Jane wondered. She had been passing hors d'oeuvres at the Gala twenty years ago when she had sensed the palpable tension between Curtis and Betsy, and had managed to sidle close behind him in time to hear his threat to Betsy. Jane knew that if Betsy succeeded in getting $25 million from Curtis, she probably would have hidden the money, as she had the jewelry, and continued her life with Mr. Powell.

If you only knew how much I know about you, Jane thought as she firmly resisted the impulse to pat Mr. Powell on the shoulder. Should I remind him that he was the one who had agreed to all this and suggest he go to the office for the day, since from what I gather, he would not be needed on camera today? But she did not touch his shoulder or suggest he go to the office. She knew he would be appalled if she took either liberty. Instead she made the symbolic gesture of offering him more coffee, and after brusquely refusing, he quietly left the room.

Yesterday she had seen that sneak Josh go through the pocket-books when the graduates were told to leave them on the table on the patio. He had removed something from one of them. She could not be sure which one, because he had been so quick about it. What had he found of interest? She had long known about his taping the people he was driving. She also knew that Betsy, "Mrs. Powell," she sneered to herself, didn't like his attitude. He wouldn't have lasted long in this job if she had lived, Jane thought.

What was it that he had taken from the pocketbook? She did know this — if it was something that would be beneficial to Mr. Powell, Josh would show it to him and, like a dog getting a friendly pat from his master, he would end up with a few hundred dollars extra in his pocket.

"Jane, I don't want to see anyone this morning," Mr. Powell said. "I will be spending a lot of time on the phone with the office. The production company is bringing their own food, so there's no reason to have an open kitchen for those people. The crew will be using the bathroom in the pool house. Let the others stay on the patio and come in and out through the kitchen to use the bathroom. I don't want any of them going upstairs or wandering through the house. Is that clear?"

What had changed so drastically from last night, when he had seemed to be enjoying himself? Jane wondered. Or was he dread-ing the one-on-one interview with that lawyer, Alex Buckley? Jane had read up on Buckley and had seen him on television discussing crimes. She knew that at some point he would be asking her questions about that night, too.

Well, I've managed to keep my thoughts to myself for almost thirty years, she thought. I'm pretty sure I can continue to keep secrets. Jane smiled to herself as she thought of the jewelry she had taken from Betsy's hiding place after her body was found. The earrings and ring and necklace George Curtis had given Betsy had of course never been worn around Mr. Powell. Betsy saved them for those quiet little get-togethers when he was out of town. Mr. Powell never knew about them, and George Curtis certainly wasn't looking to get them back.

I wonder if all these years, Curtis has been wondering if that jewelry would be found and traced to him? He did threaten Betsy that night, and he lives only a ten-minute walk away. Well, if any suspicion falls on either Mr. Powell or myself about Betsy's death, I can pretend that I just found them and let Mr. George Curtis be accused of her murder.

Satisfied with the reassuring presence of the jewelry well hidden in her apartment, Jane picked up the coffee cup that Robert Powell had put down when he left the room and, pressing it lovingly to her lips, finished the coffee he had left in the cup.

37

Claire had orange juice, coffee, and an English muffin sent up for breakfast. She was dressed and waiting long before the car arrived to pick her up and take her to the house where she had spent the nine most miserable years of her life.

She had deliberately dressed the way she usually dressed at home—a plain long-sleeved cotton shirt and black slacks. Today she did not put on makeup, nor, as was her custom at home, any jewelry. I've been fading into the background all of these years, she thought. When I was a child, my mother pushed me into it. Why should I change? Besides, it's too late for anything to change.

There was only one satisfaction in Claire's life—her job as a social worker dealing with domestic issues. She knew she was good at it, and it was only when she had helped to rescue women and children from unbearable circumstances that she had a sense of peace and fulfillment.

Why did I come back here? she wondered. What did I think I was going to get out of it? What did I think I was going to put to rest? By participating, each of the graduates risked revealing her own secret reasons for hating Betsy. Claire knew what those reasons were and sympathized with all of them. She remembered how the other three had been her strength during the high school years. When I was out with them, she thought, I could almost forget everything.

Now we're all afraid of what people might know about us. Will this program bring the truth to light, or will it simply be a messy rehash of painful memories and destroyed lives? She shrugged impatiently, then turned on the news to kill time until the car arrived. One of the items mentioned the filming of the show about the murder of Betsy Bonner Powell and how it was destined to be "the most highly anticipated event of the television season."

Claire pushed the remote control button and the screen darkened just as the telephone rang. From the lobby Josh Damiano asked in a cheery voice if she was ready to go.

Maybe I've been ready for twenty years, Claire thought as she picked up her pocketbook and slung it over her arm.

38

Chief Ed Penn had received a phone call from Leo Farley at nine o'clock on Monday evening. He could tell that Farley sounded fatigued but was shocked when Leo told him he was in the hospital. "They haven't been able to get my heart back to a normal rhythm," Leo told him. "And of course that means I'm not going to be around to keep an eye out for any potential problems."

Chief Penn's first reaction was that Leo Farley had been under the strain of the threat to his daughter and grandson for five years and was breaking under it. After pointing out what Leo already knew—that the film company had a guard at the gate of the Powell estate to keep out paparazzi and that the guard was checking everyone who attempted to get inside the grounds—Penn promised Leo he would station a squad car on the back road to be sure no one attempted to scale the fence.

Now that the program was actually being made, Penn had taken home the exhaustive file on the case and had once again been reading it through.

When Leo phoned, he had been examining the pictures of the crime scene with a magnifying glass, the beautifully appointed bedroom in the background and the incongruous sight of Betsy Powell's body, her hair loose on the pillow, her eyes staring, her satin nightgown curving on her shoulders.

The Chief read that the housekeeper had been in the kitchen when she heard the commotion upstairs and raced up to find Robert Powell gasping for breath on the floor by the bed, his hands burned from the coffee he had been carrying to Betsy.

The four graduates had rushed into the room when they heard Jane's shriek. According to them, Jane Novak had screamed, "Betsy, Betsy," even though she normally called her Mrs. Powell.

And immediately after pulling the pillow from the face of the victim, Jane admitted she had picked up the emerald earring from the carpet and put it on the night table.

"I guess it was because I almost stepped on it," she said. "I wasn't thinking about what I was doing."

What she had been doing was contaminating the crime scene, Penn thought. First by handling the pillow, then by picking up the earring.

"And then I ran over to Mr. Powell," Jane's statement continued. "He had passed out. I thought he was dead. I had watched someone do CPR on television and I tried it on him in case his heart had stopped beating. And by then the girls came in and I shrieked to them to phone the police and get an ambulance."

It was the collective calm of the four graduates that the Chief remembered noting immediately. Granted, they told him they had been up until 3 A.M. talking and had drunk plenty of wine. The lack of sleep and the excessive drinking might have numbed their immediate response to Betsy Powell's death. But it seemed to him that even allowing for the shock of it, Claire Bonner was surprisingly composed for a young woman whose mother was dead.

But then, so were the other graduates when they were interrogated.

I still don't think it was an intruder, Penn thought. I have always believed that someone in that house killed Betsy Powell.

The six people who had been there were Robert Powell, the housekeeper, and the four graduates.

They're all being questioned by Buckley, Penn thought. He's supposed to be dynamite when he's cross-examining a witness. It will be interesting to compare their initial statements with what they say now on camera.

Shaking his head, the Chief looked around his den. He felt that it was a stain on his department that the crime had never been solved. His eyes lingered on the wall with the many citations he and his department had earned over the years. There was another one he wanted.

It would be for solving the murder of Betsy Bonner Powell.

Then he glanced at his watch. It was ten minutes past nine. No more time for useless speculation. He picked up the phone to order that a squad car be stationed at the back of the Powell estate starting the next morning.

39

Bruno woke on Tuesday morning at six, aware that he was getting closer and closer to the moment of glory when he could take his final revenge.

He turned on the television as he prepared his spartan breakfast. He was allowed to keep a small refrigerator in his room. He plugged in the coffeemaker, then poured yogurt and cereal into a bowl.

After the hard news and a dozen commercials, he heard what he had been waiting to hear. "The pilot for the *Under Suspicion* series is presently being filmed at the estate of Robert Powell. Twenty years after the Graduation Gala the four honorees have gathered to appear on a television program to protest their innocence in the death of beautiful socialite Betsy Bonner Powell."

Bruno laughed aloud, a raspy, mirthless sound. Yesterday he had spoken with one of the surprisingly talkative television crew. He had said that they would be filming today and tomorrow. Tonight the graduates would stay overnight. They would be on camera, seated in the den as they had been twenty years ago. Then tomorrow morning they would be filmed at a farewell breakfast.

And while they were having breakfast, Bruno would emerge from the pool house with his rifle and take aim at her.

Bruno thought of that day long ago when, as a kid in Brooklyn, he had hung around the guys he knew were in the mob. He had a job as a busboy in the diner where some of them had breakfast every morning.

He heard a couple of them bragging about how they could shoot the apple off the head of William Tell's kid, but with a rifle, not an arrow. That was when Bruno bought a rifle and a pistol secondhand and started practicing.

Six months later, when he was clearing the table, he told the two guys who had been boasting that he'd like to show them how good a shot he was. They laughed at him, but one of them said, "You know, kid, I don't like people wasting my time with bragging. If you want to show off, I'll give you a try."

And that was how he was hired by the mob.

Bruno could take out Laurie Moran anytime, but he wanted to be sure the cameras would be rolling when she slumped over.

He slurped his coffee in anticipation of that moment.

The policeman in that squad car on the back road would come rushing over the fence and run toward the dining room. The television crew, too. When they were all past the pool house Bruno would leave by the back door and be over the fence in seconds.

It would take him only four minutes to jog to the public parking lot at the train station. The lot was only a block from the room he was sitting in right now.

He had chosen the car he would steal, a Lexus station wagon whose owner parked it at seven every morning to get on the seven-fifteen train to Manhattan.

Bruno would be driving away before they had even figured out where the shot had come from.

The owner wouldn't report the car missing until Thursday evening.

Bruno was so busy going over his plan that he did not even realize his coffee cup was empty.

What were the possibilities of failure?

Of course there were a few. A policeman might not be able to
scale the fence. In that case he'd be sure to challenge me, Bruno
thought. I don't want to have to shoot him. The noise would bring
the other cop back. But if I used the butt of the rifle, I'd have all the
time I need . . .

The element of surprise, the confusion over Laurie slumping
over, blood beginning to pour from her head—all of this would
work in his favor.

I might be caught, Bruno admitted to himself, and that would
permanently end any hope of eliminating Timmy. But if I get
away with it, I'll take care of him fast. My luck won't hold out
forever.

By hacking into Leo Farley's computer, Bruno knew that Timmy
was at camp, and even knew which tent he was in and every detail of its layout. But even if he could get into the camp during
the night and kidnap Timmy, Laurie would be notified in minutes, and he'd never be able to get near her. Timmy had to come
second.

Bruno shrugged. He was sure that old lady had heard his threat,
"Your mother's next, then it's your turn." He'd have to stick to that
plan.

He hadn't checked Leo's phone since yesterday, not that Leo had
much to say to anyone.

Bruno listened to the recording of Leo's call to the police chief
last night. *Leo Farley was in Mount Sinai Hospital in intensive
care.*

Bruno began to consider the possibilities this suggested.

Then he began to smile.

Of course, of course, it would work. It would have to work. He could pull it off.

When Laurie was at the farewell breakfast, Bruno would come out of the pool house holding Timmy's hand—and pointing a gun at his head.

40

Regina's hands were trembling so violently that she could hardly pull the T-shirt over her head. Laurie Moran had told them to dress simply. She had had replicas made of the outfits they had been wearing when the police arrived after Betsy's body was found. They had handed over their pajamas for evidence and been asked to wait in the den until they could be questioned.

Regina had been wearing a long-sleeved red T-shirt and jeans. The thought of wearing a similar outfit now was upsetting. She felt as if all the protective layers she had built around herself over twenty years were being peeled away.

Just thinking about that outfit made her remember how they had all sat huddled together, not allowed to go into the kitchen even to get a cup of coffee or a piece of toast. Jane, too, had been in the den with them, despite pleading to be allowed to go in the ambulance with Mr. Powell to the hospital.

Who had taken her father's suicide note from her pocketbook? And what would that person do with it?

If the police found it, they could arrest her for taking the letter from her father's body. She knew they always suspected that if he'd written a note, she'd taken it. She had lied over and over to them when they were investigating his death. Whoever had the note now could provide the police with everything they needed to indict her for Betsy's murder.

Regina's eyes filled with tears.

Her nineteen-year-old son, Zach, had had the brains to destroy the copy she made of the note and had tried to find the original, then begged her not to carry it with her.

What would it do to his life if she were arrested and indicted for Betsy's death?

She thought of the little boy who would come to the real estate office after school when he didn't have practice for one of his sports and want to help her by folding and mailing ads for the agency to the local communities. He was always thrilled when one of the ads resulted in a listing. They'd always been close. She knew how lucky she was on that count.

When Regina's breakfast arrived, she tried to drink the coffee and eat a bite of the croissant, but it stuck in her throat.

You've got to get a grip on yourself, she thought. If you look too nervous when that lawyer, Alex Buckley, interviews you, you'll only make things worse.

Please, God, she thought, let me be able to pull it off. The phone rang. The car was here to take her to the Powell estate.

"I'll be right down," she said, unable to conceal the quiver in her voice.

41

Alison did not go back to sleep after the sleepwalking incident. Rod felt her tossing and turning in bed and finally put his arm around her and drew her close to him.

"Alie, you've got to keep reminding yourself that you were sleepwalking that night. Even if you believe you were in Betsy's room, it doesn't mean that memory is accurate."

"I was there. She kept a low night-light on. I even remember seeing the earring sparkling on the floor. Rod, if I had picked it up, my fingerprints would have been on it."

"But you *didn't* pick it up," Rod said soothingly. "Alie, you've got to stop thinking like that. When you're in front of the camera, you've got to just tell what you know—which is nothing. You heard Jane scream and rushed to the bedroom with the others. Like the others, you were shocked. When you're interviewed, just keep saying 'the others' and you'll be all right. And remind yourself that the reason you're doing this program is because you want to have the money to go to medical school. What is it I've been telling you since you got the chance to go back to school?"

"That one day you'll be calling me the new Madame Curie," Alison whispered.

"Correct. Now go back to sleep."

But even though she stopped twisting and turning, Alison did not go back to sleep. When the alarm went off at seven o'clock, she was already showered and dressed in the slacks and polo shirt that she would soon be exchanging for the T-shirt and jeans she had worn the morning after Betsy Powell's murder.

42

Laurie, Jerry, and Grace arrived at the Powell estate a few minutes after the crew, which included a hairdresser, makeup artist, and wardrobe assistant this morning. Two new vans were on the set for their use—one to serve as a dressing room, the other for hair and makeup for those who would be on camera.

Laurie had worked well with all three crew members before. "The first scene we're shooting will be of the four graduates and the housekeeper in the clothes they put on after the body was discovered. The makeup should be light, because they wouldn't have had the time or inclination to put any on. We have a picture taken that morning by the police. Study it, then try to make them look the way they looked twenty years ago. Obviously they don't have the long hair, but they've all aged very well."

Meg Miller, the makeup artist, walked over to the window of the van to get a better look at the photograph. "I can tell you this, Laurie: they all look scared to death."

"I agree," Laurie said. "My job is to find out why. Of course you'd expect that they would look shocked and grief-stricken, but why do they all look so fearful? If Betsy was killed by an intruder, then what are they afraid of?"

The scene would be shot in the den, where the police had directed the girls to wait that morning. Incredibly, none of the furniture or draperies had been changed, so the room bore an eerie sameness to the way it had looked twenty years ago.

On the other hand, Laurie reasoned, my guess is that only Robert Powell has ever used that room in all these years. According to Jane Novak, the living room and dining room are where he does his entertaining when he has guests. From what she says, when he's alone after dinner he either goes to the den and watches television or reads, or else he goes up to his suite.

With only him living here and the way Jane keeps this place up, it's no wonder there was no need to change the interior decorating.

Or, she wondered, did Powell *want* to keep his home frozen in time, just as his wife had left it? She had heard of people like that.

She shivered as she walked quickly back to the den and entered by the patio door. The crew was setting up the cameras. There was no sign of Robert Powell. Jane had told them that he was in his office and would be there all morning.

From the beginning Powell had told her there was no need for him to equally compensate Jane. "I think I speak for her when I say we would both like a conclusion to this terrible business. Jane has always regretted the fact that after she locked all the doors for the night, the girls opened the one from the den, then when they came back in from smoking on the patio, they left it unlocked. If that had not happened, an intruder might not have been able to get in."

Maybe Powell and Jane are right, Laurie thought. After checking the cameras and the lighting, she went back out onto the patio and saw Alex Buckley getting out of his car.

Today he was wearing a sport shirt and khakis in place of the dark blue suit, shirt, and tie he had been wearing yesterday. The top of his convertible was down, and the breeze had ruffled his dark brown hair. She watched as with what was probably an instinctive gesture he smoothed his hair back and walked toward her.

"You're an early bird," he said with an easy smile.

"Not really. You should be around when we start shooting a program at daybreak."

"No thanks. I'll wait until I can push a button and see it on TV."

As he had in his office, he suddenly became businesslike. "Is the agenda still that we begin with me speaking to the graduates after you film them sitting in the den?"

"Yes. I'm doing this out of sequence because I have a strong hunch that they have all rehearsed what they're going to say to you. By starting with them all together, it may put them off guard."

"And don't be surprised at the way they're dressed. They're wearing replicas of the clothes they wore after Betsy's body was found, and then they were told to change into street wear."

Alex Buckley seldom allowed his face to register surprise, but this time he was so startled that he could not conceal it.

"You're having them wear replicas of what they wore twenty years ago?"

"Yes, for two scenes. The one in the den where they were herded with Jane as soon as the police arrived. And then one wearing gowns that are identical to the ones they wore to the Gala.

"We'll photograph the graduates against the background of films of them individually and together at the Gala. For example, when Robert Powell is toasting them, we'll have a picture of the four of them looking at him."

Alex Buckley's reply was interrupted by the limousines with the graduates arriving almost simultaneously. It was Laurie's turn to be astonished when Muriel Craig stepped out of the backseat of the second limo while her daughter, Nina, stepped out of the front passenger door. Muriel wasn't supposed to come today, she thought. Powell either called her or she's come on her own.

Either way, she's bound to make Nina edgy and angry.

Which might be good when Nina is being questioned.

43

On Tuesday morning Josh drove the Bentley to be hand-washed and detailed. Mr. Rob was very particular that it be kept in pristine order, *Or else*, Josh thought as he waited in the chair in the service center.

With a sense of satisfaction, Josh congratulated himself on solving the problem of how the graduates would be able to play the tapes he had recorded. He would put his cassette player in the powder room in the hallway next to the kitchen. There was a vanity table and bench in it for any guest who might want to touch up her makeup or hair. He would present the cassettes to Nina, Regina, and Alison and tell them they might be interested in hearing their conversations in the car, then suggest it might be worth fifty thousand dollars to have each copy destroyed.

They would be panicky, the three of them, he was sure of it. Claire hadn't said a word in the car when he drove her, so there was no cassette for her. And yet, of all of them, Josh would bet that she had the most to reveal.

He had the suicide note that Regina had hidden in her purse. Josh had debated whether to give it to Mr. Rob or try to find a better use for it. Then he found his answer: charge Regina one hundred thousand dollars, maybe even more, to get it back and tell her that otherwise he would go straight to the police. That note might take any suspicion of killing Betsy off Mr. Rob, Jane, and the other graduates.

And Josh would be a hero and good citizen if he turned it over to the police chief. But the police might ask what he was doing going through ladies' handbags. He did not have a good answer to that question, and he was hoping one would not be necessary.

Mr. Rob hadn't sent him to pick up any of the graduates this morning. Instead, sounding testy, he instructed him to come to the house after he left the service center, in case he decided to go into the office.

It was obviously unsettling for Mr. Rob to have all these people around. Not only must it bring up a lot of memories, Josh thought, but Mr. Rob must know that he's under suspicion, too, and want desperately to clear his name.

Like Jane, Josh had managed to sneak a look at Mr. Rob's will when it was on his desk. He had left $10 million to Harvard, to be used to fund scholarships for deserving students, and $5 million to Waverly College, where he had received an honorary doctorate and had already had the library named after Betsy and him.

Alison Schaefer had gone to Waverly. Josh remembered how she was the best student of the four girls and had talked about going to medical school, but then married Rod Kimball instead four months after the Gala.

Josh had always wondered why she hadn't brought Rod to the Gala that night. You never know, he told himself, they might have had an argument.

As the service manager approached Josh to tell him the car was ready, Josh concluded his line of thinking. Mr. Rob is a very sick man trying to ensure his legacy before he dies, he decided.

But as Josh got into the Bentley and drove away, he could not help thinking that there might be more reasons for Mr. Rob going ahead with the program than met the eye.

44

Leo Farley's impatience at his hospitalization grew with every passing moment. Disdainfully, he looked at the needle inserted in his left arm and the bottle of fluid connected to it dangling overhead. He had a heart monitor strapped to his chest, and when he had tried to get up a nurse came rushing in. "Mr. Farley, you cannot go to the bathroom alone. You have to be accompanied by a nurse. However, you *can* close the door."

Isn't that wonderful, Leo thought mockingly, even as he realized it wasn't right to kill the messenger. Instead, he thanked the nurse and grudgingly allowed her to follow him to the door of the bathroom. At 9 A.M. when his doctor came in, Leo was loaded for bear. "Look," he said, "I can get away without calling my daughter. She saw me last night just before I came in here, so I know she won't look to speak to me until tonight. She has two more days to finish this program, and there's a lot of pressure on her to make sure it's successful. If I have to tell her I'm in the hospital, she'll be terribly upset and probably end up coming here instead of finishing the show."

Dr. James Morris, an old friend, was equally forceful. "Leo, your daughter will be a lot more upset if something happens to you. I'll call Laurie—she knows you get these fibrillations—make it very clear to her that you're stable now and I should be able to release you tomorrow morning. I can do it before you call this evening or after. You will do her and your grandson a lot more good by staying alive and healthy than by risking a major heart attack."

Dr. Morris's beeper sounded. "I'm sorry, Leo, I have to go."

"Don't worry. We'll finish this later."

After Dr. Morris left him, he reached for his cell phone and called Camp Mountainside. He was connected to the camp administrator's office, then the head counselor, whom he had met before. "This is the pain-in-the-neck grandfather," he said. "I just wanted to know how Timmy was doing. Any nightmares?"

"No," the counselor said firmly. "I inquired about him at breakfast, and the senior camper in his bunk said he slept for nine hours straight without stirring."

Relieved, Leo said, "Well, that is really good news."

"Stop worrying, Mr. Farley. We're taking good care of him. And how are *you* doing?"

"I could be better," Leo said ruefully. "I'm in Mount Sinai Hospital with heart fibrillations. I never like feeling that I'm not available for Timmy every minute of the day."

Leo could not know that the counselor was thinking that with the strain he had been under for the last five years, it was no wonder he was having fibrillations. Instead he heard and appreciated the counselor's assurances. "You take care of yourself, Mr. Farley. We'll take care of your grandson. I promise."

Two hours later, when Blue Eyes heard the recorded conversation, he thought excitedly, He has played into my hands. Now they'll *never* doubt me.

45

❖

Jane Novak had worn the same-style plain black dress and white apron for the twenty-nine years she had been in the Powell household.

Her hair was also in the same style: combed back into a neat bun. The only difference was that it was now streaked with gray. Jane had never worn makeup and was scornful of Meg Miller's attempt to put even the lightest powder and eyebrow pencil on her. "Mrs. Novak, it's simply because the lights from the camera will wash you out," Meg said. But Jane would have none of it. "I know I have good skin," she said, "and that's because I never used any of that silly junk on it."

She did not know that even while Meg was saying, "Of course, as you wish," she was thinking that Jane indeed had a beautiful complexion and good features. Except for the droop at the end of her lips and the almost-scowling expression in her eyes, Jane Novak would be a very attractive woman, Meg thought.

Claire was the next one who would accept only a minimum amount of makeup. "I never wore any," she said. Then she added bitterly: "No one would look at me anyhow. They had my mother to rave over."

Regina was obviously so nervous that Meg did her best to pat the light beads of perspiration from her forehead with a concealer, in case she continued to sweat.

Alison, very quiet, simply shrugged when Meg said, "We're only doing a little because of the lights."

Nina Craig said, "I'm an actress. I know what lighting does. Do the best you can."

There was little that Courtney, the hairdresser, could do except to style the graduates' hair as close to how it had looked in the twenty-year-old photograph.

While Laurie waited for her stars in the den, Jerry and Grace were ready to make any adjustments Laurie thought necessary.

An enlarged picture of the four graduates and Jane, taken twenty years ago by the police photographer, rested on an easel out of the range of the camera, a template for arranging the women for their interviews. The cameraman, his assistant, and the lighting technician had already placed the cameras accordingly. Three of the girls had been sitting on the long couch, giving the appearance of being huddled together. There were two armchairs on either side of the cocktail table in front of the couch. Jane Novak was in one of them, her face grief-stricken, her eyes shining with unshed tears. Claire Bonner was sitting opposite her, her expression contemplative, but without any visible sign of grief.

Busily observing the present activity, Alex Buckley sat near the door in the leather chair in which Mr. Rob often sat at the end of the day. "It's a recliner," Jane told Laurie. "He likes to adjust it so his feet are up. His doctor said it was good for circulation."

It's a beautiful room, Alex thought as he looked around appraisingly. The mahogany paneling on the walls was the background for the vivid Persian carpet. The wall-mounted television was in the center of the bookshelves and over the fireplace. The furniture had been broken into two seating groups; the couch and chairs where the graduates and Jane Novak were now seated, and the couch and armchair with the leather recliner. The sliding glass door to the patio was on the right side of the couch where the girls were sitting and was, according to Jane, the door they had gone in and out to have cigarettes the night of the Gala, leaving it unlocked.

According to the police report, the ashtrays on the patio table had been filled to overflowing that morning. Jane indicated that at least three empty bottles of wine were in the glass disposal unit, left after she and the caterers had cleaned up after the party.

Alex listened as Laurie explained the photo shoot to the girls. "As you know, we simply want this shot of you to set the scene, with you in virtually the same outfits and in the same places as you were that morning. Then, separately, Alex Buckley will interview you in the spots where you are sitting now, to get your reflections on what you were thinking and feeling that morning. Were you talking to each other? From the old picture it doesn't look as if you were."

Nina answered for them. "We almost didn't say a word. I guess we were all in shock."

"I can understand that," Laurie said soothingly. "So just sit the way you did that morning, and we'll start taking pictures. Don't look at the cameras. Look at the picture and try to re-create the same poses."

From his vantage point behind one of the cameras, Alex Buckley could feel the tension in the room, the same kind of tension that he sometimes felt in a courtroom when an important witness was called to the stand. He knew Laurie Moran was going for dramatic impact by having the two pictures incorporated into the film, but he also knew that her goal was to unsettle the graduates and Jane until one or more of them gave a statement that contradicted what was on record. Alex watched as Meg, the makeup artist, came quietly into the den, a compact in her hand. He knew she was there in case the camera revealed anyone's face to be too shiny.

He marveled at the graduates' youthful appearances and how they all had stayed slender, and he thought that Nina, who didn't look thirty, had probably had some work done. It had been a shock to see Claire Bonner, who just yesterday had looked so glamorous and so like the pictures of her mother, by comparison look shockingly plain today. What kind of game is she playing? he wondered.

"All right, let's get started," Laurie was saying. "Grace, that pillow behind Nina, it's too far to the right." Grace adjusted it. Laurie checked the camera again and nodded to the cameraman. Alex watched as picture after picture was taken with an occasional comment from Laurie.

"Alison, try not to turn to the left. Nina, sit back the way you were in the original, otherwise you look as if you are posing. Jane, turn your head a little this way."

It was thirty-five minutes before Laurie was satisfied with what she saw in the camera's viewfinder. "Thanks very much," she said briskly. "We'll take a short break and then Alex will start interviewing you. Claire, he'll start with you. We'll be back in the den and you two will sit opposite each other in the chairs you and Jane are in now. The rest of you will have some downtime. There are newspapers and magazines in the dressing rooms. It's such a beautiful day, I imagine you will want to sit on the patio?"

One by one they all got to their feet. Jane was the first one to head for the door. "I'll put the snacks out and you can help yourselves," she said. "You can have them outside or in the breakfast room. We'll be having lunch at one-thirty."

46

Chief Ed Penn did not realize how much Leo's abiding worry about his daughter's safety while the *Under Suspicion* program was being filmed had affected him.

Even though he had ordered the squad car for the back road, he decided to take a look at the site himself. He was admittedly very curious to see how the graduates looked twenty years later.

It was around ten o'clock when, after having checked the squad car, the Chief decided to go onto the grounds and meet Laurie Moran. Of course he would not tell her of her father's concern, but on the other hand she was with six people who had been in the house on the night of Betsy Powell's murder. Penn was convinced that one of those six people was the murderer.

Robert Powell had been in a state of collapse with his hands badly burned from the steaming cup of coffee he had been carrying to his wife. He still could have killed her and figured that burns on his hands were a small price to pay for the appearance of innocence, Penn thought.

Chief Penn well knew that Regina's father had committed suicide because of the investment he made in Powell's hedge fund. A grieving daughter might very well have resented Powell for being the indirect cause of his death. The Chief was sure Regina had been lying when she claimed there was no suicide note. She had been only fifteen then, but she had withstood intense questioning, which suggested to him a steely resolve beyond her years.

Claire Bonner was a puzzle. Was it shock that made her so calm after her mother's death? He had been at the funeral. While tears streamed down Robert Powell's face, Claire had been cool, calm, and collected, as the expression went.

Nina Craig he knew less about—only that her mother constantly castigated her for introducing Betsy Bonner to Robert Powell.

Alison Schaefer seemed to be the one least likely to have a grudge against Betsy. She got married four months after Bonner's death, and, at that time, Rod had a brilliant future in football.

Penn had wondered if the paparazzi would try to get on the set. But there was no evidence of that. The guard at the gate let the Chief's car pass through, and his driver, a young policeman, parked behind the vans. "I won't be long," Penn told him and walked toward the patio, where people were gathered for lunch.

Laurie came to meet him and escorted him back to the group, where Penn immediately recognized the four graduates. They were sitting at the same table with Alison's husband and they all looked up as he approached. They all seemed startled, then defensive, but Regina was the only one who seemed to recoil as if from a blow.

He addressed her first. "Regina, I don't know if you remember me," he said.

"Yes, of course I remember you," she replied.

Chief Penn continued. "How have you been? I was sorry to hear about your mother's death right after she moved to Florida."

It was on the tip of Regina's tongue to say that her mother died of a broken heart because she never got over her husband's death, but that might open up the subject of the suicide note. Or is the police chief here because he already has it? she wondered. Hoping her hand would not tremble, Regina picked up her glass of iced tea and began to sip it as the police chief greeted the other graduates.

He turned to the table where Laurie, Alex Buckley, Muriel Craig, Jerry, and Grace were sitting.

"In a few minutes Alex will be talking with Regina about her memory of that night and the next morning," Laurie said. "Tomorrow evening when it gets dark, we will be filming the graduates in evening dresses against the background of the film of the party taken that evening. If you would like to come by and see that scene, you are welcome to come back."

It was at just that point that Robert Powell came out to the patio. "I've been working in my office," he explained. "Anyone who runs a hedge fund cannot take his eyes off the market for even a minute. Ed, how are you? Are you here to protect us from each other?"

"I don't think that's necessary, Mr. Powell."

Even though he was smiling and seemed at ease, Penn could see the fatigue around Robert Powell's eyes and the overall weariness in his body as he sat down at the table and shook his head when Laurie offered him a sandwich from the platter Jane had placed there. Muriel, who had been complaining she had nothing to do, suddenly came alive.

"Rob, dear," she said, "you've worked enough today. Why don't you and I go over to the club for a round of golf? I used to be a pretty good golfer, you know. I'm sure I can rent clubs, and I put golf shoes in my tote bag, just in case I could persuade you."

Laurie expected to hear a flat refusal, but Powell smiled. "That's the best idea I've heard all day," he said. "But I'm so sorry to say I must take a rain check. I have a lot of work to do in my office." He paused, then looked at Laurie. "You don't have anything for me to do today, I gather?"

"No, Mr. Powell. Alex will be interviewing the girls one by one. And then Jane, if we have time today."

"How long will the interviews take?" Powell asked. "I expected them to be about ten minutes each."

"They'll be cut to that time," Laurie said. "But Alex is planning to speak with each of them for about an hour. Isn't that right, Alex?"

"Yes, it is."

"Mr. Rob, are you sure that you don't want to have a snack?" Jane asked. "You hardly touched your breakfast."

"Jane takes such good care of me," Powell told the others. "In fact, sometimes she's almost like a mother hen."

Not exactly a compliment, Laurie thought. She could see from the flush on Jane's face that she didn't think so, either.

"Familiarity breeds contempt," Muriel snapped, staring at Jane as Robert Powell pushed back his chair and went into the house.

Wordlessly, Jane turned away from the table and went to where the graduates and Rod were seated. They all declined more coffee, and seeing that, Laurie pushed back her chair. "If you didn't know it before, I guess you know it now. There's a lot of waiting around in this business. Alex will start by interviewing Claire. When she is finished she can go back to the hotel, and then the same for each of you. Figure about an hour apiece."

Chief Penn stood up. "Any sign of the paparazzi or anyone trying to get in here while you're filming," he told Laurie, "give me a call immediately." He handed her his card.

Rod said to Alison, "It's getting warm out here. I guess we're not invited to sit in the living room," he added sarcastically, "and the den is being used for filming. But I suppose we can sit in the break-fast room. The chairs look comfortable there."

Laurie stood up and said to Claire, "I do think you should have a little more makeup on. With your blond eyebrows and lashes you'll end up looking terribly washed out on camera. You really need a little touch-up." She looked toward the door of the makeup van. "They're ready for you now," she said. With a brief nod, she walked over to the door that led to the den and opened it.

Chief Penn signaled to his driver and walked over to his car. He happened to glance at Bruno, who was meticulously searching for any scrap of paper or matted grass that might be disrupting the serene beauty of the grounds. Penn barely caught a glimpse of Bruno's profile, but as he got into the car he realized that something in his subconscious was bothering him. A little voice was saying, *I should know this guy, but why?*

As Alex Buckley followed Laurie into the den, he had exactly the same thought about Bruno. *I should know that guy, but why?* Alex hesitated, then reached into his pocket for his phone and snapped a photo. He made a mental note to get the landscaper's name and forward it to his investigator.

And then, for the first time, the four graduates were alone, and Josh, who had been helping Jane serve coffee, saw his chance. "I have a present for the three of you," he said, "except Claire." He looked at Claire. "I tried to talk to you in the car, but you were having none of it." Josh looked at the other three graduates. "Here is a tape I think each one of you will find very interesting. You especially, Regina. Maybe you've mislaid something I found?"

He handed separate envelopes to Regina, Alison, and Nina, then said, "There is a cassette player in the drawer of the vanity in the restroom by the kitchen. Why don't we talk after the three of you have a chance to listen to the tapes?"

Then Josh picked up the coffee cups in front of him and said: "See you all later," in a confident voice, with just the slightest undertone of threat.

47

Because his office was next to the den, where all the activity was taking place, Robert Powell chose to go back upstairs to the bedroom suite he had shared with Betsy for the nine years of their marriage. At his curt request Jane followed him with a fresh pot of coffee. Then, sensing his irritable mood, she closed the door to his bedroom so she could make up the room quickly and quietly. She skipped her usual vacuuming because she knew the sound of it would annoy him. Then she left by the bedroom door to go downstairs.

Robert was wondering once again whether he had made a drastic mistake by inviting these girls—women, he corrected himself sarcastically—to reenact what had happened twenty years ago. Had his doctor's prognosis been the reason for it? Or was it because of a perverse need to see them again, to toy with them as Betsy had toyed with them all those years ago? Had he absorbed so much of Betsy's personality that he no longer had anything left of his own, even twenty years later? Each graduate had a reason to kill Betsy, he knew that. It would be interesting to see if one of them broke down under Alex Buckley's questioning. He was sure Buckley was capable of detecting prepared answers.

Powell would bet that all the graduates had carefully practiced what they would say in their one-on-one interview with Buckley. He was sure they would start with their first impressions of what they saw when they ran into Betsy's room after hearing him shout.

It seemed like only yesterday that he had walked into her bedroom carrying the cup of coffee that she had always insisted be red-hot "to get the flavor through the coffee beans."

Rob looked down at the angry scars on his hands that had resulted from walking into Betsy's room and seeing the pillow covering her face. Betsy's long blond hair had spilled out from under it, her hands still clutching the pillow's edges. She had obviously been struggling to push the pillow away from her face.

He remembered shrieking her name and trying to keep the coffee cup from spilling before his knees buckled under him. He remembered Jane leaning over him and attempting some clumsy CPR while the girls stood around the bed like ghostly wraiths. The next thing he remembered was waking up in the hospital, conscious of nothing but the pain in his hands, and calling out for Betsy.

Robert Powell leaned back in his chair. It was time to go downstairs and make some business calls. But he hesitated for a moment as he stopped to reflect on what Claire would be telling Buckley.

He realized that what had been amusing to him was no longer amusing. All he wanted now was to have these women out of this house and to resume what little time was left of his quiet and pleasant life.

48

Alex looked at Claire Bonner across the table from him in the den. Claire had once again resisted Meg Miller's suggestion to touch up her lashes and eyebrows. Now, as Alex looked at her, he found it incongruous to compare her with the beautiful woman who had walked into this house yesterday.

It was easy to see what had made the difference. Claire's long lashes and well-shaped eyebrows were very pale, as was her complexion. She wore no lip coloring, and he could swear that she had washed the gold highlights out of her hair. I'll find out what she's up to, he thought and smiled encouragingly at her when Laurie said, "Action," and the camera's red light went on.

"I'm here in the home of Wall Street financier Robert Nicholas Powell," he began, "whose beautiful wife, Betsy Bonner Powell, was murdered twenty years ago following a Graduation Gala for Betsy's daughter, Claire, and Claire's three closest friends and fellow graduates. Claire Bonner is with me now. Claire, I know this has to be extraordinarily difficult for all of you to be here today. Why did *you* agree to come on the program?"

"Because the other girls and I, and to a lesser degree my stepfather and the housekeeper, have been under suspicion as 'persons of interest' in Betsy's death, which is the new way of saying it, for the last twenty years," Claire declared passionately. "Can you have any idea of what it's like to be in a supermarket and see your own picture on the cover of some trashy magazine with the question 'Was she jealous of her beautiful mother'?"

"No, I can't," Alex replied quietly.

"Or maybe there would be a picture of the four of us lined up, as if we had had mug shots taken of us by the police. That's why we're here today, to make the public realize how unfairly we four young women, who were traumatized beyond belief and bullied by the police, have been treated. That's why I'm here now, Mr. Buckley."

"And I assume that's why the other girls are here, too," Alex Buckley said. "Have you done much catching up with them?"

"We actually haven't had very much time to visit," Claire said. "I know it's because you people didn't want us to put our stories together. Well, let me tell you something: we have *not* boned up on each other's stories, and I think you will find that out. They'll be pretty much the same because we were together at the moment when everything was happening."

"Claire, before we discuss your mother's death, I'd like to go back in time a little. Why don't we start with your mother's meeting with Robert Powell? I understand you had only lived in Salem Ridge a short while. Is that right?"

"Yes, it is. I had graduated from grammar school in June, and my mother wanted to move up to Westchester County. Quite frankly, I know she wanted to meet a rich man. She found a rental in a two-family house, and I can assure you there aren't many two-family houses in Salem Ridge.

"I started my freshman year in high school that September, and that's when I became friends with Nina and Alison and Regina. My birthday is in October, and Mother splurged and took me to La Boehm in Bedford. Nina Craig and her mother were there. Nina spotted us, and asked us to come over and meet her mother. Of course we also met Robert Powell, who was at the table. I guess it was love at first sight for both of them, my mother and Robert. I do know that Nina's mother has never gotten over the fact that 'Betsy stole Rob from me when we were on the verge of becoming engaged,' as she put it."

"Your own father had abandoned you and your mother when you were only an infant. How did your mother manage to look after you and still work full-time?"

"My grandmother was alive until I was three years old." Tears began to shine in Claire's eyes as she mentioned her grandmother. "Then there was a series of babysitters, one after the other. If they failed to show up, Mother would bring me to the theatre and I'd sleep in an empty chair, or sometimes it would be in an empty dressing room if the play had a small cast. One way or the other we managed. But then Mother met Robert Powell, and of course everything changed."

"You and your mother had been very close, I gather? Were you ever jealous of the fact that Robert Powell came so suddenly into your life and claimed so much of your mother's time and attention?"

"I wanted her to be happy. He was obviously a very rich man. After the dinky little apartments we'd lived in all my life, it seemed like heaven to move into this beautiful house."

"*Seemed* like heaven?" Alex asked quickly.

"*Was* heaven," Claire corrected herself.

"That was quite a year for you, Claire, moving into a new area, starting high school, then your mother's wedding and moving into this house."

"It was all quite a change," Claire said with a faint smile. If you only knew, she thought. If you only knew!

"Claire, were you close to Robert Powell?"

Claire looked straight into Alex's eyes. "Right from the beginning," she said. Oh, I was close to him all right, she thought, remembering how she listened for the sound of her bedroom door opening.

Alex Buckley knew that behind Claire's smooth answers there was a land mine of smoldering anger she was trying to conceal. It wasn't all sweetness and light in this house, he thought as he decided to change his questioning. "Claire, let's talk about the Gala. What kind of night was it? How many people were here? We have that information, of course, but I'd like to hear it from your perspective."

Alex had foreseen that Claire would begin answering him in carefully rehearsed sentences. "It was a perfect night," she said. "It was an absolutely balmy evening, about seventy-six degrees, I think. There was a band on the patio, and a dance floor. There were stations everywhere with all kinds of food. Near the pool a table was beautifully decorated. The centerpiece was a sheet cake with all of our names on it and the symbols of the four colleges we went to in their school colors."

"You chose to commute to Vassar, didn't you, Claire?"

Again Alex saw a look in Claire's eyes that he could not identify. What was it? Anger, disappointment, or both? He took a shot at what he surmised. "Claire, were you disappointed that you didn't go away to college as your other friends did?"

"Vassar is a wonderful college. I may have missed out on a part of the college experience by commuting instead of boarding, but my mother and I were so close that I was happy to stay home."

Claire's smile was more of a sneer, but then she recovered herself. "We all had a wonderful time at the party," she said. "Then, as you know, the other girls slept over. When everyone was gone we put on our pajamas and robes, went to the den, and drank wine. Lots of wine. We gossiped about the party, as girls do."

"Were your mother and Mr. Powell with you in the den?"

"Rob said good night to us right after the last guests left. My mother sat with us for a few minutes, but then she said, 'I want to get comfortable, the way you all are.' She went upstairs and came back down in her nightgown and robe."

"Did she stay long?"

For a moment there was a real smile on Claire's lips and in her eyes. "My mother wasn't a drunk, never think that, but she *did* love to have a couple of glasses of wine in the evening. She had about three glasses that night before she went upstairs. She hugged and kissed us good night, which is why we all had DNA from her hair on our pajamas or robes the next morning."

"The other girls were very fond of your mother, weren't they?"

"I think they were in awe of her."

Alex knew that what Claire didn't say was that each of the girls had a reason to hate Betsy Powell. Nina, because her mother tortured her about having introduced Robert to Betsy. Regina, because her father had lost all his money in one of Robert Powell's investments. Alison, because she had lost out on a scholarship that she should have won but Betsy Bonner directed elsewhere. Robert Powell had donated a load of money to Alison's college. That donation was not forgotten when the graduate scholarship was awarded to the daughter of a woman who chaired a club Betsy was desperate to join.

"After your mother said good night to all of you, did you see her again?"

"Do you mean did I see her again alive?" Claire did not wait for an answer. "My last memory of seeing my mother alive was when she turned and smiled and blew a kiss to all of us. Of course it's a vivid memory. She was a very beautiful woman. She always wore beautiful matching nightgowns and robes. That night she was wearing a pale-blue satin set, edged in ivory lace. Her hair was loose on her shoulders, and she seemed so happy about how successful the party had been. The next time I saw her, either Rob or Jane had taken the pillow off of her face. Her eyes were wide open and staring. One hand was still clutching the pillow. I know she must have been sleepy because of all of the wine she had drunk, but I always had the feeling she put up a fight."

Alex listened as Claire spoke in a voice that seemed to be suddenly without emotion. Her hands were now clasped together, and her face had turned even paler than it had been.

"How did you know that something was terribly wrong?" Alex asked quietly.

"I heard the most terrifying shriek coming from my mother's room. I later learned that it was Rob, who was bringing my mother her usual cup of morning coffee. I think all of us girls were in a heavy sleep—we had talked and drunk until three A.M. We all got to the room at about the same time. Jane must have heard Robert's shout. She got to my mother's room first. She was on her knees bending over Robert, who had collapsed and was writhing in pain. I guess he must have rushed to grab the pillow away from my mother's face, and the hot coffee had spilled all over his hands. The pillow was to the side of my mother's head and had coffee stains on it."

Alex saw that Claire's expression suddenly turned cold. It was a startling difference from the way she had reacted to his questions about her grandmother.

"Then what happened, Claire?" he asked.

"I think it was Alison who picked up the phone and dialed 911. She shouted something like 'We need an ambulance and the police! Betsy Bonner Powell is dead! I think she's been murdered!' "

"What did you do while you waited for them?"

"I don't think it was more than three minutes later that both the ambulance and the police arrived. Then it was chaos. We were literally chased out of her room. I remember the police chief ordering us to go back to our bedrooms and change our clothes. He had the nerve to say that he could see what we were wearing and we shouldn't try to switch what we had slept in. Later we realized that those clothes would be tested for DNA as potential evidence."

"So you changed into jeans and T-shirts similar to the ones you were photographed in this morning?"

"Yes. When we had changed we were escorted downstairs here to the den and told to wait until the police questioned us. They wouldn't even allow us to go to the kitchen to make a cup of coffee."

"You're still very angry about that, aren't you, Claire?"

"Yes, I am," she said, her voice trembling with rage. "Think about it. We were all barely twenty-one. Looking back, I realize that even though we thought we were all grown up, having just graduated from college, in reality we were just frightened kids. The interrogation they put all of us through that day, and for weeks afterward, was a travesty of justice. They called us in to the police station over and over again. That's the reason that the press began to refer to us as 'suspects.' "

"Who do you think killed your mother, Claire?"

"There were three hundred people at that party. Some of them we can't identify from the photos and film we have of that night. People were going in and out of the house to use the bathrooms. Jane had put a rope across the landing at the bottom of the staircase, but anyone could have sneaked up the stairs. My mother was wearing her emeralds that night. Anyone could have picked out her bedroom and even hidden in one of those walk-in closets. I think someone waited until he thought she would be in a deep sleep, then picked up the emeralds from her dressing table. Who knows if she started stirring and he panicked and tried to put them back? One emerald earring was found on the floor. I believe she woke up. Whoever was in that room tried to keep her from calling for help the only way that was available to him."

"And that person, you believe, is your mother's murderer?"

"Yes, I do. And remember, we had left the patio door open. The four of us were smokers, and my stepfather absolutely forbade smoking in the house."

"Is that why you resent the media coverage of your mother's death?"

"That is why I am telling you that none of us here—not Rob, nor Jane, nor Nina, Regina, or Alison—had a thing to do with my mother's death. And obviously neither did I." Claire's voice became shrill. "And neither did I!"

"Thank you, Claire, for sharing your memory of that terrible day when you lost the mother you loved so dearly."

Alex reached across the table to shake Claire's hand.

It was drenched in perspiration.

49

On Tuesday morning, George Curtis got up at six thirty as was his custom and brushed Isabelle's forehead softly with his lips, trying not to wake her. He felt a desperate need to touch her. He had woken often during the night and put his arm around her. Then the guilty memory would flood his brain: *Betsy always wore satin nightgowns, too.* Inevitably his next thought was, Isabelle, I almost lost you. I almost lost the joyful life I have been living with you and our children for nearly twenty years.

That new life had begun the morning of the Gala when Isabelle told him that she was expecting twins. That incredible news was followed by Betsy demanding $25 million for her silence about their affair. I didn't mind paying her, George thought, but I knew it would be only the beginning of her threats to go to Isabelle.

These were the thoughts that were running through his head as he showered, dressed, and went down to the kitchen to make a cup of coffee. He carried the cup out to the car, placed it in the holder, and was on his way to his office, the international headquarters of Curtis Foods, ten miles away in New Rochelle.

He loved his early morning hour-and-a-half alone time in the office. It was when he could concentrate on important mail and e-mails from his district managers all over the world. But today he could not concentrate. After going over the highly favorable earnings reports, his only reaction was that he could easily have found a way to pay Betsy and bury the payment without raising any suspicion.

But I couldn't have trusted her, was the refrain that ran through his head.

When the office began to fill up just before nine, he greeted his longtime assistant Amy Hewes with his usual cordiality and crisply began to go over some e-mails he wanted answered immediately. But he knew he was too distracted to concentrate. At eleven-thirty he called home. "Any plans for lunch?" he asked Isabelle when she answered.

"Not one," she said promptly. "Sharon called and asked me to meet her for golf, but I'm too lazy today. I'm stretched out on the patio. Louis is preparing gazpacho and a chicken salad. How does that sound?"

"Perfect. I'm on my way."

As he passed Amy's desk and told her he wouldn't be coming back this afternoon, she looked surprised. "Don't tell me that you, the sought-after speaker who always wows the audience, is nervous about being interviewed this afternoon?"

George tried to smile. "Maybe I am."

The short drive seemed interminably long to him. He was so impatient to see Isabelle that he left his car in the circular driveway, bounded up the steps, threw open the door, and rushed down the long hallway to the rear of the house. Before he opened the glass door to the patio he stopped and looked out. Isabelle was sitting in one of the padded chairs, her feet on a hassock, a book in her hands. Sixty years old on her last birthday, her hair was now completely silver. She wore it in a new shorter length and with bangs. The style framed her face perfectly, with her classic features that were the product of generations of fine breeding. Her ancestors had come over on the *Mayflower.* Her slender body was already tanned. She had kicked off her shoes, and her ankles were crossed.

For a long minute George Curtis studied the beautiful woman who had been his wife for thirty-five years. They had met at a dance given by the senior class at Harvard. Isabelle had attended it with friends from Wellesley College. The minute she walked into the room, I made a beeline for her, George thought. But the first time I met her parents, I know they were underwhelmed. They would have preferred that our family had made its money on Wall Street, not by selling hot dogs and hamburgers.

What would her mother and father have thought had they known I was having an affair with my best friend's wife? They'd have told Isabelle to get rid of me.

And if Isabelle had ever known, even though she was pregnant with our twins, she would have dropped me, too.

And still would, George thought grimly as he slid open the patio door. Hearing the sound, Isabelle looked up and smiled warmly. "Was it me or the menu that inspired you to join me for lunch?" she asked as she got up and kissed him warmly.

"It was you," George replied fervently, returning her kiss and putting his arms around her.

Louis, their chef, came out onto the patio carrying a tray with two iced teas.

"Good to have you home for lunch, Mr. Curtis," he said cheerfully.

Louis had been with them for twenty-two years. He had been working as a chef in a nearby restaurant when one evening as they were having dinner there, he came to the table. "I heard that you are looking for a new chef," he had said quietly.

"Yes, our current chef is retiring," George had verified.

"I would very much like to try out for the job," Louis said. "We serve mostly Italian food here, but I am a graduate of the Culinary Institute in Hyde Park, and I promise I can offer you a wide selection of menus."

And so he had, George thought, including preparing fresh baby food every day when the twins were born and letting them "help" him in the kitchen when they were little.

George sat in a chair near Isabelle, but as Louis placed the glass next to him, he said, "Louis, will you put my tea on the table and bring me a Bloody Mary?"

Isabelle raised an eyebrow. "That's not like you, George. Are you nervous about the interview with Alex Buckley?"

He waited until the patio door closed behind Louis, then answered, "Uncomfortable rather than nervous. To me the whole idea of this program seems bizarre. I get the feeling that this is not about proving people innocent as it is proving that someone in the group was guilty of Betsy's death."

"Someone like *you*, George?"

George Curtis stared at his wife, his blood running cold. "What do you mean by that?"

"I overheard that interesting conversation you had with Betsy the night of the Gala. Even though you had pulled away from the crowd, I followed you. I was on the other side of those palms they had brought in for decoration. You didn't realize how much you had raised your voice."

George Curtis knew that the nightmare he had feared was happening. Was Isabelle going to tell him, now that the twins were raised, that she wanted a divorce? "Isabelle, I'm sorrier than you can possibly imagine," he said. "Please, please forgive me."

"Oh, I already have," Isabelle said promptly. "Did you think that I was too stupid to suspect you were having an affair with that slut? When I overheard the two of you, I decided I wasn't about to lose you. I realized we had grown apart, and I knew that some of it was my fault. I wasn't going to forgive you too easily, but I'm still glad I made that decision. You've been a wonderful husband and father, and I love you dearly."

"I was so terribly worried and guilty all these years," George Curtis said, his voice breaking.

"I know you were," Isabelle said crisply. "That was my way of punishing you. Oh, here's Louis with your Bloody Mary. I'll bet you're ready for it now."

My God, I thought I knew my wife! George Curtis exclaimed to himself as he reached for the glass Louis was putting in front of him.

"Louis, I think we're ready to have lunch now," Isabelle said as she took a sip of her iced tea.

When Louis went back to the kitchen, Isabelle said, "George, when you warned Betsy that if she ever told me about your affair with her you would kill her, I may not have been the *only* one who heard you. Like I said, you didn't realize how loud you were speaking. Then, after we came home and went to bed, I fell asleep in your arms. When I woke up at four A.M. you weren't in bed, and it was more than an hour before you returned. I just assumed that you were downstairs watching television. You always do, if you wake up and can't go back to sleep. When I heard Betsy had been smothered, I begged God that if you had killed her, you didn't leave any evidence that would lead to you. If anything comes up during the filming of this program, I'll swear that you never left our bed that night."

"Isabelle, you don't believe . . ."

"George, we live only a few blocks away from them. You could have walked to their house in five minutes. You knew the layout. And frankly, I don't *care* if you killed her. I know we can afford it, but I see no reason why you should have paid twenty-five million dollars in blackmail to that tramp."

As George held her chair for her at the table, Isabelle said, "I love you so dearly, George, and the twins adore you. Don't say anything to spoil that. Now here comes Louis with the salad. I'll bet you're hungry, aren't you?"

50

"Okay, guys, that was great. Take a break now. Alison Schaefer is next. We'll start in half an hour," Laurie said briskly. Jerry, Grace, and the camera crew knew that was Laurie's way of saying, "Get lost." It was clear to them that she wanted to talk to Alex Buckley alone. As they filed out, they closed the door of the den without asking. Then Alex suggested, "Why don't I get a cup of coffee for both of us? I know you like yours black, no sugar."

"Sounds wonderful," Laurie admitted.

"I'll be right back," he said as he unfolded his long legs and stood up.

When he returned five minutes later, coffee cups in hand, Laurie was seated in the chair where Claire had been and was busy scribbling notes. "Thanks so much," she said as he placed the cups on the table between them. "Are they all out there? I mean, is Claire talking to them about her interview with you?"

"I don't know where Claire is, but there's something funny going on with the rest of them," Alex Buckley replied. "Regina is white as a ghost, and Nina and her mother are obviously having an argument on the patio. No surprise there. Alison and Rod are taking a walk near the pool. The way he has his arm around her, I think she's terribly upset. She's holding a handkerchief and dabbing her eyes."

Astonished, Laurie asked, "What could have brought all that on?"

"When you and I left them, Claire followed only a few minutes behind," Alex said, his brow furrowed. "We left the other three waiting for Josh to bring more coffee. I'm telling you, Laurie, something happened that upset all of them. Maybe I can get it out of Alison when I interview her." His tone became crisp. "I know you want to talk to me about the interview with Claire."

"Yes, I do," Laurie said. "Why did you ask her so much about her relationship with Robert Powell?"

"Laurie, think about it. She and her mother had obviously been very tight for the first thirteen years of Claire's life. Then Robert Powell enters the picture. No matter how glamorous it may have been for her to move into this mansion, there is no doubt from everything I have read that Claire's mother and Powell were virtually inseparable. And why didn't Claire go away to college as her friends did? Claire must have been home alone a lot of nights. From what I gathered, Betsy and Powell were out almost every night on the social scene. Why couldn't Claire board at Vassar? Didn't you hear and see the way Claire's expression changed when she talked about Powell? I'm telling you right now that something was going on there," Alex said vehemently.

Laurie stared at him, then nodded.

Alex smiled. "You caught it, too. I was sure you would. Whenever I'm preparing a case for trial, I have my investigators dig into the backgrounds of the people I'm defending as well as the ones who are on the witness stand testifying either for or against my client. One of the first things I learned was to dig below the obvious. If you ask me, Claire Bonner was not as heartsick at her mother's death as she claims to be."

"At first I was attributing her reaction to shock," Laurie admitted. "Then I felt the same way. She only talked about her anger over the way the police treated her and the other girls. Not one word about grieving for her mother." Laurie changed gears. "Now, before Alison Schaefer comes in, let me give you my first impressions of her."

Alex sipped his coffee as Laurie continued. "Rod Kimball and Alison Schaefer were married four months after the Gala, and yet she hadn't even invited him as her date that night. Was she rushing into a situation because of the way they were all grilled after Betsy's death? The only other thing that I can see was that she lost out on a scholarship. It was awarded to the girl whose marks were second to hers but who happened to be the daughter of Betsy's friend. Did the fact that Powell donated a ton of money to Alison's college influence the scholarship award? Yes, I think it was the kind of scholarship donated by an alumnus, and the dean chose the winner at his discretion."

Alex nodded. "You've done plenty of your own digging, I see."

"Yes, I have," Laurie agreed. "And I've wondered whether the fact that Rod had just signed a great contract with the Giants had anything to do with Alison suddenly marrying him. But if so, when he had that accident, she certainly stuck by him, didn't she? Apparently he had always had a crush on her, from way back when they were in kindergarten. At the time they were married, he had a brilliant future as a quarterback. Even if the attraction was the fame and fortune of pro football, there had to be more to her feelings than that. The last twenty years are proof of it."

"Or is it possible she was so upset about losing the scholarship that she smothered Betsy and confessed it to Rod? That would certainly have been his hold over her for all of these years," Alex suggested.

There was a knock on the den door, and the cameraman looked in. "Laurie, are you ready for us yet?"

Laurie and Alex looked at each other. It was Alex who answered. "You bet we are. Please ask Alison Schaefer to come in now."

51

Later that morning, Leo Farley stared at the ceiling as his doctor and longtime friend checked his heartbeat. "There's nothing the matter with me," Leo said, his tone icy.

"That's your opinion," Dr. James Morris replied mildly, "but believe me, this is where you're going to stay until I discharge you. And before you ask me why again, let me explain again. You were still having heart fibrillations yesterday evening. If you don't want to have a heart attack, you'll stay put."

"All right, all right," Leo said with angry resignation. "But Jim, you don't get it. I don't want Laurie to know I'm here, and I can tell she's already guessed. She never calls me on the way to work, but she did today. She was so persistent asking me where I was last night . . . I can't have her worrying about me while she's doing this program."

"Do you want me to phone Laurie now and reassure her?" Dr. Morris asked.

"I know Laurie. If you call, it would upset her even more."

"When do you usually talk to her?"

"After she gets home from the studio. I got away with it last night, but tonight she'll expect me to go out and at least grab a hamburger with her. I don't know what my excuse will be," Leo Farley said, his voice somber but no longer angry.

"Look, Leo, I can tell you this. You had two episodes of fibrillation yesterday. If you don't have any tonight, I will discharge you tomorrow," Dr. Morris promised. "And don't forget, I still know how to reassure my patients' relatives about their health. If you let me tell Laurie that, barring any more fibrillations, I'm discharging you tomorrow morning, I think that would be the best way to go. So think about it. She can always stop in here tonight and see you. Doesn't Timmy call her between seven and eight?"

"Yes. She has him call at quarter to eight so she's sure to be free to talk."

"Then why not have her here in time to take the call, and the two of you can talk to him together? From what you tell me, he can only make one phone call every evening."

Leo Farley's face cleared. "As usual, you have a good idea, Jim."

Dr. Morris knew of Leo Farley's desperate worry about the threat to his daughter and grandson. And it won't be over until that Blue Eyes guy is rotting in prison, he thought.

He touched Leo's shoulder, but managed to close his lips before he uttered the two most useless words in the English language, "Don't worry."

52

After Josh handed the three of them the tapes, Alison was the first to go into the bathroom, take the cassette player from the vanity drawer, insert the tape, and listen to it. Aghast, she heard her conversation with Rod about her sleepwalking into Betsy's room. Near hysteria, she grabbed the tape and rushed outside. Rod had seen her from the window and hurried as fast as possible to join her.

Now, his crutches beside him, he sat on the bench near the pool with his arm around her, their backs to the production crew outside. She had managed to stop crying, but her lips were still trembling.

"Don't you see, Rod?" Alison said. "That's the reason Powell had Josh pick all of us up at the airport in that fancy Bentley at two-hour intervals, except for Claire, who arrived the night before. Powell wouldn't have done that except for one reason. The Bentley was bugged. Rod, don't you remember we talked about my sleepwalking into Betsy's bedroom?"

"Shh," Rod cautioned, then looked around. There was no one within hearing distance. My God, I'm getting paranoid around this place, he thought.

He tightened his arm around Alison's shoulder. "Alie, if they bring it up, say of course you were disappointed about the scholarship, but then it didn't matter. You'd had a secret crush on me from

the time we were in kindergarten." He paused, then thought ruefully, at least that part was true for me.

"And you asked me to marry you, even though you believed I
had been angry enough to kill Betsy Powell," Alison said flatly. "You
can't deny that for all these years you have believed I might have
killed her."

"I know how much you hated her, but I never really believed that
you could kill her."

"I did hate her. I've tried to get over it, but I can't. I still hate her.
It was so unfair," Alison said passionately. "Powell donated a ton of
money to Waverly because Betsy was desperate to get into that fancy
club. When the dean gave the scholarship to Betsy's friend's daughter, don't you think I had a good reason to kill her? Did I mention
that my fellow student flunked out her second year?"

"I think you may have mentioned it once or twice," Rod said
quietly.

"Rod, when everything you ever worked for and prayed for and
dreamed about falls apart . . . I was half out of the chair to accept that
award when the dean announced her name. You can't imagine it!"

Then she looked at him, seeing the lines of pain on his handsome face, the crutches next to him. "Oh, Rod, how stupid of me to
say that, to you of all people."

"It's all right, Alie."

No it isn't, she thought. It isn't all right at all.

"Alison, they're ready for you."

It was Laurie's assistant Jerry who was approaching them.

"Rod, I'm frightened I'm going to fall apart," Alison whispered
frantically as she stood up and bent to brush a kiss on his forehead.

"No, you're not," Rod said firmly as he looked up at the woman
he loved so dearly. Her light-brown eyes, the most prominent features in her thin face, were ablaze. The tears had left her eyelids
slightly swollen, but he knew the makeup artist would repair that.

He watched Alison as she walked to the house. In twenty years, he had not seen her so emotional. And he knew why—because she had a second chance at the career she wanted so desperately, the one that had been stolen from her.

A random thought hit him. Alie had let her hair grow longer, and now it was brushing her shoulders. He liked it that way. The other day she had said she was going to have it cut soon. He regretted that, but would never dream of saying so. There were so many things he had not told her over the past twenty years . . .

If she got through this program and received the money, Rod couldn't help but worry, would it be her ticket to freedom—from him?

53

ina was the second one who listened to her cassette. When she came back to the table her expression was almost triumphant. "This is more for you than it is for me," she told her mother. "Why don't you go in there and dwell on every word? And when you do, I don't think you'll be sobbing so much to Rob Powell that Betsy was your closest and dearest friend."

"What are you talking about?" Muriel snapped as she stood up and pushed back her chair.

"The cassette player is in the center drawer of the vanity in the hall bathroom," Nina said. "You should be able to find it."

The contented expression Muriel had been wearing turned into one of uncertainty and worry. Without answering her daughter, she hurried to the hallway. A few minutes later the slamming of the bathroom door signaled her imminent return.

When she came out her face was set in hard angry lines. Her head jerked in Nina's direction. "Come outside," she said.

"Well? What do you want?" Nina demanded as soon as the door to the patio closed behind them.

"What do I want?" Muriel hissed. "What do I want? Are you crazy? Did you listen to that tape? It makes me sound terrible. And Rob asked me to have dinner tonight. Everything is going so well, the way it was before . . ."

"Before I ruined everything for you by introducing Rob Powell to Betsy when you were practically engaged to him," Nina finished for her.

Muriel's expression became hard and calculating. "Do you think Rob has heard those tapes?"

"I don't know. I would guess he has, but that's just a guess. The chauffeur may be blackmailing us as his own little game and not telling Rob."

"Then give him the fifty thousand dollars."

Nina stared at her mother. "You have got to be joking! Rob Powell is making a fool out of you with this sudden attention. If he'd wanted you, why didn't he call you twenty years ago when Betsy died?"

"Pay that chauffeur," Muriel said flatly. "Otherwise I will tell Rob and the police that you confessed to me you killed Betsy to give me another chance at Rob. I'll say that you thought I'd be very generous to you when I became Mrs. Robert Nicholas Powell."

"You would do that?" Nina asked, white-lipped.

"Why not? It's true, isn't it?" Muriel sneered. "And don't forget that Rob's million-dollar reward for information leading to the arrest and conviction of Betsy's murderer can always be my consolation prize if you're right about his interest in me *not* being genuine. He posted that reward twenty years ago and it's never been withdrawn."

54

After she'd seen Alison rush outside and Muriel ordered Nina to go with her to the patio, Regina knew she had to listen to her own tape.

On the way to hear it, she thought, Josh must be the one to have that letter. The cassette player was on top of the vanity. She inserted the tape, then numb with fear, pressed the button. The sound of her conversation with her son, Zach, was crystal clear, even though he was calling from England.

It's as bad as it can get, Regina thought wildly. Now what happens if I don't admit that I saved Daddy's suicide note? Josh can produce it at any time. Then I could be arrested for lying to the cops when they questioned me for hours on end. He'd have both the tape and the letter to show as evidence.

Knowing she had no choice but to pay Josh whatever he was demanding, she went back to the table and pushed away her coffee, which was cold now.

Sour-faced as always, Jane promptly appeared with a fresh pot of coffee and a new cup. Regina watched as the steaming cup of coffee replaced the one she had ignored.

As Regina began to sip, the familiar nightmare replayed itself in her head. Riding her bike in the driveway of the beautiful home with the priceless view of Long Island that she had lived in for fifteen years. Tapping the switch that raised the garage door. Seeing her father's body as it swayed in the breeze that rushed in from the Sound. His jaw had slackened, his eyes were staring, his tongue was protruding. A paper was pinned to his jacket. One hand was clenched around the rope. At the last moment had he changed his mind about dying?

Regina remembered how she had felt numb and emotionless, how she had reached up for the note, unpinned it as his body moved under her touch, read it, and, shocked, stuffed it in her pocket.

In it, her father had written that he had been having an affair with Betsy and bitterly regretted it.

Betsy had told him that the hedge fund Rob had begun was about to explode in value and to invest everything he could in it. Even then, at age fifteen, Regina was sure Betsy was doing that at Powell's direction.

I couldn't let my mother see that note, Regina thought now. It would have broken her heart, and I knew her heart would be broken enough by Daddy's death. And my mother *despised* Betsy Powell. She knew what a phony she was.

Now *someone* had that note. It almost had to be Josh, who was hanging around all day helping Jane. What can I do? she asked herself. What can I do?

At that moment Josh came into the room, a tray in his hands, to clear the table. He looked around to be sure they were alone.

"When can we talk, Regina?" he asked. "And I must tell you, you should have taken your son's advice to burn your father's suicide note. I've been thinking it over. No one has a stronger motive for killing Betsy Powell than you do. Don't you agree? And don't you think that the quarter of a million dollars you're getting from

Mr. Rob is little enough to assure that no one will ever see the note or hear the tape?"

She could not reply. Her face was frozen in a look of horror and self-reproach, and her eyes looked beyond Josh to something else — her father's neatly dressed body, swaying from the rope around his neck.

55

As if by instinct, Claire raced upstairs to her old bedroom after her interview with Alex Buckley.

She knew it had not gone well. She had rehearsed her answers to the questions about the Gala, from being in the den together after the party ended to rushing into her mother's bedroom early the next morning.

It had been easy enough to re-create that terrible moment: Rob on the floor writhing in pain, the coffee splattered on his hands, his skin already raised in angry blisters. Jane shrieking "Betsy, Betsy," and holding the pillow that had smothered the life from her mother. The hair that had looked so glamorous when her mother had said good night to them was brassy in the early morning light, the radiant complexion now gray and mottled.

And I was *glad*, Claire thought. I was frightened, but I was glad.

All I could think of was that now I was free—now I could leave this house.

And I did the day of the funeral. I moved in with Regina and her mother in that tiny apartment. I slept on the couch in the living room.

There were pictures of Regina's father all over the place. Her mother was sweet and kind to me, even though they had lost everything they had because he had invested in Robert Powell's hedge fund.

Claire remembered hearing Betsy and Powell joking that Eric, Regina's father, was so gullible. *"Now remember, Betsy, I don't like you doing this, but it's necessary. It's either him or us."*

And her mother's answer: *"Better he should go broke than us,"* and laughing.

The nights I lay awake on that couch thinking that if it weren't for my mother and stepfather, he would still be alive and they would still be living in that lovely house on the Sound.

And what about Alison? She worked so hard for that scholarship and lost it just so my mother could get into some club.

Claire shook her head. She had been standing at the window looking out over the long backyard. Even with the vans from the studio discreetly parked on the left side of the property, and Alison and Rod sitting on the bench near the pool, the scene seemed as still as a painted landscape.

But then she saw movement. The door of the pool house opened, and the swarthy figure of the man who had been puttering around the garden these last few days exited.

His hulking presence broke the sense of stillness, and sent a shiver through Claire. Then she heard the click of her bedroom door opening.

Robert Powell stood there, smiling. "Anything I can do for you, Claire?" he asked.

56

Chief Ed Penn did not sleep well on Monday night. The sense of urgency that Leo Farley had imparted to him made whatever sleep he did manage to get troubled and fretful. And he had strange dreams. *Someone was in danger. He didn't know who. He was in a big empty house and, with his pistol in hand, he was searching through it. He could hear footsteps, but he could not tell where they were coming from.*

At 4 A.M., Ed Penn woke up from that dream and did not go back to sleep.

He understood Leo's concern that it was potentially dangerous to have those six people together again after twenty years. Penn had no doubt that one of those six—Powell, his housekeeper, Betsy's daughter, or one of her three friends—had murdered Betsy Powell.

Sure, the door from the den to the patio was unlocked. So what? Sure, maybe a stranger mingled with the crowd.

But maybe not.

The thing he had noticed when he arrived that morning was that among those four girls, including the daughter, he had not sensed one bit of genuine grief at Betsy Powell's passing.

And the housekeeper had kept begging to be allowed to go to the hospital to see "Mr. Rob."

Then she realized how that looked and clamped her mouth shut, Penn thought.

Powell? Few men would deliberately scar themselves with third-degree burns on their hands. Spilling coffee may have been his cover, but it's not clear what his motive would have been.

The housekeeper? Entirely possible. Interesting that the four girls had all agreed that she was screaming "Betsy, Betsy!" and holding the pillow in her hand.

Not that anyone's first instinct wouldn't be to rip the pillow off Betsy Powell's face, but Jane shrieking "Betsy, Betsy!" was another matter. Ed Penn had learned that when Betsy became Mrs. Robert Nicholas Powell and hired her friend Jane as a housekeeper, she instructed Jane to call her "Mrs. Powell."

Had Jane been burning with resentment for the nine years she had spent reduced from friend to servant?

That landscaper guy? He didn't have a record. Maybe it was just that stupid name that made him stand out. What mother with a brain in her head would give her kid the name Bruno when his last name was Hoffa and the Lindbergh case was still front page news?

Well, I guess it's better than some of the handles people are sticking their kids with these days, Ed decided.

There was no more use lying in bed. The police chief of Salem Ridge might as well get on the job. Ed thought, I'll take a ride over to Powell's place around noon and probably catch all of them at lunch.

He sat up. Then, from the other side of the bed, he heard his wife say, "Ed, will you *please* make up your mind? Either get up now or go back to sleep. The way you've been bouncing around is driving me crazy."

"Sorry, Liz," he mumbled.

As he got out of bed, Ed Penn realized that he was torn between two wishes. One, that somehow one of them would trip and reveal himself or herself as Betsy Powell's killer. The other, equally ardent, was that the filming would be wrapped up tomorrow as planned and they would all go home. The unsolved crime had been a thorn in Ed Penn's side for twenty years.

The Powell place is a tinderbox, he thought, and I can only watch it burst into flames.

When he returned to headquarters in the early afternoon, after his visit to the Powell home, his impressions had not changed.

57

Laurie decided that she had to talk to her father again. The night prior he had looked so terribly tired, and his usually ruddy face had been pale.

When she called him on her way to work, he said he was just stepping into the shower, and that he was fine.

He's *not* fine, she thought.

Now she got up and moved back to the chair behind the camera. "I'm just going to make a quick call to my father before Alison gets here," she explained to Alex.

"Of course," he said amiably.

But when she dialed the number and waited, he could sense her mounting nervousness.

"He's not answering," she said.

"Leave him a message," Alex suggested.

"No, you don't understand. My father would take a call from me if he was kissing the pope's hand!"

"What do you think he might be doing?" Alex asked.

"Maybe he's heard something about Blue Eyes and doesn't want to tell me," Laurie said, her voice trembling. "Or getting heart fibrillations again."

Alex Buckley looked compassionately at the young woman who had suddenly lost all her professional veneer of authority. Until now he had been surprised that, with her husband's murder unsolved and the threat hanging over her son and herself, she had still been able to do this program on an unsolved murder, but now he could see the degree to which she was acutely dependent on her father.

He had looked up the accounts of Greg Moran's murder. The picture of the thirty-one-year-old widow with her father's arm guiding her from the church behind her husband's casket flashed in his mind.

He knew the father had resigned abruptly from the police force to watch over his grandson.

If anything happened to Leo Farley now, any protection Laurie felt from Blue Eyes would be destroyed.

"Laurie, who is your father's doctor?"

"His cardiologist's name is Dr. James Morris. He's been my father's friend for the last forty years."

"Then phone and ask him if your father has been seeing him."

"That's a good idea."

There was a tap on the door. Alex sprang to his feet. When Grace looked in, the question she had been about to ask—"Ready for us?"—died on her lips. She saw the troubled look on Laurie's face as she held the phone to her ear and heard Alex's "Give her a minute," then closed the door.

58

"You're right, Laurie was terribly upset when I told her you were in the hospital," Dr. Morris told Leo Farley. "But I managed to calm her down. She's coming to see you straight from the filming, and as I suggested, the two of you can take Timmy's call together."

"It's a relief to know I don't have to try to figure out how to lie to her," Leo Farley said. "Did you tell her that I'm getting out of here tomorrow?"

"I told her that, barring any more fibrillations, I'll discharge you in the morning. I also told her that in forty years of practicing medicine, you're the crankiest patient I have ever had. I promise you that's what reassured her, Leo."

Leo Farley laughed a relieved laugh. "Okay, I believe that. But I'm only cranky because I feel helpless with all of these damn monitors pinning me to this bed."

Dr. James Morris took care not to let sympathy manifest itself in his voice. "Let's both hope that you don't get any more fibrillations, Leo. And I suggest that if you can force yourself to stay calm and maybe watch some game shows on television, you will be on your way home tomorrow morning."

• • •

Bruno listened with glee. Hacking into Leo's phone had been a brilliant idea. Leo had already called the head of the camp and told him that he was in the hospital. And now Bruno knew that both Laurie and her father would be on the phone with Timmy tonight.

If Leo and Laurie speak to Timmy around eight o'clock tonight, they'll be reassured and not expect to speak to him again until tomorrow night, Bruno thought.

I'll put on my police uniform and get up to the camp at ten o'clock, Bruno thought. I'll tell whoever is in charge up there that the kid's grandfather has taken a turn for the worse. If they call Mount Sinai, they'll confirm that he's a patient, but won't say anything about his condition.

It will work. Bruno was so sure of it that he began to make preparations for his little guest. In the utility room of the pool house he laid out blankets and a pillow. It would be far too dangerous to put Timmy in the bedroom in the pool house. He would have to tie him up and put a loose gag on him. He knew that it was necessary to follow the routine and have Perfect Estates pick him up in the landscaping truck and drop him off again tomorrow morning. He would bring in some Cheerios and orange juice for Timmy. He always brought his lunch in a grocery bag, so having one would not seem unusual.

The production crew had left copies of the schedule all over the place. He knew that tomorrow Powell would do the last individual interview and then everyone would be photographed at the breakfast table, as they had been for the opening segment.

That's when Timmy and I make our entrance, he thought. I'm holding his hand and have a gun to his head. I call Laurie to come out or I shoot him. Any good mother would come running out to save her little boy.

He laughed, a deep rumbling sound, then opened the door of

the pool house. The graduate with the husband on crutches was sitting on the bench near the pool.

Bruno began to studiously examine the plantings around the pool house for any sign of imperfection.

Tomorrow they'll be stained with blood, he thought gleefully. Mother and son. How appropriate that they'll die together, even if I don't get away.

59

"I was right," Laurie whispered as she turned off her phone. "Dr. Morris said that they're doing an angiogram on Dad right now, that it's just a precaution. But can I *believe* that?"

"Laurie, what exactly did the doctor say?" Alex asked.

"That Dad had heart fibrillations last night." In a halting voice Laurie explained what the doctor had told her. "I know the reason for the fibrillations. Dad was afraid of my doing this program," she said. "He thinks that one of these six people is a murderer, and could explode under pressure."

He may be right, Alex thought. "Look, Laurie," he said, "when you're finished here tonight, let me take you straight to the hospital. You don't have to wait for the company van. Let Jerry and Grace wrap up here."

Then he added impulsively, "I'll wait downstairs at the hospital until you have your visit, then we'll get something to eat, unless you have other plans."

"My plan for tonight was to have a hamburger with Dad. As ex-cop number one, he'll want to know every detail of what went on today."

"Then give him your report in the hospital and have a hamburger with me afterward," Alex said firmly.

Laurie hesitated. Given the circumstances, she could not picture

going out alone to a restaurant. Alex Buckley is a reassuring presence, she thought. And besides, I can talk to him about the interviews we'll be doing.

"Thanks, I'll take you up on that." She smiled faintly, then, as
Alex watched, she called, "Jerry, will you please tell the crew and
Alison Schaefer to come in?" Her voice was crisp and authoritative
again.

60

A grim-faced Regina went looking for Josh Damiano. She found him vacuuming the huge living room. She remembered how Betsy had grandly referred to it as "the salon." *"Until the time she married Richard Powell, the only salon she ever walked into was a beauty salon."* That's what Mother used to say about Betsy, Regina remembered.

Josh looked up and, when he saw her, turned off the vacuum. "I knew you'd be looking for me, Regina," he said with a cheerful smile.

Regina had turned on her iPhone and was recording every word they exchanged. "You have different jobs, I see, Josh. Chauffeur-housemaid-blackmailer. Obviously there is no limit to your talents."

The smile vanished from Damiano's face. "Be careful, Regina," he said evenly. "The only reason I'm helping in the house is because Mr. Powell canceled the usual maintenance service until Thursday, when everyone has gone."

"The housekeeper label isn't one you like, is it, Josh?" Regina asked. "How about embezzler? Are you sensitive about being called that?"

Josh Damiano did not blink. "I prefer to think that I am defending you from being accused of murdering Betsy Powell. Your father's suicide note gives you the greatest motive to kill her, and remember, you lied to the cops over and over again that you had not found a suicide note on or near your father's body."

"I did, didn't I?" Regina agreed. "On the other hand, I also did Robert Powell a great favor by not revealing that. Have you considered that? The note details how he let his wife have an affair with my father so she could feed him an inside tip about Powell's hedge fund. The result was that my father lost his entire fortune, and by doing so, he bailed the Powells out."

"So what?" Damiano asked.

"So I lied to my son in the conversation you taped in the car. I have another copy of my father's note. Now I'm giving you an alternative: give me back the original and we call it quits. Otherwise I take the copy and my recording of this conversation today to Police Chief Penn, and *you* land behind bars. I *assume* you taped everyone else. I'll bet they'll all produce those tapes, if pressed hard enough."

"You're joking."

"No, I'm not. I was fifteen years old when I found that note. As it was, my father's suicide was the start of my mother's slow decline. She would have gone quicker if she had known he was having an affair with Betsy as well."

Josh Damiano attempted a laugh. "All the more reason you jumped at the chance to spend your first overnight in this house, to get revenge on Betsy."

"Except that Betsy Powell wasn't worth sacrificing the rest of my life in prison. I'm a bit claustrophobic. I hope you're not."

Without waiting for a reply she left the room. Once she was in the hallway, she began to tremble violently.

Would it work? It was her only hope. She went up to the bedroom where she would spend the night, locked the door, and checked her phone.

The battery was dead.

61

Alison went into the den, outwardly calm but inwardly frantic with worry.

I was in Betsy's room that night, was the uppermost thought in her mind.

She tried to remember Rod's reassurances, but, oddly, all she could think of was that she had told him he couldn't know what it was like to want something so badly and lose it.

He couldn't? she asked herself.

She remembered the blazing headlines when he was signed by the Giants. The speculation about his brilliant future.

All the time she had spent studying, he had spent practicing football.

From kindergarten on, Rod had always been there for her.

But I was planning to marry a scientist, she thought. *We'd be the new Dr. and Madame Curie. "Dr. and Dr." Curie*, she corrected herself.

The arrogance of me. And Rod accepted it. He proposed to me and I accepted because of his promise to send me to medical school.

While he was so sick, I did manage to become a pharmacist, but I couldn't leave him. Underneath, I've always begrudged him the fact that I felt obligated to stay.

And even now, I'm thinking that if I had come here alone, I wouldn't have been talking in the car. No recording would *exist.*

"Come right in, Alison," Laurie Moran invited.

Alex Buckley stood up.

My God, he's tall, Alison thought as she took the seat across the table from him. Her body felt so rigid that she worried some part of her would break like glass if she moved too quickly.

"Alison, thank you so much for being with us on this program," Alex began. "It's been twenty years since the Graduation Gala and Betsy's Powell's death. Why did you agree to be on this program?"

The question was friendly. Rod had warned her against letting her guard down. Alison chose her words carefully now. "Do you know, or can you imagine, what it's like to be under suspicion of killing someone for *twenty years?*"

"No, I don't, and I couldn't even imagine it. As I'm a criminal defense lawyer, I have seen persons of interest live with an ax swinging over their head until a jury declared them not guilty."

"Until a jury declared them not guilty," Alison repeated, and he could hear the bitterness in her voice. "But don't you see? That's the problem. No one has formally accused any one of us, and so we are *all* treated as if we were guilty."

"You *still* feel that way?"

"How could I not? This last year alone there were two major articles in syndicated newspapers about the case. I can always tell when a new one comes out. Someone comes into the pharmacy and buys something insignificant like toothpaste and looks at me as though I were a bug under a microscope."

"Alison, that's an interesting comparison. Have you been feeling like a bug under a microscope all these years? You had hoped to earn a medical degree, didn't you?"

Be careful, Alison warned herself. "Yes, I did."

"You had every expectation of being awarded a scholarship, isn't that true?"

"I was in contention," Alison said evenly. "I came in second. It happens."

"Alison, I've done some research. Isn't it a fact that just before your graduation, Robert Powell pledged some ten million dollars to your college for a new dormitory to be named 'The Robert and Betsy Powell House'?"

"I know he did."

"Is it true that the recipient of the scholarship was the daughter of a friend of Betsy Powell's?"

Alison, you're bitter. You can't let the bitterness show.

It was as though Rod were shouting in her ear.

"Of course I was disappointed. I earned that scholarship and everyone knew it. Throwing it to Vivian Fields was Betsy's way of getting into the club Vivian's mother ran.

"But you see, all regret stopped right there. Rod had just signed a big contract with the Giants, and the first thing he did was to propose to me. We were engaged, and his wedding present to me was going to be sending me to medical school."

"Then why didn't you invite Rod to the Gala, if you were engaged to him?"

Alison attempted a smile. "Actually, it was just prior to our engagement. Rod thought I was very foolish to go to the Gala after what Betsy pulled on me."

It sounds all right, she thought. I didn't invite him because I wasn't in love with him. But then when he signed with the Giants and promised to send me to school, I agreed to marry him . . . She fought to keep control of herself.

Alex Buckley's eyes bored into her. "Alison, I would like you to close your eyes and visualize the moment you walked into Betsy's room after you heard Jane screaming."

His tone was almost hypnotic. Obediently, Alison closed her eyes.

She was in Betsy's room. She stepped on the earring, and that startled her. She heard a door open and slipped into the closet behind her. She saw someone come in and take the other pillow from Betsy's bed. Then that shadowy figure leaned over Betsy.

Through a crack in the door she watched as Betsy's body twisted and turned as the pillow suffocated her. Her muted groans were quickly stifled.

Then the figure slipped away. Was I dreaming, Alison asked herself, or did I really see a face?

She didn't know. Her eyes snapped open.

Alex Buckley saw the startled look on her face. "What is it, Alison?" he asked quickly. "You look frightened."

Alison burst out: "I can't stand this anymore! I absolutely can't stand it. I don't care what people think about me. Let them wonder if I killed Betsy. I did *not*, but I will tell you this: when I ran into that room and saw she was dead, I was *glad*! And so were the others. Betsy Powell was evil and vain and a whore, and I hope she's rotting in hell."

62

Jane was next. She was not a heavy woman, but her broad shoulders and straight carriage gave her a formidable appearance. Her constant uniform of black dress and crisp white apron seems almost a caricature, Alex thought. Except for during formal dinners, none of his friends had their help dressed like that.

She sat in the chair vacated by Alison. "Ms. Novak," Alex began. "You and Betsy Powell worked together in the theatre?"

Jane smiled thinly. "That sounds very glamorous. I cleaned the dressing rooms and mended the costumes. Betsy was an usher, and when a play closed, we would both be transferred to another theatre."

"Then you were good friends."

"Good friends? What does that mean? We worked together. I like to cook. I'd ask her and Claire to dinner some Sundays. I was sure everything they ate was takeout. Betsy was no cook. And Claire was such a sweet child."

"Were you surprised when Betsy moved to Salem Ridge?"

"Betsy wanted to marry money. She decided living in a wealthy community was her best chance. Turns out she was right."

"She was thirty-two when she married Robert Powell. Wasn't there anyone before that?"

"Oh, Betsy dated, but no one had enough money for her." Jane smirked. "You should have heard what she said about some of them."

"Was there anyone who was especially close to her?" Alex asked. "Someone who might have been jealous when she married?"

Jane shrugged. "I wouldn't say so. They came and they went."

"Were you upset when she asked you to call her 'Mrs. Powell'?"

"Was I upset? Of course not. Mr. Powell is a very formal man. I have a beautiful apartment of my own here. A cleaning service comes in twice a week, so I do no heavy work. I love to cook, and Mr. Powell loves gourmet food. Why would I be upset? I came from a little village in Hungary. We had only the barest modern conveniences—running water, sometimes electricity."

"I can see why you have been very content here. But I understand that when you rushed into Betsy Powell's room that morning, you screamed 'Betsy, Betsy!' "

"Yes, I did. I was so shocked, I didn't know what I was doing or saying."

"Jane, do you have any theory about who killed Betsy Powell?"

"Absolutely," Jane said firmly, "and in a way I blame myself for her death."

"Why is that, Jane?"

"It is because I should have known those young women would have been in and out, smoking. I should have stayed up and made sure the door was locked after they went to bed."

"Then you think it was a stranger who came in?"

"Either through the unlocked door or else during the party. Betsy had two walk-in closets. Someone could have hidden in one of them. She was wearing a fortune in emeralds, and don't forget, one of the earrings was on the floor."

Behind the camera, watching and listening, Laurie found herself wondering whether Jane was right. Claire had suggested the same thing. And from what she could see, it was entirely possible that someone might have slipped upstairs during the party.

Jane was telling Alex that she had put a velvet rope across both the main and back staircases of the first floor. "There are four powder rooms on the main floor," she concluded. "There would be no need for anyone to go upstairs, unless he or she was planning to steal Betsy's jewelry."

It's as if they all put their heads together and decided on that story, Laurie thought.

Alex was saying, "Thank you for talking to us, Ms. Novak. I know how difficult it is to relive that terrible night."

"No, you don't," Jane contradicted him, her voice even and sad. "To know how beautiful Betsy looked that night, then to see her face covered by that pillow and know she was dead, and to hear Mr. Powell moaning in pain . . . You don't and can't understand how hard it is to relive it, Mr. Buckley. You just can't."

63

Nina kept a frosty distance from her mother for the rest of the morning. When Alison went in for her interview with Alex Buckley, she joined Rod on the bench near the pool.

"Mind if I sit with you for a while?" she asked.

Rod looked startled, but then attempted a smile and said, "Of course not."

"Are you and Alison sorry you got into this situation?" Nina asked as she sat next to him.

At Rod's surprised look, she said, "Look, I got a tape, too, and so did Regina. I don't know about Claire.

"I could see that Alison was terribly upset when she played hers. So was Regina. Do you think that Josh Damiano made those tapes for himself, or do you think Rob Powell ordered him to make them?"

"I don't know," Rod said carefully.

"Neither do I. But I have to take the chance that it's Damiano's game and pay the fifty thousand dollars he's demanding. I think you should, too. I don't know what Damiano overheard you say, but that police chief is dying to solve Betsy's murder, and if he has something to run with, I'll bet he'll do it."

"You may be right," Rod said, his tone noncommittal. "But what could he possibly have on you that would make you a suspect? Certainly not the fact that your mother dated Rob Powell before he married Betsy?"

"It isn't that," Nina said, her voice friendly. "My mother is threatening to say I confessed to her that I murdered Betsy unless I pay the fifty thousand dollars to Josh."

Rod didn't think he could be any more surprised than he already had been, but now his voice was incredulous. "She's *got* to be bluffing."

"Oh, but she isn't," Nina said. "Now if Robert Powell hears that tape on which she's saying how much she hated Betsy, any chance she has with him—which I believe is nonexistent, by the way—will be over. But if this is only Josh Damiano's game, who knows? That's why she wants me to pay the fifty thousand dollars he's demanding— or else. But you see, I know Alison has much more to worry about than my mother being sure I broke up her big romance. I was very nice when the police were questioning all of us twenty years ago." She paused and looked straight into his eyes. "I didn't tell anyone that Betsy was absolutely *cruel* to Alison that night. She was gushing on and on about how proud Selma Fields was that her daughter, Vivian, had won the scholarship. She made sure to mention that Selma was throwing a fabulous party for Vivian, and then the whole family was sailing on their yacht to the Riviera. Alison was fighting back tears. When Betsy floated away, Alison said to me, 'I am going to *kill* that witch.'

"Now isn't that information worth your paying Josh Damiano the fifty thousand dollars he's demanding from Alison *and* the fifty thousand he wants from me? I want to leave here with something.

"Rod, believe me, I hate to do this, but I have no choice. I need every nickel of that three hundred thousand dollars to buy my mother her own apartment and get her out of my life. If we live together much longer, I can promise you, I will kill *her.* I know just how Alison was feeling at the Gala."

She got up. "Before I leave you, I want to say how much I admire both of you. She married you to get an education, but she stuck by you when that fabulous career you should have had disappeared. My theory is that your hold on her is she confessed the crime to you. Isn't that true, Rod?"

Rod reached for his crutches and got to his feet. His face white with anger, he said, "It's obvious you and your mother are cut from the same cloth. Alison is very smart, you know. Maybe she can dig up a few memories herself about how you were hounded for years by your mother because she kept ranting about losing Rob Powell to Betsy. Maybe you snapped and killed Betsy to make Robert Powell a widower. But there's only one problem. In a million years, Alison wouldn't murder anybody."

Nina smiled. "When do I get my answer?" she asked.

"I don't know," Rod said flatly. "Now if you don't mind, will you please let me pass? My wife is coming out of the house, and I want to go to join her."

"I think I'll just settle down on one of these lounge chairs," Nina said cheerfully as she stepped aside to let him pass.

64

Jane went straight from the interview to the kitchen. She had already prepared vichyssoise, a Waldorf salad, and cold sliced ham for lunch.

Robert Powell entered the kitchen a few minutes later. "Jane, I've been thinking. It's quite warm out. Let's eat in the dining room. How many do we have for lunch today?"

Jane could see that his mood was much brighter than it had been in the morning. He was wearing a light blue sport shirt and khaki slacks. His full head of white hair complemented his handsome face. His straight carriage belied his chronological age.

He doesn't look anything like his age, Jane thought. He's always looked like an English lord.

Lord and Lady Powell.

What had he asked her? Of course, how many would be at lunch today.

"The four graduates," Jane hesitated. "That's the way I still think of them. Ms. Moran, Mrs. Craig, Mr. Rod Kimball, Mr. Alex Buckley, and yourself, sir."

"The lucky nine," Rob Powell said cheerfully. "Or a motley crew. Which is it, Jane?"

Without waiting for an answer, he opened the patio door and went outside.

What's gotten into him? Jane asked herself. This morning it seemed like all he wanted was to get them out of the house. Perhaps knowing that they'll be on their way tomorrow is making him feel good. I don't know what the others said in their interviews, but I know *I* came off fine.

Filled with self-satisfaction, she began to set the table in the dining room.

Josh appeared in the doorway. "I'll finish that," he said angrily. "You get the food out."

Jane looked at him, surprised. "What's the matter with you?" she asked.

"The matter with me is that I'm not a houseboy," Josh snapped.

Jane had just begun placing the silverware on the table. Startled, she straightened up. Her cheeks flushed, her lips tight, she spat out the words, "For the kind of salary you get, you have some nerve to talk like that about helping out in the house for a few days. Be careful. Be very careful. If Mr. Powell had heard you, you'd have been out the door in a minute. If I report this conversation to him, the same thing would happen."

"Well, listen to the lady of the house," Josh snapped defiantly. "Whatever became of all the jewelry George Curtis gave Betsy? Don't pretend you don't know what I'm talking about. When Mr. Rob was on business trips, I used to drive Betsy to her trysts with George Curtis, and she'd be lit up like a Christmas tree when I took her to meet him. I know she kept it hidden in her room somewhere, but I never heard any mention of it being found. If there's one thing I'm sure of, Mr. Rob Powell had no idea that affair was going on."

"You don't know what you're sure of," Jane whispered fiercely. "So why don't we both agree to keep our mouths shut? Tomorrow at this time they'll all be on their way."

"One last thought, Jane. If Betsy *had* left Powell for George Curtis, she'd have taken you with her, for two good reasons. First, because you waited on her hand and foot. Second, because once she moved out of here and asked Powell for a divorce, he'd have hired private detectives to find out how long that affair had been going on and discovered that you covered for Betsy when he called her from overseas every time he was away on a business trip."

"And what do you think he'd have done to *you* if he knew you were driving her back and forth to her little love nest in his Bentley?" Jane asked, her voice almost a whisper.

They glared at each other from across the table, then Jane said in a pleasant voice, "We'd better get moving. They were told that lunch would be served at one-thirty."

65

After Alison fled from the den, Alex and Laurie did not speak until Jerry, Grace, and the camera crew were gone.

Then Alex said quietly, "Two of our graduates have now given a worldwide audience a convincing reason why one of them might have killed Betsy Powell."

"They absolutely did," Laurie said. "And who knows what Regina and Nina will have to say this afternoon? I would be surprised if all four of them don't bitterly regret getting involved in this program, even for the money."

"I'm sure they already do," Alex agreed.

"Alex, why do you think Powell insisted we all stay here tonight—and that we don't interview him until tomorrow morning?"

"Building up the pressure on all of them, hoping one of them will crack? You and I will be the chief witnesses, if that happens," Alex replied briskly. "My guess is that he's bluffing." He looked at his watch. "I'd better call my office. We're due inside in fifteen minutes."

"And I'm going to try my dad."

Alex sat back in the chair, pretending to look for something in his briefcase.

He wanted to be here for Laurie if Leo Farley did not—or *could not*—answer the phone.

66

Leo's cheery "Hello" took the edge off Laurie's panic.

"I hear you were out on the town last night, Dad," she said.

"Yes, I had a hot date at Mount Sinai. How's your show going?"

"Why didn't you call me when you went to the hospital?"

"So that you didn't come rushing over here. I've had these episodes before. Jim Morris told me to calm down by watching game shows. Right now I'm watching an *I Love Lucy* rerun."

"Then I wouldn't dream of keeping you from it. I'll be down by seven thirty at the latest." Laurie hesitated, then asked, "Dad, do you *really* feel all right now?"

"I feel fine. Stop worrying."

"You make that very hard," Laurie said wryly. "All right, go back to *I Love Lucy*. I'll see you later."

With one hand she dropped the cell phone in her pocket. With the other, she impatiently fumbled for a tissue to brush away the tears that had begun to form in her eyes.

Alex reached into his pocket and handed her his freshly pressed handkerchief. As she accepted it he said, "Laurie, it doesn't hurt to let go a little occasionally."

"I can't," she whispered. "The day I let go, I'll lose my grip for good. I keep hearing that threat ringing in my ears. The only way I have kept my sanity at all is by hoping Blue Eyes keeps his promise that I'm next. Maybe when he kills me, he'll be caught. If he gets away, maybe Dad and Timmy can change their identities and disappear; who knows? But suppose Timmy and I are outside together? Or if I die, suppose Dad isn't here to protect Timmy?"

There was no answer Alex could offer her. Her tears stopped immediately, and he watched as Laurie pulled out her compact and dabbed her eyes. When she looked up at him her voice revealed no sign of stress. "You'd better make that call, Alex," she said. " 'Mr. Rob' expects us at the table in exactly fifteen minutes."

67

Chief Penn, the graduates, Rod, Alex, Muriel, and Laurie had gathered at the dining room table when Robert Powell made his appearance.

"How quiet you all are," he remarked. "I can understand why. You are under a great strain." He paused as he looked from one to the other. "And so am I."

Jane was about to enter the dining room.

"Jane, would you please excuse us and close the door? I have a few things to share with my guests."

"Of course, sir."

Powell addressed them: "Are any of you thinking that this beautiful day is exactly the same as the day of the Gala? I remember Betsy sitting at this table with me that morning. We were congratulating each other on our good luck at having such perfect weather. Could any of us have imagined that the next morning Betsy would be dead, murdered by an intruder?" He paused. "Or perhaps *not* by an intruder?"

He waited, and when there was no response, he went on briskly, "Now, let's be sure I have the details straight. This afternoon, Regina and then Nina will be interviewed. At about four-thirty the graduates will be dressed in replicas of the gowns they wore that night and photographed against the background of films of the Gala. My good friend George Curtis will be standing with you, Alex, sharing his impressions of that evening."

He looked at Laurie. "Am I correct so far?"

"Yes, you are," she said.

Powell smiled. "In the morning I will have my interview with you, Alex—with the graduates present. I hope and expect you will all find it quite interesting. *One* of you especially." He gave a tight smile.

"As to later this evening, everyone at this table, with the exception of Chief Penn, will be staying overnight. After the last scene is finished, the graduates will be driven in individual cars to their hotels. You will pack and check out. Your luggage will be placed in your car. You will have dinner on your own wherever you wish to dine—as my guest, of course—but please return here by eleven o'clock. We will have a nightcap together at that time, then retire. I want everyone to be alert for what I have to say tomorrow. Is that understood?"

This time, as if compelled to respond, heads nodded.

"At brunch tomorrow I will present you the checks you have been promised. After that, one of you may want to use it to retain Mr. Buckley's services." He smiled a cold, mirthless smile. "Just joking, of course," he added.

He turned to Nina. "Nina, you need not share your car with your dear mother. Muriel and I are going to dine together this evening. It is time to turn the page on the past."

Muriel smiled adoringly at Powell, then shot a triumphant look at Nina.

"Enough of business. Let us now enjoy our luncheon. Ah, here comes Jane. I know she has prepared vichyssoise. You have not lived until you have sampled Jane's vichyssoise. It is indeed nectar for the gods."

It was served in total silence.

68

After leaving the dining room, Regina walked across the yard to the makeup van. The heat outside was a sharp contrast to the coolness of the house, but she welcomed it. After hearing Robert Powell's elaborate plans for the rest of the day and tomorrow morning, she was sure of only one thing: he had her father's suicide note. What more proof would anyone need that she had been Betsy's killer?

For twenty-seven years, since she was fifteen years old, even under oath she had sworn there was no such note in his pocket or around his body.

Who could have had a stronger motive to kill Betsy? she asked herself. And there was no question that Robert Powell was determined to have closure on Betsy's death. That was the whole purpose of his financing the program.

She walked past the pool. Crystal clear, reflecting the sun, brightly patterned lounge chairs scattered around it, it had the look of a stage setting. In the correspondence, they had all been invited to bring swimming apparel.

No one had.

Beyond it, the pool house, a miniature of the mansion, stood unused by anyone but the gardener, who incessantly entered and exited as he fussed over the grounds.

At the production van, Regina hesitated, then pulled open the door.

Meg was waiting, jars of cosmetics lined up neatly on the shelf in front of her.

Courtney was settled in the other chair, reading in front of a shelf of brushes, sprays, and a hair dryer.

This morning Courtney had told Regina that women would kill to have her thick, curly hair. "And I'll bet you'll say that it's a nuisance because it grows too fast."

That's exactly what I *did* say, Regina thought.

She avoided looking at the wall on her left, where the pictures of herself and the other graduates at the Gala had been blown up.

She knew what they looked like. Claire, without a trace of makeup, her hair in a ponytail, her dress high-necked and with sleeves to her elbows. Alison, whose talented mother had made her gown, as she made all her clothes—Alison's father was a produce manager in a grocery store. Nina, her dress daringly low cut, her red hair blazing, her makeup skillfully applied. Even then she looked so confident, Regina thought.

And I had on the most elegant dress of all. Mother went to work at Bergdorf after we lost everything. Even though that dress was reduced a lot, we still couldn't afford it. But she insisted I have it. *"Your father would have bought it for you,"* she told me.

Regina realized she had not spoken to Meg or to Courtney. "Hello, you two," she said. "Don't think I'm crazy. Just gearing up for my interview."

"Claire and Alison were nervous, too," Meg said cheerfully. "Why wouldn't you be? This program is going to be broadcast all over the world."

Regina sank into the chair at Meg's station.

"Thanks for reminding me of that," she said as Meg clipped a plastic sheet around her neck.

This morning, for the picture in the den depicting the four of them after the body had been found and the police had arrived, Meg had applied very little makeup, and Courtney had left their hair a touch disheveled, as it had been the morning after Betsy's death.

Now they were all wearing clothes of their own choice. "Dress as you feel comfortable," Laurie had counseled them.

Regina had chosen a dark blue linen jacket, white shell, and slacks. Her only jewelry was the string of pearls her father had given her on her fifteenth birthday.

Now she watched as with deft strokes, Meg began to apply foundation, blush, eye shadow, mascara, and lip rouge.

Courtney came over, and with a few quick movements of her brush, swept Regina's hair into a half bang and pulled it behind her ears.

"You look great," she said.

"You sure do," Meg agreed.

As Meg was unclasping the sheet from Regina's neck, Jerry opened the door of the van. "All set, Regina?" he asked.

"I guess so."

As they walked back to the house Jerry said comfortingly, "I know you're nervous, Regina. Don't be. Can you believe that Helen Hayes got stage fright every night till the moment she stepped onstage?"

"It's funny," Regina told him. "You know that I have a real estate office. Just this morning I was thinking that the day I got the letter about this program I was so unnerved I did a lousy presentation of a house I should have sold. The owner was a seventy-six-year-old woman who wanted to move into an assisted-living facility. I sold the house for her two months later, and for thirty thousand dollars less than I should have gotten for it. When I get the money for doing this program, I'm going to return my commission to her."

"Then you're one in a million," Jerry said dryly as he slid open the door from the patio to the kitchen.

Regina remembered that earlier in the morning, this patio entrance had been blocked off.

"No one on the patio now, and no sign of Jane," Jerry commented. "I guess she must take some downtime after all."

Where are the others? Regina asked herself as they walked down the hallway to the den. Are they afraid to be together?

We don't trust each other, she thought. We each had a reason to kill Betsy, but mine is the strongest.

Laurie Moran and Alex Buckley were waiting for her in the den. Laurie's assistant Grace stood to the side. A crew member was still adjusting lights. The cameraman was in his place.

Without being invited, Regina sat at the table opposite Alex. She began to clasp and unclasp her hands. Stop it, she warned herself. She heard Laurie's greeting and returned it.

Alex Buckley was welcoming her, but she was sure his attitude was hostile. When would he produce her father's suicide note? she asked herself.

"Take one," the director was saying, and began to count. "Ten, nine, eight, seven, six, five, four, three, two, one." There was the clap of the slate board, and Alex began.

"We are now speaking to the third of the four honorees at the Graduation Gala, Regina Callari.

"Regina, thank you for agreeing to be with us on this program. You grew up in this town, didn't you?"

"Yes, I did."

"And yet, as I understand it, you haven't been back since shortly after the Gala and the death of Betsy Bonner Powell?"

Try to sound calm, Regina warned herself.

"As I'm sure the others have told you, all four of us were treated as murder suspects. Would you have hung around after that?"

"You moved to Florida shortly after. Your mother followed you there?"

"Yes, she did."

"Wasn't she very young when she died?"

"She was just turning fifty."

"What was she like?"

"She was one of those women who did a lot of good, but hated the limelight."

"What was her relationship with your father?"

"They were one soul."

"What was his business?"

"He bought failing companies, turned them around, and then sold them for huge profits. He was very successful."

"Let's go back to that later. I want to talk about the night of the Gala, starting with when you were all in the den together."

Laurie listened and observed as Regina told the same story as the other girls. They had filled their wineglasses again and again. They had discussed the evening, laughing at some of the dresses of the older women. Exactly as the other girls had, she described the finding of Betsy's body.

"We were young. You must know that we all had our own issues with the Powells," Regina was saying. "By then I know I was relaxed and enjoying being with the others. We refilled our wineglasses, going in and out for smokes. Even Claire was joking about her stepfather being so finicky about smoking. 'Please,' she said, 'don't light up until you are at the end of the patio. He's got the nose of a bloodhound.'

"We were talking about our plans. Nina was going to Hollywood. She always played the lead in the plays in high school and college, and, of course, her mother was an actress. She even joked about the fact that her mother was still riding her because she called Claire and her mother over when they were in the same restaurant, and that's how Betsy met Rob Powell."

"How did Claire respond to that?" Alex asked quickly.

"She said, 'You are lucky, Nina,' " Regina answered.

"What do you think she meant?" Alex asked quickly.

"I have my suspicions," Regina answered honestly. "But I just don't know."

"Let's go back a little," Alex said. "I've seen pictures of your home. It was *very* beautiful."

"Yes, it was," Regina said. "And more than that, it was a warm and comfortable home."

"But then, of course, everything changed when your father invested in Robert Powell's hedge fund."

Regina realized where he was going. Be careful, she warned herself, he's building a motive for you to have killed Betsy.

"It must have been hard not to resent the fact that virtually all of your dad's money was lost in that investment."

"My mother was sad but not bitter. She told me my father had something of a go-for-the-gold mentality, and he put too many eggs in one basket several times. On the other hand, he had never been reckless."

"But you still maintained a close friendship with Claire?"

"Yes, I did, until we all left Salem Ridge. I guess by unspoken agreement we didn't want to stay in touch after Betsy's death."

"How did you feel coming to this mansion after your father's death?"

"I was very seldom here. I don't think Robert Powell liked having Claire's friends around. We were more likely to get together at the rest of our homes."

"Then why would he have the Gala for all of you?"

"My guess is it was Betsy's idea. Some of her friends were having graduation parties for their daughters. She wanted to outshine them."

"What were you thinking the night of the Gala?"

"Missing my father. Thinking how perfect that beautiful night would have been if he were still here. My mother was a guest as well—I could see in her eyes that her thoughts mirrored my own."

"Regina, at age fifteen you discovered your father's body," Alex continued.

"Yes, I did," Regina said quietly.

"Would it have been easier for you if he left a note? If he had apologized for his suicide and the financial disaster? If he told you one last time he loved you? Do you think that would have helped you and your mother?"

The vivid memory of feeling so happy, riding her bicycle up the long driveway, the salt air filling her senses, pushing the button to open the garage door, the sight of her handsome forty-five-year-old father swaying from the noose, one hand around it as if perhaps he changed his mind too late, shattered Regina's fragile composure.

"Would a note have made any difference?" she asked, choking out the words. "My father was dead."

"Did you blame Robert Powell because your father lost everything in his hedge fund?"

Her last shred of composure crumbled. "I blame both of them. Betsy was up to her neck in deceiving my father, just as much as Powell was."

"How do you know that, Regina? Wasn't it because your father *did* in fact leave a note?"

Alex waited, then went on firmly. "He *did* leave a note, didn't he?"

Regina heard herself trying to whisper a faint "No . . . no . . . no," as he stared at her, his eyes sympathetic but demanding.

69

Bruno's excitement rose to a fever pitch after he heard Laurie's call to her father. Gleefully, he reflected on how everything was falling into place.

Leo Farley would be in the hospital until tomorrow morning.

Leo and Laurie would take the call from Timmy in the hospital room.

Two hours later, I pick up Timmy, Bruno thought. Leo had already told the director of the camp that he was in the hospital. I'll be in a cop's uniform.

I can pull it off.

I can probably even get away with it.

But if not, it's worth it. The "Blue Eyes" murder case had been in the newspapers for years; still was. If they only knew that I spent five years rotting in prison after I shot Laurie's husband. And all for a lousy parole violation. But in a way, it was *worth* it. Leo Farley and his daughter have spent these five years wondering and worrying about when I'll strike again. Tomorrow their waiting will be over.

Bruno dropped the phone into his pocket and went outside in time to see the police chief's car pulling up behind the studio vans. He was here for lunch.

Bruno walked to the putting green, as far from the chief's line of vision as humanly possible. Here, the chief could not get a clear look at his face.

There was one thing Bruno knew—most cops have long-term memories of faces, even when people age or alter their facial hair.

Or are dumb enough to put themselves on Facebook.

Bruno laughed out loud at that thought.

An hour later he was carefully examining the flower beds alongside the pool when the police car drove away.

That meant the chief wouldn't be back until tomorrow.

Just in time for the Big Show, Bruno thought gleefully.

70

Nina and Muriel did not speak after lunch. Muriel had obviously asked Robert Powell to have a car ready for her for the afternoon, because it had parked at the front door and was waiting for her.

Nina knew what that meant. The expensive new outfits her mother bought on her credit card were about to be put aside in favor of new ones—ones that would also be purchased on Nina's credit card.

Nina went up to her room to try to collect her thoughts until it was time for her own interview.

Like all the others it was a large bedroom, with a sitting area that offered a couch, an easy chair, a cocktail table, and a television.

Nina sat on the couch, taking in the cream-colored draperies behind the bed, the way their edgings picked up those on the panels at the window, and the way the rug and pillow shams coordinated and harmonized. An interior designer's dream, Nina thought.

She remembered that about a year before her death, Betsy had commissioned a complete redecorating job. Claire had told the girls about it.

Claire had said, *"I've been told to bring you over to see it. My mother is giving the grand tour to everyone."*

The "grand tour" came up after she died, Nina remembered. In fact, a college friend majoring in pre-law had warned me it would be a factor in the defense if anyone was accused of Betsy's murder: many, many people knew the layout of the house exactly—and that Betsy and Robert had separate bedrooms.

What is going to happen? Nina asked herself. I'm sure Robert is bluffing. He's making a fool of my mother, and she will turn on me again. Would she honestly be vindictive enough to claim I confessed to her that I killed Betsy?

No, even *she* couldn't do that, Nina decided.

Or could she?

Nina's cell phone rang. She picked it up, and her eyes widened as she saw the number. Quickly she answered, "Hello, Grant."

His voice was warm as he spoke her name.

Nina listened as he told her she wasn't to make any plans with anyone else for Saturday night. He wanted her to go to a dinner party with him at Steven Spielberg's home.

To go with Grant to a dinner party at Steven Spielberg's home! This was the crème de la crème of Hollywood society.

Suppose her mother accused Nina of confessing to Betsy's murder? Or, almost as bad, returned to California with her and picked up where they had left off: living with her, screaming at her all the time, the condo always a mess, wineglasses all over the place, the smell of cigarette smoke heavy in the air.

"Can't wait to see you Saturday night," Grant said.

Don't sound like Muriel, simpering and fawning, Nina warned herself. "I'm looking forward to it so much, too, Grant," she said warmly, but without undue excitement in her tone.

After she disconnected, Nina sat, no longer even aware of her surroundings.

No matter which way she does it, my mother is going to ruin the rest of my life, she thought.

The phone rang again. It was Grace. "Nina, would you mind going over to makeup?" she asked. "They'll be ready for your interview in about half an hour."

71

Laurie and Alex sat in the den and compared notes after Regina's interview.

"Was I too rough on Regina?" Alex asked.

"No, I don't think so," Laurie said slowly. "But when you were finished, I don't think anyone would doubt that there was a suicide note. But why would a fifteen-year-old have taken it?"

"You have your own theory, I know," Alex said. "Don't think I haven't noticed that whenever you ask me my theory, you already have one of your own."

"Guilty as charged." Laurie smiled. "My theory is that there was something in that note that Regina didn't want her mother to read—and that it involved Betsy. Maybe the fact that her father was having an affair with her. That's what I see. Remember how Regina described her parents as being 'one soul'?"

"And that opens up the question—perhaps Betsy influenced her father's reckless business decision to put everything he had into Powell's hedge fund," Alex suggested. "Doesn't that give Regina a strong motive to take a God-given opportunity to punish Betsy?" he added.

"If I were in her shoes and had lost my parents and everything I had because of Betsy Powell," Laurie told him, "I could kill. I know I could."

"You *think* you could," Alex corrected. "Now, tell me what you thought of Robert Powell's speech at lunch. I'm telling you right now that I think he's bluffing, but if one of the people at that table *did* murder Betsy Powell, he or she may believe his threat. He's playing a dangerous game."

72

⤬◇⤬

Nina looked in the mirror as Meg clipped the vinyl sheet around her neck.

"Now, Meg," she cautioned, "this morning you were told to make us look like rag dolls."

"I was told to make you resemble the way you looked the morning Betsy's body was discovered," Meg said matter-of-factly. "Even then you looked better than anyone else."

"I looked passable, but for this interview I want you to make me look a little like her." Nina held up a picture of Grant with his late wife, Kathryn.

Meg studied it carefully. "You resemble her," she observed.

"I *want* to resemble her," Nina said flatly.

She had googled everything she could find on the subject of Grant Richmond. For a major producer, he led a quiet behind-the-scenes life. He had married at twenty-six. His wife had been twenty-one.

They had been married for thirty years before she died two years ago of heart failure from a lifelong condition.

No children, and not a whiff of scandal about them.

So Grant had been a one-woman man, and he had been alone for two years. By now he was probably lonely.

He was pushing sixty.

Nina held up her camera and looked at a second picture. "Who does this look like?" she demanded.

Meg studied it carefully. "This is the same lady, Nina. Is she a relative?"

Nina nodded in satisfaction. It's not just that I'm a good dancer, she thought. I resemble his wife.

"Look, Meg," she said. "She's not a relative, but I want to look like her when you do the makeup."

"Then I can't put that heavy liner and shadow on you."

"That's fine with me."

A half hour later Meg said, "That's it."

Nina looked in the mirror. "I could be her sister," she said. "Perfect."

"My turn, Nina, it's getting late," Courtney said briskly.

"I know." Nina moved into Courtney's chair. Holding the picture, she said, "She had short hair. I don't want to cut mine."

"Don't," Courtney said. "I'll put it up in a twist; same effect."

Five minutes later, Jerry knocked on the door of the van. When he came inside, he was startled by the change in Nina's appearance.

"Ready, Nina?" he asked.

"Yes, I am." She gave herself a final look in the mirror before she got up. "These two are miracle workers," she said. "Don't you agree, Jerry?"

"Yes, I do," he said honestly. "By that I mean for giving you a different look, not a better one," he added hastily.

Nina laughed. "Good you added those last few words."

As they left the van, Jerry compared the graduates. He liked Nina best. The others seemed to be trapped in their own shells. For women who had been close friends until they were twenty-one, they seemed to have very little to say to each other. When they were on the patio in between shoots, they all grabbed for a book or their smartphones from their purses.

Nina did, too, except when Muriel insisted on talking. She always paid attention when Muriel gushed about what a wonderful man Robert Powell was, and how Betsy had been her dearest friend.

It's as if Muriel is always hoping that Powell can hear her, Jerry thought. She's overplaying her role. I've been around enough film sets to know that.

He and Nina were walking past the pool. "I wouldn't mind taking a swim on a day like this," he commented. "How about you?"

"I'd like to be taking a swim in the pool at my condo. I do that every day, or evening if I work late," Nina said.

What am I going to say? she was asking herself. What kind of questions are they going to ask me? What's going to happen tomorrow when Robert Powell shows us the door? Would my own mother use that moment to swear that I confessed to killing Betsy to her and claim the reward?

You bet she would!

I won't let it happen.

Jerry did not attempt to keep up the conversation. Unlike Regina, Nina did not seem nervous, but he was sure she was preparing herself for the interview.

But then she suddenly said, "There's Creepy Crawly again." She pointed to Bruno, who was at the far end of the grounds behind the house. "What's he doing? Chasing bugs on the plants?"

Jerry laughed. "Mr. Powell is a perfectionist. He wants every shot of the grounds to display them in their normal pristine condition. Yesterday when we were taking pictures of the four of you in different locations back here, he looked shocked when the equipment made tracks in the grass. Then, as you saw, Creepy Crawly, as you call him, came running to the rescue."

"Oh, God, do I remember that he was a perfectionist!" Nina exclaimed. That last night when we were all going back and forth from the den to the patio and Regina put out her last cigarette, she deliberately missed the ashtray on the table and ground it out on the tabletop. I don't think anyone else saw her.

Should I tell *that* story when I'm interviewed?

Again the patio and kitchen were empty.

Grant will be watching when this is on television, Nina told herself as she and Jerry walked down the hallway to the den. I certainly have the least reason to have killed Betsy. No sane person would think that I did it. The fact that my mother blames me for introducing them would never be a strong enough motive for murder.

She stood for a moment at the door of the den. Well, this is it, she thought. Alex and Laurie were waiting for her. I wonder what the others were feeling when they walked in here? Nina asked herself. Could they possibly have been as terrified as I am now?

Come on, I'm an actress. I can carry this off. She gave a brief smile and, with an air of confidence, took the seat opposite Alex.

"Nina Craig was the final graduate being celebrated on the tragic night of the Graduation Gala," Alex began. "Nina, thank you for being with us today."

Her mouth too dry to speak, Nina nodded.

His voice friendly, his smile warm, Alex asked, "What does it feel like to be here again in Salem Ridge, reunited with your old friends after twenty years?"

Be honest whenever you can, Nina warned herself. "It's awkward, even strange. We all know why we're here."

"And why is that, Nina?"

"To try to prove that none of us murdered Betsy Powell," she said. "And that she was killed by a stranger who came in. On the other hand, we all know that you're hoping that one of us will blurt out a confession or give herself away. I certainly think that's what Robert Powell is hoping. And, of course, in a way I can't blame him."

"How does that make you feel, Nina?"

"Angry. Defensive. But I think we all have been feeling like that for the last twenty years, so it's nothing new. I've certainly learned the hard way that you can get used to anything."

Listening and observing, Laurie found it hard to conceal her surprise. Nina Craig was not responding to Alex's questions the way she had expected at all. Somehow, she had expected a more belligerent response from her. After all, Nina had the least reason of all of them to have suffocated Betsy, but her attitude now was one of regret, even when she confessed to anger. And she *looks* different, too, Laurie thought. Softer. What's the reason she had her hair styled in an up-sweep? With all the research we've done on her, I've never seen one picture without the flowing locks. She's playing a game, but what is it?

Nina was taking Alex through her childhood.

"Alex, as you obviously know, my mother, Muriel Craig, is an actress. I was kind of born in a trunk. We moved all over in those days."

"What about school?"

"Somehow, between the East and West Coasts, I graduated from grammar school."

"What about your father? I know your parents were divorced when you were very young."

He couldn't stand her, either, Nina thought. But he got away fast. "They married young and divorced when I was three."

"Did you see much of him after that?"

"No, but he did contribute to my college education." A little, she thought, a very little—what Mother could squeeze out of him in court.

"Actually, you saw very little of him from the time of the divorce, isn't that true, Nina?"

"He tried his hand at acting, didn't make it, then moved to Chicago, remarried, and had four more children. There wasn't much room in that for me."

Where is he going with this? Nina asked herself frantically.

"Then you never had a father in your growing-up years?"

"I think that's obvious."

"Why did you and your mother move to Salem Ridge, Nina?"

"My mother was dating Robert Powell."

"Wasn't she also offered the leading role in a pilot that became a series and ran for six years, and has been on reruns ever since?"

"Yes, that's true. But Powell told her that he didn't want to be married to anyone who would be working all the time."

"Even when her relationship with Powell ended, the two of you stayed in Salem Ridge. That seems curious to me."

"I don't know why. She had rented a condo. There was a very nice old couple next door, the Johnsons. When she broke up with Robert Powell, my mother was offered a flurry of jobs. I had started high school. She paid the Johnsons to look after me when she was working."

Don't dwell on how lonesome it was after the Johnsons poked their heads in to say good night and I was left by myself for the night, Nina thought. And then when Mother got home from a job, she'd start ranting about how hard she was working, and how it was all my fault, over and over again. I'd miss her when she was away, then when she came home I'd wish she was away on a job anywhere else in the world.

"Your mother kept the condo until you went to college, didn't she?"

"Yes. By then all the jobs were on the West Coast. She had bought a condo out there."

"So you spent your semester breaks and vacations with her?"

"Whenever possible. But I was getting summer-stock jobs and grabbed them whenever they were offered."

"Nina, let's talk about the Gala."

Laurie listened as, in different ways, Alex asked the same questions he had asked the other girls. Her answers were virtually the same as those of the other graduates. She, too, insisted that an intruder had to have been the culprit.

"Let's go back," Alex suggested. "Were you surprised when Claire called and told you that her mother and Robert Powell wanted to have a Graduation Gala for the four of you?"

"Yes, but it was a good chance to see the girls again."

"Your mother was invited to attend as well?"

"Yes, but she didn't."

"Why not?"

"She couldn't take the time off. She had an audition coming up."

"Nina, wasn't it because Betsy scrawled on the invitation that she and Robert couldn't wait to see her, and how blessed she was that you had called her over to the table that wonderful day she and Robert met?"

"How do you know that? Who told you that?"

"Actually, your mother did," Alex said amiably. "Shortly before lunch today."

She's building up to saying that I confessed to her that I murdered Betsy, Nina thought. No matter whether anyone believes her or not, that will be the end of any chance I have with Grant.

What was Alex Buckley asking her? How would she describe her feelings about Betsy Powell?

Why not tell the truth? Why not?

"I loathed her," she said. "Especially after I read that note. She was mean. Make that cruel. There wasn't a decent bone in her body, and when I looked down on her dead face, I had to force myself not to spit on it."

73

George Curtis arrived at the Powell mansion at three-thirty. He had been asked to wear the same kind of evening attire he had worn at the Gala. He had a virtual replica of it in his closet. Because it was so warm, he carried his white dinner jacket, shirt, and bow tie on a plastic-covered hanger.

Before going to the club to play bridge with her friends, Isabelle had given him a cautionary note. "Just remember, you think you kept your little romance pretty quiet, but if I was suspicious, don't you think anyone else was? Maybe even Rob Powell? Just be careful and don't fall into a trap. You had the strongest motive of anyone to have Betsy dead." Then, with a kiss and a wave of her hand, she stepped into her convertible.

"Isabelle, I swear to you—" he had begun.

"I know you do," she said. "But remember, you don't have to convince *me*, and I don't care if you did it anyway. Just don't let yourself get caught."

The temperature had dropped a little, but it was still very hot. George parked his car in the front driveway, picked up the clothes hanger, and walked around to the back of the house. A flurry of activity greeted him. The production crew had their cameras aimed at designated spots on the grounds. He guessed that was where the graduates would be standing while he talked in the foreground with

Alex Buckley. He had been told that the background would be a rolling shot of scenes from the Gala.

Laurie Moran approached as soon as she spotted him. "Thank you so much for agreeing to do this, Mr. Curtis. We'll try not to keep you too long. Why don't you wait inside with the others? It's too hot out here."

"That's not a bad idea," he agreed. He crossed the patio with reluctant steps and went into the house. The four graduates were in the main dining room, dressed in the gowns that he recognized were replicas of the ones they had worn that night. Even with the skillfully applied makeup they were wearing, the tension in their faces was unmistakable.

He did not have long to wait. Laurie's assistant Grace came in to take the graduates outside. When she came back for him, he saw that they were all in place, standing like statues against what he knew would be the background of films of the Gala. He wondered what they were thinking. He wondered if every one of them didn't feel as he had that night. I was terrified that Betsy had the power to ruin my marriage just as the children Isabelle and I had prayed for were becoming a reality, he thought. Alison had to have been bitter. She had lost out on her scholarship because of the donation Rob had made to her college. Occasionally I would pick up something in the grocery store where her father worked, and he would always brag about how hard Alison was studying . . .

There's no one in town who didn't hear Muriel tell the story of how Betsy stole Rob from her, and the fact that it was all because of Nina. And from what I hear, Claire had desperately wanted to board at Vassar, but neither Betsy nor Rob would hear of it. "A *waste of money when she has such a beautiful home*," as Betsy put it. And Regina's father committed suicide because of his investment in Rob's hedge fund.

Who among those girls, amid all the extravagant display, could have avoided feeling bitterness that night? And from the next day on, for twenty years, they had lived under a cloud of suspicion.

George Curtis felt a deep sense of shame. I *did* come back here the night of the Gala, he remembered. It was about 4 A.M. I stood here on this spot. I knew where Betsy's bedroom was. I was crazed with fear that Isabelle would divorce me if Betsy ever told her about us. But then I could see the reflection of someone moving in Betsy's room. There was a light in the hallway, and when the door opened I was almost sure I could tell who it was.

I still think I know who it was. I *know* who it was. When Betsy's body was discovered I wanted to tell, but how could I explain why I was here at that time? I couldn't. But if I had admitted to what I saw, everyone else who has been under suspicion wouldn't have been going through this hell for twenty years. He felt the guilt wash over him.

Alex Buckley was walking to him. "Ready to go down memory lane, Mr. Curtis?" he asked cheerfully.

74

"How do you think that went?" Laurie asked with concern as she stepped into Alex's car.

Alex was starting the engine and putting up the top of his convertible. "I think we could use some air-conditioning. To answer your question, I think it went great."

"I think it did, too. But it's twenty of seven. I'm so afraid that if we hit traffic we won't be at the hospital when Timmy calls, and Dad will miss talking to him."

"I checked the traffic report a few minutes ago on my iPhone. It's okay. I promise I'll get you to the hospital by seven-thirty."

"One more left," Laurie sighed as Alex drove out of the grounds of the Powell estate. "And now the usual question. What's your take on George Curtis?"

"He's a class act," Alex said promptly. "He's the kind of guy people look up to. Well, why not? He's been on the cover of *Forbes* magazine."

"And it doesn't hurt that he is downright handsome," Laurie said. "Think about it. Curtis is a billionaire, charming, good-looking. Compare him with Robert Powell, at least as far as money goes."

"There is no comparison, Laurie. Powell may be worth half a billion, but Curtis is worth billions."

"Now, think of that frame in the Gala films where George Curtis and Betsy look pretty serious, almost as though they're arguing."

"Are you using that in the background, Laurie?"

"No. That wouldn't be fair. But I do know this: the George Curtises of this world don't get involved with this kind of program unless they have something to hide. Think about that."

"Laurie, you continue to amaze me. I *did* think about it. And once again, I agree with you," Alex told her.

Laurie pulled out her phone. "I'll just alert Dad that we're on our way."

Leo answered on the first ring. "I'm still alive," he said. "I'm now watching *All in the Family*. Another golden oldie. Where are you?"

"On our way down. Traffic is good so far."

"Didn't you say Alex Buckley was driving you here, then back to the Powell place?"

"That's right."

"Don't let him cool his heels in the car. Bring him up. I'd like to meet him."

Laurie looked at Alex. "Would you be interested in meeting my dad?"

"Of course I would."

"Alex accepts with delight, Dad. See you."

75

$\diamond$

Bruno was putting on his police uniform when he listened to the call. Countdown! he said to himself. After all these years, I get my revenge. There shall be wailing and gnashing of teeth, he thought. Oh, Leo, how sad you are going to be. Your daughter. Your grandson. And all the while they've been searching through hospital records to see if the doctor had made a mistake on a patient. *You* were the one who made the mistake, Leo. When you were a tough young cop. Too tough. You could have given me a break when you arrested me but you wouldn't. You wrecked my life. You cost me thirty years in prison and then another five for good measure.

Bruno stood in front of the full-length mirror on the closet door of his shabby apartment. He had been renting it month to month because, as he had explained to the landlord, he wanted to be sure that his job with Perfect Estates worked out. The landlord, happy to avoid necessary repairs for the present, was delighted with his temporary tenant.

He wouldn't care that I left suddenly, especially since I paid him to the end of the month, and I'm not going to claim the month's security.

As if anyone could damage this dump, Bruno thought.

76

As Laurie and Alex were driving out, the production crew was closing down for the day.

The graduates had changed from their gowns, and all of them as one turned down the offer to keep them. "Laurie really wants you to have them," Jerry explained. "And I can tell you, they were very expensive."

Nina spoke for all of them. "That's just what we need, another reminder of that night."

Their cars were waiting to drive them to their hotels.

When Rod and Alison arrived at their room, they happily closed the door behind them. Then Rod reached for her. "Alie, it's all right."

"It's not, Rod. It's not all right. You know what's on that tape. You know what Josh can do with that." She turned from him and angrily reached into the closet, grabbing clothes from their hangers and throwing them on the bed.

Rod sank onto the couch and unconsciously began to massage his aching knees. "We are going to have a scotch now," he said emphatically. "Then we are going to order a fabulous dinner, either here or out—your choice. We'll order the most expensive items on the menu, courtesy of Robert Powell."

"I couldn't eat a thing!" Alison protested.

"Order it anyhow."

"Rod, you make me laugh when I have no reason to."

"Alison, that's what I'm here for," Rod said cheerfully. He was not about to tell her that he absolutely shared her concern about Josh's tapes—not because of the money, but because of what it would do to Alie if, once again because of Betsy Powell, her chance to go to medical school without taking on a heavy financial burden, was snatched from her.

77

Regina carefully packed the few new clothes she had brought in preparation for the program. *I may be trading these for an orange jumpsuit,* she thought bitterly. *Score one hundred for Robert Powell. He ruined my life when I was fifteen years old, and now he has his big chance to ruin the rest of it. I wouldn't be surprised if he put Josh up to going through my bag.*

But in the note Dad accuses him and Betsy of deliberately setting him up for a scam. *Why would Robert want that to come out? Josh must be doing this on his own. I've got to pay him off,* she thought. *How ironic—I have publicly made myself more likely to be accused of being Betsy's murderer than if I'd stayed home selling real estate.*

Efficiently, she packed her overnight bag and a large suitcase. *Now where?* she asked herself. *I don't feel like calling for room service. I've got a car downstairs, courtesy of Mr. Powell. Should I?*

Yes, she decided, *why not?* She would have him drive her past her old house, then take her to the restaurant where she and her parents used to go regularly for dinner.

Auld lang syne, she thought.

78

One more night in the house she hated! Why did I do this to myself?

It was a question Claire had been asking herself since the plane landed. Had it been stupid to make herself up to resemble her mother that first morning? Had she done it to stick it to "Daddy Rob"? Maybe. He'd had the nerve to open the door of her bedroom right after her interview this morning to ask her that very question. Why didn't I ever press charges against him in all these years? she asked herself. Why don't I do it now?

She knew the answer. Because it gave me a perfect reason to kill my mother, and because, with his battery of lawyers, Daddy Rob would have held me up as a demented liar, and my mother would have loved backing him up. That's why I became a counselor, she thought. I wanted to help other girls in my situation. But not many of them told me that *their* mothers accepted the fact that their stepfather came sneaking into their room at night. I know that until I go into therapy myself, I'll never move forward with my life, Claire conceded. He's held me hostage all these years.

There was one way she could get to him. Tonight and tomorrow morning she would again wear makeup and style her hair to accentuate her remarkable resemblance to his dear Betsy. As if that makes a bit of difference in the grand scheme of things, Claire thought bitterly as she picked up the phone to order room service. *I wonder if Nina will faint again when she sees me.*

And why was she, of all people, the one to faint in the first place?

79

Nina packed, then had room service send up dinner. As she list-lessly took a bite of cordon bleu, her phone rang. To her astonish-ment, it was Grant.

"Couldn't help wondering how the interview went," he said. "Alex Buckley is notorious for shaking up witnesses."

"Well, he did an Oscar-worthy performance on me," Nina said. "Wait until you see it."

"Hey, you sound pretty down."

"I guess I am," Nina admitted.

"Try not to be, but I understand. I was a witness in a fraud case twenty years ago. It wasn't pleasant."

Pleasant! That's a good word, Nina thought as she listened to Grant tell her he was looking forward to seeing her and wished her a good flight.

Nina took a large swallow of vodka from the tumbler beside her dinner plate. Maybe if I promise my mother to give her all the money left after paying Josh, she'll be satisfied, she thought. Espe-cially if she knows that an A-list producer like Grant is dating me!

80

In Mount Sinai Hospital, Leo was looking at his watch with growing impatience. It was twenty to eight, and Laurie still wasn't there. But just as he was sure she would have to take Timmy's call in the car, Laurie appeared in the doorway. The tall, impressive-looking guy behind her was instantly recognizable as the famous Alex Buckley.

Laurie rushed to hug him. "Dad, I'm so sorry. They should take the East River Drive and bury it at sea. There was a fender bender at 125th Street. You would have thought it was a terror attack for the traffic jam it caused."

"At ease," Leo said, "or you'll be the next one in here with heart fibrillations." He looked up at Alex. "Wouldn't you agree with that, counselor?"

"I certainly agree that your daughter is under a lot of stress," Alex said carefully as he pulled up a chair at Leo Farley's bedside. "But she's doing a great job with this program, I can promise you that."

"Now, before you ask me again, Laurie, yes, I feel fine, and yes, I get out tomorrow morning," Leo Farley declared. "What time do you wrap up this witch hunt you're on?"

"Hey, Dad, that's not exactly what I would call having respect for my work," Laurie protested.

"I have every respect for your work," Leo said. "But if I had gotten away with murder for twenty years and now I was under a spot-light where every word I said in front of a national viewing audience could be picked over by all the amateur sleuths in the country, I might be driven to do whatever it took to cover my tracks."

Alex saw that both Leo and Laurie kept glancing at their watches. It was five to eight.

"Timmy's late calling. I'd better call the office at the camp again and check to see if anything is wrong," Leo said.

"Dad, you've been calling the office at the camp?" Laurie asked.

"You bet I have. That way I can keep them on their toes and make sure that there's no lapse in security there. What do you think, Alex?"

"In your situation, if I were the parent or grandparent, I would do exactly the same thing," Alex agreed.

The ringing of Laurie's phone brought a collective sigh of relief. Before it rang again, she and Leo were saying, "Hi, Timmy."

"Hi, Mom," a happy young voice answered. "I was worried that you wouldn't get home in time to have Grandpa with you when I called."

"Well, we're both here," Laurie said.

Alex listened as Timmy described his activities of the day. He was on the "A" swim team. He liked the three other guys in his tent. Camp was fun. It was only at the end of the conversation that his tone became wistful. "I miss you guys. Are you really, really coming up on visiting day?"

"We are really, *really* coming up on visiting day," Laurie promised.

"You bet we are," Leo said emphatically. "Have I ever broken a promise to you, big guy?"

"No, Grandpa."

"Do you think I'm going to start now?" Leo demanded with mock severity in his voice.

The wistful note was gone.

"No, Grandpa," Timmy said happily.

When they said their final good-bye, Laurie looked at Alex. "That's my little guy," she said proudly.

"He sounds like a great kid," Alex said honestly.

"And now I want you two to go get something to eat and start back to Robert Powell's place," Leo said firmly. "You'll be late enough as it is. Laurie, I hope you're going to take a couple of days off after you wrap up this program."

"That's the last thing I'll be doing, Dad. In fact, that's almost funny. Postproduction can be the toughest part of it. But I agree with you—emotionally, this one has been tough. I have to tell you, I hope I'm never under suspicion of having committed a murder."

Alex knew which way Laurie and her father's thoughts were turning. "I'll defend you, ten percent discount," he promised. They both laughed, and when Alex said good-bye to Leo he heard himself saying, "I defended some people in cases about which I'd love to have your opinion. Would you want to have dinner sometime?"

"Sure I would," Leo agreed.

"Can I come?" Laurie laughed.

"There's no question about that," Alex said, his tone now serious.

With a final good-bye to Leo, they went downstairs and left the hospital.

"I love Manhattan," Laurie sighed. "It's home sweet home."

"So do I," Alex agreed. "Look, we don't have to be back to that mausoleum until eleven, and it's only eight thirty now. Why don't we have a relaxed dinner?"

"We were talking about grabbing a hamburger."

"Forget it. Marea on Central Park South is one of the best restaurants in New York. It's always full, but by this time the theatre crowd has gone. Okay with you?"

"Perfect," Laurie said. Relaxed now that Leo looked good and Timmy sounded happy, she knew she would enjoy the evening dining with Alex.

At that very moment, Bruno was crossing the Tappan Zee Bridge on the way to Timmy's camp.

81

Twenty-four miles away in an equally expensive restaurant in Westchester County, Robert Powell and Muriel Craig were sipping champagne. "To our reunion," he whispered.

"Rob, dear, I've missed you. Oh, how I've missed you." Muriel reached across the table for his hand. "Why didn't you ever call me in all these years?"

"I was afraid to call you. When we broke up I was very unfair to you. I know you had given up the chance to be in that series, and it became so successful. I owed you so much, I didn't know where to begin."

"I called and wrote to you," Muriel reminded him.

"That only made me feel more guilty," Robert Powell confessed. "And I haven't told you yet how absolutely lovely you look tonight."

Muriel knew that was not flattery. She had prevailed on Meg and Courtney to do her makeup and style her hair. She had found a beautiful dinner suit in an exclusive boutique in Bedford. The fact that she had already bought a beautiful dinner suit with matching accessories on Rodeo Drive in Hollywood did not trouble her. She was carrying Nina's credit card.

Robert was saying, "I think we'd better order."

Throughout the dinner, he skillfully intermingled compliments with subtle questions. "I was so flattered to hear that you blamed Nina for calling Claire and Betsy to the table that day, Muriel."

"I could have killed her," Muriel admitted, her voice thick and a little loud. "I was so in love with you."

"And I often thought of you over the years and wondered how stupidly carried away I was, and how much I came to regret it." He paused. "And then, when Betsy was mercifully off my hands, I wish I could have known who to thank."

Muriel looked hesitant, then glanced around the dining room to be sure that the occupants at the surrounding tables were absorbed in their own conversations. Satisfied, she bent forward and leaned across the table as far as she could, getting a smear of butter on the lapel of her new suit.

"Robbie, do you mean you were *glad* when Betsy was smothered?"

"Promise not to tell anyone that," he whispered.

"Of course not. It's our secret. But you know how close my daughter, Nina, and I have always been?"

"Of course I do."

"Well, she was so upset with what Betsy wrote on my invitation, you know, how she wanted me to see how happy you two were and how glad she was that Nina had introduced you . . ."

"I learned about it later, and I was shocked."

"I was hurt, but Nina was furious at her. She knew how much I loved you. Rob, I think Nina was the one who killed Betsy. She did it for me so that I would have another chance with you."

"Are you sure, or are you guessing, Muriel?" Robert Powell's eyes were suddenly alert, his tone of voice sharp.

Muriel Craig looked at him, vaguely aware of the change in his manner. "Of course I'm sure, Robbie. She called me. You remember, I was in Hollywood and she was crying over the phone. She said, 'Mommy, I'm scared. They're asking so many questions.

" 'Mommy, I did it for you.' "

82

$\diamond$

Jane checked the bedrooms for the last time before they all got back. She had opened the bar in the den and laid out a platter of hors d'oeuvres just as she had done the night Betsy was murdered. She thought, Oh, to be rid of all of them at last!

After several days of all this activity, she was unused to the blessed silence in the house. Mr. Rob had taken that impossible Muriel Craig out to dinner. No question, she looked beautiful, but there was no doubt she already had a few under her belt.

And there was a faint smell of smoke in her bathroom.

Mr. Rob scorned anyone who drank too much or smoked.

Mr. Rob was toying with Muriel. Jane knew the signs. It was similar to the way Betsy had toyed with Regina's father, until she got him to sink every nickel he had into the hedge fund.

Oh, they were quite the pair of experts at cheating people, she thought with admiration. Plus, Betsy was a two-faced fraud. She had skillfully hidden her little dalliances from Mr. Rob.

That was why Betsy had slipped me little gifts to keep my mouth shut, Jane thought.

But she was worried now. She had missed the fact that Josh had been playing his own little game, blackmailing people he taped in the car.

If Mr. Rob knew she had covered for Betsy, she would be fired at once. He must never know. But who would tell him? Not Josh. He'd lose *his* job, too.

I still have the jewelry that George Curtis gave Betsy, Jane thought as she turned down the beds for the visitors and lowered the shades in their rooms, a job she hadn't done in twenty years— except, of course, for Mr. Rob. Sometimes she put a chocolate on his pillow, just as they did in hotels.

Mr. Curtis had been here this afternoon. Boy, he must have been squirming, she thought, talking to Alex Buckley about the Gala.

After the Gala, Jane had fixed the platter of hors d'oeuvres for the girls and brought them to the den. I was in and out for the first half hour or so and listened to all of them until they really let go on Betsy. Then they started to look at me and I said good night.

If push came to shove, I could make a case against any one of them, she told herself.

She laid her head on Mr. Rob's pillow, just for an instant. Then she pulled herself up and with rapid fingers plumped it again.

Tomorrow night at this time she and Mr. Rob would be alone again.

83

"It's time to get back," Alex said reluctantly. For the last ninety minutes, in between thoroughly enjoying chatting with Laurie over an excellent dinner, he had found himself telling her stories of his own background—how his mother and then his father had died when he was in college, how at age twenty-one he had become his seventeen-year-old brother's guardian.

"He became my 'little guy,'" he said, and then, appalled at his own words, said, "Laurie, I'm sorry. There's no comparison with your situation."

"No, there isn't," Laurie said matter-of-factly. "But I hate it when people weigh and measure every word they say to me. It's a continuing factor of my life. But your brother grew up and is a successful lawyer, and someday Blue Eyes will be captured and this awful burden will be gone. My one comfort is that Blue Eyes swore he'd get me first." She sipped a taste of champagne. "I can drink to that!" she said.

"Put down that glass," Alex said forcefully. "Let's drink to Blue Eyes being captured and rotting in prison for the rest of his life." He did not add, Or being shot between the eyes in cold blood, as he murdered your husband, Dr. Greg Moran.

Reluctantly, Alex signaled for the check.

Fifteen minutes later they were driving toward Westchester on the Henry Hudson Parkway.

Alex could see that Laurie was struggling to stay awake. "Look, why don't you close your eyes?" he suggested. "You told me you didn't sleep last night because you were worried about your dad, and I doubt you'll sleep much tonight, either."

"You're absolutely right," Laurie sighed. She closed her eyes and in less than a minute Alex heard the sound of her soft, even breathing.

He glanced over at her from time to time. From the outside lights of the parkway he could see her profile, and then was pleased when, in her sleep, her head turned toward him.

He thought about how worried Leo Farley was about her being under the same roof as these people, one of whom was surely a murderer—but which one?

And there was something familiar about that gardener. What was it? He had snapped his picture yesterday when he was out on the patio and sent it to his investigator. He had also called Perfect Estates. He had told the person answering the phone that, for security reasons, he was just verifying the names of everyone on the property.

Robert Powell's speech at lunch was clearly an attempt to frighten one of them into making a move, Alex thought, and whoever that person is may take a last, desperate chance to stop him.

Thirty minutes later he tapped Laurie's arm. "Okay, 'Sleeping Beauty,'" he said briskly. "Time to wake up. We're here for the night."

84

Bruno was in the office at the camp. The counselor on night duty had been summoned from his cabin.

Toby Barber was twenty-six years old, a good sleeper, an early-to-bed type. Rubbing his eyes, he came into the office to confront Bruno, authoritative in his police uniform, a concerned look on his face. "I'm sorry to disturb you, Mr. Barber," he told Toby, "but it's very, very important. Commissioner Farley has had a major heart attack. He may not make it. He wants to see his grandson now."

Bruno was a good actor. He stared straight into the young counselor's eyes.

"We've been warned to take particular care of Timmy," Toby said, trying to come fully awake, "but I do know that his grandfather called the head counselor today and told him he was in the hospital with a heart condition. I'll call my boss right away on his cell to get his permission. He's visiting friends at a birthday party."

"Commissioner Farley is dying," Bruno said, his voice laced with fury. "He wants to see his grandson."

"I understand, I understand," Toby said nervously. "Just one phone call."

There was no answer on the phone.

"He probably doesn't hear it," Toby said worriedly. "I'll try again in a few minutes."

"I am not waiting a few minutes," Bruno thundered. "The commissioner is a dying man who wants to see his grandson."

Thoroughly intimidated, Barber said, "I'll get Timmy. Just let me help him change."

"Don't change him. Put on his bathrobe and slippers!" Bruno ordered. "He has plenty of clothes at home."

"Yes, of course. You're right. I'll get him."

Ten minutes later Bruno was holding the hand of a sleepy Timmy and putting him in his car.

His mind was racing with a combination of triumph and anticipation.

85

Robert Powell arrived home to receive the first of his overnight guests.

Muriel rushed upstairs to change her jacket. Horrified when she looked in the mirror, she freshened her makeup and brushed her hair. She walked downstairs trying not to show that she was unsteady on her feet. When she came into the den, she saw that Nina was the next to return. She saw the expression of contempt in her daughter's eyes. Wait till you see, she thought as she went over to Rob to kiss his cheek. He put his arm around her tenderly.

Claire, Regina, Alison, and Rod arrived within a few minutes of each other. Laurie and Alex were last, but within ten minutes all had gathered and were in the den.

Jane stood at the bar to pass out wine and cordials.

Robert Powell held up his glass. "I cannot thank you all enough for being with me, and I apologize that you have had to endure this ordeal for twenty years. As you know, I, too, have been under a terrible cloud of suspicion. But I am happy to say that tomorrow morning, during my interview, I will announce to the world that I now know who killed my beloved Betsy—and I will name that person. So let us have this final toast to the relief that is to come, and say good night to each other."

There was absolute silence in the room. The platter of hors d'oeuvres, so carefully prepared by Jane, was ignored.

Everyone put their glasses down without speaking and began to leave the room.

Josh was hovering in the hallway, ready to assist Jane with collecting the glasses and turning off the lights.

Laurie and Alex waited until the others were upstairs to say good night to Robert Powell.

"That was a pretty strong statement, Mr. Powell," Alex said flatly. "And very provocative. Do you really think it was necessary?"

"I think it was absolutely necessary," Robert Powell said. "I have spent many years going from one to the other of those four young women, trying to imagine who went into my wife's bedroom and stole the breath from her body. I know Betsy had her faults, but she was exactly right for me, and I have missed her for twenty years. Why do you think I never remarried? Because she is irreplaceable."

Where does that leave Muriel Craig? Laurie wondered.

"And now I wish you a very good night," Powell said briskly.

Alex walked Laurie to the door of her room. "Keep your door locked," he said. "If Powell is right, someone is right now trying to decide what to do. Crazy as it sounds, someone might blame you for setting up this program."

"Or blame you for driving every one of them to admit she hated Betsy, Alex."

"I'm not worried," Alex said quietly. "Go to bed and lock your door."

86

Regina sat on the edge of the bed. I know he means me, she thought. Josh must have given him the suicide note. I wonder if I'll still get the money. I can use it for my defense. For twenty years I've wanted an end to this. Well, I have it now.

In robotlike fashion she changed into pajamas, went into the bathroom, splashed water on her face, turned off the light, and went to bed. Then, sleepless, she stared into the dark.

87

Alison and Rod lay side by side, their hands clutched under the light covers.

"I did do it," Alison said. "I know I was in Betsy's room, and I was in the closet watching."

"Watching what?" Rod asked quickly.

"Someone holding the pillow over Betsy's face. But Rod, it wasn't someone, it was me."

"Don't say that!"

"I know it's true, Rod. I know it's true."

"You don't know it's true. Stop saying that."

"Rod, I'm going to go to prison."

"No, you're not. And for one reason: I couldn't live without you."

Alison stared into the darkness and came to realize the truth that anger had hidden from her. She said, "Rod, I know that you have always felt that I married you so that you could send me to medical school. I may have believed that myself. But you weren't the only one who fell in love the first day of kindergarten. I did, too. It's a terrible thing, but I know I have wasted twenty years hating Betsy Powell."

She laughed mirthlessly. "If only I had had the satisfaction of knowing what I was doing when I killed her."

88

Claire sat on the couch in her bedroom, making no attempt to sleep.

So he actually did love my mother, she thought. From the time he started coming into my room less than a month after we moved in here, I allowed it for her sake. I could see that she was so happy, and I wanted to keep her that way. I was sure that if I told her, she'd move out of here, and then where would we be?

Back in a tiny apartment. She dated men along the way, looking for what Robert Powell could give her. We were so close when I was little. I felt I owed it to her. It was my big secret, making that sacrifice for my mother. Counting every night he didn't come near me as a blessing. Then I overheard them talking. He was telling her about the night before, and she was pleased I was so responsive.

Damn her, damn her, damn her.

I smothered her in my mind from the time I was thirteen. If I was the one who did it that final night and somebody saw me and is saying so now, so be it, so be it.

89

Nina did not attempt to go to bed. Instead she sat, legs crossed, replaying in her mind the events of the day. Was it possible that her mother had carried out her threat? She's a good actress, Nina thought, and who wouldn't believe her?

I didn't know that Robert Powell was so bulldozed by Betsy that he didn't see her for what she was. Or maybe he *did* see her for what she was and found it thrilling.

If Rob has been playing up to my mother these couple of days, she's obviously been fool enough to fall for it. If she's said I confessed to killing Betsy, it's impossible for me. And when Rob shows her the door tomorrow, she can go straight to the police chief to claim the reward. What, if anything, can I do about it?

90

As the last light went out in the house, Bruno got out of the car. He had given Timmy a sleeping pill and now had him slung over his shoulder. Carefully he climbed over the fence, moving slowly to be sure not to disturb him. He carried him into the pool house and opened the door of the utility room. He laid him on the pile of blankets he had prepared for him and loosely tied his hands and feet.

Timmy stirred and murmured a protest when Bruno tied a relaxed gag around his mouth, then fell back into a deep sleep.

Bruno knew he had to be picked up tomorrow morning by the landscaper's truck. There would be no explanation for him not being there. But the kid should be okay until I get back, he thought. Even if he wakes up, he can't get out and he can't pull the gag off. His hands are tied behind him.

Now that the end was near, he knew that he was not only deadly calm, but would *stay* deadly calm. He looked down at Timmy's sleeping face. There was enough light from the full moon that he could see it clearly. "You would've looked just like your daddy someday," he said, "and your mommy is right in that house and doesn't know you're here. Wait till she finds out you're missing."

He knew he should leave but could not resist reaching into his pocket and taking out a tiny case. He opened it and took out shiny bright blue lenses and put them in his eyes. He had worn them that day because they would stand out just in case anyone got close enough to describe him. He remembered how he had heard Timmy's wail five years ago: *"Blue Eyes shot my daddy."*

Yes, I did, he thought. Yes, I did.

He took out the lenses, saving them for tomorrow.

91

Leo Farley could not sleep. The cop in him was sending him a warning. He tried to brush it off.

Laurie is okay, he reminded himself. I'm glad Alex Buckley is in that house. It's obvious that he likes Laurie, but more important, he knows she's facing a potentially explosive situation tonight with that bunch in the same house.

Timmy sounds great, and I'll see him Sunday. Then why in hell am I so sure that something is seriously wrong? Maybe it's just all these heart monitors on me. They'd drive anyone crazy.

The nurse had left a sleeping pill on his night table. "It's not strong, Commissioner," she had told him, "but it will take the edge off and let you get some sleep."

Leo reached for it, then threw it back on the table. I don't want to wake up half-groggy, he thought angrily.

And anyhow, I know it won't help me go to sleep.

92

At three o'clock in the morning, Jane got quietly out of bed, opened the door of her room, and padded along until she reached the room where Muriel Craig was sleeping.

Her noisy snoring was sufficient proof that she was under the influence of excess liquid refreshment. Jane tiptoed over to the bed, bent over, and raised the pillow she was holding. Then, with a sudden quick movement, she jammed it over Muriel's face and clasped it down.

The snoring stopped with an abrupt gagging sound. The strong hands of her attacker held the pillow like a vise. Muriel began to gasp for breath.

Her hands flew up and she tried to push the pillow away. "Don't bother," someone whispered.

Any remnant of the fog in her brain disappeared.

I don't want to die, Muriel thought. I don't want to die.

Her long fingernails dug deep into the back of her assailant's hands, and for a moment their grip loosened. Muriel pushed away the pillow and screamed. But then the pillow came back even more forcefully over her face. "You didn't think I'd let you have him," Jane hissed, her voice ragged and her tone vicious as she again clasped the pillow tightly over Muriel's face. "Maybe they know I killed Betsy, but you won't get a chance at him. *He's mine. He's mine.*"

Throughout the second floor, everyone heard the scream and felt utter disbelief.

Alex arrived first, wrestling with Jane and throwing her to the floor. As he turned on the light, he saw that Muriel's face was blue. She was not breathing. He pulled her out of the bed, laid her on the floor, and began CPR.

As Robert Powell ran down the hall, Rod and the four graduates came rushing from the other direction. Wild-eyed Jane looked from one to the other of them and began to flee, still clutching the pillow.

"You?" Powell shouted and began to follow her. "It was *you?*"

Stumbling and gasping, Jane ran down the stairs and through the kitchen. Shoving the patio door aside, she ran into the darkness, not knowing where to go. She was beside the pool when Robert Powell grabbed her.

"It was you," he said. "All this time it was *you?* For twenty years I have seen you every day and never suspected for one minute that you killed my Betsy."

"I love you, Rob," she moaned. "I love you, I love you, I love you."

"You can't swim, can you? You're afraid of water, aren't you?" With a sudden motion, he shoved her into the pool, then buried her frantic pleas for help by shouting: "Jane, Jane, don't be afraid, we'll help you, Jane, we'll help you. Where are you?"

When he was sure that she was sinking, he continued running past the pool house and down the driveway until, exhausted, he sank onto the ground. That was where he was found when a squad car came roaring around the driveway. A policeman knelt beside him. "It's all right, Mr. Powell, it's all right. Do you know which way she went?"

"No." Robert Powell's breathing was labored, his complexion ghastly white. Just then the outdoor lights burst on, and every corner of the grounds became visible. "Maybe the pool house," he breathed. "Maybe she's hiding in there."

Sirens screaming, other squad cars began racing down the driveway. Ed Penn was in one of them.

"Look in the pool house," the policeman with Powell shouted.

One of the officers raced to the door of the pool house and was pushing it open when another cop shouted, "She's down here."

He was standing by the pool looking down. Jane, faceup, was lying at the bottom. Her eyes were open and her fists were closed as if she were still grasping the pillow. The officer dove into the pool and struggled to bring her to the surface. The other officers helped him drag her out of the pool and they positioned her on the ground. They pumped her chest and applied CPR. After several minutes they stopped their futile attempt to revive her.

Inside, Alex had managed to get Muriel's heart beating. The graduates and Rod were standing motionless in the room. As Muriel fought her way back to consciousness, she moaned, "Rob, Rob."

Nina's hysterical laughter could be heard through the house.

93

Bruno stood on the sidewalk for a full fifteen minutes before Dave Cappo pulled up in the grounds van promptly at 8 A.M. Dave was bursting with excitement as they headed for the Powell estate.

"Did you hear everything that's going on?" he asked.

"What's that?" Bruno asked, saying to himself, I don't care.

"Somebody tried to kill somebody at the Powell place last night."

"What?"

"It was the housekeeper. She killed Powell's wife twenty years ago," Dave said breathlessly. "She tried to do it again to someone else last night, but she got caught in the act. She tried to get away and fell in the pool—turns out she couldn't swim."

Did they find Timmy? Bruno thought in terror.

"What do you think of that?" Dave was asking. "I mean, for twenty years those four graduates have been under suspicion, and it turns out none of them did it."

"What's happening up there now?" Bruno asked. If they found Timmy, I can have Dave take me home right now. I can say I don't feel well. I can be out of this town in minutes. Timmy doesn't know who picked him up. But they'll come looking for me fast . . .

"Oh, just the usual stuff," Dave said. "The medical examiner took away the body. From what I hear, the housekeeper was standing there holding the pillow over the face of the mother of one of the graduates. Her name is Muriel Craig. She's an actress."

Bruno knew he had to respond. "Oh, I've heard of her." They haven't searched the pool house, he thought. They wouldn't have any reason to start searching now. I'm going to see it through.

Usually Dave dropped him off in the driveway. "I don't know if they'll let you in, but we can try. Then you can tell us everything that's going on now."

The car was stopped by a policeman. "I'll have to check inside," he said. He phoned and received the answer.

"Mr. Powell says to let him in. He can start working on the putting green that's outside the area the police have roped off."

Trying to look casual, Bruno got out of the car and walked slowly to the pool house. He passed the pool. The body was gone. He went in, closed the door, and rushed to the utility room. Timmy was awake. He was squirming on the mound of blankets. Tears were running down his cheeks. Bruno knelt beside him. "Don't cry, Timmy," he said. "Mommy's coming soon. I'm going to give you some cereal and let you go to the bathroom. Then Mommy will take you to see Grandpa. Is that okay?"

Timmy nodded.

"Now you have to promise me that you won't try to call out when I let you eat. Is that a promise?"

Timmy nodded his head again.

There was a small bathroom off the utility room for the use of any of the grounds help. Bruno carried Timmy into it and stood with him over the toilet. "Let it go," he said. It'll be your last time, he thought.

He placed Timmy back on the blankets, went into the kitchen, and brought out Cheerios, milk, and orange juice.

"I'm going to pull down the gag," he said. "I'll let you eat, but make it fast."

His eyes terrified, Timmy obeyed.

When he was finished, Bruno retied the gag, again being sure that it was not too tight. He pushed Timmy down on the blankets. "If you try to make any noise, no one will hear you," he warned. "If you're very, very quiet, I promise Mommy will come to pick you up."

Bruno reached for a rake, carried it out of the utility room, closed the door, and locked it.

He went outside and began to poke at the grass around the putting green with the rake.

94

Before the police responded to the 911 call, Josh had rushed to Jane's apartment, where he searched for and found the hidden jewelry George Curtis had given Betsy. Now it was securely in his pockets with no one the wiser. He had been surprised that Jane was the one who had killed Betsy, even though he had always suspected she was crazy about Mr. Rob.

At nine o'clock everyone who had stayed overnight came down for breakfast. They barely spoke to each other. The realization that they were now free of any suspicion that one of them had taken Betsy's life was just beginning to sink in.

Muriel had refused to go to the hospital and stayed in bed until the medical examiner had left with Jane's body. Her throat swollen, her voice husky, she had already begun to realize that now Robert was really alone, and he would know that she had lied to him about Nina's confession. But on the other hand, she thought, maybe he will understand that I lied because I love him so much. To that end, she finally got up, showered, carefully made up her face, and brushed her hair. When she was finished, she dressed in a light sweater, slacks, and sandals. She hoped the rapidly spreading bruises on her throat would show Rob how much she had endured for him.

Chief Ed Penn and other detectives had spent the hours after the incident individually questioning everyone in the house. All of their accounts were consistent. From all initial appearances, Jane had acted alone in trying to kill Muriel. From all initial appearances, Jane had accidentally fallen into the pool as she fled from the house.

Under these circumstances, he reluctantly agreed to the fervent request by Laurie and Alex to allow them to finish the program. "The investigation is not over," he told them firmly. "Everyone will have to come in to give formal statements. But as long as no one tries to go into the roped-off areas, I'll let you continue."

In the den, Laurie and Alex were waiting to hold the final interview with Robert Powell.

The others had been invited in to watch. By then they were all packed and dressed, desperate to be away. Still hardly able to believe that the nightmare was over, they filed into the den and sat behind the cameras, waiting for Robert Powell.

95

Mark Garret, the camp director at Mountainside, stared incredulously at Toby Barber. "You mean you let Timmy Moran leave with a stranger last night?" he asked.

"His grandfather is dying. A policeman came for him," Toby said defensively.

"Why didn't you call me?"

"I did, sir. You didn't answer your phone."

With a sinking heart, Garret realized that Toby was right. He had taken off his jacket, and in the noise of the party could not have heard his cell phone ring.

I spoke to Leo Farley yesterday, he tried to reassure himself. He told me he was in the hospital.

But he also warned me that the person who killed Timmy's father had threatened him and his mother. Suppose he was the one who picked up Timmy?

Desperately afraid, Garret picked up his phone. Leo Farley's number was on his desk, ready to reach at any time in case a threat to Timmy materialized. He could only hope and pray that Leo Farley had indeed been in an emergency situation.

Farley answered on the first ring.

"Hello there, Mark," he said. "How are you doing?"

Garret hesitated, then asked, "How are you feeling, Commissioner?"

"Oh, I'm okay now. In fact, I'm getting discharged this morning. I spoke to Timmy last night. He's having a great time with you at the camp."

There was nothing Mark Garret could do except blurt out, "Then you didn't send a cop for him last night?"

It took seconds before Leo could absorb what he was hearing. His nightmare was happening. It could only be Blue Eyes who had taken Timmy.

"You mean despite all my warnings you let my grandson go away with a stranger? What did he look like?"

Garret asked Toby to describe the policeman.

In despair, Leo heard a description matching the one that elderly Margy Bless had given to the police five years ago of Greg's murderer: below average height, kind of bulky-looking . . .

Leo asked, "Did he have blue eyes?"

"I asked Toby. He didn't notice. He was very tired."

"You fool!" he shouted as he broke the connection.

He ripped off the wires that were monitoring his heart. In his mind he could hear the words Blue Eyes had shouted to Timmy: *"Tell your mother that she's next. Then it's your turn."*

Frantically he dialed Ed Penn's phone. If he kept to his threat, Blue Eyes would kill Laurie first. He had to be heading for her now—and pray God, with Timmy still alive!

96

Robert Powell, haggard and worn but impeccably dressed in a shirt and tie and summer-weight jacket, quietly listened to the greeting from Alex. The graduates were stationed behind him.

"Mr. Powell, this is hardly the way I expected this program to end. Did you ever know or suspect that Jane Novak had murdered your wife?"

"Absolutely not," Robert Powell said wearily. "I have always suspected that it was one of the graduates. I was not sure which one, and I wanted the answer. I wanted closure. I *needed* closure. I am not a well man; my days are numbered. I have just learned that in addition to my other medical problems, I have a fast-moving form of pancreatic cancer. Before too long, I will be joining my beloved Betsy in heaven or in hell."

For an instant, there was silence.

"I am planning to leave five million dollars to each of the graduates. I know that, in different ways, Betsy and I have damaged each and every one of them."

He turned to look at them, expecting expressions of gratitude.

Instead he stared at identical expressions of contempt and disgust.

97

"It's time," Bruno said. "We're going to have you call Mommy." He had put the shiny blue contact lenses back in his eyes.

Timmy looked up into the blue eyes that had haunted him for more than five years of his young life. "You shot my daddy," he said.

"That's right, Timmy, and let me tell you why. I didn't want to be a criminal. I wanted to break away from the mob. I was only nineteen. I could have had a different life. But your hotshot grandfather caught me driving drunk. I begged him to let me go and told him that I was reporting to the army the next day. But he arrested me. Then the army wouldn't take me, and I got back with the mob. I broke into a house, and the old lady in it had a heart attack when she saw me. She died. I got thirty years."

Bruno's face became contorted with anger. "I could have done anything. I can build computers. I can break into any computer or phone. I had figured out how to get even with Leo Farley. I was going to kill the people he loved—his son-in-law, his daughter, and you. I got your father, but they sent me back to prison on a stupid parole violation for another five years. Now you know, Timmy, and it's time to call Mommy."

•　•　•

Laurie and Alex watched as the graduates walked out of the room, leaving Robert Powell sitting alone. Silently Laurie nodded to the crew to pack up. There was nothing more to be said.

Alex felt the vibration of his phone ringing in his pocket. It was his office; the investigator he had assigned to find out about the landscaper.

"Alex." His voice was urgent. "The landscaper you asked us to check out. He is not Bruno Hoffa. He's Rusty Tillman, who served thirty years in prison. He got out five and a half years ago, a week before the doctor was shot. He went back to prison on a parole violation, and got out five months ago. We ran his picture—"

Alex dropped the phone. Unbelieving, he stared at Laurie. She had been about to step out onto the patio. He heard her phone ring as he frantically shouted, "Wait, Laurie!"

She was already out on the patio, her phone to her ear.

"Timmy, you're not allowed to call me during the day," she said. "What's wrong, honey?" And then she looked up.

The pool house door was opening and Timmy, in his pajamas and robe, was coming out, hand in hand with the gardener. He was holding a rifle pointed at Timmy's head.

With a shriek Laurie began to race across the lawn.

Chief Ed Penn was roaring toward the Powell estate. "Don't turn on the sirens," he warned his driver. "We don't want to alert him. Tell all units to report to the Powell estate."

The policeman in the squad car behind the estate had received the urgent message, had cut through the woods and was climbing the fence. Although a highly skilled marksman, Officer Ron Teski had never fired his weapon in the line of duty. As he sprinted toward the backyard, he realized this might be the day he had trained for. Blue Eyes dropped Timmy's hand and, laughing, let him run to Laurie, who was running toward them from eighty feet away.

The squad car carrying Ed Penn came racing around the circular driveway. Penn, his gun in hand, frantically took aim at Blue Eyes. The shot missed its mark.

By now Laurie had reached Timmy and was bending over to pick him up. Wanting to finish the task the way he had envisioned, Blue Eyes took aim at Laurie's head. As he was about to fire, Officer Teski's first shot cut into his shoulder. Spinning, Blue Eyes raised the rifle and tried to point it in Laurie's direction. His finger was on the trigger as he felt an explosion rip through his chest.

Blue Eyes' body fell to the ground accompanied by the sound of breaking glass. The bullet he had fired crashed through the window of the den where Robert Powell was still sitting. With a puzzled expression, Powell raised his hand to what remained of his forehead and then fell from the chair.

Seconds later, in a foreshadowing of what was to come, Alex Buckley was wrapping Laurie and Timmy in his arms.

Epilogue

Six months later, there was another reunion of the graduates—this time on a much happier note.

It was Alex who suggested they get together at his apartment on New Year's Eve. The developments in their lives had been extraordinary, and he said it was time to share them.

They sat together and compared notes over cocktails while Ramon prepared dinner.

Claire had gone to a therapist, able at last to talk about what Robert Powell had done to her. "It wasn't my fault," she was now able to say with conviction. She had started to use makeup again and was quietly content to no longer conceal her resemblance to her mother. Now she sat, a very pretty woman, laughing with her old friends and telling them about her new social life.

Regina's first action when she received the money from the Gala Reunion had been to return the commission Bridget Whiting had paid her. The real estate business had picked up, and a bigger home with an office attached was within her grasp. It gave her enormous pleasure to know that her ex-husband and his rock-star wife were in the midst of a bitter divorce. Zach spent almost all of his free time with her.

Nina was engaged to Grant Richmond. She had willingly turned over her share of the Powell and production company money to her mother, with the proviso that they never have any contact again. Muriel, typically, was telling everyone how much Robert had loved her, and that they had planned to be married before the dreadful accident that took his life.

Alison was attending medical school in Cleveland, commuting from home. She joked that it was hard to keep up with her fellow twentysomething students. She shared the joyous news that she was three months pregnant. Rod had stunned her by saying he was going to be her fellow student. For years, it turned out, he had wanted to become a pharmacist himself.

The four graduates were all saying that Robert Powell was shot before completing his final attempt to make up for what he had done. They were asking each other whether, if he had lived, they would have taken his money. They admitted to each other that they would have accepted it after all they had been through.

George Curtis had been invited to the party, too. Listening, he realized he had gotten off easy. Robert Powell had never suspected his relationship with Betsy. Isabelle had forgiven him. He could have saved twenty years of anguish, but had been too much of a coward to do so.

At the dinner table George smiled as he thought about the announcement he was about to make. Robert Powell had promised to give the graduates five million dollars but had died before he could change his will. George was going to give each of them the five million that would have come from Powell. George knew in his heart that he was trying to make up for the damage his twenty years of silence had inflicted on them.

Three of the graduates had gone to Chief Penn with the recorded threats from Josh, who was now out on bail, awaiting trial. A search warrant had revealed the jewelry Jane had stolen in his apartment. Since Jane had taken it from Betsy, it was now part of Betsy's estate.

When Josh's trial and his appeals were over, it would be released for Claire to dispose of as she wished.

Alex, listening to the four graduates, marvelled at their resilience, and then he looked at Laurie. For the first time in the nearly six years since Greg's death, she and Leo had left Timmy with a neighbor who was a babysitter. He saw how their faces now were transformed by the easy laughter they shared with the others. It had been incredible for them to learn that a seemingly routine DUI arrest Leo had made as a young patrolman had been viewed by Blue Eyes as the event that had ruined his life—driving him to Greg's murder and forcing them all to live under the threat of violence for so long.

The *Under Suspicion* series had taken off, as Laurie had predicted.

Alex knew it was too soon to let her know how deeply in love with her he was. She still needed time to heal.

I can wait, he thought, as long as it takes—however long that is.